Praise for Laura Lee Guhrke and the Scandal at the Savoy Series

"The best in historical romance!"

—Julia Quinn, *New York Times* bestselling author of the Bridgerton series

"Laura Lee Guhrke has a lively style that sizzles."

—Jane Feather, *New York Times* bestselling author

LADY SCANDAL

"With appealing protagonists and some convincingly steamy scenes, this will appeal to fans of Julia Quinn and Amanda Quick."

—*Publishers Weekly*

"A captivating, delightful read, full of humorous moments and characters who feel real enough for readers to genuinely care about how their story will end."

—*Library Journal*

"A top-notch historical romance."

—*Kirkus*, starred review

BOOKSHOP CINDERELLA

"Packed with chemistry and fun, this is a fairy-tale treat."

—*Publishers Weekly,* starred review

"It has been a while since Guhrke's last superbly written historical romance, but her latest artfully constructed literary confection is well worth the wait. George Bernard Shaw himself would appreciate Guhrke's clever riff on his classic, *Pygmalion,* not to mention her sprightly prose and sparkling, champagne-fizzy wit."

—*Booklist,* starred review

"A promising start to a cheery new Victorian romance series."

—*Kirkus*

"A great mix of wit and attraction as opposites clash and romance blooms."

—*Library Journal*

Bad Luck Bride

ALSO BY LAURA LEE GUHRKE

Lady Scandal

Bookshop Cinderella

Bad Luck Bride

LAURA LEE GUHRKE

FOREVER
New York Boston

This book is a work of fiction. Names, characters, places, and incidents are the product of the author's imagination or are used fictitiously. Any resemblance to actual events, locales, or persons, living or dead, is coincidental.

Cover design by Daniela Medina. Cover photo by Ilina Simeonova / Trevillion

Forever
Hachette Book Group
1290 Avenue of the Americas, New York, NY 10104
read-forever.com

First Edition: July 2025

Forever is an imprint of Grand Central Publishing. The Forever name and logo are registered trademarks of Hachette Book Group, Inc.

Print book interior design by Taylor Navis

Library of Congress Cataloging-in-Publication Data

Names: Guhrke, Laura Lee, author.
Title: Bad luck bride / Laura Lee Guhrke.
Description: First edition. | New York : Forever, 2025.
Identifiers: LCCN 2025004202 | ISBN 9781538722664 (trade paperback) |
ISBN 9781538722671 (ebook)
Subjects: LCGFT: Romance fiction. | Novels.
Classification: LCC PS3557.U3564 B33 2025 | DDC 813/.54—dc23/eng/20250204
LC record available at https://lccn.loc.gov/2025004202

ISBNs: 978-1-5387-2266-4 (trade paperback), 978-1-5387-2267-1 (ebook)

Printed in the United States of America

LSC-C

Printing 1, 2025

1

The Savoy Hotel, London, 1898

She shouldn't. She really, really shouldn't.

Lady Kay Matheson stared at the breakfast plate before her, her hand still holding the silver cover she'd just pulled from the tray, and she felt the paralyzing agony of sudden temptation. And who could blame her?

Before her were all the elements of a traditional English breakfast—eggs, bacon, baked beans, fried potatoes, and mushrooms sautéed in lovely, lovely butter. No fried bread was on the tray, but there was a basket of French croissants, along with a pot of jam. Raspberry jam—her favorite. Naturally.

Kay's empty stomach rumbled.

This was not, she reminded herself sternly as she set aside the plate cover, her breakfast. She slid her gaze across the table to the other tray, then to the one being carried away by her mother's maid, Foster.

Either of those, Kay knew, could contain her own breakfast, which consisted of a single piece of melba toast, a few paper-thin shavings of cold ham, and a boiled egg. She opened her mouth to call Foster back, then stopped.

Just one slice of bacon, she thought, as the maid disappeared into Mama's bedroom.

Unable to resist, she moved to take a piece from the plate in front of her, but then a vision of white satin, lace, and tulle sprang into her mind, and the first notes of Mendelssohn's wedding march sounded in her imagination. She snatched her hand back and sat on it, reminding herself of the fabulous wedding gown Lucile was making for her and how it would never look right if it had to be let out at the seams. Desperate to marshal her willpower, she took a deep breath, but she was immediately overwhelmed by the delicious scent of bacon.

Willpower went to the wall, and Kay capitulated, sliding her hand from beneath her hip just as the door of her bedroom opened. Quick as lightning, she snatched the bacon off the plate and shoved it into her mouth, then slammed the plate cover back over her sister's breakfast.

"I smell breakfast," Josephine said as she crossed the sitting room to the table where Kay sat.

"Morning," Kay mumbled rather indistinctly as her sister crossed the sitting room and approached the table.

"Morning," Josephine responded, sliding into the opposite chair, her hand lifting the cover off the tray in front of her, exposing Kay's meager bits of food. "What the—"

Josephine paused, looking up, her emerald-green eyes widening a little, her exquisitely shaped lips curving at the corners. "Stealing my breakfast, are you?" she said teasingly.

Kay's answering glance was apologetic even as she savored the heavenly taste in her mouth. "Only a bit," she said once she had chewed and swallowed the stolen treat. "Sorry, but I just couldn't help myself."

"Perfectly understandable." Josephine gestured to the full plate in front of her sister. "Have the rest, do."

Kay sighed. "I can't. I felt my corset growing tighter with every moment I spent looking at those fried potatoes of yours."

"You've been banting for months. You've been so terribly strict with yourself, in fact, I'm surprised you haven't fainted dead away at some point. It won't hurt to indulge yourself just this once."

"Won't it, though?" Kay gave her sister a rueful glance across the table. "If that dress of mine shows the tiniest bulge, the gossip rags will shred me into spills. And giving them any excuse to employ their poisonous pens is something I will never do again. So..."

She paused, shoving the tray toward her sister before she could change her mind. "Take it," she urged, making a face. "And give me my bread and water."

The trays were exchanged, but before either of them could pick up a fork, their mother's voice entered the conversation.

"It's a miracle, my darlings!" Magdelene cried, coming toward them in a negligee of pink silk, a newspaper in her hand and a pair of gold-rimmed pince-nez perched on the tip of her nose. "An absolute miracle!"

Always flamboyant, Magdelene paused beside Kay's chair, lifted the paper higher, and began to read. "'Lady Kay Matheson, as we all know, was one of London's least impressive debutantes the year she came out—'"

"What *are* you reading, Mama?" Kay cut in, though given the words her mother had just recited, she feared she already knew.

"*Talk of the Town.*"

"Delilah Dawlish's column?" Her fears confirmed, Kay made a sound of exasperation and disdain. "Awful woman. Why do you read her malicious rubbish? We already know she hates me—"

"Ah, but she doesn't," Magdelene said triumphantly, waving the paper in the air. "Not anymore."

Kay gave a snort of disbelief. "Since when?"

Magdelene merely smiled, held up the paper and continued, "'Because of her scandalous attempt at elopement fourteen years ago, we thought reckless, foolish Lady Kay was forever doomed to shame, disgrace, and spinsterhood. But—'"

"That's what you deem a miracle, Mama?"

"*Listen*, won't you?"

"Must I?"

Magdelene ignored that wistful plea, gave a theatrical little cough, and went on, "'But things may at last be changing for poor Lady Kay. She was spied Tuesday last in the showroom of Lucile. And what, you ask, was she doing? Selecting bolts of satin. White satin, my dears! Can it be that society's longest-suffering jilted bride has finally found some much-deserved happiness?'"

"I admit, that's an agreeable change from her usual dreck," Kay said, working to keep her voice light. "I wonder how long it will last."

"Permanently, I hope," Magdelene replied, tapping the newspaper with one decisive finger. "It's taken years, but all the other society pages have been slowly coming around, especially once dear Wilson began showing his interest in you."

To her mother, Kay's fiancé was always "dear Wilson." The American millionaire was saving her family from the dismal fate of genteel poverty, after all. Even if he proved to be the greatest villain since Napoleon, Mama would probably still call him a dear.

"Delilah Dawlish was the last one holding out on you," Magdelene said, as if Kay needed that particular reminder, "but it appears that even she is finally ready to forgive and forget your great mistake."

Kay's disastrous attempted elopement with a stone-broke fortune hunter had been a mistake, no doubt, but given the humiliating way she'd been forced to atone for it, she felt her mother's hopes about Delilah Dawlish were somewhat premature. Granted, she was finally going to be washed clean by becoming respectably married, but she'd seen her name dragged through the mud of the gutter press too many times in the past to think anything was going to change before she got to the altar.

"You're so optimistic, Mama," she said wryly. "Fourteen years ago, if you recall, I was the plain, freckled, chubby girl no man would ever look twice at. Is it any great surprise that I eloped with a fortune hunter? I thought," she added before her mother could reply, "after I'd come to my senses, that we'd be able to hush it all up. But no. Just as I was on the verge of marrying Cousin Giles, the elopement scandal came out, Giles called things off, and I was ruined, shamed, destined—so *Talk of the Town* and all the other gossip rags reminded everyone daily—for permanent spinsterhood, forever spurned by the bachelors of good society."

As she paraphrased bits from the stories that had been written about her over the years, Kay could not quite hide her past pain nor her contempt for both the ravenous journalists and the despicable scoundrel who had given them such rich meat to feed on at her expense. "And we can all thank Devlin Sharpe—"

She stopped, her utterance of his name like a hand around her throat, choking her.

Magdelene sighed, giving her daughter a censorious glance over the rims of her pince-nez. "We do not mention That Horrible Man," she reminded, giving the devil his due in obvious capital letters. "Not ever."

"Quite right, Mama," Kay replied, shoving thoughts of Devlin out of her mind. "But I can't imagine what on earth has brought about this transformation of me into the—how did the Dawlish woman put it?—the 'longest-suffering jilted bride' deserving of happiness."

"Does it matter? You cannot deny that Mrs. Dawlish speaking in your favor is a splendid turn of events. For both of you," she added with a glance at her younger daughter.

"Very splendid," Kay agreed. "Especially with Jo coming out this season. But I'd still dearly love to know what has inspired this change of heart about me."

"Dear Wilson," Magdelene murmured with a sigh. "Such a wonderful man. Handsome, successful, and so, so generous."

It was the final part of that assessment that gave Kay a hint as to what her mother meant. "Are you saying Wilson bribed that sordid scandal sheet to write something nice about me?"

Even as she spoke, Kay knew such an action would not have been out of character for her fiancé. He did tend to think money could solve any problem. That, she supposed, was a luxury of the very rich.

"No, no, darling. That's not how it came about. Not at all."

Kay found her mother's choice of words anything but reassuring. "How then?" she asked, growing uneasy.

Magdelene gave a deprecating shrug. "Wilson and I have been corresponding regularly during his visit home to New York, and in one of my letters, I happened to mention that Sir Adair Sloane owns *Talk of the Town*. And," she added, ignoring her eldest daughter's aggravated sigh, "I explained that it is London's most influential society paper, that it has been very cruel to you in the past, and that it still seems inclined to harp on some... ahem... unfounded rumors about your past. Upon his return yesterday from New York, he must have called on Sir Adair and resolved the problem."

"Unfounded rumors?" Kay echoed and laughed. "I know we've had to deny everything and pretend to society that the elopement never happened, but there is no point in whitewashing things to Wilson. When he proposed to me in January, I told him that the rumors about me were true."

"You did?" Magdelene stared at her in dismay. "But why? That is the same mistake you made with Giles, and look how that turned out. Why would you do such a thing a second time?"

"So I should accept a man's proposal under false pretenses?" Kay shook her head. "No. Don't worry, Mama. Wilson, unlike Giles, didn't care a jot. Like nearly everyone else, he knew our denials were all a hum just to save face."

Her mother sighed. "Really, my dear. There is such a thing as too much honesty."

"Since we've all been living a futile lie ever since the rumors began circulating eleven years ago, I found being honest a refreshing change."

"Oh, did you? You might have stopped to consider the risks. What if Wilson had done what Giles did and cried off? What would happen to Josephine's chances of a good marriage? And what about you and me? Where would we live? We'd end up scraping by on Giles's charity, in a horrid little cottage somewhere. Did you think of that?"

"I'm never allowed to stop thinking about it, with you constantly reminding me," she countered, and immediately regretted it as her mother's face took on the appearance of a wounded kitten. "But how," she said, deciding it was best to divert the conversation, "did telling Wilson about Sir Adair's dirty little paper impel that rag to have a change of heart about me?"

Thankfully, her ploy succeeded. "Ah, well," Magdelene said, "I happened to mention to dear Wilson that Sir Adair's favorite charity is a most worthy one. Widows and orphans. What, I asked him, could be more worthy of a contribution than that?"

"You're so public-spirited, Mama. I suppose I should be grateful that you didn't actually come right out and ask Wilson to bribe Sir Adair."

Magdelene had the temerity to look affronted. "I would never be so crude as that."

"Nor, I suppose, would you have to be. Wilson didn't become one of the wealthiest men in America by being slow on the uptake. Your hints were enough, I daresay. Tell me," she continued, almost afraid to ask, "did you and Wilson do this with all the papers, or just this one?"

"It wasn't necessary with the others." Magdelene set down the paper and patted it with once hand. "As I said, the other papers have already softened their stance toward you quite a bit. And I'd have expected you to be relieved that *Talk of the Town* is finally saying nice things about you."

"I am, I am," she replied at once, holding up one hand in a show of capitulation. She might not care much for her mother's methods, but if they had the happy result of Delilah Dawlish no longer shredding her into spills, Kay supposed she could live with it, especially given how much it would help Jo make a successful debut this season. "I know you and Wilson were both acting for my benefit, so go on." She gestured to the paper in her mother's hand. "Finish reading me the result of your joint efforts."

Magdelene returned her attention to the page and continued, "'Lady Kay, we have observed, is looking quite fashionably slim nowadays. No doubt that is what inspires her to look at white satin.'"

"A moment of madness," Kay muttered, took a sip of her unsugared tea, and grimaced.

"It wasn't," Josephine assured her at once. "It will make a lovely wedding dress. You'll be the most beautiful bride in London."

Kay knew that was sisterly loyalty talking, but nonetheless, she felt a fierce wave of affection for her young sibling rising up inside her. "You're a darling, but I wonder if I ought to have picked the chiffon instead? I know it's not as fashionable as the satin, but—"

"Only the plump girls wear chiffon," her mother cut in, "and you are most certainly not one of those. At least not anymore."

"Thank you, Mama."

The dryness of her reply was lost on her mother. "Besides, Wilson prefers the satin. I asked him. Don't swear, dear," she added as Kay muttered an oath. "He told me quite clearly that he wanted to be kept informed of all the wedding plans while he was away."

"What?" Kay cried, tossing down her napkin, now truly exasperated by her mother's interfering ways. "Oh, Mother, really!"

"Isn't the dress supposed to be a surprise for the groom?" Jo asked.

Magdelene ignored them both and resumed reading. "'We thought that Lady Kay might have caught Mr. Wilson Rycroft's eye during his first visit to England last summer. But when he returned to America for the holidays and no engagement was announced, we could only conclude we were mistaken. But he is back in London now, and giving us cause to wonder anew if a certain red-haired spinster with a checkered past is what has pulled him back to our shores. We are certain it is no coincidence that well before the season, he and Lady Kay are both residing in the same London hotel. No engagement has been formally announced yet, but the bolts of satin at Lucile rather give the game away, don't you—'"

Magdelene broke off as Foster placed a tray of food in front of her. "What's this?" she asked, removing the pince-nez from her nose to study the half-empty plate with surprise and a hint of distaste.

"It's half past ten, my lady. I thought you might wish to finish your breakfast."

"No, no." Magdelene, still quite slim at the age of fifty-five, waved a hand over the tray in an uninterested way that her famished eldest daughter could only envy. "I'm quite finished. And I don't have time, in any case, if it is half past ten. I don't want us to miss our first appointment of the day."

"What appointment?" Kay asked as Foster took the offending tray away. "We aren't returning to Lucile until this afternoon, I thought."

"I'm not talking about Lucile. I scheduled a meeting for us with the Savoy florist at eleven to discuss the wedding flowers."

"But why? We're not having the wedding banquet here, unfortunately. Not now."

"Who says so?"

Kay stared at her mother in surprise. "Delia said so. The only room the Savoy has that's large enough for us is the Pinafore Room, and because of that muddle between her and Lord Calderon in January, our reservation got pushed aside for another wedding."

"It was quite unforgivable of Calderon to pull the Pinafore out from under us for someone else! That is why, after we meet the florist, I am paying a call on Mrs. Carte to discuss the situation with her."

"I realize Mrs. Carte is now in charge of the Savoy, but I don't see what good talking to her will do."

"Delia had mentioned before she left for Paris that she had another plan in the works that might allow us to still have the wedding banquet here."

"But that was before the Savoy fired her, along with most of the other members of staff. Lord Calderon resigned, leaving Mrs. Carte in charge. And since that woman hates Delia, it's clear any plan she had for us is out the window. And now that she's had to go to Paris—"

Her mother interrupted with a sniff. "It was very inconsiderate of Delia to go off like that and abandon us."

Mama was nothing if not self-absorbed. "Delia's had her own troubles, Mama. She did get fired, after all. Still, I am sure she hasn't abandoned us. She said she was only staying a fortnight, so she'll be back any day. And she did give us a list of possibilities to investigate in her absence. Not that it's done us much good," Kay added with a sigh. "We've looked everywhere, but there doesn't seem to be a single ballroom or banquet hall anywhere else for the seventh of June that's large enough to accommodate us."

"Just so. We have no choice but to discern if Delia's plan—whatever it was—can still be managed. Failing that, we might see if the party that stole the Pinafore out from under us can be persuaded to change their reservation."

"Never say die," Kay said solemnly. "Perhaps like Sir Adair, they have a favorite charity Wilson can donate to."

"My thoughts, exactly," Magdelene said with complacence.

"Mother!" Kay cried in vexation. "I was joking."

"I wasn't."

Kay groaned, and for a moment she wondered if a second attempt at elopement might be in order. But she shoved that mad idea aside. This wedding had to be right out in the open, for everyone who mattered to see. For Jo's sake as well as her own, it had to be the biggest, most opulent social event of the season, the event everyone spent the rest of the summer talking about, not because it was a scandal, but because it wasn't.

That was why, despite Wilson's desire not to formally announce the engagement before he returned, they had informed all their relations of the news. Happily relieved that their most disgraced relation was about to be washed clean, all of them had agreed to attend, hence the need for such a large banquet room. Making her wedding a social success was why she'd chosen fashionable satin for her dress when she preferred chiffon, why she starved herself with minuscule breakfasts, and why she was willing to accept the embarrassing efforts of her mother and Wilson to bribe the society papers—it would all be worth it in the end. Once she walked down the aisle in honorable fashion in front of all of society, her past would be well and truly behind her at last.

"Either way," she said, returning to the vital point, "I doubt even

Wilson's money can be counted on to persuade the party reserving the Pinafore Room to vacate it."

"I think we are obliged to explore all possibilities. We simply must find a room that will seat everyone."

That was an inarguable point.

"So," her mother went on in the wake of her silence, "I asked Mrs. Carte if we might call on her to discuss the matter. She suggested half past eleven, but now, I wonder..."

Magdelene paused, considering. "I wonder if that gives us enough time. We shall have barely a quarter of an hour to see the florist before we have to dash off. Perhaps you could see about the flowers while I pay that call on Mrs. Carte. Orchids would be lovely, darling, by the way."

"Very lovely," she agreed, her gaze straying to her desk where the unpaid bills were piling up with alarming rapidity. "And very expensive."

"But we don't have to worry about expenses, darling. Not anymore."

Yes, there's nothing like marrying a millionaire to solve all a girl's problems.

That rather cynical reply hovered on Kay's lips, but as she looked up, noting how her engagement to one of America's richest tycoons had smoothed away the lines of worry that had been etched into her mother's face since her father's death a year ago, any impulse Kay had to say those words vanished.

Giles, being the new earl, had wanted—quite rightly—to move into the house. He had half-heartedly offered to let them continue living there with him and his wife, but that would have been terribly awkward, to say the least, and they had declined. For the past year, they had been drifting all over England, from hotel to hotel, trying to make their minuscule quarterly allowance from the impoverished estate last by ducking their bills and evading their creditors. Had Wilson not come along, had he not proposed, they'd eventually have had to go abroad.

But Wilson had come along, and when he proposed, Kay's relief had been so great, she'd nearly fainted for the first time in her life. The creditors could all be paid, Mama would be secure, and Josephine would be able to have her first London season at last.

London, of course, was expensive, but the Savoy had always been known to have fairly liberal terms of repayment, at least as far as members of the aristocracy were concerned.

"Yes," her mother said, breaking into her thoughts, "orchids would be best, I think."

She wanted gardenias, but for a June wedding, gardenias would be almost as much as orchids. On the other hand, did it really matter? After all, the dresses were from Lucile, the Savoy was costing the earth, and the pricing estimates for Jo's debutante ball had made her gasp in shock, but perhaps her mother was right to not be worried. After all, Wilson was one of the richest men in America, and once her engagement to him was formally announced, the bank would be happy to give her a loan based on her expectations. And once she and Wilson married, the marriage settlement he'd agreed to pay would cover everything. They'd only be in trouble if the wedding didn't come off.

"Not orchids," she told her mother. "I prefer gardenias."

"Gardenias? No, no, dear. I know they are your favorite, but they are white, and your dress is white. No, orchids will be better. Pale green ones, with your coloring."

"I'll have both, then," she said, making the compromise. "But either way, I don't have to pick them today. I'd rather go with you to see Mrs. Carte," she added, hoping there might be a way to prevail upon the wife of the Savoy's founder for the Pinafore Room without attempts at bribery. "After all, the room is more important. We have plenty of time to choose the flowers."

"But we don't, Kay. That's just it. June seventh is only ten weeks away, dear. The season will be full-on by then, with flowers of all sorts in short supply. And with this being Josephine's first season, things will be a whirlwind for us as well. Best to have all the wedding plans made well in advance. I will call on Mrs. Carte, and you will see the florist. Your sister can accompany you."

Kay capitulated, knowing her mother was right. "Very well. When Jo and I have finished, we'll come fetch you, have lunch at the Criterion, and go on to Lucile from there."

A frown marred Magdelene's smooth forehead. "I'm not sure that's wise. I don't want anyone to see you two on your own and think you're gallivanting around London unchaperoned."

"A valid point, Mama, but a five-minute ride in a growler with my sister is hardly gallivanting. And it's silly for you to come back here when Mrs. Carte's office is right on the way to the Criterion. Don't fuss."

"Oh, very well, but you'd best stop dawdling and eat your breakfast," Magdelene said as she set down the paper and rose from the table. "You've only half an hour, and you still have to dress."

Kay turned toward her sister as their mother started toward her room with Foster on her heels. "You don't mind helping me with the flowers this morning, do you, Jo?" she asked, casting a covetous glance at Josephine's croissants as she picked up her napkin.

"Don't call your sister Jo," Magdelene admonished over her shoulder without so much as a backward glance. "And, Kay, I'd suggest that you not sponge off your sister's plate," she added, making Kay wonder—not for the first time—if her parent had eyes in the back of her head as well as the front. "Satin is so unforgiving. What will people think if the dress doesn't fit?"

Despite this echoing of what Kay already knew, she couldn't help a wistful sigh as she picked up a slice of melba toast. "I wish I didn't have to care so much what people think."

"It's not for much longer," Josephine said. "Only until June. Once you're married, you can eat whatever you like and wear whatever you like and go where you like, and no one will care, not even Delilah Dawlish."

Jo was right, of course, but as Kay took a bite of hard, dry toast, she grimaced. It was like eating sawdust. June, she decided, could not come fast enough.

"Devlin?"

At the sound of his name, Devlin Sharpe looked up from the paper he was reading to find Pamela coming toward him across the lobby of the Savoy. It had been two months since he'd seen her, and as he watched her approach, he appreciated—not for the first time—her ethereal blond beauty and the grace with which she seemed to float across the floor. She reminded him a bit of the angel one might put atop one's Christmas tree.

But appearances could often be deceiving, and Lady Pamela Stirling was no exception. The only child of a marquess, Pam had all the well-bred arrogance that came from high position. But Devlin didn't mind that. Born into the same aristocratic world she inhabited, he was used to it. In addition, Pam had been raised as the center of her parents' universe and was a bit spoiled in consequence, but Devlin didn't mind that, either. These days, he had the blunt to give her anything she wanted, and in return, she was happy to put his wishes above even her own, a trait he found both surprising and quite gratifying. In Devlin's entire life, no one had ever put him first, not his own family, and certainly not his previous fiancée, and he found his second fiancée's willingness to do so a welcome change from all the people in his past experience, even if he was paying for the privilege.

Besides, angels had never held any charms for him. His father hadn't nicknamed him the devil's spawn for nothing. And Pam was quite a catch for a man of his position. The disgraced fifth son of a baron didn't usually warrant the attentions, much less the hand, of a marquess's daughter, even if said marquess was stone broke.

He wasn't in love, but that was quite all right with him, too. Love, as he knew from bitter experience, was painful, messy, and highly overrated, and he wanted nothing to do with it ever again.

He'd admitted as much to Pam upon proposing, of course, and much to his relief, she'd accepted him anyway and expressed a similar view of love to his own. She was fond of him, she'd said, but she'd never have agreed to marry him if he hadn't had money. Her brutal, clear-eyed honesty about herself and what she wanted from life was another thing he liked about her, and another refreshing contrast to his first fiancée.

"Are you all right?" Pamela asked, smiling a little as she paused in front of his chair.

"Of course," he said, setting aside the *Times* and rising to his feet. "Should I not be?"

"You're staring at me as if you've never seen me before."

"Well, it's been two months since we parted in Cairo," he reminded. "And if I am staring, can you blame me?" he added, giving a nod to the hotel guests around them who hurried to and fro across the Savoy's elegantly appointed lobby. "Half the men here are staring at you. I'm just one amid the throng."

"Hardly," she said, laughing, but beneath that amused, dismissive reply was a complacence that indicated she was well aware of her own feminine appeal.

How could she not be?

With her wheat-gold hair, brown doe eyes, and stunning face, Pamela had been deemed one of the most beautiful women in London during her debut two years before, and even if society hadn't been so fulsome in their praise, one glance in the mirror and she'd have had to be blind not to see the blessings fortune had conveyed upon her. Rather surprising that she hadn't been snapped up by the end of her first season. But then, Devlin knew there was a rebellious streak in Pam's nature, one he guessed had led her to reject the men her mother had deemed suitable for introductions. Pamela's mother did not find him the least bit suitable, and that, he supposed, was part of his charm as far as Pam was concerned.

"When did you arrive from Yorkshire?" she asked, interrupting his thoughts.

"Late last night."

"And how is your family and the estate?"

"My brother Thomas and his family are well enough. And Stonygates is ticking along as if it's still 1820. What about you? Lord Walston's estates in fine form?"

"Well enough, under the circumstances. Papa was quite pleased since we'd been away nearly a year. Speaking of fathers..." She paused, giving him a hopeful look. "I note you don't mention yours. How is he?"

"I wouldn't know," Devlin replied with a shrug, pretending a lightness he didn't quite feel. "He refused to see me and departed within an hour of my arrival for his hunting lodge in Scotland. Thomas showed me round the old place."

"I'm sorry to hear that, but he will come around eventually."

"I'm sure he will, once Thomas tells him I'm engaged to you."

"That's more than we can say of my mother."

As she spoke, a faint, almost imperceptible smile tipped the corners of her mouth, confirming his suspicion that Pamela relished twisting her mother's tail whenever possible.

"Enough about our absolutely impossible families." Devlin eased a bit closer to her. "What's important is that I'm finally able to see you again. Pity I arrived from Yorkshire so late last night. Had I arrived earlier, I'd have come running to pay a call on you straightaway."

Her smile widened. "I was so glad to see your invitation to lunch on my breakfast plate this morning."

"And I'm glad you were free to accept." He glanced past her. "Where is your mother, by the way? Isn't she joining us?"

Pam heaved a sigh. "Yes, unfortunately. You and I can't go to lunch alone, even if we are engaged."

"That would be unthinkable," he said with a pretense of gravity. "Capital offense."

"It is for my mother," Pam said, making a face. "But our luncheon reservation isn't until half past twelve," she added, brightening, "so Mama won't be down for at least half an hour."

"Well, then…" He paused, smiling a little, his gaze honing in on her small, rosebud mouth. "Dare I hope you sought me out for a little passionate necking in an empty corridor somewhere before Lady Walston joins us?"

Pamela blushed, looking the picture of maidenly modesty. "Devlin," she said with reproof, "you mustn't say such things."

"Darling, you love it when I say such things."

In the wake of that, Pamela proved herself no angel at all by slanting him a flirtatious look from beneath her lashes and saying, "Perhaps I do. But," she added at once, shredding any hopes he might have been harboring of a deliciously illicit interlude, "that's not why I came down early. I must see the florist. I have a few questions about the wedding flowers before I decide which ones I want."

"You're already choosing the flowers? But the wedding isn't until June."

"And that's less than three months away, so I simply must make a decision now. Besides," she went on before he could even get his mind to understand the need to choose one's wedding flowers ten weeks in advance, "you need to pick a flower for yourself."

He looked at her askance. "The groom has to have a bouquet, too?"

"Not for the wedding, silly. We're going to lunch, remember? At Rules." She tapped a fingertip against his lapel as he remained unenlightened. "And your buttonhole is empty."

He looked down to find she was right. "So it is," he conceded. "Too many years in the wilds, my dear."

"You should hire a valet."

He laughed. "My darling, whatever for? We'll be returning to Egypt in just a few months."

She frowned as if puzzled. "Longer than that. We'll be in Italy for our honeymoon, you know. And a gentleman," she added before he could point out that a two-week honeymoon made their return to Cairo exactly three months hence, "especially once he is married, should always have a proper valet. Even in Africa, the rules of proper dress must be observed. And you can't argue that having a valet wouldn't be quite a convenience here in London."

Humoring her, he decided, was his best bet at this point, since he didn't much care either way. "It would be handy," he agreed. "Having been away so long, I sometimes forget the absurd requirements of fashion."

"They aren't absurd, Devlin. Not here, not when everything one does is seen and remarked upon."

"Yes," he said with feeling. "I'm well aware."

Pam immediately looked stricken. "I didn't mean—"

"It's quite all right," he interrupted. "Please, darling, don't apologize. I know I have to be on the straight and narrow these days, now that I'm about to be a married man. And I'm happy to toe the line, for your sake. So," he added, offering his arm, "with my nefarious plan to spirit you away definitely off the table, shall we go see the florist together?"

Her stunning smile was his reward. "Excellent idea. I can help you choose a boutonniere."

Out of nowhere, he felt a flash of irritation at the offer. That made no sense, of course, since they were engaged. Pamela had every right to a bit of wifely supervision where her future husband was concerned. And no one could argue that she did not have excellent taste.

She slid her arm through his, and together they crossed the opulent lobby. As they entered the shop of the Savoy florist, the various scents of the flowers seemed overpowering, and the clouds of pink, yellow, and white blossoms all around them made Devlin wish, not for the first time, that he'd been able to talk Pam out of a wedding in England. After fourteen years away, being here made him feel smothered, trapped, and strangely off-balance.

"Why don't you look at these stems while I see Monsieur Lavigne?" Pamela suggested.

She gestured to a wrought-iron rack nearby, where single stems of flowers reposed in galvanized pails of water, waiting to adorn the lapels of London's dandies. He studied them, feigning vast interest as Pamela walked away toward the back of the shop, going up and down the rows. Bachelor's buttons, rosebuds, gardenias. He stopped, and in his mind, an image of a white gardenia in a girl's copper-colored hair flashed through his mind. He shoved it out again and moved on to the diminutive pink, white, and red carnations in the next row.

He selected a red carnation from the pail nearest him, but then he remembered vaguely that red carnations were only acceptable if your mother was alive. Or maybe that was white? Uncertain, he fingered the carnation, cursing himself for procrastinating about hiring a valet. But then, it had been easy to procrastinate during his two months at Stonygates when he'd had one of his father's footmen to do for him. Now, however, with the season coming, and the wedding, he'd best get on with finding someone. Because Pam was right: in London, everything, even the wrong flower in a man's buttonhole, was cause for comment. And he'd been cause for comment enough already in his life.

Best to err on the side of caution, he decided as he put the red carnation back and reached for a bright blue bachelor's button instead.

He'd barely pulled it out of the bucket, however, before a feminine voice floated to his ears. It was not Pamela's voice, but it was familiar—a voice from long ago, a voice that went with red hair and gardenias, a voice he knew as well as he knew his name, even though he hadn't heard it, except in dreams, for nearly fourteen years.

Devlin froze, suddenly paralyzed.

"I want to have a look at the gardenias," the voice said, coming to him over a trellis densely packed with vines of pink bougainvillea. "I might want one for my hat. Why don't you go and have the doorman order us a cab? I'll follow you in a minute."

It's not possible, he told himself, his fingers clenching around the dripping stem in his hand, his guts tightening with dismay. *I'm imagining things.*

That rather desperate thought had barely crossed his mind before the owner of the voice came around the trellis, and as she stopped a few feet away, the sight of her shredded any optimistic notion that he'd been imagining things.

Standing amid buckets and bouquets, her flaming hair a vivid contrast to the pink flowers and greenery all around her, was the woman it had taken him many long, hard years and the kisses of many other women to forget.

Kay.

There was no mistaking those bright curls peeking out from

under a wide-brimmed hat of pale yellow straw, or those strangely beautiful silvery-green eyes surrounded by dark red lashes, or that pale, porcelain skin. And there was definitely no mistaking the freckles spattered across her nose and cheeks that always made her look as if a mischievous fairy had come along in the night and dusted her face with brown sugar.

She didn't look exactly the same, however. She was thinner than the girl he remembered, he realized as he glanced down over a fashionably slim figure in blue wool.

What a pity.

She probably wouldn't agree with him there. Kay had always hated her curves. Why that was so, he'd never understood, but then, most women had ridiculous ideas about what constituted feminine beauty. Torching their hair with hot curling tongs, picking at their food like finicky little birds, squeezing and pinching their waistlines with corsets until they looked like wasps, bleaching away their pretty freckles with lemon juice.

For Kay, of course, using hot tongs had never been necessary. Her hair had always been a mass of unruly corkscrew curls. And using lemon juice would have been a futile endeavor, for her freckles were everywhere. Her shoulders, her arms, cresting the tops of her breasts—

Memories assailed him, of brushing brilliant copper tresses back from her shoulders, of tracing star constellations across the golden-brown dots along her clavicle above the edge of her white chemise, kissing the ones scattered across her shoulders. With those memories came an onslaught of other emotions, emotions he hadn't felt for years, emotions he thought he'd conquered and killed long ago.

Desire, anger, frustration, pain—they caught him unawares, like a knife in the dark, slipped between his ribs, piercing his lungs, robbing him of the ability to think or even breathe.

He looked up, watching her big sage-colored eyes narrow to slits, demonstrating that he wasn't the only one thinking of the past, though if her face was anything to go by, the biggest thing it made her feel was contempt. The lips of her wide, generous mouth were pressed together in a tight, unforgiving line. Her pert freckled nose was wrinkled up as if she'd caught a bad smell. One auburn eyebrow arched upward in unmistakable disdain.

Damn it all, he thought, the knife twisting deep inside his chest. *Damn it all to hell.*

2

She ought to have known, she supposed, that this moment would come one day.

After all, in a city populated by a mere six million people, of course she'd be bound to stumble upon the only man she'd ever loved, the man who'd left her flat, broken her heart, and ruined her life. Yes, indeed. Her luck was just that good.

But she hadn't known. He'd taken her father's bribe and gone off in that craven way for Africa, and after more than two years with no word from him, after watching helplessly as the rumors of their botched elopement had spread far and wide, destroying her reputation and her future, after over a decade with no indication that he ever intended to return to England, she'd been lulled into the heavenly belief that she'd never see the contemptible cad again.

So now, as Kay stared into Devlin Sharpe's face, she felt all the shock, all the pain, all the humiliation of the past come rushing back in a flood. Heat rose in her cheeks, rage burned like fire in her chest, and she could only stare at him, paralyzed into immobility.

In appearance, he looked different somehow from the man she remembered. His eyes were still that extraordinary shade of turquoise blue, but in a face bronzed by the African sun, their color seemed more vibrant, more startling than ever. Beneath the brim of his hat, his hair was still the color of a moonless midnight, but at his temples, there were a few faint strands of silver amid the black, marking the passage of time.

His face was still lean and angular, the planes of his cheekbones as sharply chiseled as ever, but there were faint smile lines at the corners of his eyes and the edges of his mouth that made him seem mellower somehow, less hard, less rebellious and defiant than the man she'd known so long ago. His once-straight Roman nose was ever so faintly out of place, showing that it had been broken at some point, probably by a hard right hook he no doubt richly deserved.

His face wasn't the only thing that had changed, she realized, her gaze sliding down. He still topped her five-foot, four-inch frame by a good ten inches, and he still had the same wide shoulders and mile-long legs, but during the past fourteen years, the gangly, whipcord thinness of his youth had filled out, transforming his body to a more powerful, muscular one than that of the younger man she remembered.

His gray wool suit and gray homburg hat were commonplace attire for an upper-class Englishman, and yet, somehow, his appearance reflected not the isle of his birth but the continent from which he'd just come. He looked strong, primitive, and almost laughably out of place in the civilized confines of a London florist's shop.

One thing about him, however, had not changed at all, Kay noted in chagrin as she lifted her gaze again to his face. He was still the best-looking man she'd ever seen.

How nauseating.

"You," she said with soul-deep loathing.

"Well, well," he drawled, tipping his hat to her with a bow, "if it isn't Lady Kay."

The contemptuous way her name rolled off his tongue shredded any notion she might have had that he had mellowed with time. It also flicked her on the raw. What grudge was he nursing, in heaven's name? She'd been the injured party all those years ago, not him.

She scowled. "What in blazes are you doing here?"

"Isn't it obvious?" He gestured to their surroundings, and her shock deepened as she realized what he meant.

"You mean…" She paused, appalled by the implications. "You don't mean you're staying here at the Savoy?"

"Staying at a hotel is rather a novel concept, I know. But there it is."

Kay recovered her wits with an effort. "I didn't know a hotel of this caliber allowed dogs."

He laughed. "Why, Kay, what a thing to say. Are you angry with me for some reason?"

That question was too much. "Don't pretend, you bastard," she choked. "If I'm angry, you know exactly why."

Something glittered in those brilliant blue eyes, the triumph of knowing he'd gotten under her skin, and she cursed herself for giving him that sort of satisfaction.

"Do I?" he murmured, his voice low and mocking. "And even if I do know, society doesn't, do they?"

She stiffened, looking away, knowing he had a point, hating him all the more for it.

When their elopement had become public knowledge and sordid fodder for the gutter press, each of them had chosen the only possible course: denial. They'd claimed that they hardly knew each other, that the elopement had never happened, and that the rumors were nothing more than ill-founded gossip. Their simultaneous efforts hadn't mattered, sadly, since most people hadn't believed either of them. Nonetheless, the course had been set, and there was no changing it now.

Granted, the odds were low that anyone they knew was watching them at this particular moment, but if he was in London for the season and staying at the Savoy, there would surely come an occasion when someone they knew would see them encounter each other. If she displayed any hint of her animosity and contempt for him, it would only serve to confirm society's long-held suspicions. She might as well stand on a rooftop and shout out to the world the humiliating admission that yes, he really had ruined her and jilted her, and she hated him for it.

No, however hard it might be, polite indifference was the only choice open to her.

Resolved, she looked up, but the smile curving the edges of his mouth fractured that resolve at once, and she wondered what would happen if she just hurled sensibilities and propriety and playing safe and watching eyes to the wind, hauled back, and slapped that faint, insolent smile right off his arrogant face.

"You want to know what I think?" he asked, breaking into her turbulent thoughts.

She forced herself to offer a polite smile. "Not really, no."

His smile widened a fraction, showing that her offhand reply hadn't fooled him for a second. "I think the sight of me makes you angry because you still care."

Of course that's what he'd think, the conceited scoundrel. "That must be it," she countered brightly. "I'm absolutely pining. Can't you tell?"

He flashed her a grin, his teeth startlingly white in his bronzed face. "Glad to hear you admit it."

Kay's palm began to itch.

Thankfully, however, she had no chance to give in to her temptation to do him violence, because another voice entered the conversation at that moment, saving her.

"Devlin?"

Both of them turned as a woman came to his side, a young blond beauty with a face Kay recognized. About the same age as Josephine, Lady Pamela Stirling had attended the same finishing school as Kay's young sister and had been the acknowledged beauty of the season during her coming out two years before. She was also from one of Britain's finest, most influential families, a family Kay could not afford to antagonize.

As Kay wondered how a girl of barely twenty even knew Devlin Sharpe, much less knew him well enough to call him by his Christian name, Devlin turned to the girl, his impudent grin softening.

"Darling," he greeted, his voice low and unmistakably tender.

Darling? Kay's mind echoed the word in shocked disbelief. *Darling?*

"I need to make introductions, I would imagine," he went on, and when he looked at Kay again, she forced herself to don an expectant smile of greeting. "Lady Kay, allow me to present my fiancée."

Fiancée? She stared at the couple, thinking she must have misheard, but then, Pamela's fingers curled around Devlin's arm in a clearly proprietary gesture, and Kay realized she had not misheard anything.

"There's no need for introductions," Pamela said, returning Kay's pasted-on smile. "Lady Kay and I already know each other."

"You do?" Devlin asked, sounding surprised.

He wasn't the only one, she thought. Her own wits seemed to have disintegrated, and she couldn't seem to stop staring at Lady Pamela's hand tucked intimately into the crook of his arm. But when he pressed his palm over Lady Pamela's gloved fingers in an obvious show of affection, smiling at the girl as if utterly besotted, Kay stiffened, her considerable pride coming to the fore and reminding her that a warm, friendly demeanor was absolutely vital. Anything less would only reinforce Devlin's conceited presumptions, and that was something Kay refused to allow.

"Of course we know each other," she answered his question with a pretense of hearty good cheer. "We met at Willowbank Academy, if I remember rightly."

"School?" Devlin gave a disbelieving laugh. "You two could never have been at school together."

For some reason, Pamela found that amusing. "Of course not, silly," she replied with a tinkling laugh of her own. "Lady Kay graduated many years before I was ever there."

Inwardly, Kay grimaced. *Ouch.*

"No," Pam went on, "I was at Willowbank with Lady Kay's sister, Josephine. We were friends there. Lady Kay and I met during the graduation ceremonies."

Other than a brief introduction during the event in question, Kay could not recall Jo making any mention at all of Lady Pamela, so the two girls being friends was a doubtful prospect, but Kay had no choice but to give Pamela the benefit of the doubt. "All of you looked so lovely that day in your white caps and gowns."

Pamela laughed again. "We thought ourselves so grown up in them, I daresay. Although to someone your age," she added, "we must have seemed terribly young."

Biting back a sarcastic rejoinder about being older than Methuselah, Kay kept her smile in place, but the effort of doing so was already making her jaw ache, and she wondered just how long she had to stand here with these two, making small talk, before she could escape. Fortunately, Fate chose that moment to come to her aid.

"Kay?" Josephine's voice called behind her. "I've got a growler waiting for us. If we don't go soon, we'll be late meeting Mama. What on earth is taking you so— Heavens, it's Pamela!"

That surprised exclamation bolstered Kay's resolve even more. After all, like the couple in front of her, she too had moved on to a better life and future.

"What a nice surprise, isn't it, Jo?" she said, almost wincing at the forced heartiness of her own voice as her sister came to a halt beside her. "Running into your friend Lady Pamela this way? And you'll never believe who's here with her! Mr. Devlin Sharpe."

Faced so unexpectedly with the man who had ruined her sister, Jo couldn't quite hide her shock, nor her resentment on Kay's behalf. Her eyes widened, then narrowed.

"I'm sure you don't remember Mr. Sharpe," Kay said quickly. "He's so much older than you, after all," she added, getting a bit of her own back for Pamela's earlier remark. "Why, I think you were only a toddler when he went away to Africa all those years ago."

Devlin perceived her emphasis on the wide gulf between his age and Pamela's, for a wry smile twisted one corner of his mouth.

Josephine, heaven bless her, recovered, taking Kay's cue. "A pleasure to meet you, Mr. Sharpe," she said. "And Pamela, too. What an extraordinary surprise this is."

"Lady Pamela and Mr. Sharpe are engaged to be married," Kay went on, putting just the right amount of congratulatory pleasure into her voice. "Isn't that wonderful news?"

In profile, she saw Jo's lips part in astonishment, but again, Jo managed to play up beautifully. "Congratulations to both of you. Goodness, Kay," she added, her voice taking on a lively tone, "it's weddings, weddings everywhere this year, isn't it?"

"What's this?" Lady Pamela cried as Kay shot her sister a grateful glance. "Josephine, don't tell me you're getting married, too?"

"Me?" Jo laughed at that. "Good heavens, no. I'm out, I suppose, but it's not official until I make my debut in May."

"Didn't you come out last year? I was away in Europe, but I thought you had. I know you didn't come out with me the year before. Illness in the family, wasn't it?"

"Our father, yes. I would have come out the following year, but then our father died."

"Lord Raleigh's dead?" Devlin asked Kay as Pamela left off clinging to him like a limpet and moved closer to Jo. "I'm sorry, Kay," he added as Pamela murmured similar sympathies to Jo.

"Are you?" Kay murmured, her voice tight and too low for the two others to hear. "I don't recall you being particularly fond of my father."

"I barely knew him, but nonetheless, I'm sorry for your sake," he answered quietly, a kind reply that stung because he sounded like he meant it. "I know how fond you were of him."

He knew nothing of her complicated relationship with her late father, but either way, she didn't want him to be kind. No, damn it all, she wanted him to be rude and uncivil and awful, which didn't make any sense, especially given how necessary it was to maintain this charade of friendly politeness.

"Yes," she said with quiet dignity, "I was very fond of him."

"I almost envy you."

Kay understood at once what he meant. "You and your father haven't made amends, I take it?"

"Has the sun started rising in the west?"

She caught the bitter note behind the lighthearted question, but before she could think of how to reply, Lady Pamela broke off her conversation with Jo and returned her attention to Kay, offering the appropriate sympathies before reverting to the previous topic of conversation. "But if Jo's not getting married, then who is?"

The possibility that Kay might be the bride in question had clearly not occurred to the girl, and she supposed that as a disgraced and ruined spinster, firmly on the shelf for more than a decade, she ought to be used to that sort of dismissal. But nonetheless, it stung, particularly since the girl's own fiancé had been the cause of Kay's fall from grace.

"The one who's getting married is me," she said, savoring the news as she said it. "The wedding is in June."

"You?" The younger woman blinked. "You're getting married?"

Kay raised an eyebrow. "You seem surprised, Lady Pamela," she purred sweetly.

Pamela's skepticism was immediately concealed. "It's only that I don't recall seeing a wedding announcement in the papers."

"My fiancé has been in New York, and we wanted to wait until his return before we made the announcement. You'll see it within the next few days, I imagine."

"Well, this news is just too, too wonderful," Pamela said, turning to the man beside her. "Isn't it wonderful, Devlin?"

"Yes, wonderful," he said, his voice indifferent, his face impossible to read. "Who is he?"

"Oh, no one you know, I'm sure," Kay replied. "His name is Wilson Rycroft."

For some reason, that seemed to take him aback. "Rycroft?" he said, blinking. "You don't mean the American millionaire?"

A slight frown drew his brows together, indicating that he wasn't as indifferent to the news of her own engagement as he pretended to be, a fact that gave Kay immense satisfaction. She was so glad now that a show of amiability had been required of her. Until this moment, she'd never truly appreciated just how rewarding it could be to take the high road.

"The very same," she said, her pretense of a smile widening into a genuine one. "It sounds as if you know him?"

"We've met."

With that unmistakably terse reply, Kay decided this was the perfect time to make her exit.

"Indeed? How lovely," she said with wicked, heartfelt sincerity. "And now, Josephine and I really must be going. If we don't, we'll be late meeting our mother for lunch. And then we're off to the modiste. Wedding gowns need so many fittings to be just right, don't they?"

Pamela expressed wholehearted agreement with that sentiment, then farewells were said all around. At last, with profound relief, Kay turned and ushered Josephine out the door.

As they crossed the lobby, all the chaotic emotions that had been swirling around within Kay from the moment she'd laid eyes on him began fading into a vague sense of unreality, as if the whole ghastly episode had been nothing but a dream.

"Goodness, that was awkward," Josephine pronounced. "Of all the unexpected encounters. Too bad you couldn't have ducked out of the shop before they saw you."

"I would have done, believe me," Kay assured her, "but there was no time. I came around a trellis and there he was. A moment later, he was introducing me to his fiancée." As she spoke, her sense of unreality about the whole thing grew stronger, enveloping her in a strange numbness.

"How awful. What did you do?"

Kay shrugged. "In cases such as these, there's only one thing one can do, really."

"Which is?"

Kay waited until they had passed through the plate-glass door held open for them by a Savoy doorman before she replied. "Be civil, of course."

"Bor-ing," Jo said with obvious disappointment, falling in step beside her as they walked to the cab waiting for them in the courtyard. "Was it terribly hard?"

The question planted Kay's smile back in place. "Why should it have been?"

"Well," Jo began, but Kay forestalled her.

"Naturally, it was a bit of a shock, seeing him again after so many years. And meeting her, too, of course." Kay paused as the driver opened the door. "But I got over all of that almost at once."

"So you're all right, then?"

All right? The question caught her off guard, and she nearly stumbled as she stepped into the carriage, but when she answered, her voice was firm. "I'm quite all right."

Jo didn't seem convinced. "Are you sure?" she asked as she followed Kay into the cab. "The fact that he's engaged to be married doesn't bother you? Not even a little?" she added as Kay shook her head.

"After fourteen years? Don't be silly." Kay bent down, hiding her face from her sister's disbelieving stare, buying time as she settled her skirts around her feet. "Why should it bother me after all this time?"

"I can think of heaps of reasons," Jo muttered. "Abandoning you so abominably, for one thing. Telling people about your elopement nearly three years after it happened, spreading malicious rumors from thousands of miles away. And why? Out of spite and jealousy, that's why. He heard you were going to marry Giles, and he wanted to pay you out."

Kay couldn't disagree, for what else was there to believe? But it served no purpose to rehash it all now, especially with her young, impressionable sister. "Perhaps, but—"

"The horrible part is that it worked," Jo went on before Kay could redirect the conversation. "Giles broke the engagement when the scandal broke. Oh, I know Sharpe publicly denied the elopement had taken place," she added as Kay opened her mouth to reply. "But it's obvious that was just a belated, lame attempt to exonerate himself from being the cause of all your troubles. And his own father disowned him right after, didn't he? I'll wager Sharpe hadn't expected *that* to happen."

Kay frowned. "How do you know all this? You were only six when I eloped and nine when the whole mess became public knowledge. You shouldn't know all these sordid details. Who's been talking?"

"No one. But I can read, can't I? The scandal sheets still write about it even now, as we both saw only this morning."

"Josephine, really!" As the elder sister by a substantial margin, Kay felt obliged to issue a reprimand. "You know that Mama has forbidden you to read the gossip rags on your own."

Josephine made a sound of derision between her lips, showing what little effect their mother's rules had on her. "No one believed his denials about the elopement, of course," she resumed. "And why would they? He didn't even bother to come home to deny it all in person. He just sent that Delilah Dawlish a statement for her nasty little paper by letter, and that was all he did. The scoundrel."

That was, no doubt, an accurate assessment of Devlin Sharpe's character, but again, her responsibility as the elder sister held sway. The fact that she'd been so reckless and foolish at Jo's age obligated her all the more to be a good influence on her young sibling now. "That was a long time ago, dearest. It's all water under the bridge. We've both gone on with our lives. And if he and Lady Pamela are happy, I'm happy for them."

Even as she spoke, she could hear the chirpy brightness of her voice and the sickening sweetness of her words.

Jo evidently heard it, too. "And everything in the garden is lovely?" she asked skeptically.

"Well, it is!" Kay insisted. "Because I'm quite happy, too. But," she added, smiling as Jo continued to eye her with concern, "I do confess, I enjoyed it thoroughly when you pointed out that Lady Pamela wasn't the only one getting married."

Jo grinned back at her, appeased. "That was good, wasn't it?"

"Rather. Are you really friends with her?"

"With Pamela? Who says so?"

"She did."

"Did she?" Jo seemed vastly amused. "We weren't what I'd ever call friends. We were in a few classes, of course, and we were on the fencing team together. That was about all. She could parry all right, but she couldn't lunge for toffee."

To Josephine, who was mad about fencing, the inability to lunge was a grievous sin indeed, but the girl's fencing ability wasn't what Kay wanted to know about.

"And what..." Kay paused, gave a cough, and then said diffidently, "What's your opinion of her?"

"Of Pamela? Oh, she's all right, I suppose. She can't help being a perfect fool."

Kay laughed merrily at that description.

"And if you really mean it that everything's all right, then I'm glad," Jo went on. "Even though it shows you're a far nicer person than I am."

"Oh, I wouldn't say that." Kay gave her sister a rueful look, wrinkling up her nose. "For a second or two when I first saw him, I admit I was sorely tempted to slap him across the face or bash a bunch of carnations over his head."

Jo laughed cheerfully at the prospect. "Either of those would have been something I'd have loved to see."

"I resisted the impulse," she said sternly.

"What a shame."

"On the contrary, it's a very good thing. We're bound to run into Devlin and Lady Pamela again and again during the course of the season, so it's best to be polite. Especially since in the eyes of the world, we have no reason not to be."

As she spoke, her resentment and rage flickered up again, just as they had when she'd first seen the mockery in his face, and she wondered how she could keep up pretenses when everything in her wanted nothing but to heap on him the contempt and scorn he deserved.

"I don't see how that's possible," Jo said, breaking the sudden silence, reflecting her own thoughts. "Especially for Mama. She adores making scenes."

At the mention of their overly dramatic mother, Kay once again snuffed out the old anger. It served no purpose to indulge it.

"Mama will have to restrain herself," she said firmly. "And she will. She knows what's at stake. The scandal rags still watch me like circling vultures, and I have no intention of giving them any meat to feed on. All Mama's machinations with *Talk of the Town* notwithstanding, my scandal won't truly be over until I'm safely married to Wilson. And with you coming out a month before that, we can't afford to put a foot wrong."

"I know, I know," Josephine conceded, giving in with a sigh. "It's best all around if we can all be civil. Won't be easy, though."

"No," Kay agreed with a sigh. "But this is how it has to be. We've no choice."

Josephine eyed her with sympathy. "Maybe it will get easier as time goes on."

"It will," Kay replied, hoping that was true. "Now that the initial shock is over."

"And who knows what might happen?" Jo said, settling back beside Kay as the cab jerked into motion, circled the fountain, and made its way out of the Savoy courtyard and onto the Strand. "You and Sharpe might even be able to bury the hatchet before it's all over."

"I'll never be *that* nice," Kay countered at once, giving a sniff as she settled back beside her sister. "I'll be civil, because I must. I'll be polite. But the only way I'll ever truly bury the hatchet with Devlin Sharpe is if I can put the blade right into his despicable, deceitful heart."

3

Devlin stared at the empty doorway of the flower shop, a slew of emotions seething inside him like a caustic stew.

Surprise at seeing her, however, was not one of those emotions. Pam's desire for a big society wedding here in London at the height of the season had all but guaranteed that he and Kay would meet again. All three families were part of the ton, after all, and regarded doing the season as a necessity of life.

Not that he cared much how his own family would feel. His mother had died giving birth to him, a fact for which his father had never forgiven him. And since his disastrous elopement with Kay, he hadn't even been on speaking terms with the old man.

Devlin would have liked to heal that particular breach for Pam's sake, but his trip to Yorkshire had not made much headway in that regard. And if he did succeed, he was under no illusions that it would be due to his efforts. The fact that he was allying their insignificant barony with the powerful Marquess of Walston would do far more to bring about a truce with his father than any olive branch he might hold out.

As for Devlin's four older brothers, only two were left. Roger and James were dead, killed in a cholera epidemic half a dozen years ago. Stephen, the only one who'd made an effort to keep in contact with him after the debacle with Kay, was settled in Australia now. As for Thomas, well…he was the eldest, the heir, and as he'd done all their lives, he would take his cue from their father. The rest of Devlin's relations would do the same.

Still, no matter which way the chips fell with his family, he and Kay would be running across each other, and probably more often in the weeks before his wedding than either of them would welcome. He'd been prepared for that. What he hadn't been prepared for was all the powerful emotions his first sight of her had evoked.

Absurdly, what had come first was desire, flickering to life inside his body, demonstrating that the wild, uncontrollable passion he'd had for her in his youth was a flame that, despite his best efforts to extinguish it, had never quite gone out.

Then, like paraffin tossed onto the spark of that old desire, had come anger, anger that had flared up with sudden, undeniable life. He thought of those early days in Africa—his travels from Cape Town to the bush of East Africa, to Cairo, as he searched for an occupation, a career, a way to make good and prove to Kay's family that stealing her hand wasn't all he was capable of, that he was worthy of her, that he would be able to support and take care of her and make a life for her, even if that life was on another continent. He thought of all the letters he'd written, how careful he'd been to give particulars of where she could write back, but she never had. Even after he'd finally settled permanently in Cairo, he hadn't given up. No, like a fool, he'd sent more letters; he'd even sent cables, but as one year became three with still no word, his hopes had become harder and harder to prop up.

And while he'd been going through all of that, what had she been doing? Letting another man push in and take his place.

With that reminder, he once again felt the pain, the pain of her unfaithfulness, hitting him just as hard now as it had the day he'd read in an old copy of the *London Times* of her engagement to her cousin Giles. In hindsight, he supposed the fact that she'd thrown him over shouldn't have been much of a surprise. Not only had Giles had far more money than him at the time, he'd also been heir to a title—the Raleigh title, to be precise—and a title was something Devlin was unlikely to ever possess.

He'd been tossed aside without a word, and though she and Giles had called off the engagement a few months later when the elopement rumors had begun to surface, that had been no consolation to Devlin's betrayed and devastated heart.

Now she was engaged again. He had no reason to resent her for that, of course, but when he thought of how she'd looked moments ago, telling him of her engagement with that gleeful little smile on her face, it felt like salt poured into ripped-open wounds.

Suddenly he hated her for that, hated her for proving that even now, after all this time, even engaged to someone else, he still wasn't completely free of her.

And if all that wasn't enough to drive a man to the brink, there was the identity of her new fiancé. Of all the wealthy, eligible men in the world, he thought in aggravation, she'd had to pick Wilson Rycroft? A hard-drinking man from the wilds of America's Midwest, richer than Devlin and Giles combined, old enough to be Kay's father, Wilson Rycroft also happened to be, like Devlin, one of the investors in his friend Calderon's new hotel. Had he known of Kay's engagement, he'd have refused his friend's offer to be a part of this new venture, but he hadn't known. Had Rycroft known about him? he wondered. Either way—

"Devlin?"

Engrossed in his own thoughts, he barely heard Pamela's voice. Perhaps he ought to bow out of this hotel investment group? He had plenty of investments in Northern Africa—his touring company, his hotels in Cairo and Luxor—he didn't need anything like that here. Backing out would be letting Simon down, but to be involved in any sort of business venture with Kay's future husband could prove awkward, even if he was only here for the next few months. If Simon had only told him, warned him. But then, Simon probably hadn't known of her engagement, either—

"Devlin?"

This time, the sound of Pamela's voice penetrated his thoughts, and he opened his eyes to find her watching him in puzzlement.

"Are you..." She paused, frowning a little. "Are you all right?"

"Of course. Shouldn't I be?"

"Well, I've been talking and talking, and you've been standing there like a statue."

"Sorry. I was thinking."

"I daresay," she countered, pouting a little. "It must be a matter of great importance, since you haven't heard a word I've said."

"It's a matter of business." He hesitated, wondering what to tell her, knowing he could be walking onto rather thin ice. "About that new hotel venture I'm involved in."

"The one here in London with your friend Lord Calderon and the Duke of Westbourne?"

"Yes." He wavered, then added, "We decided to expand the venture beyond one hotel, and to raise funds for that, we put shares in the corporation on public offer just two days ago. Wilson Rycroft is one of those who bought in. I didn't think anything of it at the time, of course, but now..." He paused again, studying Pam's face, not sure from her placid expression what she was thinking. "Now that I know Rycroft is engaged to Lady Kay, I'm wondering if I should bow out?"

"Bow out?" Pamela's smooth forehead crinkled a bit as if in puzzlement. "But why on earth should you do that?"

"Well...given all that gossip years ago," he began, but to his amazement, Pamela laughed.

"You mean because you and Lady Kay once scandalized society by trying to elope?"

He blinked at her matter-of-fact tone. "I told everyone that it never happened."

"Of course you did. Quite right of you."

"But you don't believe my declaration was the truth?"

Pamela gave him a look of pity. "Dearest Devlin, no one believes it."

That, he appreciated with a grimace, was probably true. "Perhaps that's all the more reason to bow out. The first hotel is set to open in a few weeks, and Simon wants a big, grand ribbon-cutting for it with everyone in society stopping by. I'm expected to be there, and I'd like my fiancée there by my side. No doubt," he added, studying her face, watching for any signs of feminine jealousy, "Rycroft will be thinking the same."

Not a flicker of concern disturbed her perfect countenance. "Of course. And...?"

"There are sure to be other events, too, while we're here in London—dinners, parties, and the like—and there's the season, too, of course. We're bound to see the two of them. It could be awkward. I should hate for you to be uncomfortable in any way."

"But why should I be?" Pamela seemed genuinely bewildered. "That whole business between you and her was ages ago. Why, I was only a child. It's silly to be bothered by things like that. And it certainly shouldn't have any impact on our plans or your business arrangements."

"An admirable attitude."

The dryness of his voice seemed to penetrate Pam's complacency, and her eyes widened as if in surprise. "Did you think I'd be jealous? Of her?"

"I suppose I did, rather," he confessed, bemused.

"My darling." She smiled, the confident smile of a girl who knew her own appeal, a smile tinged—perhaps—with just a hint of conceit. "Lady Kay is no threat to me."

He looked into her face, the face of a woman who was barely twenty and beautiful enough to stop traffic, who was able to bring dozens of men running with a snap of her fingertips, and he supposed it was understandable that she wouldn't regard a woman who was older than she, who had been deemed a spinster, as a threat, even if her fiancé and that woman had a past. As she'd said, it was a long time ago.

"I see," he said slowly, not sure what else to say. "Then there's no reason for me to bow out of this thing?"

"None at all. Now, then," she added and patted his lapel, "you'd best pick a flower, and let's be going. If we're late, Mama will squawk like an irritated hen. She hates when people are unpunctual."

"Right." Still bemused by her utter lack of jealousy, and a bit humbled, too, if he was being honest, but also heartily glad to leave the subject of his first love behind, he turned and pulled a bachelor's button from the bucket of flowers beside him. "What about this one?"

She laughed, shaking her head as if he were a hopeless business. "Far too plebeian."

"I'm so glad I have you to steer me in the proper direction about these things," he said, returning the bachelor's button to its place and selecting a small white carnation instead. When he shot her an inquiring glance, she nodded approval, and he broke the stem to shorten it.

"Are you?" she asked, as he tucked the flower into the buttonhole of his morning coat.

"Am I what?"

"Are you glad?" she asked, adjusting the stem, then letting her hand linger against his chest. "Truly?"

Encouraged, he leaned closer. "Are you certain we have to go to lunch?" he murmured. "I prefer my idea of some passionate necking."

He planted a kiss on her perfect retroussé nose, causing her to cast an apprehensive glance around the shop. "Devlin," she chided, though he could tell she wasn't really displeased. "You shouldn't do things like that."

"Why not?" he countered, catching her hand in his as it fell to her side. "Because people will see? Let them."

"But—"

"We are engaged, after all."

"But no one knows that. We haven't announced it yet."

"Now that we are both here in town, I think it's time we did."

"Mama won't like it," Pamela warned, but even as she spoke, it was clear the notion was not unpleasing to her. "She's been so insistent we not announce it until the season starts. I fear she's stalling, hoping I'll change my mind about marrying you."

"No doubt," he agreed, supposing wryly he ought to be used to a lack of parental approval by this time. "Is she—" He paused, meeting her eyes. "Is she justified in that hope?"

"Devlin! You know she's not." Her lower lip jutted out a little, showing hints of a rebellious streak in her nature. "Mama loves arranging my life to suit her, but I have no intention of allowing it."

A feeling he knew well. Lifting her hand, he pressed a kiss to her gloved fingers. "Then let's put the announcement in the papers so that everyone, including your mother, will know it's official."

Her wide, radiant smile was his reward. "This week?"

"Perfect."

He paid for his purchase, and as they left the florist, he was relieved to note that all the tumultuous emotions evoked by his encounter with Kay had disintegrated. Pain and anger were gone. Sanity had returned.

The only thing he felt now was a strange lightness of heart, and he realized that unbeknownst to himself, he'd been on tenterhooks about his inevitable encounter with Kay from the moment he'd set foot in England again. But that particular moment had come and gone, and now that it was over, he could be sure that she was well and truly in the past.

So what, he thought, if they couldn't avoid her? So what if she was marrying a man Devlin had business dealings with? As Pam had rightly pointed out, it didn't affect them. And it would only be for the next few months, anyway, and then he and Pam would be going back to Africa. As for Kay, she could marry an American millionaire nearly twice her age, or her titled cousin, or a toad covered in warts, for all he cared.

Nonetheless, he took a quick glance around as he and Pamela reentered the lobby, and he gave a sigh of relief that Kay was nowhere in sight. The past might at last be buried, but the less he and Kay Matheson saw of each other during the next few months, the better for everyone's peace of mind.

Despite Magdelene's efforts, Mrs. Carte made it clear that there would be no banqueting room at the Savoy for Kay's wedding dinner, a fact that was no surprise to Kay. Her mother, however, still seemed unable to accept it.

"I just don't understand why the woman can't honor whatever plan Delia had in mind for us," Magdelene said for perhaps the tenth time that afternoon. "It was the Savoy's muddle, after all. They ought to feel obliged to make up for it."

Preoccupied with her own thoughts, Kay scarcely heard.

Devlin was back.

Hours later, that fact seemed even more appalling than it had when she'd first set eyes on him in the flower shop. The shock of running into him so unexpectedly after so long had struck her with the force of a lightning bolt, and being introduced to his fiancée hadn't helped her recover. Somehow, however, amid the polite conversation she'd been forced to make and the pretense of amiability she'd been forced to don, a feeling of numbness had overcome her initial shock, and by the time she and Jo had stepped out of the hotel and into their waiting carriage, the whole ghastly episode had seemed like nothing more than a dream, enabling her to believe her assurance to her sister that she was quite all right.

But was she?

Kay bit her lip, staring down with unseeing eyes at the book of fashion plates in her lap as her mother's voice droned on beside her.

"Impossible woman. Why, she would not even tell me the identity of the party who managed to steal the Pinafore Room out from under us. I dropped hint after hint, to no avail."

Kay's feeling of numbness had persisted during their cab ride to Mrs. Carte's office and all through lunch with their mother at the Criterion, but now, with Jo in one of the fitting rooms at Lucile being measured for her bridesmaid's gown, and herself ensconced in the dressmaker's main showroom with nothing but her mother's faintly complaining voice to distract her, memories of the past were coming back in force, burning away the fog of numbness and exposing deeper emotions—emotions she hadn't felt for years, ones she had hoped never to feel again.

The agony of divided loyalties ripping her apart when she'd defied her family and eloped with Devlin to Gretna Green. The resentment and the relief when her friends had pulled her back from the brink of that irrevocable decision. The pain of looking into Devlin's blue eyes when he'd stood with her in the room of that roadside inn with her friends standing by, and the last words he'd said to her.

If you don't come away with me now, you never will.

He'd been right about that. What he hadn't told her was that he never intended to give her another chance to try.

"Delia must have said something to the woman, surely. I wonder if I should cable Delia in Paris and ask her. What do you think, dear?"

Knowing a question had been asked of her, Kay roused herself just enough to offer a reply. "Oh, absolutely, Mother."

Satisfied, Magdelene prattled on, and Kay resumed ruminations of the past.

She could still vividly recall those awful months after her return home and Devlin's departure for Africa. Her father's anger and disappointment, her mother's tearful recriminations, her banishment to the family's most distant estate in Wales, and the dreary winter months she'd spent there with no one but her mother and baby sister for company.

She'd tried to be strong, holding on for two years with nothing to sustain her but faith that Devlin would write, that he'd tell her when he'd be coming back to court her properly and honorably, her insistence to her father that she would wait for the man she loved to the end of time...but then her exasperated father had shown her irrefutable proof of her lover's betrayal, and her faith had been shattered. The pain of heartbreak that had followed in the wake of that discovery seemed as fresh now as it had the day her father had shown her the canceled bank draft he'd written with Devlin's signature of endorsement on the back.

Two thousand pounds. Devlin had given her up, deserted her, and sold her love for two thousand pounds.

From out of nowhere, a sob rose up. She tried to catch it back, pressing a gloved hand over her mouth, but it was too late.

"Kay, darling, what is it?" Magdelene asked, turning on the velvet settee to look at her. "Are you all right?"

"Of course," she said at once, trying to regain the numbness she'd felt in the cab with Jo, but it was too late for that, so the only thing to do was invent an excuse. "I have a bit of a headache, Mama. That's all."

Fortunately, Magdelene accepted this explanation without question. "So that's why you've been so quiet and diffident this afternoon," she said with a nod. "I knew something was wrong."

Magdelene, of course, had no idea of the cause. In the cab on the way to Mrs. Carte's office, Kay and Jo had agreed not to tell their mother about the encounter with Devlin. Upon hearing of it, Magdelene would have given in to her innate need for drama and collapsed in a faint. Upon being revived with smelling salts, she'd have then wailed about That Horrible Man, cried about Kay's past shame and disgrace, and made dire predictions that all her good work to restore Kay's reputation would surely be undone by some nefarious deed on Devlin's part. Not wanting to endure any of that, Kay and Jo had decided to let Mama find out from someone else that Devlin Sharpe was back in town.

"Yes," Kay agreed, putting a hand to her head and wincing in what she hoped was a convincing show of pain. "I really could do with a phenacetin powder and a cold compress."

"Oh, my dear! I do hope you'll be all right by this evening."

"This evening?"

"Don't tell me you've forgotten? Dear Wilson is taking us to the opera at Covent Garden tonight. He told us about it yesterday when he arrived back from New York."

Since admitting the fact that she'd forgotten her own fiancé had just returned after a three-month absence would probably earn her a disappointed look and a lecture, she knew dissembling was her best course. "Silly Mama, of course I haven't forgotten," she lied, pasting on a wan smile. "It's just this beastly headache making me woolly-headed. I'm sure I'll be fine by tonight, if I could just lie down for a bit. Perhaps—"

She paused, looking at her mother in a way she hoped was appropriately apologetic. "I'm sorry, Mama, but I really think I must return to the hotel and have a rest."

"Of course." Magdelene rose. "I shall fetch Josephine, and we'll go at once."

Magdelene started to move toward the changing rooms, but Kay put a hand on her arm, stopping her. She couldn't bear any more of her mother's unceasing stream of repetitive conversation. Not just now. She badly wanted to be alone.

"Oh, no, Mama, there's no need for that," she said. "What with the wedding and her first season coming, Josephine needs so many gowns. We'll never have them all chosen in time if we delay. No, you stay here with her, and I will take a hansom back to the Savoy. Don't fuss, Mama," she added as her mother started to protest. "I'll go straight back, and it's barely a ten-minute carriage ride. Besides, I very much doubt Delilah Dawlish is skulking about the Savoy lobby waiting to catch me out. Thanks to your good work, of course."

Mollified, Magdelene consented with a nod. "Very well. But go straight up to your room when you arrive. No dillydallying."

Fortunately, Kay had already turned away and started for the door, so her mother didn't hear her sigh. "Of course," she called back. "I am in no mood for dillydallying, I promise you."

Despite that assurance, Kay did not take a cab back to the hotel. Instead, she chose to walk. It was a fine spring afternoon, and by the time she reached the Savoy, the cool, crisp air had done much to restore her equilibrium.

Out from under Mama's watchful eye, with no desire to sit in her room nursing a fictional headache, Kay instead took a stroll through the hotel. She passed the American Bar, noting the men sipping cocktails there with both envy and curiosity. She'd never had a cocktail. Given Wilson's rather domineering personality and old-fashioned ideas, she doubted she ever would.

Still, a glance into the dining room on her way to the front desk to fetch her letters reminded her that many freedoms would be accorded her once she was married that even Wilson wouldn't blink an eye at. Lingering over afternoon tea in an elegant restaurant with her friends, for one.

Thoughts of marriage brought thoughts of the wedding, reminding her that they still had nowhere to hold the wedding banquet. If they didn't find something soon, they'd have no choice but to pare down the guest list. Given Mama's conversation with Mrs. Carte, that possibility seemed more likely than ever, and Kay knew it might be wise to take a second look at some of the Savoy's smaller banqueting rooms.

Tucking her letters into her handbag, Kay left the front desk and retraced her steps through the lobby and past the American Bar, then turned down the corridor of banqueting rooms that were reserved for the private parties of those who could afford them.

Not the Mikado, she realized, with one look through the doorway. Even if she cut her guest list to the absolute minimum and used both the banqueting room itself and its adjoining reception room to seat everyone, there would still not be enough space. Kay gave up on the Mikado and moved on, but she was soon forced to discard both the Penzance and the Gondoliers for the same reason. Just as she'd feared, all these rooms were just too small.

As she passed the Pinafore Room, she stopped, staring through the doorway of the reception room to the banqueting room beyond with a hint of wistful longing. Pointless, she knew, to wish for what might have been, and yet...

Irresistibly drawn, she stepped through the doorway into the Pinafore's reception room. Plenty of space for guests coming from the church to mingle here before the meal. Standing here, she could picture many of those who had once judged and condemned her happily sipping champagne punch from pewter cups and sherry from slim cordial glasses, gladly toasting the bride and groom, magnanimously forgiving Kay for her past sins. People adored stories of redemption.

Kay moved to the adjoining room, where waiters were setting tables for some big affair that evening, and as she watched them, she imagined them serving the twelve delicious and elegant courses she had planned so carefully with the Savoy's head chef.

Such a meal would have been a shining triumph, the perfect way to close the door on a decade of shame, the perfect entrée into her new role, the role every girl dreamed of and all parents of a daughter hoped for: that of the married woman.

Perfect, she thought with a pang as she fingered one of the precisely folded napkins. This room would have been so perfect.

"Lady Kay?"

She looked over her shoulder to find the maître d'hôtel standing nearby, watching her in some perplexity. "Can I be of help, my lady?" he asked.

"No, no, not really." She gave him a rueful smile as she turned around. "Not unless you know how I might turn two of your smaller banqueting suites into one larger one?"

His brow cleared, as if he'd heard that wish expressed before. "I'm afraid not, my lady."

"Never mind then," she said. "There's nothing I need, thank you."

Satisfied, he gave a bow and walked past her, crossing the long banqueting room and departing through the open doorway into the corridor beyond.

Kay turned in the opposite direction, intending to retrace her steps out of the Pinafore, but she had barely passed through the doorway leading back into the reception room before another voice, a nauseatingly familiar feminine voice, sounded from the banquet room behind her, and she paused.

"Oh, Mama, look! Won't this be just perfect?"

Lady Pamela Stirling.

This echoing of her own thoughts by Devlin's fiancée was more than she could bear just now. Kay resumed walking toward the door, quickening her steps in her desire to get away, but she'd only made it halfway across the reception room before Pamela's next words brought Kay to a halt.

"I am so glad Devlin was able to reserve it for the wedding."

Kay turned, frowning. Devlin and Pamela had managed to secure the Pinafore for their wedding, but she would be stuck settling for something not half as nice for her own? Life, she thought in aggravation, was just not fair.

"It will have to do," another female voice replied in grudging agreement. "It's pretty enough, I suppose. For a hotel."

"Now, Mama," the girl said in a wheedling voice, "you know we can't have the wedding at home in Durham. The house is leased. Besides, with the wedding set for June, everyone will be here for the season, so it's much more convenient to marry from here, making a hotel the best solution. And the Savoy has the biggest banquet room in town, so we can have a proper sit-down dinner."

"Stand-up breakfasts are more fashionable."

"They are only fashionable because so many people are pinching their pennies these days."

"So are we."

"Maybe so, but I refuse to announce the fact to the world. Besides," she added as her parent started to interrupt, "Devlin thinks stand-up breakfasts are silly, and so do I. Sipping soup out of cups and nibbling on canapés? No, a banquet here at the Savoy is a much more desirable option. And this room is perfect."

"It will certainly seat all the guests we wish to invite," Lady Walston countered, her voice dry. "We can say that much."

"Mama, you really mustn't be this way. As I said, a banquet room here is the most sensible course, and I'm so grateful we were able to secure this one. It was quite clever of Devlin, I think, to make the arrangements and secure the room so far in advance."

The older woman gave a huff in reply, making it clear that she didn't think much of her future son-in-law or his cleverness.

Kay smiled, taking what was probably an uncharitable amount of pleasure in that thought, and she abandoned any notion of retreat. In fact, wild dogs couldn't have dragged her away at this point, and she moved to one side of the open doorway, straining to hear more.

"Dear Mama, please don't frown so disapprovingly. It was clever. Admit it. You know we'd never have acquired a banqueting room of this size for the seventh of June had we waited until now to begin looking for it."

The seventh of June?

Kay's momentary amusement vanished, and she stared at the open doorway, aghast, hardly able to believe what she was hearing. *Devlin* was the one who'd gotten the Pinafore Room, taking it away from her for his own wedding? Devlin was the reason she and Mama were now scrambling so desperately to find a suitable replacement? But how had he managed it? And why hadn't Delia told her about it?

Kay had barely asked herself these questions before Pamela's voice came again, giving her at least some answers.

"Another party wanted the room, I understand, but Devlin easily took care of that. What a fortunate thing that he and Lord Calderon are such good friends."

"Oh," Kay breathed, a sound of outrage that was—fortunately—too low for the women in the adjoining room to hear.

So like him, she thought, her hands curling into fists at her sides, to do something like this. His special gift seemed to be that of dashing her hopes and spoiling her dreams, even if in this case it was just a bizarre, awful coincidence.

But was it? Kay tensed, her nails digging into her palms as another appalling thought struck her. Was it a coincidence, or had Devlin done this on purpose?

The latter theory would presuppose he'd known of her engagement two months ago. She had accepted Wilson's proposal at Christmas, but they had decided not to announce it until after his return to London.

Still, Giles and his family and the handful of her other scattered cousins had all been told once the date had been fixed, and though they'd been sworn to secrecy until the season began, a secret known by more than one person didn't usually remain a secret. Devlin, she supposed, could have learned of it somehow, and decided to steal a march on her. But would he really be so low, especially after all this time?

That question had barely crossed her mind before her sister's words from this morning echoed through her mind.

Spite and jealousy…he heard you were going to marry…he wanted to pay you out.

He'd given her up for money, and she had no doubt he'd been the source of the rumors that had sabotaged her wedding plans with Giles and ruined her reputation. Was it really all that hard to imagine him making trouble for her again now, even over a decade later?

She thought of her first sight of him in the flower shop and the mockery and resentment she'd seen in his eyes.

"That bastard," she whispered, choking on the words. "That despicable, conniving bastard. What a malicious trick to play."

All the pain and anger Kay had been working so hard to snuff out since this morning came roaring back, stronger than ever. And though she didn't know how he could have learned of her wedding plans, she was damn well going to find out. And when she did, she thought, tears of outrage stinging her eyes, she was going to tell that man exactly what she thought of him, his mockery, and his petty, mischief-making schemes.

Blinking back tears, rage still seething through every fiber of her being, she turned away from the two women in the adjoining banquet room, escaped out into the corridor, and made her way back to the lobby. But as she approached the front desk, she appreciated the fact that an unmarried woman could not just walk up to a hotel clerk and openly ask for a man's room number.

She stood for a moment, lost in thought, then she veered away from the front desk and entered the Savoy's reading room instead. Crossing to one of the writing desks, she sat down and opened the center drawer, helping herself to an envelope and a sheet of the hotel stationery that was always available to guests.

Back in the lobby a few minutes later, she watched from a short distance away as the bellboy she'd asked for assistance took her sealed envelope with a blank sheet of paper tucked inside to the front desk and gave it to the clerk. When the clerk put the note into one of the cubbyholes of the massive wall cabinet behind him, she noted the number on the brass plate above it: room 506.

Her ploy successfully accomplished, she turned around and made her way out of the lobby and down a side corridor to the electric lift that would take her to the fifth floor.

It was time—long past time—for a showdown with Devlin Sharpe. She could only hope that he was in, he was alone, and there wasn't a hatchet anywhere in the vicinity.

4

Pamela was right. He needed to hire a valet, even if it was only temporary.

Devlin straightened from the trunk he'd just opened, staring in dismay at the rumpled mess that only yesterday had been two stacks of neatly folded evening clothes.

All his things had been packed with meticulous care by a footman at Stonygates before his departure, but the contents of this trunk, at least, were now a mess. Worse, he realized in chagrin, it was his own fault. Due to his failure to secure the interior straps after pulling out a spare handkerchief at the last minute, all his evening clothes had been left to become a hopeless jumble during the journey from Yorkshire to London.

Devlin tossed aside the dress shirt in his hands and picked up another, only to find it was as wrinkled as the first. The same could be said of all his other evening coats, waistcoats, and trousers. Not a thing in this trunk was fit to wear.

He glanced at his watch, noted it was half past five, and did a few quick calculations. Half an hour or so for the Savoy laundry to iron his clothes—if he was lucky—then a quarter hour to dress. Then another quarter hour to arrive at Lord Barton's house for dinner before the opera.

"That's cutting it close," he muttered.

His future mother-in-law already didn't approve of him, and he very much feared that arriving late to her brother's dinner party would do him in forever as far as she was concerned. On the other hand, showing up in wrinkled clothes was probably an even greater sin. For the former, he could at least invent some excuse.

He pressed the call button beside his bed to summon a footman. When the servant arrived, Devlin handed over his best evening suit, requested the quickest service humanly possible, and gave the young man a very generous tip, hoping for the best.

The tip, he appreciated a short time later, must have done the trick, for he'd just finished scraping away the day's beard stubble from his face when there was a knock on his door.

Suitably impressed, Devlin set aside his razor, retrieved his discarded trousers from the floor, and pulled them over his naked hips. He then did up the buttons, snagged a towel from the rack on the wall, and left the bathroom. He wiped traces of shaving soap from his face as he crossed the sitting room of his suite, happily relieved that the Savoy laundry was so much more efficient than he'd anticipated.

But when he opened the door of his suite and saw that the person standing in the corridor was not a Savoy footman with his evening suit, Devlin's relief evaporated, and a mingling of astonishment and consternation took its place.

"Kay?" He glanced past her, noting no one else in the corridor. "What the devil?"

"Ssh. Not so loud. Are you alone?"

He blinked, his surprise deepening at the abrupt, rather suggestive question, but even putting everything in their past aside, the expression on her face was enough to make it clear she wasn't here for the usual reason a woman came to a man's room. That dangerous, silvery glint in the depths of her green eyes, the proud tilt of her chin, and the determined set of her jaw were all very familiar to him, though he hadn't seen them for years. Kay had always had a quick temper, and right now, she was mad as hell. It was obvious, for some reason he couldn't fathom, that he was the cause, and that alone made the temptation to needle her irresistible.

"Why, Kay, you naughty girl," he murmured, smiling. "I've only been back in town a day, and here you are at my hotel room door asking me questions like that? I'm flattered, my sweet, but you know I'm already engaged to someone else."

A wave of pink washed into her pale cheeks. "Don't be absurd."

"Is it so absurd?" He paused, dabbing the last bit of soap from his chin, then he slung the towel across his shoulders and went on, "What else is a man to conclude from a visit like this, and at this particular time of day, too?"

"I didn't come for a *cinq à sept*! Especially not with the likes of you. I'd rather be tortured on the rack."

"You mean you didn't come here to ravish me?" He shook his head, putting on a show of mock regret. "How disappointing. What did you come for, then?"

"We need to talk. It's important," she added when he didn't reply.

"I daresay," he conceded. "To bring you alone to my hotel room, it must be."

"Well, then?" she prompted when he fell silent. "May I come in?"

He didn't jump to let her. Instead, he tilted his head to one side, studying her through the open doorway, unable to imagine what she could possibly want to discuss with him now that was so important she'd take this sort of risk. Still, whatever her reasons, from the look on her face, he was sure letting her in would be something he'd regret.

"I'm not sure that's wise," he said at last, compelled to remind himself and caution her. "Someone might find out, and that would start tongues wagging about us all over again. If anyone sees you here, the scandal would be—"

"The longer you make me stand here in the corridor," she said, flattening a hand against his chest, "the greater the risk becomes."

Even through the cotton of her glove, he could feel the heat of her palm, and his stomach dipped as if he'd just started down in the Savoy's electric lift. When she pushed, her hand pressing against his heart, arousal flickered dangerously within his body, and even as he tried to suppress it, he allowed himself, for some stupid reason he could not fathom, to be pushed backward into the sitting room.

"Besides," she assured him as she followed him in, closing the door behind her, "scandal is nothing new to me, thanks to you."

Guilt shimmered through him at that reminder, for he knew he deserved a good part of the blame for what had happened, though not all of it, by any means. Either way, a chap had his pride, and Devlin decided he'd rather be damned for all eternity than allow Kay to see any pangs of conscience on his part.

"Is that why you came?" he asked instead, shoving aside any foolish emotions of guilt or desire, reminding himself the days of both were gone for good. "About fourteen years too late for us to talk things through, isn't it?"

"Your despicable conduct in the past is not what I want to talk about. I'm here about the present. And no one's going to find out I've been here, unless you tell them." She paused, her eyes narrowing. "Not that such conduct from you would be much of a surprise."

The accusation that he would pull such a dirty trick flicked Devlin on the raw. "Now, wait a damn minute—" he began, but she cut him off.

"I came here because there's something I simply must know. Did you—" She stopped abruptly and swallowed hard, her anger suddenly, inexplicably faltering. "That is . . . I mean to say, if you—"

She stopped again. Lifting her hands, she hooked the fingers of one hand with the fingers of the other, took a deep breath as if bracing herself, and opened her mouth to try again. But then she tossed up her hands as if in surrender.

"I can't," she declared as she let her hands fall to her sides. "I simply can't have a conversation with you when you're in this state. Will you please put on a shirt?"

At that question, his anger faded, and amusement took its place. "No, Kay," he answered, grinning, immensely gratified by her obvious discomfiture. "I don't believe I will. Why should I?"

"Because it's not decorous. It's not . . ." She paused, and though she didn't look down, her tongue darted out to lick her lips. "It's not decent."

"So much maidenly modesty," he murmured. "I never knew you were such a prude."

She didn't reply, and he grasped the ends of the towel around his neck in a deliberate move to draw her eye, provoking her for reasons even he couldn't quite understand. "After all, it's not as if you've never seen my naked chest before. Remember?"

Just as he'd intended, her gaze slid down to his chest. As he watched the blush in her cheeks deepen, his mind flashed back to the last—and only—time she'd seen his bare chest. That fateful night at a roadside inn just north of Birmingham was as close to Scotland as they'd managed to get before her friends, the Duke of Westbourne's sisters, had come swooping in to rescue her from his nefarious clutches. Looking at her, he wondered if she was thinking of that night, too.

Not that it mattered, he supposed, for when she looked up at him, her expression made it clear that if she was thinking about that night, it was not with any tender regard or lingering passion or even regret about her choice to leave him there and return home.

He shouldn't be surprised by any of that, he supposed, and yet, it stung. Because for him, the memory of what they'd felt for each other fourteen years ago was as vivid as if it had all happened last month. He kept his gaze on her face, for if he looked down, his imagination would begin stripping her down to her chemise and drawers, just as he had that fateful night on the road to Gretna Green, reminding him of how close he'd stood to paradise, and how it had slipped through his fingers.

And that, he realized, was what compelled him to goad her so mercilessly. To cover his own weak spot, a weak spot he'd had from the first moment he'd ever laid eyes on her lined up at one side of a London ballroom with all the other wallflowers, a weak spot that he'd only realized he possessed when he'd pulled her into his arms on the ballroom floor and those strange, haunting eyes had looked at him as if he were king of the earth, a weak spot that even after all that had happened and all the years that had passed was still there inside him, making him as much of a fool at thirty-four as he'd been at twenty.

"Do you, Kay?" he asked softly, breaking the silence, closing the distance between them, savoring the alarm that rose up in her eyes. "Do you remember?"

Her chin jerked, her shoulders squared, and her eyes were cold enough to freeze the fires of hell. She leaned back, away from him, but to her credit, she didn't retreat. "I can see that you are determined to be uncivil. What a surprise."

"You pushed in," he reminded, straightening away from her with a shrug of nonchalance that he could only hope was convincing. "It's hardly my fault you interrupted me while I was in the midst of getting dressed. Speaking of which—"

He paused, making an exaggerated show of glancing at the clock on the mantel. "I have plans this evening with my fiancée's family to celebrate our engagement. And I'm already late, so I'd appreciate it if you'd come to the point and then get the hell out of my room."

If he'd hoped his mention of Pam would get a rise out of her, he was disappointed.

"Very well. Back in January, did you or did you not know about my engagement?"

Of all the things he might have thought she would say, that particular question wasn't one of them. "I beg your pardon?"

"If so, how did you learn of it? Did someone tell you, and if so, who was it?"

He frowned, hearing the rising urgency in her voice but unable to pinpoint the cause.

"Does it matter?" he countered, buying time. "Why should it matter to you when I learned of your engagement to Rycroft? Or who might have told me of it?"

"Damn it, Devlin, stop toying with me and just answer my question."

"I see no reason why I should. At least not until you tell me why you want to know and why it's so important that you would risk coming to my room this way to find out."

Their gazes locked, hers imperious, his unyielding, as the clock on the mantel ticked away the seconds.

At last, it was she who capitulated, breaking the silence with an aggravated sigh. "Back in January, I reserved the Pinafore Room here at the Savoy for my wedding banquet. But then I was told my reservation had been canceled and that the Pinafore had been given to someone else. This afternoon, I discovered that that someone was you."

"What?" He blinked, taken aback. "Really?"

She folded her arms. "You seem surprised."

"Well, of course. I mean, that's quite a coincid—" Devlin broke off and stiffened, suddenly wary as he began to realize what all this was about. "Just what are you implying?"

"Lord Calderon canceled my reservation. Calderon is your very close friend, is he not?"

His suspicions confirmed, Devlin felt anger rising again, higher, hotter, a rekindling of all the resentment, hurt, and disillusionment that had been smoldering for years under the ashes of their dead romance.

"And you think that I stole it from you?" he demanded, his voice strident to his own ears, any pretense of indifference now beyond him. "That I did it to spike your guns and ruin your wedding plans, or something along those lines?"

"Why shouldn't I think it?" she cried, unfolding her arms,

clenching her hands into fists at her sides. "It's not as if such a thing would be out of character for you."

"That tears it," he cried, whipping the towel from his neck and tossing it aside as his smoldering emotions flared to blazing life.

He must have looked a formidable sight at that moment, for when he stepped forward to once again close the distance between them, she stepped back, her eyes widening in alarm as her back hit the closed door behind her.

"I've had it to here," he said through clenched teeth as he stopped in front of her, "with having insinuations and accusations about the past thrown in my teeth as if I bear all the blame for what happened and you bear none. I've had enough of that from my own relations, including my father, who disowned me, cut off my share of income from the estate, and who, to this very day, still isn't speaking to me because of what happened between us. I don't need to stand here and tolerate the same accusations from you."

She didn't reply, and her silence only sent his fury rising higher.

"When we eloped, you knew full well what it all meant. We talked about the ramifications in detail, including the risks if we were caught. I was scrupulously honest in warning you—"

"Honest?" she cut in, a sudden quiver in her voice that seemed at odds with the scorn in her eyes. Her face twisted, going awry, and she looked away. "You? Is that supposed to be a joke?"

The pain he saw in her countenance hit him square in the chest, but he set his jaw and ignored it, reminding himself that she wasn't the only one who had suffered.

"You may have a point there," he conceded, his voice tight. "I did lie, and quite blatantly, too, when the news eventually got out. If you recall, I denied to anyone who would listen that the elopement ever happened. I even gave interviews to the gossip rags. I lied myself blue in the face to salvage your reputation."

"An attempt that dismally failed, perhaps because you made these denials by letter from thousands of miles away, instead of coming home to face them in person. How brave of you. How noble."

He couldn't help a laugh. "So, let me see if I have this right. I was not only obligated to lie about our elopement ever having happened, but I was also expected to abandon my business interests in Africa just as they were beginning to bear fruit, travel halfway back around the world, and utter those lies in person, all so that I could watch you marry another man?" He laughed again, a raw, caustic sound that made both of them wince. "You'll have to forgive me, Kay, but I'm just not that big of a hero."

"Hero?" she scoffed, the contempt in her voice razor-sharp, cutting him to the quick.

"You thought so, once," he muttered, and it was his turn to look away.

"Then I was a fool, for it's clear you don't even know what the word means. I was ruined because of you, and your weak attempt at lying on my behalf from the other side of the globe didn't do a thing to stop it."

"An unfortunate outcome that is hardly my fault. I did what I could to mitigate the damage, but—"

"Mitigate the damage?" she echoed. "Mitigate the—"

She stopped as if too outraged to continue, and Devlin took advantage of the moment to point out the obvious. "Had you married me as we had planned, you wouldn't have been ruined. We'd have raised some eyebrows, and that would have been the end of it. Calling me out for not rushing to your side three years after the fact is a bit thick, don't you think, since you didn't even have the courage to marry me when you had the chance. Oh, but you were happy to marry your cousin, the heir to the title, weren't you, when the opportunity arose?"

"So that *is* why you did it." She stared at him as if surprised, though he hadn't a clue why. "Well, there we are, then," she whispered. "Jo was right after all."

"Right about what?" he asked, his own anger giving way to sudden uncertainty. "What does your little sister have to do with any of this?"

She shook her head and laughed, but there was no humor in it, and none of her previous scorn, only what might have been disbelief.

"Not only her," she said. "But my parents, too, and some of my other relations, and the few friends I had left. Everyone on my side tried to tell me that's why you did it, but despite everything, I never quite believed them, not really. I couldn't believe that even you could be that low. How naïve of me."

He still had no idea what she was talking about, but he did know everyone in her family and his had deemed him entirely to blame for the whole ghastly business, and he was weary of it. He hadn't kidnapped her, for God's sake.

"I've taken as much of this as I can stomach," he shot back, any shred of patience he possessed now utterly gone. "Will you stop talking in riddles and tell me what you're driving at? What were you urged to believe? Among my many sins," he added when she didn't reply, "just which one are you referring to?"

"Those rumors about our elopement started up three years after the fact." She lifted her chin, her gaze boring into his. "Right after Giles and I became engaged."

"I'm quite aware of that, thank you. Since, being a gentleman, I'm the one who was obligated to refute those rumors, it's quite unnecessary for you to remind me of the date I was forced to do so. What does that have to do with any—"

He stopped, realizing the answer to his question before he'd even finished asking it. "Wait," he ordered, taking a step back from her, his mind reeling as he appreciated what she was really accusing him of. "You think I'm responsible for the news of our elopement getting out? And that I did it because you threw me over for your cousin?"

"Threw you over?" she echoed. "Is that how you justify yourself? By claiming that *you* are the injured party in this? Of all the unmitigated gall."

"I don't have to justify anything! God knows, I have plenty of reasons to hate your guts, but I am in no way responsible for the news of our botched elopement getting out. You want to lay blame for that, you'll have to look elsewhere."

"And just where would I look?"

"Damned if I know. Your friends, the Duke of Westbourne's sisters, seem the most likely suspects."

"They would never have told anyone." She shook her head. "Never in a thousand years."

"The duke himself, then."

"He admitted the truth to my father because it was dawn before he and his sisters got me safely back to the house party, and by then, Mama had noticed my absence, found my note, and told Papa I'd run away. But no one else knew. And my parents certainly wouldn't have let such news get out."

"Then it was your maid. Or one of the duke's servants. Or," he added as she again shook her head, "perhaps someone that one of us knew saw us together on the train to Birmingham, or at the train station, or at the inn where we stopped that night. Maybe the chambermaid at the inn or another servant there put it all together and got a nice bit of money for telling Delilah Dawlish all about it. How does anyone know how secrets like this get out? But they often do. It's quite obvious that someone told, but it was not me. The only person on my side to whom I have ever confessed the truth about what happened was Calderon."

"Well, then, we know how the scandal got out, don't we?"

"Not possible. I didn't even admit to him my denials were a hum until long after the whole mess was public knowledge. Besides, Calderon would never have told anyone what really happened. He's straight as a die."

"Not so straight, since he discarded my reservation of the Pinafore Room and gave it to you."

"I'm sure it was just a mix-up. We didn't steal the blasted thing out from under you. Hell, I didn't even know you were engaged again until you told me the news yourself this morning in the flower shop."

"So it's just a coincidence that Lord Calderon, your closest friend, took away my reservation for the Pinafore Room and gave it to you?"

"Since I never asked Calderon to take it from you, and since Calderon would never comply with such a dishonorable request anyway, even for my sake, then, yes, a coincidence is exactly what it is. And in any case, it's just a banqueting room. I can't see why that is something to make a fuss about—"

"Don't you?" she cried. "Then allow me to enlighten you on the subject. When the rumors got out, I was ruined, jilted by my fiancé, abandoned by most of my friends, and shunned by nearly everyone in society. I was in virtual exile. No man would look at me twice. It's taken me over a decade to rebuild my reputation."

He pressed his lips together and looked away. He tried to take refuge in his own righteous indignation with the reminder that she wasn't the only one who had suffered the consequences of their mutual decision to elope, but he found little consolation in that.

"I'm fully aware of what you've endured, Kay," he said at last.

"You may be aware of it, but you can't possibly know what it's been like."

"No," he admitted, the concession bitter on his tongue. "I suppose not."

"Well, it's been hell. Mud slung at me, doors slammed in my face, me having to bow and scrape to anyone in society who'll give me half a chance, watching everything I do and every word I say, knowing I can't afford to make a single misstep. I have finally managed to be grudgingly accepted again, but not by everyone. Even after all this time, though not a whisper of scandal has touched my name in over a decade, there are those who still see me as damaged goods, who ridicule me behind my back, or pity me, or look down their noses at me. It's a miracle I found any man willing to marry me at all. The only way I will ever be able to lay this sordid episode to rest for good is to have my wedding be the event of the season, with as many of the people I've been bowing and scraping to in attendance as I can muster, both at the ceremony and at the wedding banquet afterward. But that plan is curtailed now, thanks to you."

"If you've been so disgraced, what makes you think all those people will come to your wedding anyway?"

The smile that curved her lips was a bitter one, ironic, without a shred of humor. "Because we English have such a deep-seated sense of fair play. People will climb over themselves to come and watch me be washed clean. And afterward, they'll gladly toast my future happiness and nod wisely to each other, and say, 'Well, my dear, I never believed those silly rumors about her to begin with.'"

That, he supposed with a grimace, was a pretty fair take on the British character. "We English are awful humbugs, aren't we?"

"Yes. The more people there to witness my rehabilitation, the stronger it will be. But that requires St. Paul's Cathedral, and a banquet room that can seat all the influential people I've spent a decade bowing and scraping to. Thanks to you, however, I now have to decide who I must cut from my guest list because there isn't another banquet room available in any decent part of London that is large enough. I know that because I've spent the past two months looking for one."

He set his jaw, working to don the armor of indifference as he forced himself to look at her again. "All that's a shame, and I am very sorry for it, Kay, I truly am, but I did not take the Pinafore from you on purpose. As for the rest, I am not responsible for how word about our elopement got out any more than you are, believe me."

Uncertainty flickered across her face, but when she spoke, her voice was unrelenting. "I don't see why I should believe you about anything."

He gave it up. "Then we seem to be at an impasse, for I see no reason to stand here all night rehashing the matter and engaging in round after round of no-I-didn't and yes-you-did. It would be a waste of breath."

Her chin lifted, and that, he well knew, meant trouble. "I can think of a way you could convince me."

He drew a deep breath, knowing he had to ask, sure he would regret it. "How?"

"Tell your fiancée the truth."

Devlin frowned, uncomprehending. "What purpose would that serve? Like everyone else, she already knows my denials about the elopement were lies, so—"

"That's not what I mean."

"What, then?"

"Tell her that she can't have the Pinafore Room because, due to some muddle, the room was already taken by someone else when you made the reservation."

"The someone in question being you, a fact she is sure to discover in very short order."

She shrugged, clearly indifferent to the hot water that would land him in. "You're a glib fellow, God knows. You'll think of a palatable way to break it to her."

"Right," he replied with a laugh. "I'm to tell my current fiancée—who, by the way, desires a banquet room every bit as big as yours—that she can't have the Pinafore because my former fiancée wants it and I'm giving it to her. Is that how this is supposed to go?"

"You aren't giving it to me. I already had it when you reserved it. I'm merely asking you to explain that to her. And I think you owe me that one little favor, at least."

He thought back to those first years in Africa, all the hard work he'd done, thinking he was making a future for them only to read in a newspaper that she was throwing him over to marry her cousin, a man who had money and a title and her father's approval.

His heart turned to ice.

"Go to the devil." He paused to retrieve his towel from the floor and loop it back across his shoulders. "I owe you nothing more than what I've already done."

She shook her head. "Selfish to the end."

"So it would seem." He reached around her, nudging her to one side as he opened the door. "Now, as I said before, I have an engagement. So unless you want me to use force and shove you out into the corridor, you'd best depart of your own volition."

She exhaled a sharp sigh, but much to his relief, she turned away to depart.

"So delightful of you to come by," he said to her back as she walked out into the passage. "We really must have another visit soon."

Her reply was to pull the door shut behind her with a loud, decisive bang.

Devlin turned away from the closed door and started back toward the bathroom, but he'd barely reached the other end of the sitting room when there was another tap on the door.

With an oath, he retraced his steps and reached for the door handle. "By God, Kay," he said as he opened the door, "if you've come back to flay me again—"

He broke off at the sight of the Savoy footman standing in the corridor with Devlin's clothes draped over his arm.

"Your evening suit, sir. Would you care for valeting assistance?"

"I would," he replied, relieved by the offer of help, though it was probably already too late for a few minutes of assistance to matter.

And his relief was short-lived, in any case, for as the footman assisted him to dress, he had little to do but stand still and hear Kay's anguished words echo through his mind.

I was ruined... it's taken me over a decade to rebuild my reputation.

Devlin's conscience, pesky devil that it was, nudged him again, and he hated that even after she'd broken his heart and forsaken him for her cousin, she could still make him feel as if he were the villain.

He stirred, restless, shifting his weight, and the footman looked up from the stud he was fastening into the bib of Devlin's shirt. "Sir?"

"It's nothing," he assured the fellow. "Carry on."

The stud snapped into place, but even as the footman helped Devlin into his waistcoat, knotted his white tie, and assisted him in sliding his arms into the sleeves of his evening coat, Kay's words still pounded his conscience like a drumbeat.

Mud slung at me, doors slammed in my face, me having to bow and scrape to anyone in society who'll give me half a chance...

"Your hat, sir."

Relieved by the distraction, Devlin came out of his reverie and accepted his top hat. "Thank you..."

He let his voice fade, giving the footman an inquiring look.

"Myers, sir," the young man supplied.

"Thank you, Myers. Will you be able to assist me when I return? It'll be late, well after midnight."

"That's all right, sir," the servant replied, slinging Devlin's evening cloak over his shoulders. "I'm here until nearly dawn anyway. Just ring downstairs and ask for me."

After handing over another tip, Devlin followed the footman out the door. Along with half a dozen other guests, he took the lift down to the ground floor, but even the lively conversation that swirled all around him as they descended to the lobby was not enough to drown out Kay.

Even after all this time, though not a whisper of scandal has touched my name in over a decade, there are those who still see me as damaged goods, who ridicule me behind my back, or pity me, or look down their noses at me.

The lift came to a stop with a little jerk, and he stepped out into the lobby with the others. Rather like salmon in a river, they streamed toward the doors, Kay's voice overriding talk of the theater and the opera that swirled and eddied around him.

The only way I will ever be able to lay this sordid episode to rest for good is to have my wedding be the event of the season…

The doorman held back the plate-glass door, and Devlin stepped out into the cold, damp spring night.

But that plan is curtailed now, thanks to you…

"Damn," he muttered, stopping in his tracks, rubbing a hand over his forehead. "Damn, damn, damn."

Ignoring the curious stare of the doorman, Devlin turned around and recrossed the lobby, noting grimly how late he was with a glance at his pocket watch as he made his way to the front desk.

"May I help you, Mr. Sharpe?" the clerk asked.

Devlin shoved his watch back into his waistcoat pocket and looked up with a resigned sigh, wondering how late he was going to be due to the inconvenient pangs of his conscience and if that would put him irretrievably beyond the pale with his future mother-in-law. "Where can I find a telephone?"

5

When Kay left Devlin's hotel room, she was even more stirred up than she had been when she'd arrived, and her anger, frustration, worry, and pain did not abate once she reached her own suite. It was a powerful combination of emotions she found hard to conceal from her mother and sister when they returned from Lucile, a combination that, sadly, Wilson's perceptive eyes cottoned onto the moment he saw her coming toward him across the Savoy lobby that evening.

"What's the matter?" he asked in his usual blunt American style once preliminary greetings had been exchanged. "What's wrong?"

"Not a thing," she lied. "I had a bit of a headache earlier, but it's gone."

"Dear Wilson," her mother said, pausing beside her, Josephine behind them. "So lovely to see you again. And you needn't worry about Kay. She's right as rain now."

Wilson ignored her mother. Instead, his steely eyes beneath silvery-gray brows searched Kay's face. His features, craggy rather than handsome, seemed harsher than usual, whether due to his painstaking scrutiny of her at this moment or due to the fact that he had just endured a long transatlantic journey, she couldn't have said. "Just a headache?" he said, his voice sharp. "That's all?"

Her heart gave a jolt of alarm, and she wondered wildly if Wilson could have known of Devlin's arrival, the flower shop, or her rage-fueled venture to Devlin's room. But there was no way Wilson could know about any of that, surely.

He studied her for a long moment, tapping his top hat thoughtfully against his thigh, and she had to resist the urge to squirm beneath this perusal. But at last, he nodded as if satisfied. "I'm glad you're feeling better. How are the wedding plans coming along?"

Kay was both relieved by the change of subject and reminded of the current problem. "Don't ask," she said with a sigh.

"Still no place for the big shindig?"

"No. Speaking of the wedding," she said, "now that you're back, I suppose we should formally announce the event. That way we can send the invitations out. After all," she added, pride forcing her to keep her voice indifferent when so much was at stake, "it's less than three months away."

"By all means, announce it. But stop fretting about the wedding. Hell, I don't care if we get married at the registry office and eat our first meal together in the Savoy restaurant. Would be far less fuss, that's for sure. I know—" He paused, leaning intimately closer, as if they were suddenly the only two people in the Savoy lobby. "I know why you want a big affair," he said, his voice softening a fraction. "But it doesn't matter to me."

"I know. And I adore you for that. But, you see, it matters to me."

"Well, since I don't much care either way, I'll let you have this big society wedding, though I don't really see the point of it." Wilson gestured to the door with his hat. "I have a carriage waiting. Shall we go?"

The four of them started for the exit doors, Kay and Wilson falling in step behind her mother and sister.

"How was New York?" she asked. "And how is Charlene?" she added, referring to his fifteen-year-old daughter.

"Willful. She resents like hell being treated like a child, but treat her like she's grown-up and she resents that, too."

She noted the baffled impatience in his voice and hastened to reassure him. "At her age, that's perfectly normal. She'll grow out of it."

"Hmm…so her governess tells me. But it's hard to know what to say to her. She rebels at everything, so much so that I've got the governess watching her like a hawk, day and night."

Kay knew, better than most, how obsessively watching over one's daughter might only increase her desire to rebel, but she didn't say so. "What about your merger?" she asked instead. "Did you get it all arranged the way you wanted it?"

"Of course." Wilson turned his head to give her a smile, a hard smile that made her wonder if she'd imagined the tenderness in his face a few moments earlier. "I always get what I want in the end."

"Always?" she countered lightly. "Goodness. How impressive."

He laughed. "Is it really a surprise to you?" he asked, as they passed through the exit doors and into the courtyard. "After we met at those yacht races last summer, I did manage to swing invitations to three of the house parties you attended in the autumn."

Startled, she stopped in the courtyard, staring at him. "You got yourself invited because of me?"

"Of course," he said, stopping beside her. "I see something I want, I go after it, and I get it. It's that simple. Did you really think it was just a coincidence I was in all the same places you happened to be?"

"Well, no, not exactly. I just..." She paused, running a finger around the inside of the Roman pearl choker at her throat, feeling oddly uncomfortable all of a sudden. "I suppose," she said at last, forcing a little laugh, "I just assumed we knew all the same people."

"So we did, once I made their acquaintance. I told you, Kay," he added when she didn't reply, "when I see something I want, I go after it, and I always get it in the end."

With those words, she felt a sudden, smothering tension, the reason for which she couldn't quite account, and she didn't know what to say. Fortunately, her mother spoke up at that moment, saving her from a reply.

"Come along, you two. Stop dawdling or we'll be late."

Kay turned, following her mother and sister into the luxuriously appointed carriage, and though the short journey from the Savoy to Covent Garden gave her little time to think about what Wilson had told her, once they were in the opera box, the lights had dimmed, and the performance had begun, she couldn't stop her thoughts from returning to it.

What he'd done sounded romantic, she supposed, but strangely, it didn't feel that way. Perhaps that was because through most of her life, she'd been watched over so closely by her parents, particularly her father. Or perhaps it was because ever since her great mistake, her mother had continued to obsessively hover over her to make sure something like that never happened again. Or perhaps it was because she knew Wilson was not a romantic sort of man.

Even his marriage proposal had been one of practicalities—how he had what she needed (security—he hadn't been sordid enough to say money), what he needed that she had (blue blood, even if it was a little tainted), how they could build a transatlantic dynasty, how highly he regarded her, how much his young daughter needed a stepmother.

He was fond of her, he thought very highly of her, and admired her pluck—whatever that was—but there had been no mention of love. She hadn't minded that, of course, for love had gotten her no end of trouble and anguish, and she was quite happy to leave it far behind her. For the second time since Devlin Sharpe had smashed her life to bits, she had been presented with a way forward. Like her cousin Giles once had, Wilson offered her a position and a place in the world, one that allowed her to wipe the slate clean of the stupid mistake she'd once made for love. Thankfully, Wilson hadn't cared about her past or whether she was damaged goods. That could be considered romantic.

Couldn't it?

Wilson wanted her despite her past, wanted her enough that he'd followed her all over Yorkshire like a besotted schoolboy.

Or like a hunter stalking prey.

Kay shifted in her chair, telling herself not to be absurd. So what if he'd scraped acquaintance with people she knew just to get closer to her? Just as he'd said earlier tonight, he'd wanted her, and Kay knew that was a good thing, especially since she wanted him, too.

Didn't she?

At that traitorous question and the sudden pang of doubt that accompanied it, Kay slid her gaze sideways to the object of her thoughts. The light was dim here in the Royal Opera House, but she could see him clearly enough—his thinning silver hair, the creased lines of his profile, attractive in a ruthless kind of way. Her gaze moved farther down, over his sloping shoulders and down his barrel chest to his stomach, resting on the ever-so-slight paunch of middle age that his elegant clothes couldn't quite hide.

She looked away, impatient with herself. For heaven's sake, nearly three months had passed since they'd become engaged, and not once had she felt a speck of doubt about her decision to accept him. So why was she having doubts now?

As if in answer, an image of Devlin earlier that day came into her mind, his naked chest and muscled abdomen, his dark lashes lowered over vivid blue eyes, his insolent smile.

Hating him, exasperated with herself, she squeezed her eyes shut to blot him out, but that didn't work. Opening her eyes again, she leaned forward in her seat, forcing her attention to the stage, but as she stared at the performance going on below, a London ballroom came to mind, the fifth ball of her first season without more than five dances in total to her name.

Instead of the notes of Verdi's opera, she heard the lively notes of a Scottish reel. Instead of opera singers on a stage, she saw couples kicking up their heels on a parquet dance floor. And in the midst of it all, she imagined herself, sandwiched between her hostess, Lady Rowland, and her mother: a chubby, freckled, tongue-tied girl with her back pressed against the wall and her lace gown itching like mad, hating every moment of this horrible ordeal called the London season, feeling an utter failure, wishing she were anywhere else on earth.

And then, the dance had ended, the couples had cleared the floor, and there he'd been on the other side of the room, his eyes scanning the crowd where she stood, going right past her like every other man at every other ball, and then…and then swerving back to look again.

So long ago, and yet, she could remember everything about that first glimpse of Devlin Sharpe. The light of the chandeliers above glinting off the unruly strands of his midnight-black hair. His eyes, the only eyes she'd ever seen that were truly the color of turquoise, lighting on her. His dark brows lifting, as if the sight of her somehow surprised him, and then, a faint smile curving the corners of his mouth as if the surprise was a very nice one indeed.

And then, he'd moved, heading straight for her, those brilliant eyes riveted on her face as if nothing else in the world existed. His deep, well-bred voice asking Lady Rowland for an introduction and then asking her for a dance. When he'd held out his hand to lead her to the floor, Kay had felt the sweet, stinging pain of hope, and gratitude, and joy, and sheer, stark terror. And when he'd turned and taken her in his arms, her heart had seemed to leap out of her chest, tumbling right into his grasp.

Three months later, after only seven conversations and six stolen kisses, she'd agreed to give up everything in her safe, tidy world, to elope with him to Gretna Green and make a new life by his side on the other end of the globe.

They'd never made it to Africa, of course, or even Scotland, but long after the duke and his sisters had found them, persuaded her home, pulling her back from the brink of a wild, irrevocable decision, and returning her to sanity, her love for Devlin and her faith in him had remained unshaken.

If you don't come with me now, you never will.

She hadn't realized what he'd really meant by his fateful words that night in Birmingham: that if she didn't come now, he'd leave her behind for good. She'd thought he would see that the duke's sisters had been right, that it was far better to engage in an honorable courtship, however much her parents disapproved, than to sneak off in the night. She'd assumed he loved her enough to follow her home and patiently win her, that he would at least try to gain her father's permission, or if that failed, that he would at least be willing to wait the three years until she was twenty-one and parental permission wasn't needed.

Even when she'd been confronted by her father, when she'd faced his anger and disappointment with her, even when he'd banished her to their remotest estate in Wales, her love for Devlin had remained unshaken. Even when she had learned he'd departed for Africa without her, even when twenty-six months had gone by with no word from him, she had still refused to believe he had abandoned her. Until the day her father, impatient with her unwillingness to give Devlin up and exasperated by her intransigent refusal to consider marrying her cousin Giles instead, had told her the truth and showed her the proof of Devlin's betrayal. Staring at the canceled bank draft, she had been forced to realize what an idiot she had been.

The singing stopped, the music ended, and all around her, the crowd applauded, forcing Kay out of her contemplation. As the lights came up, she came out of the past and into the present, away from the man who'd ruined her and toward the man saving her. Away from the man who'd let himself be bought and toward a man who could buy anything, a man who could give her children and a secure future, who would provide for her mother and sister. A man who, by his own words, thought very highly of her. That, she thought, turning to look at him again, was so much better than love.

Wasn't it?

"Kay?"

She blinked, realizing Wilson had just said something to her. "Hmm? Sorry, what did you say?"

"You're staring at me awfully hard." He laughed. "As if you've never seen me before."

"Am I?" She echoed his laugh with one of her own, touching her fingers to her forehead. "How rude. I was lost in thought, I'm afraid."

"Thoughts about what?"

"About you, of course," she said lightly. "Now," she added with a deep breath as she stood up, "I think I'll take a turn downstairs while I have the chance. If everyone will pardon me?"

Wilson rose at once. "I'll come with you."

Suddenly, she felt stifled again, just as she had in the Savoy courtyard when he'd told her about following her across Yorkshire, just as she had felt with her mother in the dressmaker's, and she wondered in chagrin if it was her destiny to be followed and hovered over and watched every minute of her entire life from birth to death.

"Oh, no, please. I'd prefer to go alone." The moment the words were out of her mouth, she realized how they must have sounded, and when Wilson frowned, she hastened into speech again, hoping she hadn't hurt his feelings. "I doubt you'll wish to accompany me into the ladies' withdrawing room," she murmured, trying to look embarrassed at having to refer to such a delicate topic.

At once, Wilson's face relaxed back into an expression of tolerant amusement. "I'd rather not."

"That's just as I thought. I'll try to be back before the end of intermission."

"I should hope so. It's thirty minutes."

She gave him a look of pity. "Really, darling. Women take forever in these matters. You've been married before. Surely you know that?"

"I've been a widower so long, I'd forgotten," he admitted, took up her hand, and cupped it in both of his. "But is it wrong that I'll miss you?" he asked.

She smiled. "If it is wrong, I don't care. Miss away."

"Heartbreaker."

With a laugh, she pulled her hand free and left the box, joining the stream of people making their way to the lobby. She made use of the ladies' withdrawing room, and though it did not take as long as she'd implied to Wilson, the first warning gong had just sounded by the time she returned to the lobby, signaling only ten minutes until the end of intermission. She started back toward the wide, sweeping staircase to return to her seat, but she'd barely taken three steps in that direction before she heard an airy feminine voice behind her calling her name.

"Kay, my dear!"

She turned to find a tall, slim brunette in burgundy velvet coming toward her, just the person she needed to speak with.

"Delia?" she cried in happy relief. "I thought you were in Paris."

Before she could say more, however, she was engulfed in a soft wave of delicate French perfume and enveloped in an affectionate hug.

"I just got back a few days ago," Delia said as they drew apart. "And it's been an absolute whirlwind since I stepped off the boat. I shot a letter off to you at once, but of course, I didn't know you were already here in town. If I had, I'd have already called. Oh, Kay, I have so much news to tell you. For one thing..."

She paused and took a deep breath. "I'm engaged."

Kay laughed. "What, again?"

Delia made a face. "Don't tease. I suppose it is in rather bad taste, my marrying again, having been widowed three times in my life already, but that man is impossible to resist. Speaking of Calderon," she added, glancing around, "I wonder where he's got to. He went off to order sandwiches and champagne for my box, and—"

"Calderon?" Kay interrupted in dismay, hoping she'd heard wrong. "You don't mean Lord Calderon, who you had to work with at the Savoy?"

"The very same."

"But—" Kay broke off, shaking her head, trying to assimilate this bit of news. "Last time we spoke, back in January, you told me how awful he is. You couldn't stand him, you said."

"I know, I know," Delia replied, holding up her hands in a helpless gesture. "What can I say? It was all true at the time, but he wore me down, Kay." She gave a deep, rapturous sigh. "He absolutely wore me down until I just couldn't hold out against him any longer."

In other circumstances, Kay might have laughed at such a declaration, for if anyone were prone to wearing anyone down, it was Delia. But at this moment, she didn't feel much like laughing.

"I don't know what to say," she murmured at last. "And if you're happy, of course I'm happy for you. But I confess, I don't feel inclined to like your Lord Calderon very much. Not today, anyway."

"Goodness, I know Simon drives me mad on occasion—which is probably why I adore him so much—but what's he done to you? And I didn't even know you'd ever met him."

"I haven't, but I learned just this afternoon that he's friends with Devlin Sharpe. Did you know that?"

"Well..." Delia paused, shifting her weight, tugging on one diamond-bedecked earlobe, a gesture she was always inclined to do when caught out.

"And while we're on the subject," Kay went on in the wake of her friend's guilty silence, "why didn't you tell me Devlin is the one who took the Pinafore from me?"

Delia grimaced. "Found out about that, did you?"

"I did. What I want to know is why I didn't find it out from you."

"I wanted to wait until I could present you with an alternative. I thought that might take the sting out of it, so to speak."

"When I found out, it was quite a shock. And now to find out that you're engaged to his best friend, the man who helped him take it. And you didn't tell me any of this? Really, Delia! You should have told me."

"I know, I know. My mistake, but surely, his friendship with Sharpe is no reason for you to dislike Simon, I hope? We all have friends our other friends don't like, and we tolerate it. If we didn't," she added, laughing, "I'm sure we'd have no friends at all!"

"Delia, this isn't funny," she chided. "Especially since it's clear Lord Calderon is the reason I don't have the Pinafore Room. He canceled my reservation and gave it to Devlin, didn't he?"

"What?" Delia's amusement faded at once, and she shook her

head vehemently. "No, no, you've got the wrong end of the stick there. The whole thing was just a muddle between Simon and me, as I already told you. I assure you, dearest, it wasn't deliberate in any way. We each reserved the room and forgot to tell the other. But there's nothing to worry about now anyway, because we've got an absolutely divine alternative for your wedding banquet, big enough to seat everyone."

"You do?" Kay blinked, taken aback, her frustration fading. "Really? Are you sure?"

"Yes. It's all arranged, I promise you."

With those words of reassurance, Kay's relief was so great, she felt weak in the knees, making her realize just how worried she'd really been all these weeks since the Pinafore had been snatched away.

"But where is it?" she managed at last. "Did that plan you were developing for us at the Savoy work out after all, the one you were so mysterious about? Even though you're not there any longer?"

"Oh, no, it's not at the Savoy, but speaking of the Savoy, my crowd is going to supper there after the opera. Why don't you join us, and you and I can talk about it all?"

Kay looked at her askance. "The Savoy? You're giving them your business after they fired you?"

"Yes, well, Simon still does business with some of the investors there, and one hates to burn bridges in business. You'll learn that soon enough once you marry your American millionaire. Besides, you know as well as I do that the Savoy serves the best opera suppers in town. So will you come? That way, I can pull you aside and we can discuss all the details."

"I'd love to, but I've got my mother and sister with me. And Wilson, of course."

"Oh, that'll be all right. I've already got such a crowd, what's four more? Now, I see Calderon standing by the staircase, beckoning me and tapping his pocket watch. He's such a stickler for punctuality. But he's probably right to nag me. I've got heaps of people in my box tonight, and they'll surely be wondering what's happened to us if we don't go up. Besides, abandoning one's guests is terribly poor form, so I should probably toddle."

"Wait," Kay implored as her friend moved to go. "You can't just tell me it's all arranged and go dashing off before you tell me where!"

"Oh, didn't I say?" Delia smiled. "How does Westbourne House suit you?"

"Your cousin's house in Park Lane? But I thought it wasn't available. We talked about it in January, and you said the duke had already leased it for the season to some American family."

"So he had! But Max is here in town just now, and he told me himself only a few hours ago that we could have Westbourne House for you after all, if we still wanted it. Only for the weekend of the wedding, but I told him yes, of course. I hope that was all right?"

"All right?" Kay laughed, her emotions ricocheting back once again to relief, making her feel a bit dizzy in consequence. "My wedding banquet in the duke's ballroom? How could that not be all right?"

"Well, that's just it. You may not want the ballroom after I've told you my other idea."

"I don't understand. What other idea?"

"You remember I told you I had a way we might be able to keep your banquet at the Savoy? Well," she went on as Kay nodded, "my vision was to build a glass-walled banqueting room on the roof of the hotel."

"What a wonderful idea! How did you ever think of such a thing?"

"If you remember, Max built an immense hothouse on the roof of Westbourne House for Evie when they got married, and that was the inspiration for my idea. Of course, if you would prefer to use Max's ballroom instead of Evie's hothouse, we could do that."

"No, no, I love the idea of having the banquet in a conservatory. All the benefits of a garden setting, without relying on the fickle English weather. Oh, Dee, how clever you are. No wonder you were so marvelous at planning parties for the Savoy."

"The hotel didn't agree. I got fired, remember? Anyway, with Max's house already leased for the season, I thought my idea was completely out the window, and I was just sick to think you were being left high and dry. I was determined to find you something, of course, but now I don't have to, and it's all settled, thank heaven."

"But how did the duke manage to persuade his tenants to vacate for a week in the midst of the season?"

The second gong sounded before Delia could reply, warning the crowd still milling about the lobby they had only five minutes to find their seats before the performance resumed.

"That's the second gong, so I simply must go, dearest. I'll see you at the Savoy later?" she added over her shoulder as she turned away.

Kay nodded. "Of course. Thank you, Delia. Thank you, thank you."

Delia gave her a rueful smile. "Don't thank me, darling. I'd love to take the credit, but I wasn't the one who arranged it. I came back from Paris prepared to beg, borrow, or steal a banquet room for you somewhere, but as it turned out, I didn't have to."

Kay nodded in understanding. "I'll be sure to write the duke tomorrow and thank him."

"Max isn't the one you should be thanking either, I'm afraid."

"But who then?"

"Brace yourself. It was Devlin Sharpe."

"What?" Kay stared at her. "You're joking," she said with a laugh.

"Would I joke about something like that?" With those words, Delia dashed off, leaving a bemused, completely bewildered Kay staring after her.

6

Due to Delia's revelation, Kay paid even less attention to the second half of *Don Carlo* than she had the first. Instead, she spent the remaining ninety minutes of the performance wondering how, in the space of only a few short hours, Devlin Sharpe could have arranged for Westbourne's tenants to vacate his luxurious ducal residence in Park Lane during the height of the upcoming season.

He and the duke scarcely even knew each other. And why would Devlin do such a thing? Remorse? Guilt?

Go to the devil. I owe you nothing more than what I've already done.

Those defiant words did not indicate a man suffering any pangs of conscience. If he even had a conscience, and that was something Kay found hard to credit.

By the end of the opera, however, she had come to one definite conclusion. Regardless of how or why this had come about, she was not going to tell anyone that Devlin was the person responsible. Josephine was young and impressionable, and the less said to her about Devlin Sharpe, the better. And Wilson would hate the idea that his fiancée might be beholden to Devlin in any way.

As for her mother, if Magdelene learned That Horrible Man

was somehow behind it, she'd faint dead away from the shock, and upon being revived with smelling salts, she might declare that they were obligated to refuse it, since Devlin must be playing some sort of cat-and-mouse game, and it would not do to be in his debt. Kay knew her mother was probably right, but she couldn't afford to turn down the duke's splendid ballroom, despite who had arranged for it.

During the carriage ride back to the Savoy, Kay informed everyone of Delia's news and her invitation to supper, hedging around the details, and by the time they reached the hotel, the other three members of her party had the distinct impression that Delia was solely responsible for securing the duke's ballroom, accepting Kay's explanations at face value, much to her relief.

That relief, however, vanished only moments after they had returned to the hotel. As they started down the long corridor of reception rooms to the Mikado, she found that Devlin, Lady Pamela, and Lord and Lady Walston were walking directly ahead of them, and that she was not the only one to notice the fact.

"Kay," Josephine whispered to her, pulling her back to let Wilson and her mother go in front of them, "do you see him? Do you?"

"Shush," she replied in a sharp whisper, "or Mama will hear you. Yes, I see him. He's going to a supper party, too, obviously. What of it?"

"What of it?" Josephine glanced ahead, then back at her. "I doubt you'll be asking that in a second or two."

Puzzled, Kay turned from Jo's worried face to the corridor ahead, just in time to watch Devlin and his party join the queue of Delia's guests gathering at the door to the Mikado Room.

"What in heaven's name is he doing?" she muttered in horror. "Crashing Delia's party?"

"Maybe he intends to make a scene or something?" Jo whispered back. "Perhaps we should leave?"

"An excellent idea." With that, she lunged forward and grabbed her mother by the arm, pulling her back from Wilson's side. "We have to leave, Mama. Now. At once." But before Kay could say more, the matter was taken out of her hands. And by a most unlikely source.

"Mr. Sharpe," Wilson called, causing Magdelene to gasp and Josephine to groan under her breath. For her part, Kay could only stare, appalled, as her fiancé stepped forward to give Devlin what appeared to be an amiable clap on the shoulder as he declared, "Good to see you again so soon."

So soon? Kay's mind echoed. What on earth did that mean?

"And you, Mr. Rycroft." Devlin shook the other man's hand without even glancing in her direction. "Have you met Lord and Lady Walston? And their daughter, Lady Pamela? You know that Lady Pamela and I are engaged to be married?"

Beside her, Magdelene sagged, letting out a low moan, and Kay nudged her with one foot. The last thing they needed right now was any of her mother's histrionics.

"Of course I do," Wilson was replying. "Why, I heard you discussing it with Lord Calderon this very afternoon."

This afternoon? Wilson and Devlin had seen each other this afternoon?

Kay could only watch, dumbfounded, as her fiancé was introduced to Lord and Lady Walston, and she felt as if she were Alice from the children's story, instead of stepping through the doorway of the Mikado Room at the Savoy, she'd just stepped through the looking glass and straight into Wonderland.

Wilson turned, beckoning to her, and rather like a marionette whose strings had just been pulled, Kay jerked forward, too dazed to do anything else.

"Have all of you met my fiancée, Lady Kay Matheson?" Wilson asked, his voice so nonchalant that it was almost as if he were unaware of the events of fourteen years ago.

Left with no choice, Kay donned a polite, friendly air. "Lord and Lady Walston," she greeted. "I believe the last time we saw you was at Lady Pamela's graduation from Willowbank? Lady Pamela, good to see you again as well. Mr. Sharpe," she continued, the rigorous training in social graces drummed into her during her own years at Willowbank coming to her aid and enabling her to sound casually indifferent. She even managed a nod in his direction, though she did not quite meet his eyes. "Congratulations on your engagement. All of you remember my mother, Lady Raleigh, of course, and my sister, Lady Josephine?"

Josephine was a brick, taking her cue from Kay perfectly, but her mother looked ready to live up to all Kay's expectations and sink to the floor. In the end, however, good breeding prevailed over Magdelene's natural instinct for drama, and more stilted greetings were exchanged as the line moved forward and they entered the Mikado Room.

Ahead of her, Kay could see Delia and Calderon greeting the arriving guests, and she did not miss the shock on Delia's face as Devlin reached her. She cast a frantic glance in Kay's direction, then at her other guests, who had not failed to notice the newest arrivals and were watching this scene unfold with avid curiosity.

Delia, left with little choice, took Devlin's outstretched hand, giving Kay a look of apology.

"We shall have quite a crowd this evening, it seems," she said after greeting him and the other members of his party. "I hope we'll have enough room for everyone. Heavens, Simon," she added, giving a tinkling, bell-like laugh as she turned to the tall, blond man beside her. "I do wish you would warn me when you invite more people."

Calderon glanced down the line, saw Kay, and raised an eyebrow. "I might say the same," he murmured.

"If we're to be married, darling," Delia chided with another laugh, "we really must learn to communicate about these things in advance."

"If it's a problem," Devlin said, "I can see the maître d'hôtel about finding my party a table in the restaurant."

His offer was negated at once, and by the last person Kay would have expected. "No, no," Lady Pamela said, "that won't be necessary, surely?"

Everyone, including her own parents, looked at her in surprise. Except Magdelene, who put her face in her hands and groaned again, earning herself another gentle kick of Kay's evening slipper.

"After all," Pamela went on, seeming oblivious to the disconcerted reactions around her, "it's a bit silly, isn't it, all of us trying to avoid each other, and for no reason other than some silly gossip from years ago? Doesn't it make far more sense for all of us to be friends? There's a London season ahead, and since Devlin and Lord Calderon and Mr. Rycroft are all doing business together now—"

"What?" Kay gasped, cutting the girl off mid-sentence, shock momentarily overcoming good manners.

"Sorry, my dear," Wilson interjected smoothly, turning to her with a laugh. "I haven't yet had the chance to tell you. Mr. Sharpe and I are both investors in Lord Calderon's new hotel venture, along with a bunch of bigwigs you probably already know, like the Duke of Westbourne. We held a meeting earlier today to discuss some of the details, approve a board of directors, that sort of thing."

Westbourne, too? Kay opened her mouth, but for the life of her, she could think of nothing to say.

"You don't mind, of course?" Wilson went on, his gray eyes fixed on her in one of those hard, pointed stares of his, and with an effort, Kay gathered her wits.

"Mind?" she echoed, feigning surprise at the very idea, feeling as if she was fooling no one. "Why on earth would I mind?"

Wilson gave a slow, approving nod, as if she'd passed some sort of test, while Pamela clapped her hands together like a delighted child.

"It's all settled, then," the girl declared. "We'll all stay. That is," she added, turning to Delia, "if our hosts don't mind? If it's a problem of place settings or something—"

"Oh, that's nothing," Delia said with a wave of her hand. "This is the Savoy, after all. They can easily seat a few more. But I should hate for anyone to feel..." She paused again, looking at Kay. "Uncomfortable."

Suddenly, it wasn't only Delia looking at her, but everyone in the room, and Kay wanted to shout that feeling uncomfortable was an understatement. But, of course, she couldn't do that. She had to play the game. It was the role she'd chosen in those first moments in the flower shop, one Wilson obviously wanted her to play now, one that would serve her best in the long run.

"I don't see," Kay said, meeting Delia's inquiring gaze, "why anyone should feel uncomfortable. But if we are," she added, forcing herself to make light of it all, "that means we're all in desperate need of a drink."

Thankfully, all the guests laughed at that, except her mother, of course. Despite Magdelene's appalled expression, however, the tension seemed to break, and Delia signaled for a waiter to begin serving vermouth, sherry, and other aperitifs.

"That seemed to go all right," Jo murmured as the others moved away. "Better, at least, than I thought it would. Ooh, sherry!" she added, plucking a glass of sherry off the nearby waiter's tray.

"All right?" Magdelene echoed, too upset by what had just happened to check the girl.

Kay pulled the glass out of Jo's hand. "No spirits," she said over her sister's indignant protest, handing her a glass of lemonade from the tray instead. "You're not really out until your debutante ball in May."

"I'm practically out now. I'm here tonight, aren't I? Besides, I should have been out two years ago. And, anyway, it's only sherry. I'm always allowed to have wine with dinner."

"A few sips of wine with each course at dinner," Kay corrected. "This is not dinner, and a full glass is not a few sips."

"This is so silly," Jo muttered, rolling her eyes. "I'm not a baby. I'm three months from being twenty."

"How can you say this went all right, Josephine?" Magdelene wailed, reverting to the former topic. "This is a disaster. What are Wilson and Westbourne thinking, to be associating with That Horrible Man?"

"It's business, Mama, and I am marrying a man of business," Kay said, a stern reminder to herself as well as her mother. Taking a look around to be sure no one was watching her, Kay lifted the glass of sherry she'd taken from Jo to her lips and downed the entire contents in three gulps. God knows, she'd earned it.

"I don't understand you, Kay. I really don't. How can you stand to be in the same room with him after what he's done? And how can you expect me to be civil after everything that's happened—"

"Because nothing happened," she cut in incisively, giving her parent a meaningful glance to remind her of the position they'd taken years ago. "Remember? Therefore, Devlin's presence here has no effect on us," she added as her mother tossed her head with a huff. "And it's vital that we demonstrate the fact."

"I suppose so, but oh, how I'd love to give That Horrible Man a piece of my mind."

"I daresay you would, Mama." She had no doubt Magdelene had spent years inventing and rehearsing the scene in which they met Devlin again, one in which she would heap withering scorn and contempt upon the blackguard who had started those vicious rumors about her daughter and ruined her chances, and she was clearly displeased at being deprived of the opportunity by the prying eyes all around them. But though Kay understood how tempting it was to dress Devlin down publicly, she knew it would never do.

"If you make a fuss, Mama, people will take it as proof that there's something to that old business after all. And," she went on as Magdelene tossed her head with a grudging snort, "Wilson wouldn't like it if we made any sort of a fuss. There's some sort of business deal involved here, and if we queer the pitch, he will be angry, and that is a complication to my life I can do without. So pipe down, Mama, and at least try to be civil. Now," she added, glancing across the room, "there is one friend of ours I simply must talk to. If you will excuse me for a moment? And for heaven's sake, don't let Josephine have any wine until we sit down to supper. She's not used to spirits, and her getting tipsy is the last thing we need.

So, young lady," she added, giving her sister a stern look, "no wine until we eat."

"You never let me have any fun," Jo grumbled as Kay turned away, plucked a second sherry off a nearby tray, and started across the room toward her hostess.

Noting her approach, Delia excused herself from the guests she was speaking with and met Kay halfway. "You have a steely look in your eye that tells me I'm about to be raked over the coals," she murmured, taking Kay's elbow and propelling her into the adjoining dining room, away from prying eyes. "But darling, I swear, I did not know Sharpe was coming."

"I believe you, and if I'm looking grim, it's not because of you. Still, I have to ask. What is he doing here?"

Delia gave a helpless shrug. "He and Simon are old friends. Simon saw him at the opera with Lady Pamela and her parents, and unbeknownst to me, he asked them to join us. He didn't know I had invited you. As I told everyone, that man and I need to learn to communicate better."

"Clearly," Kay replied, a dry response that made Delia wince. "But enough about that. There are other things we need to discuss. How is Devlin responsible for getting me the duke's ballroom? And what is this business deal and why did your fiancé drag mine and Devlin and the duke—of all the mad matches in the world—into it? What was Calderon hoping to achieve with this? A more peaceful world?"

Delia smiled. "Well," she began, but Kay forestalled her.

"How did Calderon ever persuade the other three to become involved? And why did no one bother to tell me about it? And why does Lady Pamela not seem to care a jot? She even wants us to be friends. Friends? What a joke."

"Heavens, with that barrage of questions, where do I begin?" Delia laughed, but her laugh ended in a little cough when Kay did not laugh with her. "As to how they all ended up in business together, it started when I got fired from the Savoy a few weeks ago and Simon resigned his position on the board. Rather at loose ends, he decided to start his own hotel venture, and he pulled in Devlin as the first investor, then Max. Simon was aware that my cousin is always looking for new investments. Any peers with sense always are, given the state of land rents nowadays. So Simon presented Max with this opportunity, and Max jumped on it."

"Even though he knew Devlin was involved?"

"I think he decided that after fourteen years, it might be time to make peace. Simon feels much the same. They're right, I suppose. You don't mind, do you, darling? Surely not, not after all this time?"

She reminded herself that she had no right to mind. Who Westbourne and Calderon chose to do business with was not for her to say.

"What about Wilson?" she asked instead. "Did Calderon really have to pull in my fiancé as well? Not that I really mind, of course," she added at once, trying to assume an air of nonchalance about it. "Business or not, we probably won't see much of them."

"More than you think, I'm afraid."

Kay's stomach lurched with sudden dismay. "Nonsense. Why should we?"

"There's the season, for one thing."

Kay shrugged, her sudden tension easing. "Oh, well, we can easily avoid each other there. It's not as if anyone will be so ill-bred as to invite us to the same parties. At least not on purpose," she added, giving Delia a meaningful glance.

Delia wrinkled up her nose in rueful fashion. "As to that, I must warn you that all of you will be invited to my wedding. Devlin Sharpe is Simon's best friend, so he'll no doubt be best man, and whether it's ill-bred or not, I'd like you to be my maid of honor. Of course, if you don't want to do it," she added at once, "I'd understand."

"Stuff. I will adore being your maid of honor. Devlin Sharpe and I may hate each other, but I daresay we can both manage to be civil for one afternoon."

Delia bit her lip in apologetic fashion, telling Kay there was worse to come. "It'll be more than one afternoon, darling, I'm afraid. They're all in business together, you know, and these ventures always involve masses of social obligations."

Kay's hand tightened around her glass, bracing herself. "Such as?"

"Dinner parties, hotel openings . . . that sort of thing. Wilson will no doubt expect you to attend at least some of these, even before you're married. Sharpe will expect the same of Lady Pamela. Don't worry, darling," she added as Kay didn't reply. "It's not as if the men will talk about you over the port. I daresay even Sharpe wouldn't be caddish enough to tell your fiancé the elopement really happened."

"You have more faith in Sharpe than I do," Kay replied. "But he can say whatever he likes about the elopement. I already told Wilson the truth."

"You did?"

"If you're going to lecture me," Kay replied with a sigh, "please don't. You should have heard my mother when she learned I had told him. You'd have thought I was about to confess to murder. But I felt it only right to give Wilson the true story. And now, in light of what you've told me, I'm especially glad I did."

"I wouldn't dream of lecturing you. I think you were quite right. And since Rycroft must have known about Devlin's involvement when he bought shares in the new company, he clearly isn't worried or jealous."

"No," Kay agreed, lowering her gaze to her sherry glass, staring meditatively into the amber depths. Somehow, given how he'd traveled all over the north of England last autumn in pursuit of her, she would have thought he would be jealous. It seemed odd that he wasn't.

"Sorry, Kay," she added, misinterpreting her silence. "Stings a bit, I suppose?"

"Not at all." Kay lifted her head. "I am a bit surprised, that's all. It doesn't seem... quite in character for Wilson."

"What do you mean?"

She thought of the things he'd said tonight as they'd left the Savoy, the implication of possessiveness in his voice. Perhaps she'd imagined it. Or perhaps he welcomed the chance to flaunt her in Devlin's face. "Nothing," she answered. "I'm actually relieved. Besides, when I accepted Wilson's proposal, I knew what I was getting."

"A man of business?"

"Just so. And because of that, I appreciate that going into a lucrative business venture with a duke and a viscount is a deal Wilson would never let pass by."

Delia frowned, uncomprehending. "But why should their rank matter? What does he care?"

"Because of Charlene. His daughter. She's fifteen, so she'll be coming out in a few years. But with Wilson being such new money, the poor girl won't ever be accepted in New York. So he wants to bring her here when the time comes, and to do that, he needs connections here. That's why," she added, "he came to England in the first place."

"Kay!" Delia's eyes widened, making her regret she'd been so frank. "You mean Rycroft's marrying you for your connections?"

"Of course not," she replied with asperity, suddenly on the defensive. "If British connections were all he wanted, he could have found much better ones than I can offer. I'm ruined, remember?"

"In the eyes of some people, I know that's still true," Delia was forced to concede. "But not everyone feels that way."

"Thanks in part to my powerful friends," Kay replied, holding up her glass in acknowledgment of Delia's influence and that of her cousin, the duke, and, to a lesser extent, his sisters. "I will always be grateful to you for standing by me."

"We always will. But, dearest, if your connection to us is the reason Rycroft's marrying you—"

"Listen to you," Kay scoffed lightly. "What conceit."

Delia's answering gaze was steady. "Is it conceit?"

"Of course. Titled fathers all over Britain would love to get their daughters married off to American millionaires. Wilson could have had his pick, I daresay, but he chose me."

"Which only shows his excellent taste."

Kay smiled at her friend's show of loyalty. "Thank you, Dee, but we both know I was never the catch of the season, even when I was young and unsullied. Now, it's different. And I don't even have a dowry to offer."

"What? Your father left you nothing?"

No point in trying to dissemble. "Not a farthing," she confessed. "We knew things were a bit tight, of course, but we didn't learn until after he died that everything that wasn't entailed was mortgaged to the hilt." Kay took another swallow of wine. "That was rather a shock."

"Oh, Kay," Delia murmured, giving her a look of compassion she found almost unbearable. "My dear."

Appreciating she'd said more than she'd ever intended, probably due to the sherry, Kay set aside her glass. "So all's well that ends well," she said lightly. "Wilson is rich as Croesus, so he hardly needs his future wife's dowry. As for me, I can rest easy, knowing Mama will be taken care of. Josephine will have a very generous portion when she marries, a dowry fat enough to take the sting out of her husband having a disgraced sister-in-law. As for me, I will be washed clean. I will also have a home, children, and a secure future. It's more than I ever thought I'd get."

Delia opened her mouth to reply, then closed it again.

"Don't look so stricken, Dee," Kay said gently. "Wilson is very fond of me, I promise you. And I'm fond of him. He's a good, decent man, and he'll be good to me, and that's more than a lot of women can claim. Now, enough about that," she added sternly before her friend could ask any more inconvenient questions. "There's still one thing you haven't told me. How did Devlin Sharpe get me the duke's ballroom? Does he know Westbourne's tenants, or something?"

Delia shrugged. "Your guess is as good as mine. Max told me the news only a few hours ago, but he was on his way to some sort of political meeting tonight for the Lords, and I was on my way here, so I had no chance to obtain any details. But he told me Sharpe is the one responsible."

Before Kay could reply, a cough from the doorway to the reception room had both of them turning in that direction to find the subject of their conversation standing there.

"Ladies," Devlin said with a bow. "I hope I'm not interrupting."

As he straightened, the movement drew Kay's gaze to his chest, and at once, the image of him half naked came again into her mind—the washboard ripples of his abdomen, the striations of sinew and muscle in his powerful arms, the honey-bronze color of his skin—and tongues of heat curled in her belly.

"Not at all, Mr. Sharpe," Delia was saying. "We don't mind, do we, Kay?"

Kay couldn't quite find her voice to reply. The heat in her midsection was rushing upward like a wave, flooding her face. It took all the will she had to lift her gaze, a stupid and humiliating move, for the knowing curve of his lips and the tiny smile lines at the corners of his eyes told her he knew exactly what she'd been remembering.

Cursing him, his splendid chest, and her own fair complexion, Kay forced herself to meet his amused gaze head on. "Of course not," she lied. "Join us, Mr. Sharpe, by all means."

"No, no," he replied. "As I said, I didn't mean to interrupt your tête-à-tête. I'm here on behalf of Lord Calderon. The maître d'hôtel is asking him about the seating arrangements, Lady Stratham, since there are more guests than expected. I know my friend well, and from the look on his face, I fear he's a bit lost."

"I daresay he is," Delia replied in amusement. "The poor pet hasn't a clue about the nuances of seating. He'd just be dogmatic about it, and follow precedent to the letter, which means the two of you would probably end up next to each other."

At that ghastly prospect, the heat inside Kay was instantly doused, and sanity returned. Devlin must have felt pretty much the same way she did, for his knowing smile vanished at once.

Delia, of course, perceived their mutual dismay. "Heavens, my darlings," she cried, laughing a little, "no need to look so horrified. I was only joking! But I'd best see the maître d'hôtel anyway, just to be sure. In the meantime," she added with mock severity as she turned away, "do try not to kill each other. And, Kay, if you want to know how you got Max's ballroom, why don't you just ask the man who arranged it?"

Watching as Delia started for the door, Kay felt an absurd jolt of panic at the idea of being left alone with this cretin. "I'd prefer to come with you, Dee," she said hastily and started to follow, but Devlin's amused voice stopped her before she'd taken two steps.

"Running away? But I thought you wanted to know about the duke's ballroom? Of course," he went on when she didn't reply, "if you'd rather scurry off like a frightened rabbit..."

The idea that he thought her afraid of him was too much to bear. Kay stopped and whirled around, shoving down the silly panic of a moment before. "I'm not the least bit afraid of you," she said coldly. "I merely detest the sight of you. There's a difference."

"Kay, Kay," he said, shaking his head, his eyes crinkling with amusement at her expense, "is that any way to talk to your fiancé's business partner?"

She made a sound of derision through her teeth. "I can't think how you managed the blunt for such an investment. Lady Pamela's dowry, I suppose?"

If she thought her words would sting, she was disappointed, for Devlin grinned. "Careful," he warned. "I may have done you a favor by arranging for you to have the duke's ballroom, but I can also un-arrange it."

"It was hardly a favor," she countered tartly. "Since you're only replacing what you stole in the first place."

"As I told you this afternoon, I didn't steal it."

She gave a skeptical sniff, but there was no point in arguing about it. Best to just ask him about the duke's house, thereby proving she was no timid rabbit where he was concerned, and then get the hell away from him before he could bait her any further. "Either way," she said, "how did you persuade the duke to get his tenants out of the Park Lane house? Especially in the space of one afternoon. And," she added, unable to resist asking the even more puzzling question, "why did you do it?"

"Oh, well, as to the how, that was absurdly simple." He paused, taking a sip of wine. "After you departed my suite this afternoon in a whirlwind of righteous indignation, I telephoned Westbourne and presented a possible solution to your little problem, whereupon we then made use of both telephone and telegraph. Within an hour, we'd arranged for the Robinsons—that's the American family leasing the duke's house—to be invited to a country-house party put on by Lord Linville, the duke's neighbor in Gloucestershire, the weekend of June seventh."

"Does Linville know the Robinsons?"

Devlin's smile widened. "Not yet. But he will meet them this weekend when he goes up to the duke's estate for a spot of fishing. Robinson, the duke tells me, is an avid fisherman."

Kay frowned, still confused. "But why would Linville invite people he doesn't even know to his house party? And why would the Robinsons accept such an invitation to the country in the midst of the season?"

"Lord Linville, as you may know, is a marquess with two unmarried sons and a mortgaged estate. Robinson is new money, obscenely so, and he has four very pretty, very eligible daughters.

A marriage between their families means no mortgage for Linville and at least one of Robinson's daughters off his hands and married to a future marquess. Both of them jumped at the chance. As for you, you get use of Westbourne's ballroom, his kitchens, his French chef, and a few of his servants for your wedding banquet. Winning all round for everyone, wouldn't you say?"

Kay didn't know quite what to reply. "And the duke did this just because you asked him to, even after…after everything that happened?"

"We're in business together now. It's in his best interests and mine if we can rub along. As I said, it was simple to arrange. The simplicity, however, doesn't really negate your obligation, does it?"

Dissembling, she decided, was her best option. "Oh?" she said, pretending bewilderment. "What obligation would that be?"

"Oh, Kay, don't be coy." He paused, tilting his head to one side, looking so infuriatingly pleased with himself that she felt again the almost irresistible temptation to slap him. "I salvaged your grand wedding affair. I think that pretty much puts you in my debt, doesn't it?"

"Debt?" she echoed with lively scorn. "Of all the arrogant, conceited, idiotic—"

"Careful," he cut in, his eyes on her face, his grin widening. "We're being watched."

She glanced toward the doorway, dismayed to see that he was right. Several people were observing them through the opening, heads together, whispering.

She looked at him again and offered her prettiest smile in return. "As I already pointed out, it's not a favor to give back what you stole."

"Indeed? So, since I stole it from you, what possible reason could I have for trying to make it up to you now?"

"Heaven only knows why you do the things you do. Probably just to give yourself the chance to crow."

"That must be it," he countered with a shrug and took a sip of his drink.

She frowned, the light tone of his voice giving her sudden pangs of doubt about her theory, despite the fact that crowing was exactly what he'd been doing for the last five minutes. "Why, then? I can't believe it's pangs of conscience."

He made a scoffing sound. "Hardly that, since I have nothing to feel guilty about."

"As I said this afternoon, you're such a hero."

His smile didn't falter, but his eyes flashed, a glimmer of anger and something more, something she couldn't quite identify, something that, if she didn't know better, might have been hurt. It vanished, however, before she could be sure, and when he spoke, his voice had resumed its light, airy tone.

"Either way, my motives don't really matter, do they? Your problem is now solved, and all's well that ends well. You and your American millionaire can host the swankiest wedding banquet since Queen Victoria, and he can keep you in the style to which you've always been accustomed, something I certainly couldn't have provided you at the time. Your father would be so proud."

She felt compelled to defend her parent. "My father loved me. He did," she insisted as Devlin raised an eyebrow. "He always had my best interests at heart."

"A husband with money being your father's definition of what's in your best interests?"

"His refusal of your suit wasn't only due to your lack of money! I deserved a proper courtship, not an elopement in the dead of night. Had you stayed and made your case patiently, he would have eventually allowed you to court me in honorable fashion and prove yourself worthy of me. And he'd have given his blessing in the end."

"You know," he said slowly, "there was a time when I badly wanted to believe that."

She lifted her chin, giving him the haughtiest look she could manage. "Whether you believe it or not," she said with dignity, "it's the truth."

"We decided to elope, if you recall, because we knew he would not give his permission. But he was happy to give it for Giles, wasn't he? Whether it was because of Giles's wealth, or his title, it rather makes his motives and aspirations regarding you pretty plain, don't you think? How bitter his disappointment must have been when you and Giles called things off."

There was a glimmer of truth in his conclusions about her father, of course, for Papa had always favored her marriage to her wealthy cousin. She had no intention, however, of acknowledging the fact, nor admitting that Giles had broken their engagement because she was damaged goods. Even if he already knew all that, admitting it to him now would be too humiliating.

"An accusation of mercenary motives on anyone's part is laughably hypocritical, coming from you," she shot back instead, her voice shaking, even as she worked to hide her resentment of him from any watching eyes. "After all, we both know what you're willing to do for money."

He had the gall to look as if he didn't know what she was talking about. "What the devil do you mean by that? If you're referring to Pamela's dowry again—"

"Lady Kay?"

Both of them turned at the interruption to find the Savoy's maître d'hôtel nearby, making her wonder wildly what the man might have overheard.

"And you asked me earlier," Devlin muttered, "how secrets get out? This is how."

Though she was loath to admit it, he had a point, and she realized in chagrin that yet again, he had managed to provoke her into forgetting discretion, goaded her into doing and saying things that put her at risk, and gotten her all stirred up over resentments that were all in the distant past. It seemed to be, she thought grimly, his special gift.

With an effort, she ignored him, tamping down the resentment roiling within her, and addressed the maître d'hôtel. "Yes, Monsieur Latrec? What is it?"

"My apologies for interrupting, my lady, but dinner is about to be served, and we need to finish preparing the banquet room."

"Of course," Devlin said before she had the chance. "We wouldn't dream of delaying you. Lady Kay?"

He offered her his arm, but when she looked at it as if it were a venomous snake, he gave a low, unexpected chuckle.

"Don't worry, Kay. I won't bite you. I can't. After all, we've no reason for animosity, remember? And besides, we'll all be mingling in society together this season. Your fiancé wants that, and so does Pam, apparently, so we have to be matey, and affable, and all friends together."

"Ugh," she groaned. "Saints preserve us."

Still, he was right that neither of them had a choice in the matter, so she put her hand on his arm as lightly as possible. "Very well. Let's get this over with."

"That's the spirit."

Her face a mask of serene amiability, her hand in the crook of his arm, she accompanied Devlin back through the doorway, but the moment they were once again in the reception room, she pulled free, for the last thing she wanted was to be forced by proximity to accompany him in to dinner. Before she escaped his company, however, she couldn't resist offering one last parting shot.

"I may have to put up with you for the sake of this hotel investment business you're involved in with Wilson, but as for us ever being friends..."

Aware that all eyes in the room were fixed upon them, she paused to give him one more smile, though she only managed it through clenched teeth. "I'd rather be friends with Lucifer."

She turned away, but if she'd hoped her parting words would leave a mark, she was disappointed, for his amused laughter followed her all the way across the room.

7

In the fortnight that followed his encounter with Kay at Simon and Delia's opera supper, Devlin barely had time to breathe. Countless discussions with lawyers, accountants, and the other board members about the new hotel, helping Simon with the final arrangements for the Mayfair's opening, and meeting Pam's dozens of relatives took up every waking moment of his time, but sadly, none of that stopped his mind from returning to Kay again and again and her barbed implications.

I can't think how you managed the blunt for such an investment. Lady Pamela's dowry, I suppose…

Did she really think he was marrying Pam for her money?

The opposite was closer to truth, since Devlin's future father-in-law was mired in debt, with a portion for his daughter of less than a thousand pounds. Devlin's current balance in his London bank alone was a hundred times that much, but Kay, it was clear, didn't know any of that. They'd been interrupted before he could set her straight about his finances, but he damn well intended to do so at the very first opportunity.

And she had brass to criticize him for having mercenary

motives when she had not only thrown him over for her wealthy cousin but she was now marrying a man who was not only obscenely rich but also twice her age. He could believe she'd been fond of Giles, but what was her motive for marrying Rycroft? True love? Not bloody likely. He'd be sure to tell her that, too, next time they met.

"How's that sound, Devlin?"

"Hmm?" Roused from his contemplations by the sound of his name, he looked up to find both the duke and Simon looking at him expectantly.

"Excellent, excellent," he replied with no idea what he was praising.

The other two, however, seemed satisfied, and the conversation moved on to the question of a menu for the Mayfair's grand opening celebration. Devlin paid attention just long enough to agree with making it a stand-up affair, with champagne and claret cups and canapés served on trays before his mind wandered again to Kay's insinuations.

We both know what you're willing to do for money.

Granted, her father had not approved of his daughter marrying the impecunious fifth son of a baron, but Kay hadn't seemed to care a bit about his lack of money. Not then, anyway. That she felt compelled to rub his face in it now stung a bit, he had to admit. But thinking back on the other night, he was dismayed to realize that her poor opinion of him wasn't what really hurt.

No, what hurt was that even as she'd stood there, shredding him into spills and freezing him with those glacial green eyes, even as he'd teased her and countered her accusations with a show of indifference, all the old passion for her had been there, too, rumbling deep down within him, ready to rise up again at the slightest provocation. Hell, their prospective marriage partners had been in the very next room, and yet Kay had still managed to ignite his desire quick as lighting a match.

That's really why he resented her so. Because despite everything, he was still not free of her. Fourteen years, he thought in self-disgust, and yet she could still infuriate him and hurt him and arouse him like no other woman ever could. It had always been that way. It probably, he appreciated grimly, always would be.

What a galling thought.

She'd moved on with her life, and he thought he had as well, and yet now he wondered if he'd only been fooling himself.

What did Kay have to do for him to stop feeling this way? he wondered. Push him off a cliff? Shoot him with a pistol? And what about Pam? At the thought of his fiancée, Devlin's frustration deepened. He had a future with Pam, he could build a life with her. The only thing he and Kay had ever built was a bonfire of passion and an ash heap of regrets.

"The twenty-third of April, it is, then." Simon stood up, Westbourne with him, and Devlin, roused from his contemplations, jerked to his feet. "I shall have Delia make all the arrangements and send the invitations straightaway."

"Now that we've settled that question," the duke put in, "might I suggest some luncheon? We can finish going over the changes to the incorporation papers while we enjoy an excellent joint of beef at the same time."

Simon concurred with that suggestion, but given that Devlin had no idea what changes had been proposed during this meeting that still required going over, he was relieved that he had other plans.

"Sorry," he replied. "I can't stop. I'm meeting Pamela and her mother for luncheon, and she has some outing planned for us afterward. You two can manage the remaining details on the incorporation without me, I trust?"

Assured on this essential point, Devlin left the Mayfair and returned to the Savoy, where he found Pamela waiting for him in the lobby, and at the sight of her, looking sweet and lovely, with a welcoming smile on her lips, Devlin's tumultuous thoughts about Kay faded away, replaced by a sureness that he was doing the right thing. It was the same feeling he'd had the first evening Pam had come to dinner at his villa in Cairo with her parents. When he'd watched her coming up the steps of his home, he'd seen his future. He had no intention of throwing that away because of his past.

"Darling," he greeted. "How pretty you look. New dress?"

"Delivered by the dressmaker's this morning." Smiling, she lifted her hands, palms toward the ceiling, and twirled, giving him a full view of her gown, a chocolate-box confection of pink-and-white stripes.

"I'm not sure I need lunch," he said. "Because you look good enough to eat."

She laughed, clearly pleased, but before she could reply, another, far less agreeable voice intervened.

"Mr. Sharpe."

"Lady Walston." He turned, freezing his smile in place to greet Pamela's mother.

His prediction that being tardy to dinner would only worsen things with his future mother-in-law had proven true. She'd been disapproving before; now she was barely civil. They lunched at the

Savoy, but be he ever so charming, she continued to eye him as if he were a bug she needed to squash. Thankfully, however, when they took a stroll through the nearby Victoria Embankment Gardens afterward, she complied with her daughter's thinly veiled hints and moved out of earshot, giving them some privacy.

"So what is this outing you've got planned for us this afternoon?" he asked as they strolled between beds of bright yellow tulips and purple pansies, her mother following them at a discreet distance. "Punting on the lake in Hyde Park? Hiring a motor for a drive in the country? It's a perfect day for either," he added, glancing upward, where for once not a single cloud marred the sky. "And it would be nice to see something of dear old England before we sail back to the other side of the world."

"No, no, not a drive in the country, though we could do that tomorrow if the weather holds. But for today, I had rather a different plan in mind. One that involves the indoors more than the out."

"Now, you've intrigued me, I confess. What is this plan?"

She stopped walking, causing him to stop as well, and turned toward him, smiling a little. "I thought," she murmured, taking his hands in hers, "we might perhaps look at some London houses."

"London houses?" he echoed in surprise. "Whatever for?"

Pam looked up, fixing that limpid brown gaze of hers on his face. "Once we're married, I expect we'll need one."

"I don't see why, since we'll be living in Egypt."

"Of course," she agreed at once. "But you have this hotel venture with your friend, Lord Calderon now, and I thought—"

"Yes?" he prompted when she fell silent and looked down.

Pam didn't reply for a moment. She pulled her hands from his, apparently distracted by an undone glove button, and as she moved to remedy the problem, he studied her bent head, wondering just what was going on inside it.

"I thought," she said slowly as she worked to push the button at her wrist back through its hole, "you'd want to stop on here for a bit longer than we'd originally planned. You know, until the new hotel is well established. I heard you tell Papa at dinner the other night that things there are at a crucial stage right now."

"Well, that's true enough, but by the wedding, it will all be sorted. And afterward, Simon will have my proxy for anything the board needs to vote on. He can easily cable me in Cairo if any sort of emergency decision has to be made, or if he comes across other properties the company may wish to purchase. We can't stop on here too long. I have other hotels to run."

"I see," she said with a nod, but still preoccupied with her glove, she didn't look up, and he began to feel uneasy. "So there's no need to visit Cook's and change our itinerary?"

Was that really her only concern? he wondered. "No need at all. We'll spend the wedding night at the Savoy, just as we planned, then leave for Paris on our honeymoon the next day. We'll spend a few days in Paris, a couple weeks in Italy, then we'll continue on to Constantinople, then Cairo."

As he spoke, he thought suddenly of Kay and the plans they'd made to go to Africa together, and how she'd balked at the last minute, and he wondered with a sudden flash of alarm if history was going to repeat itself. Was Pam getting cold feet? Granted, he'd made it very clear that Africa was where they'd be living, but then…he'd made that clear to Kay, too, all those years ago. Would Pam, like Kay, shy at the jump and decide living in England was more important than he was? Could he find himself jilted at the altar a second time?

"Cairo is where the vast majority of my business interests are, Pam," he felt compelled to remind her. "So that's where we'll have to live. I told you that when I proposed. Surely you remember?"

"Of course," Pam agreed. But though she'd finished fiddling with her glove, she didn't look at him, and when she started to turn as if to resume their walk, he put his hands on her shoulders, stopping her and turning her once again to face him.

"Afraid you'll be homesick?" he asked gently.

That made her smile a little. "How well you understand me. I suppose it stems from being in England again after so long away. Seeing all my friends, knowing it may be a long time before I see them again…well, it's giving me a bit of a pang to think of leaving them so soon. We were only in Egypt a couple of months during our tour, you know. It wasn't long enough to make any real friends there."

"Don't I count?"

"You know what I mean," she said, her smile widening a bit at his teasing. "I didn't make any female friends."

"But you will," he assured her. "There's a substantial number of British people living in Cairo these days. You'll have a whole coterie of bosom companions before you know it. And we British love to spend our winters in warm climates. You know that yourself. Remember what it was like for you and your parents when you were staying at my hotel there? You were always running into people you knew."

"True. But they weren't staying. Like me, they were on holiday. Besides, we won't be living in your hotel."

"No, but we'll only be a short carriage ride away. And you've seen my house several times already, so you know it is every bit as luxurious as my hotel. Electricity, hot and cold laid on in the bathrooms, and plenty of servants for you to boss around."

Unexpectedly, she laughed. "I remember thinking the first time we dined there how much more modern your house is than any of Papa's estates here."

"And the first time I saw you coming up the steps of the veranda there, do you know what I thought?" Despite the fact that he could feel her mother's disapproving gaze boring into his back from the other side of the flower beds, he moved closer to Pam, close enough that her skirt hem brushed the toe of his boot. "I remember thinking that with you there, my house finally felt like home."

"You did?" she asked, looking surprised, her voice wistful. "Did you really?"

"Really. You won't be homesick, at least not for long. And it's not as if we'll never come back to England again. I shall have to come home occasionally to tour the hotels with Simon, see how things are going, that sort of thing. When I do, I daresay you'll want to come with me."

"Can I?"

"Of course you can come with me, darling. I'd be lost without you. So you see? There will be opportunities for you to see your family and your friends. But, to return to the subject that started this discussion, we don't need a house in London."

"No," she agreed. "Not yet. But..." She paused, smiling, slanting him an unmistakably flirtatious look even as she blushed. "We will need one when the children come."

As agreeable as the thought of making babies might be, his

uneasiness once again came to the fore. "Why," he asked, treading carefully, wondering if he was about to get into deep waters, "should the children make any difference there?"

Her eyes widened, flirtation giving way to surprise at the question. "Because we'll want our sons educated at Eton and Oxford, of course. Surely you agree, being an Etonian yourself?"

He thought of his Eton education, an education that had proven of little practical use. Hell, if he hadn't insisted on breaking with family tradition and enrolling in London's Royal School of Mines to study mining engineering, he'd probably still be stone broke, and Pam would be marrying some other chap.

Pam, however, gave him no chance to express his opinion. "They'll scarcely be twelve before Eton," she went on. "We can't just ship them off halfway around the world on their own at that age."

"Of course not. We'll come with them to see them settled at school, of course, but that doesn't mean—"

"And what about our daughters?" she interrupted. "When they are ready to make their debut, what am I to do? I can't bring them out from Cairo. If I do that, their marriage prospects will be dismal."

The marriage prospects of his as-yet nonexistent daughters had never occurred to him, though admitting that fact was clearly not going to score him any points with Pam.

"Perhaps you're right," he said instead. "But all that's a long way off, and even if we do decide to live here during that period, it won't be permanent, no matter what happens."

"Oh, no," she agreed quickly. "Of course not."

"Then aren't we getting a bit ahead of ourselves, talking about things that won't be happening for at least a dozen years?"

"Hmm...perhaps you're right. And if you'd rather wait, of course we will. But the more time that goes by, the higher the prices on London properties will become."

That was an irrefutable point. "So you think we ought to buy a house now?"

"That's up to you, darling. I just thought it would be an excellent business investment, even if we only rarely use it ourselves."

He almost laughed at that, for he'd never known Pam pay any attention to business investments before, his or anyone else's. Nonetheless, she wasn't wrong, and as he considered her idea, he appreciated that acquiring a London property did make a certain amount of sense.

"It's not necessary for us to purchase something now, of course," she went on when he didn't reply. "As you said, the possibility of living here is a long way off."

"If we did buy something now," he said slowly, thinking it out as he spoke, "we could lease it. That is, if we can find a decent one."

"It's amazing how we think so much alike!" she cried, giving him a delighted smile. "Because that's just what I thought, too. So..." She paused, reaching into her skirt pocket and pulling out a folded sheet of paper. "So I took the liberty of finding some we might look at."

"Did you, now?" he murmured, her words of a few minutes ago flashing through his mind.

I thought you'd want to stop on here for a bit longer than we'd originally planned.

How long, he wondered suddenly, before she was pointing out other London investments that he might wish to consider?

Studying her face as she looked down at the sheet in her hand, he thought of her ready acceptance of his business investment with

Kay's fiancé, and he wondered suddenly if her encouragement and approval there stemmed not from business and social considerations but from a desire to tie him to England in as many ways as possible. But what about Kay?

Lady Kay is no threat to me.

The memory of those words in the flower shop deepened the uneasy feeling clenching his guts.

"Do you want to look over this list?" she asked, bringing him out of his reverie.

"You seem to have put some serious thought into this, my dear," he said, watching her, trying to tell himself he was being absurd.

"It's always best to plan ahead, don't you think?" she asked serenely and returned her attention to the sheet in her hands. "Most of the prospects are from house agents, of course."

"You've been visiting house agents? Without consulting with me first?"

She looked up, her eyes innocently wide. "Only because I have so much more free time than you do. But it hardly matters, anyway, since the best prospect is one I learned about quite by accident. It's Lord and Lady Shrewsbury's house in Eaton Square. They want to sell it, Lady Shrewsbury told me, once the season is over. She said we were welcome to see the place any time we like. But I'm not sure you'll like it, though."

"Does it matter if I like it?" he countered, wondering what she'd say. "Since we'll be leasing it?"

Her eyes widened further. "Of course it matters. You are a far better judge of investment property than I am, darling. And prospective tenants aside, if we ever do decide we want to live in it for a few years while our boys are in school and our daughters do the season, it will have to suit us as well. So it's important that we both like it."

Devlin was only slightly reassured by her use of the words "if" and "we," and he felt compelled to be blunt. "You aren't changing your mind, are you, darling? About living in Egypt? Because marrying me requires that, you know. Or perhaps it's me you're having second thoughts about?"

The astonishment in her face turned to dismay. "Changing my mind? About you? Heavens, no! Goodness, if I ever thought you'd think my little jaunt around London with house agents was motivated by that, I'd never have done it. Darling!"

With those words, Devlin forced aside his alarming speculations about her motives, speculations, he reminded himself, that had no basis in fact. His past experience with Kay was just making him imagine the worst, that was all. Pam wasn't Kay, nothing like, and it was stupid to worry about his future with her based on the nightmare experiences of his past.

"Eaton Square, eh?" he said. "Sounds all right, I suppose. Why do you think I might not like it? No bathrooms? Bad drains?"

"No, no, all that's all right. But the furnishings..." She paused and shuddered. "Ghastly. And the drapes are rotting, they're so old. Even so." She paused again, biting her lip with an apologetic look. "They want the earth for the place, I'm afraid."

"Anyone selling a London house in Eaton Square would want the earth for it. And in that location, the furnishings won't matter all that much if we're leasing it out."

"I'm sure you're right. It ought to bring a very high rent, don't you think?"

"Obscenely high, I daresay."

"So..." She paused, folded the list and put it in her pocket, then took his hands, biting her lip as she looked up at him hopefully. "Should we call on Lady Shrewsbury this afternoon and see if she'd be willing to give us a tour of the place today?"

Marriage, he reminded himself, required compromises. As she'd pointed out, a London residence would certainly be desirable later on, and in the meantime, it was a sound investment. "Why not?" he answered. "It never hurts to look. Why don't you fetch your mother," he added, nodding to where Lady Walston was studying a splendid flower bed of narcissus, "while I secure us a cab?"

Her radiant smile was his reward, but as he stepped onto Northumberland Avenue to hail a growler, Devlin couldn't quite shake off his uneasiness, and he decided that if he and Pam did purchase a London house, he'd best arrange for a tenant and sign a lease straightaway, before she started asking his preferences in furniture and measuring for new drapes.

In the days that followed the opera supper, Kay saw nothing of Devlin, much to her relief. It was three weeks later, when an invitation came in the afternoon post, that Kay was reminded she could not avoid him altogether. Kay gave a sigh, staring down at the penned words of the card without enthusiasm.

The Duke of Westbourne
Requests the honor of your presence at a soiree
To celebrate the grand opening of the Mayfair Hotel
The Twenty-Third of April

Eight o'clock in the Evening
The Victoria Room
Mayfair Hotel
12 Hamilton Place, Mayfair

The Mayfair was that hotel of Devlin's, the one that Wilson was also involved in, and Kay's mind immediately began fashioning reasons to refuse the invitation. A conflicting engagement (which was always possible), or the illness of dear Mama (who would be happy to play at having a cold in order to avoid any event where That Horrible Man was sure to be), or perhaps womankind's most convenient excuse and one she had used on her mother only a few weeks ago (the sudden headache).

Kay tapped the card against her palm, but as she considered which of these options would be most convincing, an image of Devlin's face came into her mind, his insolent smile, the knowing gleam of amusement in his eyes, and she appreciated that whatever excuse she gave, none would be convincing enough to fool him.

Kay yanked her pen from its holder, telling herself it didn't matter what Devlin thought. That reminder had barely gone through her mind before a question followed it.

What about Wilson? How would he feel if she refused to attend this affair?

She remembered quite clearly how her fiancé had hauled her forward that night at the Savoy supper, and she very much feared he would insist she attend. If she balked, whatever the reason, he could be very displeased. He might even be angry.

Kay's gaze strayed to the stack of unpaid bills on the corner of her desk. Angering Wilson was not something she could afford to do. Kay sighed again.

"Is something wrong?"

Kay glanced at Josephine, seated at the nearby table, frowning at her over the stack of her own letters, then she looked over her shoulder at the half-closed door into their mother's bedroom where Magdelene was taking her usual rest after tea. "Of course not," she answered. "Why do you ask?"

"You've sighed at least three times in the last fifteen seconds. What's the trouble?"

Kay hesitated, but the faint sound of Magdelene's snoring reassured her that her mother was sound asleep. "I have an invitation here from the Duke of Westbourne. I've no doubt Mama got one, too, and since the duke's family knows you're out, I expect you've got one as well."

"Me?" Josephine instantly dropped the letter she'd been opening and began rooting through her pile of correspondence. "What sort of event is it? Oh, do say it's a ball."

"Sorry, no. The duchess is expecting a baby, so she and the duke are not doing the season this year, remember? He just comes down, I understand, for the Lords, or for events like this soiree. It's for the grand opening of that new hotel of his, the Mayfair."

Josephine's hands stilled and her eyes widened as she looked up. "The Mayfair?" she cried, her voice rising in surprise. "Isn't that Devlin Sharpe's hotel, too?"

"Shush," Kay ordered, casting another glance at Mama's bedroom. "Keep your voice down. Mama's sleeping."

"Sorry. But that is the one, isn't it?" she added in a whisper as she rose and crossed the room to Kay's side. "Or have I got it mixed up?"

"No, you're quite right."

Josephine paused beside her chair, looking thoroughly let down. "Well, then, we certainly won't be going."

Kay made a face. "We might have to. Wilson's involved in that hotel as well, if you recall."

"Mama won't like it if we go."

"No," Kay agreed. "And Wilson won't like it if we don't. You remember how he practically dragged us into that opera supper." Again, she glanced at the bills on her desk. "No, dear sister, I'm afraid Wilson's wishes trump Mama's."

"What about you?" Josephine asked. "What do you want to do?"

"Do you need to ask? I'd rather have teeth drawn than be anywhere near Devlin Sharpe."

"Well, then, refuse it. Wilson surely won't want you attending an affair you don't want to attend."

"Won't he? Still..." Kay paused, considering, then reached for a sheet of stationery, her mind made up. "You're quite right. Why should I go to something I don't wish to?"

The matter settled, Jo returned to her own letters, and Kay inked her pen, but she'd barely written the words, "With regret," before Devlin's amused voice echoed through her mind.

Running away?

Kay paused and set her jaw, working to shove his provoking words out of her mind.

Of course, if you'd rather scurry off like a frightened rabbit...

She was not a rabbit, and she certainly wasn't afraid of *him*. It was both galling and infuriating that he thought so. Suppressing an oath, Kay shoved aside the sheet of paper, reached for a fresh one, and before she could change her mind again, she had accepted the duke's invitation and sealed her acceptance inside an envelope.

Her mother would be a trial, and the evening would be unpleasant, but Kay consoled herself with the knowledge Wilson would be pleased, and pleasing Wilson was her most important duty.

Nonetheless, as she gave the letter of acceptance to her mother's maid to post, she knew full well the real reason she was accepting had nothing to do with pleasing her fiancé. No, she was going to this soiree because she had no intention of letting Devlin Sharpe ever accuse her again of being a coward. She'd hurl herself onto the train tracks before she'd ever let him have the satisfaction.

Kay knew, probably better than anyone, that impulsive decisions could lead to surprising and unintended consequences, a fact that was brought forcibly home to her that evening when Wilson called at her suite on his way to a business meeting, and she launched the topic of the Mayfair.

"I hear this new hotel of yours is opening in less than a fortnight," she began as she poured him a whiskey.

"Yes, I know. Calderon's got some big grand opening party on in honor of it." He paused, giving her a look that was almost apologetic as he took the offered glass of whiskey from her. "My attendance will be required, of course."

"Of course," she agreed as she poured a small glass of sherry for herself. "No doubt that is why I also received an invitation."

Wilson stilled, his glass halfway to his lips. "You got one?"

"Yes. So did Mama, of course, and Josephine. Would you care to fetch us in your carriage, or shall we meet you there?"

He lowered his glass, staring at her as if she'd suddenly grown a second head. "My dear Kay, you won't be going."

She stared, not sure she'd heard right. "I beg your pardon?"

"As I said, I must attend, but there's no reason for you to be there."

She thought again of that night at the opera supper when he'd insisted on hauling her forward to converse with Devlin, his fiancée, and his future in-laws, and her confusion deepened. "I'd have thought you'd want me to be there," she said slowly. "But you don't want us to go?"

"Of course I don't. What a question. I don't want you anywhere near that scoundrel Devlin Sharpe."

"But...but...the other night..." She paused, laughing a little at the vagaries her fiancé possessed. He really was the most unpredictable man. "Three weeks ago at the opera supper, you practically dragged me into Calderon's supper party and behaved as if we were all happy as clams together."

"Of course I did." Wilson shrugged and took a sip of whiskey. "But only because at that point there was no graceful way to bow out. When you told me Lady Stratham had invited us to supper, I was quite glad to attend, with her fiancé being a business partner of mine. And she's got a lot of influence in society as well, so keeping in with her will be good for Charlene down the road."

Kay winced at her fiancé's opportunistic way of putting things. Once they were married, she hoped she'd be able to help him smooth over those rough edges.

"And she's the duke's cousin," he went on. "Cozying up to her helps me get closer to him."

As he spoke, Delia's words of that night at the opera flashed through Kay's mind.

You mean Rycroft's marrying you for your connections?

"I see," she murmured, a bad taste suddenly in her mouth.

"It never occurred to me that Sharpe would be there. That's the worst of these impulsive, last-minute invitations. One never knows who one might encounter. Had I known Sharpe was going, I would have insisted you send Lady Stratham a note with some excuse. Sudden illness, or something like that."

Kay was now totally confused. "But isn't Sharpe a business partner, too?"

"Yes, but surely you realize that's not the same thing. Sharpe's not a social acquaintance. He's got no title and no social influence. And the man's a bounder, as we both know. I refuse to allow you anywhere near him if it can be avoided."

"Refuse to allow?" Kay echoed with a little laugh. "Indeed? How terribly medieval of you, darling."

Wilson did not laugh with her. Instead, he frowned. "You can't possibly think I'd feel any other way?"

"I did think just that," she confessed. "It being a business dinner, I thought you'd want me by your side."

"Women should never think about business matters. You always get things wrong."

Kay was a bit irritated by this sweeping generalization about her sex, but, tactfully, she didn't show it. Instead, she stuck to the topic at hand. "You just said how important keeping in with the duke is, so I thought—"

"That's what I don't get," he interrupted. "What was the duke thinking to even invite you? Seems in thoroughly bad taste to me."

Kay shrugged. "Not really. I've known the duke all my life. His sister Idina, Lady Rothmere, and his cousin, Lady Delia Stratham, have long been friends of mine. We all came out together. I'm sure one of them did the invitations. They probably felt as I did, that you'd want me there."

"If so, it was damned silly of them, and you. I'm surprised at you, Kay. You will write immediately and refuse the invitation."

She stiffened, her irritation deepening at this criticism of herself and her friends, and by the peremptory way he dictated what her actions would be. "Are you forbidding me to go?"

"Since you put it that way, yes."

Kay thought of all the times her father had forbidden her to go to an event, of the rigidity with which she'd been controlled as a girl, of the two years she'd spent banished to Wales, and something rose inside her, a feeling she hadn't felt since the summer she turned eighteen—a sudden flash of rebellion, the same sort of rebellion that had sent her careening off to Gretna Green with Devlin. She knew the high price one could pay for such impulsive decisions, but despite that, and despite the fact that she had not initially wanted to go to this soiree in the first place, the idea of being ordered not to go impelled her to debate the point.

"Well, I'm sorry if that's how you feel about it," she answered. "But I'm afraid it's too late to refuse. I already accepted the invitation."

"What?"

"As I said, I had thought surely you would want me to go. It never occurred to me that you would object. Now I have to go."

"Nonsense. Write again and take back your acceptance."

"I can't do that," she said, feeling an incomprehensible hint of pleasure in conveying that bit of news. "One does not renege on an accepted invitation, especially not to a duke."

He shrugged. "You can think of something that won't offend him. You forgot you had a prior engagement. Or something unexpected has occurred. Or feign illness. He can hardly take offense to you being ill."

All of these were excuses she herself had considered, but Kay had no intention of exercising any of them now that her acceptance had been tendered. "Lie to the duke?" she said. "I'm astonished that you would suggest such a thing."

"Your astonishment is of no account."

Kay stiffened at those dismissive words. "But—"

"You will write to the duke," he cut in, "and refuse the invitation, or I will do it for you."

The tenor of his voice brooked no opposition. His displeasure with her was palpable, warning her it was best not to antagonize him further, but before Kay could invent a reply that would both enable her to stand her ground and defuse his anger, another voice entered the conversation.

"I hope this isn't a disagreement I'm hearing," Magdelene said brightly as she entered the sitting room, Josephine on her heels.

Kay took a deep breath and turned to her mother, grateful for the interruption. "Not at all, Mama. The Duke of Westbourne is having a soiree for the opening of his new hotel, and we've all been invited. But because Mr. Sharpe also owns part of the hotel, he's sure to be there as well."

"What an appalling prospect," Magdelene cried, giving a shudder. "We can't possibly go."

"Just what I was saying, Lady Raleigh," Wilson interjected

before Kay could reply. "I have explained to Kay that she will have to make some excuse."

"And I explained to Wilson," Kay put in, "that I have already accepted the invitation."

"Kay!" Magdelene cried. "What were you thinking?"

"I thought," she said uncompromisingly, "that Wilson would want me to accept."

"That's true," Josephine put in, coming to her defense. "She did. We discussed it."

Josephine was ignored.

"Well, now we have to go," Magdelene wailed. "Oh, dear. Oh, dear. This is a fine kettle of fish."

Wilson's glass slammed down on the top of the liquor cabinet loudly enough to make all three women jump, but when he spoke, his voice was silky—dangerously so. "Kay is not going. I refuse to allow it. I hope," he added, turning to her mother, "that's clear?"

Mama visibly wilted. Swallowing hard, she nodded.

Just like with Papa, Kay thought, dismayed by the realization. Some things never changed.

"Now," Wilson said, breaking into Kay's suddenly bleak thoughts, "I have to be going. I have a dinner meeting."

"Wait," Kay implored, following him as he started for the door. "Can we not at least discuss this?"

He paused, turning to give her that hard stare of his, but Kay didn't want to become her mother, not if she could help it. She didn't wilt. Instead, she took a deep breath and improvised. "I'm thinking of Josephine. She really ought to be allowed to go."

"Of course she can go," he said as he opened the door into the corridor. "Magdelene can take her. You will stay here with a sick headache."

"But, really—"

"My dear Kay." He paused, the door half open, and leaned close to her. "I'm thinking of Josephine, too," he said so softly that only she could hear. "I'm thinking of the dowry she'll need to marry well."

He had just played the trump card, and they both knew it.

Once again feeling a bit like a puppet on a string, Kay forced herself to smile. "Of course. Shall we see you on Friday for the Royal Academy opening?"

He gave a nod of agreement and departed, much to Kay's relief, but the door had barely closed behind him before Magdelene let out a wail.

"Oh, Kay," she cried, "you mustn't antagonize him. You simply mustn't!"

"I hadn't meant to," she murmured, rubbing a hand over her forehead with a sigh.

"If he breaks the engagement, what will happen to us? How will we pay our bills? Where will we live? Without Wilson, we'll be destitute." Her voice was rising dramatically with every word, but Kay knew that Magdelene was not merely giving in to her histrionic instincts. The fear her mother felt was deep and genuine.

"And what about Josephine?" Magdelene continued when she didn't reply. "How will she ever—"

"Don't bring me into this!" Josephine cried. "Kay needs to do what's best for her. We'll be all right, whatever happens."

"Thank you, darling," Kay said, but she knew Jo was being naïve.

She sank into a chair, suddenly, terribly tired. "Don't worry," she added, giving her sister a reassuring smile. "It's all a fuss about nothing. After all, I didn't really want to go to the blasted party anyway."

She didn't add that she also knew when she was beaten. That admission was too wretched to make out loud.

8

During the two weeks that followed, neither Kay nor Wilson referred to their discussion about the upcoming Mayfair soiree. Wilson seemed to regard the matter as closed, but it did not escape Kay's notice that her fiancé also began keeping a very watchful eye on her, particularly during those occasions when Devlin was known to be anywhere in the vicinity.

The Royal Academy exhibition was always the launching point of the London season, so of course Devlin was there with Pamela and her parents, but as they strolled about the galleries, if Kay happened to come within ten yards of the other group, Wilson instantly began steering her away in the opposite direction. At the Chelsea Flower Show, Devlin had barely come within noticing distance before Wilson was suggesting that Kay might like some ice cream from the confectioner's shop six blocks away.

In other circumstances, it might have been amusing to think her fiancé could be jealous of Devlin Sharpe, particularly since Devlin was the last man on earth Kay would have chosen to keep company with. And she ought to have been relieved that her fiancé was there to save her from any contact with a man she couldn't stand.

Many women, she supposed, would adore this sort of protectiveness on the part of a fiancé. But, oddly, Kay felt none of that. Instead, every time Wilson hauled her away, she felt again the same smothering sensation she'd experienced upon learning he'd deliberately followed her all over Yorkshire last autumn. Between him and her mother, Kay spent a great deal of time feeling like a prisoner. It was almost like being in Wales all over again.

Adding to her frustration, this sort of jealousy was clearly a one-way street. At Lord Walston's ball, when Kay took the floor with their host, Wilson, who hated dancing, didn't hesitate to claim Lady Pamela for a turn about the floor. In Wilson's view, it seemed wholly acceptable for a man to be possessive of his woman, but a woman was not allowed that privilege about her man. Kay had never been one to march for the vote or chain herself to a railing, but as the days passed, her fiancé's obvious double standard began to grate on her already raw nerves.

Still, there was little she could do about it. Devlin was the last man in the world for whom she'd risk Wilson's ire and endanger her sister's marital prospects, her mother's security, or her own still fragile reputation.

When the evening of the Mayfair soiree came, Josephine offered to stay home with her, and Magdelene would have been quite delighted to send a note that all of them were ill, but Kay negated these suggestions.

"Don't be absurd," she said for the third time, shooing them both toward the door. "The season has begun, Jo is out, and she needs to meet as many new people as possible. This Mayfair business is a perfect opportunity for that, since Delia's invited half the ton, including some very eligible young men."

When the two of them had departed for the West End, Kay ordered a meal brought up from the kitchens, and afterward, with her corset tossed aside for the comfort of a nightgown and peignoir, she curled up in the suite's most comfortable chair for what she hoped would be an agreeable evening alone with a book.

Reading, however, proved little distraction. She stared at the pages, but her mind insisted on veering off into visions of her future, a future that seemed dishearteningly reminiscent of her past, where a man told her what to do, where to go, and with whom she could associate. Stern reminders that husbands who behaved this way were as common as blades of grass didn't cheer her much.

She tried to console herself with the knowledge that beggars could not be choosers. Unless she wanted to face her future alone, childless, and living in poverty, unless she wanted her sister to share a similar fate, unless she wanted to spend the next few decades listening to her mother complain incessantly and blame her for the dismal state of their life, Wilson was her best option.

No, she corrected at once, her gaze straying to her desk and the unpaid bills still waiting there for her attention. Wilson was her only option.

She'd known that all along, of course. Wilson's proposal had been such a relief, it had almost made her weak in the knees. And it wasn't as if she'd agreed to marry a man she didn't like. Quite the contrary. From their first meeting last August, she had liked Wilson very much. She had respected his strength, his keen mind, and his business acumen. He seemed fond of her sister, and he was able to tolerate her mother. In addition, she had appreciated his solicitous regard for her. His desire to be near her had been like a balm to her wounded feminine heart. She'd been happy—thrilled, even—to accept his proposal, for it meant she wouldn't die a spinster and would perhaps now be able to have children, and her family would never have to worry again about how the bills got paid. So, why now, only four months after agreeing to marry him, were thoughts of her impending wedding making her feel so unutterably depressed?

That question had barely gone through her mind before the image of a pair of turquoise blue eyes gave her a possible answer, and Kay shut her book with an aggravated snap. It was Devlin's return that was muddling her all up, twisting her into knots, filling her mind with doubts, and turning Wilson into some sort of obsessive, dictatorial limpet. Had Devlin not come back, none of this would be happening.

Or would it?

Fortunately, a knock at the door interrupted that disturbing question, and Kay looked up in surprise. The Savoy's room service had already brought her meal, and she'd dismissed Foster for the evening.

The only possible conclusion, she thought as she set aside her book and stood up, was that Mama had forgotten her key. That was not an unusual circumstance, but as Kay started across the sitting room to open the door for her parent and sibling, a glance at the clock deepened her surprise. Mama and Jo hadn't even been gone two hours.

The knock came again, and Kay reached for the door handle. "Back already?" she called, laughing as she slid back the bolt and opened the door. "It must have been a terribly dull par—"

She stopped, staring in astonishment, for instead of her mother with Josephine, it was Devlin standing in the corridor. Still dressed in white tie and tails from the party, with a thunderous scowl on his face, he managed to look both urbanely handsome and savagely primitive at the same time.

"Devlin? What on earth—"

"Are you all right?"

Given her dispirited thoughts this evening, and the fact that because of them, she didn't feel the least bit all right, his abrupt question startled her. The moment they'd first met, she had felt as if this man could see into her very soul. With his question hanging in the air, she wondered if, even after all this time, he still could.

"I beg your pardon?" she murmured, having no clue what else to say.

"I heard you were ill."

Before Kay could reply, a door opened farther down the passage, and she grabbed Devlin by the sleeve to haul him inside before anyone could see him hovering in the corridor.

"I'm not ill," she said, shutting the door behind him.

"Sure?" His eyes raked over her, reminding her that she was wearing nothing more than a thin lawn peignoir and an even thinner nightgown. At once, heat flooded her face, and she instinctively reached up one hand to pull the edges of her peignoir together as she worked to marshal some cool dignity.

"I think I'd know if I were ill or not."

"I heard your mother tell Simon you were practically knocking at heaven's gate."

"That's not surprising," she said wryly. "My mother loves drama."

"I see." His fierce expression relaxed, and a faint smile curved the edges of his mouth. "So all your shivers and flutters and heart palpitations are fiction?"

"Pure fiction," she assured him. "I'm surprised she didn't say I was quarantined with some bizarre fever no one's ever heard of before. Nonetheless, I'm perfectly well. Is that why you're here?" she added. "Because you were worried about me?"

Even as she asked the question, she knew it was absurd.

His amusement vanished. He met her gaze, shaking the dark hair back from his brow like a defiant stallion. "Yes, as a matter of fact, I was."

Her lips parted, but no words came out. With that one word, the warmth of embarrassment intensified, spreading outward, transforming into something else entirely, something that made her feel as if she'd just downed a snifter of brandy. Beneath the hem of her nightgown, she curled her bare toes into the plush Aubusson carpet.

"So if you're not ill," he went on when she didn't reply, "then why aren't you at the party? Unless—"

He broke off, and with mercurial suddenness, his amusement returned. "Still running from me, are you?" he asked, folding his arms and rocking back on his heels, smiling, looking far too pleased with himself all of a sudden. "What are you so afraid of?"

Had he dumped ice water over her head, he couldn't have doused the warmth inside Kay more effectively. "Don't be ridiculous," she said coolly. "I'm not the least bit afraid of you. If I were," she went on as he made a sound of disbelief, "I'd never have let you in just now."

He lifted his hands in a self-evident gesture. "Well, then, why are you here, avoiding me, instead of at the party?"

"Listen to the man!" she cried, rolling her eyes. "My decision to not attend the party has nothing to do with you, you conceited oaf."

"No?"

"No! I'm not at the party," she added crossly as he continued to stare at her in obvious skepticism, "because I wasn't allowed to go."

"What?" He gave a laugh. "Kay, you're not a child. You're not even the adolescent girl who was so sick at the idea of disappointing and disgracing her parents that she left me flat in a Birmingham inn. You're a woman of thirty-two," he added, ducking his head to study her face when she looked away. "Isn't it time to cut the apron strings?"

"Oh, for heaven's sake," she shot back. "It was not my mother who forbade me to go to the party. It was—"

She stopped, sensing she was heading into deep waters, but when she saw his humor vanish once again, she knew she'd given the game away.

"Wait," he ordered, holding up one hand, palm toward her, his expression one of disbelief. "You mean, it was Rycroft? He ordered you not to come?"

She didn't reply, because, after all, what could she say?

"And you knuckled under?" Devlin went on in the wake of her silence, his voice low, vibrating with sudden anger. "To *him*?"

"I didn't knuckle under," she denied, even as she knew that was precisely what she'd done. "I chose," she went on, working to muster her dignity, "to honor his request that I not attend."

The frown on his face deepened to an absolute scowl. "My God," he muttered, shaking his head, "fourteen years, and nothing's changed with you, has it? You're still letting your life be dictated by what other people want and expect of you."

That accusation touched on her already raw mood and ignited her temper, mainly because she knew there was some truth in it. "You don't know anything about me," she cried. "Or my situation, or what I'm forced to do—"

Again, she stopped, hand over her mouth, but it was too late. What was it about this man that always loosened her tongue? she wondered in aggravation. He could pull secrets out of a sphinx.

"Forced how?" The words out of his mouth were like a whip, cracking in the air.

She tried to turn away, but he put his hands on her arms to stop her. "What's that bastard doing to you?"

"Nothing." Kay took a deep breath, striving to regain a sense of discretion. "It's not what you think."

"No? Then what is it? The money? You just want to marry a millionaire, is that it? Is staying in the lap of luxury worth selling yourself?"

She jerked free. "That's a laughable question, coming from you."

"Are we now talking about my reasons for marrying Pam? Because," he added as she pressed her lips together and didn't answer, "last time we met, you practically accused me of marrying Pam for her money, so let me set you straight about that. Pam's father is absolutely flat. She's got no dowry to offer."

"I'm not talking about her." Kay drew a deep breath. "I'm talking about you and the money you took."

"What money?"

"What money do you think? The money my father paid you to go away, of course!"

"What?" He blinked, looking utterly taken aback. "Is that what you think? That I allowed your father to buy me off?"

"Don't bother denying it. I know what happened."

"Apparently you don't."

"I saw the canceled bank draft, Devlin. Papa showed it to me about two years after you left, because he was tired of how I was still stupidly mooning over you. I saw your signature on the back, plain as plain."

Her voice was shaking now, but she forced herself to continue. "'Two thousand pounds was all it took for you to give me up."

"Damn it, Kay, I didn't give you up. That money was a loan."

"Oh, please."

"But it was! After you left me in Birmingham, I went to see my father, and I told him about us. I asked him if he would help me by giving me a bigger allowance so I could reassure your father that I could support you even if I stayed here, but of course, my father refused to help. So I went to Yorkshire to see you so that we could discuss what to do next, but your father said you'd gone to Wales. He said the duke had told him about us and our attempt to elope, and that you were all muddled up about it, and he suggested that you go to Wales for a bit to think things through."

"I'm not sure it was really a suggestion."

"You mean he forced you to go?"

"He didn't tie my hands, shove me in a carriage, drag me to Wales, and lock me in a garret, if that's what you mean." She sighed, lifting her hands in a helpless gesture, letting them fall. "He said how disappointed he was in me. How the fact that I had gone behind his back in this clandestine manner had broken his heart."

Strangely, Devlin smiled a little at that. "You always cared far more about your father's opinion than I ever did about mine."

Kay refused to be diverted. "And the money? What about the money he gave you?"

"I told your father we were in love and we still intended to marry, and I asked for his permission."

"And he refused, of course. I told you he would. That's why we decided to elope in the first place."

"But that's just it. He didn't refuse. He admitted quite frankly that he didn't approve of the match. How could he, he asked, given that I had no prospects? I explained why we'd decided to go to Africa, told him some of my ideas for what I could do there, and to my amazement, he listened."

"He did?"

"Yes. He said that I seemed to know what I was doing, and that if I could make good on my plan, and if I had proven by the time you were twenty-one that I could take care of you, he'd give his blessing to our marriage and wouldn't fight it. He said he understood how hard it was for a younger son to get on in the world. He'd been the younger son, too, before his brother's death, so he appreciated the difficulties I was facing. He said that for your sake, he was willing to give me a chance, and he offered to stake me."

"Did he?" Kay murmured faintly, a sick knot forming in her stomach.

"That's what the two thousand pounds was for. It was a loan, Kay, a loan I paid back within three years. Every penny, with interest. And I don't know why I'm even having to tell you all this again."

"Again?" she echoed, bewildered. "What do you mean? You never told me any of this."

"I damn well did. Before I left for Africa, I went to Wales to see you. Your mother said you didn't want to see me, that you wanted time apart to think. So, I wrote you a letter, explaining the arrangement I'd made with your father. Then I caught the boat out of Liverpool. I wrote again when I reached Cape Town, telling you where I was and how you could contact me. I wandered a lot in those early days, but I always made sure to inform you of where I was—"

"Devlin," she interrupted, her mind reeling at this news, "in three years, I never received a single letter from you. Not one. I wrote to you at Stonygates, but I never heard back. I only knew where you were because Delia came to visit me, and I asked her to find out where you'd gone. That's how I got your address in Cape Town. I wrote you again and again, but you never answered me. Not...even once."

"I moved on from Cape Town in less than a year, but as I said, I kept you informed. I wrote you every week." He stopped abruptly, studying her face. "You never got any of my letters, did you?"

She shook her head. "No, but if you wrote, then my mother must have—" She broke off, unable to quite voice that suspicion out loud.

Devlin had no such compunction. "She suppressed them," he said flatly.

"Oh, God." Kay pressed a hand over her mouth, realizing in dismay what her mother must have done. "How could she—how could they," she amended, knowing her mother would never have done this without orders from her father, "have done that to me? To us?"

"I wrote to you in Yorkshire as well as in Wales. I even sent cables. They must have suppressed those as well. Damn it all," he added explosively. "I should have known he would never allow you to marry me, but he sounded so sincere when he put it to me, insisting the money was only a loan as he handed me the bank draft. He even wrote a promissory note, detailing the terms and interest rate. I don't suppose he showed you that."

"No. He told me he offered you money to go away. He said it was a test," she added as he muttered an oath. "If you were honorable, you wouldn't have taken it."

"Borrowing that money seemed my only choice at that point.

Having listened as the duke's sisters pointed out to you how disappointed your family would be if we eloped, seeing you go wobbly and change your mind because of that, I feared the only way I'd ever have you at all was to get your father on my side."

"That was probably true," she conceded. "Defying my father," she added in whisper, "was never an easy thing for me."

"I know that. I decided that the only chance I had was to prove I could support you. As I said, I tried my father first, but he wasn't obliging. When your father offered to stake me a loan, I thought it was the perfect solution."

"Oh, yes, perfect," she murmured, sick at how skillfully her father had manipulated both of them.

"But when I didn't receive any letters from you," he continued, "I began to fear that your time to think had made you go off me altogether. I didn't want to believe that, but given that you never replied to any of my letters, it was hard not to. And then..." He paused and swallowed hard. "Then I read you'd gotten engaged to Giles, and that confirmed all my worst fears. It rather put *finis* to the whole thing."

"And I thought my father was right about you, that you'd allowed yourself to be bought off, and your lack of letters seemed to prove it. When he showed me the bank draft, he said if you loved me you wouldn't have taken the money. You'd have stayed and courted me in proper fashion. And that, he said, was why he didn't want you for a son-in-law. You had your eye on the main chance and taking the money proved it. I was angry with my father for testing you that way, but I hated you far more because you had proved him right."

"While I blamed you for abandoning me, for choosing your rich cousin instead of me."

"So—" She broke off, overcome by the emotions engulfing her—disbelief, disillusionment, bitterness, and rage. Rage, most of all. She tried to tell herself that she had no reason to believe Devlin over her own parents, and yet, now, in this moment, she knew that Devlin was telling her the truth. She didn't know how or why she knew. She just did.

"So all this time," she whispered, wrapping her arms around her ribs to hold in the onslaught of feelings that threatened to overwhelm her, "all this time, when we were both thinking we'd been betrayed and abandoned by the other, it was just a big misunderstanding engineered by my parents to drive us apart."

"I guess it was." He laughed suddenly, a harsh sound that made her wince. "I knew your father didn't approve of me, but I really couldn't blame him. I knew he had you under his thumb, but God help me, I never thought he'd sink so low as to deceive us both. And I certainly didn't think your mother, who seemed merely an amiable nitwit, was capable of such duplicity."

"Blame her talent for drama." Kay rubbed a hand over her forehead, feeling suddenly tired. "It enables her to tell very convincing lies. Sometimes, I think even she believes them."

"Evidently. But from my point of view, the news of your engagement shredded me. I felt as if you'd reached across three thousand miles and stuck a knife in my chest. It hurt like hell," he added pensively. "It hurt for a long, long time."

"I was feeling pretty much the same. Oh, we ought to have known!" She looked at him, anguished. "Why didn't we know? Why didn't we see?"

He thought about that for a moment. "Well, we were both terribly young. You can be damned stupid when you're young. And speaking for myself," he added slowly, "it wasn't that hard to believe I'd be abandoned, since my own father had pretty much done that the day I was born."

She nodded in commiseration. "And I was a social failure, chubby and plain, so—"

"You were never plain," he interrupted. "Or chubby. Damn it, Kay, don't denigrate yourself that way. I hate that."

That made her almost want to smile. "You always hated that." She paused, then laughed a little, shaking her head. "What fools we were, to be so quick to lose faith in each other. Although perhaps it's not that surprising," she added thoughtfully, "for we didn't know each other all that well when we decided to run off."

"No, I don't suppose we did, but—" He broke off and gave a laugh. "The odd thing is, from the moment we met, I felt as if I'd known you all my life. That made the news of your engagement that much worse."

She bit her lip, for she'd once had similar feelings. "By the time I got engaged to Giles," she said after a moment, "I didn't even think you'd care."

He nodded, accepting that. "In any case, I don't suppose any of it matters now. Not after all this time."

"No," she agreed. "It doesn't matter now."

With that, an odd sense of anticlimax seemed to come over the room. They stared at each other, neither of them seeming to know what to say next. They both knew the true facts now, and that was all well and good, but as he'd said, it didn't matter anymore. Too much time had passed. Too many years to think and blame, too much believing the worst and hating each other, too many tears of heartbreak, too much pride and hardening of hearts.

"Well," he said at last, "now that we've got all that sorted, how about you answer my question?"

She shook her head, bewildered, unable to remember what they'd been talking about before. "What question was that?"

"Your father spent your whole life controlling you."

She couldn't argue with that, especially now. "He always did like being the master of his universe. But that was only because he was so sure he knew what was best for me."

He groaned. "Oh, Kay."

"What?"

"Please don't tell me everything your father did was out of love."

"Perhaps my father was a bastard. And there's no doubt that he was controlling and domineering. But he was my father, and—" She broke off, lifting her chin proudly. "And though it may be a flaw in my character, I loved him. I still do. I shouldn't, I suppose, but I do."

"He had a damned poor way of showing his love for you."

"Even so..." She paused, thinking of herself as a little girl and of her father opening his arms to her, catching her up, spinning her around and laughing with her. Of all the times he'd read her bedtime stories, and taught her games like backgammon and chess, and dried her girlish tears. "However flawed his actions, I do believe he thought he was doing what was best. To him, marrying Giles was the best way to secure my future. Besides," she added before he could argue the point, "you said the past doesn't matter anymore."

"No, except that one ought to learn from the past, don't you think, and not keep making the same mistakes?"

Kay stiffened, suddenly wary. "I assume there is some specific mistake on my part that you're referring to?"

"You assume correctly." He took a step toward her, closing the distance between them. "Your father's gone, Kay," he said, his voice gentler than she'd heard it for a long time. "So why are you now deciding to let history repeat itself?"

"What?" She stepped back, staring at him, aghast. "Is that what you think I'm doing?"

"Isn't it? Whether he loved you or not, whether his actions were motivated by that love for you or by his own self-interest, it doesn't alter the fact that he was a bully, and you spent your entire life giving in to him. The one and only time you ever rebelled—by throwing in your lot with me—you lost your nerve because you were sick at the idea of losing his good will."

"That wasn't why I changed my mind about eloping with you. At least," she amended when he raised a skeptical eyebrow, "that wasn't the only reason."

"I don't know if you're right about your father," he went on as if she hadn't spoken, "but even if you are, that fact made him no less determined to get his way. So do you really want to spend the future repeating the past? Do you really want to live your life letting a second man dictate to you where you'll go and what you'll do? Do you really want to marry a man who will decide for you what friends you'll have and what parties you'll go to?"

"Says the man who tried to spirit me off to Africa in a clandestine manner and was angry as hell when I changed my mind about letting him do it!"

"Of course I was angry. You were throwing away your chance at happiness and mine and running back to what was safe, familiar, and had never made you happy. What man wouldn't be angry?"

"Thank you for proving my point. Only a man trying to control me would conclude that he knows better than I do what I need to be happy. Deciding my happiness wasn't your office then, and it certainly isn't your office now."

"But it's Rycroft's?"

The disdain in his voice was more than she could bear. She whirled around, stalked to her writing desk, and yanked open a drawer. "You want to know my reasons for giving in to Wilson's request?"

"Request? Or command?"

She ignored that. "You want to know my reasons for being compliant and obedient?" she asked as she pulled out a fat sheaf of papers and retraced her steps. "Here are my reasons. All four thousand nine hundred and eighty-two of them."

She slapped the sheaf of papers against his chest. When his hand came up to take them, she drew her own hand away.

"What's all this?" he asked.

"Bills," she told him. "Nearly five thousand pounds' worth. And that's only about half of what we owe," she added as he glanced down at the papers in his grasp. "When Papa died, I learned the estate was bankrupt. Giles got anything that was entailed to the estate, of course, and creditors took the rest."

"Wasn't your cousin able to help you?"

"Not much. He had money, but his first obligation was to the estate, and that took nearly every cent of his fortune. He provides us with a small income of a hundred pounds a year and a dress allowance."

"That's all?"

"Creditors didn't take our jewels, but only because Mama and I sold them before the creditors could get their hands on them. If you see me or Mama wearing any baubles this season, don't look too closely, because the pearls are Roman pearls and the diamonds are zircons. Sadly, however, the money we got from selling our jewels is gone now, and as you can see, the debts are piling up. To put it bluntly, Devlin, we are destitute."

"So, then, why—" He stopped, but his glance around told her what he hadn't said.

"Why the Savoy?" she said, finishing his question for him. "Why stay at London's most luxurious hotel when you're broke? Is that what you were going to ask?"

"There are less expensive lodgings to be had in London, even at this time of year."

"Of course. We could go live in a flat in Soho or Lambeth and save a few hundred pounds. But that's a drop in the bucket, given what we owe. And when your little sister is finally going to make her come out after two years of waiting, and you're hoping a successful season will enable her to find a worthy husband, you need a respectable address. After all, what gentleman is going to call on a young lady living in some dingy little flat above a store? And don't tell me love would conquer all, because we both know it wouldn't."

"But surely you have relations somewhere who can help—"

"Most of them are distant cousins we hardly know and most are as strapped as we are. You know how hard things are for those who make their income from land rents. Anyway, Giles kindly offered to let us make our home with him, but somehow, I just couldn't stomach the idea of living in the same house with the man who had once jilted me for being a slut."

He grimaced.

"Giles's wife," she went on mercilessly, "didn't seem to like the idea much, either."

"What about your friends?"

"Most of our friends turned their backs on us when I became damaged goods. It's better now than it was eleven years ago. Time has enabled me to become somewhat rehabilitated. But even so, how can I ask those who slammed their doors in my face then to take me in now? Even if they agreed, it would be humiliating." She shook her head. "We've attended house parties whenever possible, of course, but there haven't been many invitations there, as you might imagine."

"Then where have you been living since your father died?"

"We lived on the estate at first, but of course Giles wanted to move his own family in. We could have taken a cottage somewhere, but we've been living in hotels instead, because it's less expensive that way."

"Less expensive? That's not possible."

She gave him a brittle smile. "It is when you're able to duck out and move on without paying the bill."

Her cheeks burned at the confession, for she knew how wrong it was. "For the past year, we've been all over England, going from hotel to hotel and avoiding our creditors. But then, I met Wilson at the Henley Regatta, and he took a shine to me. When he proposed, it was like the answer to a prayer."

Devlin studied her for a long moment, his mouth a grim line. "And you think Rycroft is a good way out of the mess?"

"No, Devlin," she said, her voice hard to her own ears, "I think he's the only way. But if you've any other suggestions, I'm willing to listen. Being a woman, I can't run off to Africa or some other outpost of empire to make my fortune. And with my sordid past, no one would hire me to be a governess or lady's maid. Perhaps I could work in the Savoy laundry or be a chambermaid? Perhaps my mother could indulge her talent for drama and become an actress? Oh, wait, I know!" she added with bright, biting sarcasm. "Josephine could become a nursery governess. That would bring in about fifteen quid a year, and we wouldn't have to pay for her food and lodgings. Someone might be willing to hire her to care for their children, because unlike me, she's unsullied."

Devlin looked away, rubbing a hand over his jaw. "God, Kay," he muttered.

"Don't you dare pity me!" she ordered fiercely.

"I'm not. I just..." He paused and took a breath. "I just wish I'd known."

"And if you had known, what difference would it have made? What could you have done for me?"

He opened his mouth, then closed it again.

"Exactly," she said, his silence making her point with painful clarity. "There are only two ways a man can help a woman out of a situation like mine—one honorable and one not—and neither of those solutions would have been acceptable to either of us. Besides, I'd have refused any form of help from you, honorable or otherwise, because I hated you as much as you hated me."

"Still, you don't have to do this, Kay. You don't have to marry Rycroft. I can give you a loan."

That was more than she could bear. "No. I'd never be able to pay you back."

"That doesn't matter."

"It matters to me. I won't take charity from my friends. Do you think I'd take it from you? As for these," she added, snatching the sheaf of bills out of his hands, "my engagement has been formally announced, so I will be able to pay them. Banks, I have discovered, are quite willing to loan you heaps of money when you're officially engaged to an American millionaire. And everything will be all right once I marry Wilson. The marriage settlement will pay off all our debts, and my family will never have to worry about money again. Josephine's future will be secure."

"It's not worth it, Kay."

"Not worth what? Missing a party or two?"

"That's not what I mean, and you know it. It's not worth selling yourself."

"I am doing no such thing!" she cried, affronted.

"No? Are you so much in love with Rycroft, then?"

That question felt like a blow to the chest, and it took her a moment to reply.

"I'm very fond of Wilson," she said at last, her voice prim as any maiden aunt's. "And he's very fond of me."

"So, no, you're not in love with him."

She made a sound of impatience and looked away. "I'm fighting for my family's future as best I can."

"By capitulating to a man you don't love who is a controlling, domineering bully?"

She set her jaw and looked at him again. "Your rudeness never ceases to surprise me."

"Don't make this about me," he said, seeing right through her. "The point is you are choosing to marry a man just like your father. The more things change, the more they stay the same."

That stung, mainly because she'd thought that exact same thing as she'd watched her mother cave to Wilson's wishes about the soiree.

"A man who can control you is what you know," he went on. "It's what you're used to, what you understand. And I would imagine doing this is also a very good way to—how shall I put it?—atone for what you see as your own past sins."

She opened her mouth to reply, but the furious denial she wanted to offer stuck in her throat, because he was right, damn him.

"My motives are my own business," she said, striving not to show he'd hit a nerve. "And whether Wilson is like my father or not is irrelevant. We may not be love's young dream, but Wilson is the only man who has offered me marriage since Giles threw me over. He's the only chance to marry I'll ever have."

"You don't know that. And even so—"

"As for your accusation of selling myself," she cut in, "marrying for a dowry is a time-honored and perfectly acceptable tradition. Many women and men have done it," she added as he turned away with an oath of exasperation and started for the door. "When they've had no other choice."

"What you really mean," he shot over his shoulder, "is that the choice you're making is one your mother and society would approve of. You care far more about pleasing others than you do pleasing yourself." He paused by the door and turned to look at her. "You always have."

"I am working to ensure that my family is safe, secure, and happy," she countered, baffled—not for the first time—by his selfish outlook on life. "What is wrong with that?"

"Nothing's wrong with it, unless it's always at your own expense."

"Well, you'll have to forgive me, but I happen to like being safe and secure, too! I like knowing I won't have to spend my life ducking creditors. I like being able to pay my bills for a change. And it is a great comfort to me to know that my mother, my sister, and my future children will be taken care of. But you're right about one thing, Devlin. You're right to point out that the more things change, the more they stay the same, because I remember us having a very similar conversation to this one fourteen years ago. I remember you persuading me to rebel, to put my own happiness first and run off with you, a selfish decision that, despite the fact that I changed my mind, ended up costing me everything."

"And you don't think marrying this man will cost you at least as much, and perhaps far more?" He turned to open the door, shaking his head as if he was as baffled by her point of view as she was by his.

"What's it to you?" she cried. "Even if all you say is true, what difference does it make to you what I do or who I choose to marry? After all this time, why do you care?"

He stopped at the question, but he didn't reply straightaway. Instead, his gaze raked slowly down over her, and when he looked into her face again, something in the brilliant depths of his eyes made Kay's heart slam against her ribs with enough force to rob the breath from her lungs.

"Damned if I know, Kay," he muttered as he turned and walked out. "Damned if I know."

9

In the wake of Devlin's departure, Kay's head was in a whirl, her emotions a scrambled, unholy mess. The revelations they had shared and the conclusions drawn from them had left her baffled, frustrated, and angry. And yet, as she thought about it, she knew her present feelings, whatever they might be, were of little consequence.

Unless she wanted to toss her sister's welfare aside, marrying Wilson was her only real choice. Wilson was also her best chance to escape being a childless spinster for the rest of her life. And having spent the past year in the agonizing uncertainty of genteel poverty, she knew that a lifetime of that was no better guarantee of happiness than her present course.

No, though her conversation with Devlin may have cleared up a few mysteries from the past, she'd appreciated almost immediately that knowing what had really happened fourteen years ago didn't change a thing now.

There was, however, one aspect of the past that did have to be addressed, and she tackled it first thing the following morning. Up before the others, she dressed, went downstairs to the Savoy florist, and booked an appointment. Upon her return, she found that her mother was awake. Hearing voices from the older woman's room, she tapped on the door and entered.

She found her mother in bed, reading the paper and eating her breakfast.

"Ah, there you are," Magdelene cried, looking at Kay above the pince-nez on her nose. "I've been frantic wondering where you'd gone. I sent Foster to go in search of you."

"I needed a walk."

"Alone?"

"Of course not," she said at once. "I took the bellboy with me. I'm sure everyone who's anyone saw us together and rumors will fly in tomorrow's *Talk of the Town* that I'm dallying with a much younger man, but what can I say? He's a charming fellow."

Magdelene, of course, did not appreciate the sarcasm. "There's no need to be snippy, miss."

Given the revelations she and Devlin had shared, Kay felt more than snippy. "Mama, I need to speak with you about something. It's rather important."

Magdelene reluctantly put aside that morning's edition of *Talk of the Town*. "Of course. What is it?"

"Kay?" Josephine called from the other room. "Are you back? I need your help."

"I'm in here, darling," she called back and turned again to her mother. "I don't want Jo to overhear our conversation," she said in a lower voice, "so I'm sending her downstairs on an errand."

"How mysterious," Magdelene murmured as Jo entered the bedroom.

"There you are!" Jo said, pausing in the doorway, "I woke up and you were already out and about. Foster's gone looking for you, you know."

"I only went for a walk."

"Well, either way, since Foster's not here, I need you to button me up." Jo turned, presenting her back.

"By the way," Kay went on as she pushed the younger girl's long auburn tresses over her shoulder and began slipping the carved ivory buttons of Jo's dress through their corresponding holes, "I've made an appointment for you with the Savoy florist to choose the flowers for your debutante ball."

"You mean I get to pick the flowers?" Jo turned her head in surprise, looking first at Kay, then at their mother, and then at Kay again. "Really?"

"Of course you get to pick," Kay replied before Mama could do so. "It's your ball, after all. Why wouldn't you choose your own flowers?"

"Well..." Josephine paused. "The two of you usually do things like that for me."

"Do we?" Kay hesitated, remembering her instructions to Jo about wine the other night, and she realized to her dismay that she had been smothering Jo the same way she had always been smothered.

The more things change...

"I suppose we have tended to hover over you too much," she admitted. "But you're out now, and you deserve some freedom to make your own decisions. And," she rushed on before her mother could object, "Mama and I have no doubt you'll choose the perfect arrangements. But the only appointment Monsieur Lavigne had available this week was for half past nine this morning, so you'll have to hurry."

"I should say so," Jo said, laughing. "It's twenty past nine now."

"I know, and I'm sorry I didn't tell you sooner, but I forgot. While you're downstairs, you might also see the maître d'hôtel to be sure the other decorations coordinate with the flowers you choose. There," she added, patting her sister's back. "You're all done up."

Jo left the bedroom, and Kay watched from the doorway, waiting until Josephine had left the suite, then she turned around. "What," she said, wasting no time on preliminaries, "happened to my letters?"

"Letters? What letters?"

"My letters to Devlin Sharpe fourteen years ago, and those he sent to me."

Magdelene looked away, touching a hand to the side of her neck, adjusting the collar of her nightdress in an obvious attempt to stall. "I'm sure I don't know what you mean," she said at last.

"Don't play the innocent, Mama. I wrote Devlin dozens of letters, but he never got them. He also claims he often wrote to me—"

"And how do you know all this? Have you been talking to That Horrible Man? Oh, Kay, really!" she added on a wail. "What is wrong with you? Have you no sense at all?"

"Don't make this about me. What happened to those letters? You suppressed them, didn't you?"

In confronting her mother with this, Kay had thought Magdelene would immediately fall back in a faint or go into hysterics. Instead, to Kay's surprise, Magdelene lifted her chin, settled against the brass headboard behind her, and faced her accusation with surprising equanimity. "Yes," she admitted. "I did. What of it?"

Kay breathed a humorless laugh at her mother's unexpected candor. "At least you are honest enough to acknowledge your contemptible deceit when faced with it."

"Contemptible?" Magdelene tossed her head. "I was trying to save you from making an irrevocable mistake."

"A task at which you ultimately failed."

"And whose fault was that, pray? Given his character," she added as Kay made an impatient sound, "I suppose your father and I ought to have known Sharpe would spread vicious rumors about you upon your engagement. But that thought never occurred to us."

"They weren't rumors, Mama," she reminded uncompromisingly. "They were facts. But Devlin didn't cause those facts to become known."

"Is that what he told you?"

"Yes. And I believe him."

"Oh, Kay! How can you be such a fool? He's lying."

"A grievous sin you seem to know a great deal about," she countered. "Nonetheless, he says he did not start those rumors, and I believe him. As for who you were trying to save, please don't pretend you were motivated by any motherly concern for me. You were trying to save Papa and yourself. I was merely the means by which you chose to do so."

"We were trying to save the estates, which was also saving you, young lady, and your baby sister, and hundreds of other people. Or would you have preferred we let Raleigh Grange fall to pieces and watch our tenants and our servants and the village suffer without trying to save them just so that you could marry for love? Love," she added with disdain. "No eighteen-year-old girl even understands what love is. You'd known That Horrible Man less than three months. Love? Don't tell me."

"What about Papa? Wasn't saving the estates, taking care of us, and ensuring everyone's future supposed to be his office?"

"He tried!" For the first time, a quaver came into Magdelene's voice. "You know the income from land rents is dismal nowadays. These beastly agricultural depressions, tenants giving up their farms to work in factories... all that puts a peer in an almost impossible position. When your father realized that mortgaging the estates wasn't going to be enough to carry us through, he put what money we had left into funds and investments, but then..."

"But then," Kay finished for her, "he lost it all."

Magdelene sniffed. "Your father was an earl, Kay, not a financier."

"So I became the only card he had left to play. He refused to allow me to consider Devlin as a suitor, but that wasn't because Devlin didn't have the money to support *me*."

As she spoke, the girlish delusions she'd clung to about her father began breaking apart and falling away, and she was astonished at how liberating that felt. "No," she continued, "it was because Devlin didn't have the money to bail him out of the mess. He needed to sell me off."

"I refuse to allow you to denigrate your father in this ungrateful way!"

"Ungrateful?"

"Yes!" Magdelene cried. "It was not your father's fault that things happened as they did. You have no idea how it worried him that he was not able to take care of us. All the sleepless nights he went over and over the account books, trying to make the money we had stretch a little further. And none of this was his fault. Most of the money had dried up long before he even became the earl."

"So you and Papa transferred the burden of responsibility for our future onto me without even consulting me on the subject."

"Our fortune was gone. We were practicing every economy possible, paring staff down to the bone, making over clothes season after season, cutting house parties to one a year. You have no idea how hard it was."

"Only one house party a year?" Kay echoed. "Oh, well, I'm sure I don't know how you managed to hold your head up in the county."

Magdelene drew herself up with injured dignity. "There were far worse things than that, things we never told you. Did you ever go into the attics at Raleigh Grange? No?" she added when Kay shook her head. "Shall I tell you what they contained? Bowls, pots, and buckets everywhere to catch the rain from the roof, a roof that leaked like a sieve and could not be repaired because there was no money to do so. Cracks in the very foundations of the house that we had no money to fix. We mortgaged everything we could, but it still wasn't enough."

She sniffed and lifted a corner of the counterpane to dab at her eyes. "The tenant cottages were in need of repairs, too, but we couldn't afford any, so we had to lower the rents. That, of course, meant even less money coming in." Her mother's voice was shaking, and Kay braced herself for the inevitable bout of weeping that was about to commence. "There were times when Mrs. Jones was at her wits' end to make a decent meal on the food budget we had to give her. We were teetering on the brink of destitution long before your father died, Kay. We hid it from you, of course, but now, after a year of living with what I had endured for two decades, surely you have come to understand the hard reality of our situation?"

"Given that I am now marrying a man I do not love to save us from poverty, I can assure you that I understand the situation quite well, Mother."

"Love," her mother said with a sniff as she tucked her handkerchief back in her pocket. "You keep throwing that word around as if it is the only thing that matters. Going without food and a roof over your head would be worse, young lady."

Kay didn't know if her mother was exaggerating what she'd put up with during her years at Raleigh Grange. With Magdelene, one could never tell where truth ended and fiction began. But she did know that her childhood had not been one of money being extravagantly flung about. Even when she was a little girl, there had been economies. She also knew that her mother was right. Love was all very well, but it didn't pay the bills.

Despite that, however, she could not forgive her parents' deceit so easily. "You lied to me. You and Papa lied, and you schemed, and used me. You put the burden of saving us on me."

"Who would you suggest carry that burden, if not you? Would you prefer to lay the responsibility on Josephine?"

Kay sucked in a deep breath, that question like a punch in the stomach. "Giles," she said after a moment, "would have saved the estates with his money when he became the earl, with or without marrying me. I don't see why you needed me."

"We were still hoping for a son. And our hopes were justified when I became pregnant again."

"What?" Kay stared at her parent, aghast. "When was this?"

"Right after you eloped. Why do you think your father and I did what we did? Why we were so desperate for you to marry someone suitable? Were we to leave our son with a bankrupt, decrepit estate?"

"And I," Kay murmured bitterly, "was to be the sacrificial lamb for this potential son and heir."

"Don't pretend you don't understand how families like ours work! Daughters must take second place. But then, I lost the baby, and we knew all was probably lost for us as well. But we still hoped to secure your future and your sister's. That was why your father was pushing you so hard to marry Giles, and why we had to keep you away from That Horrible Man. With Giles, your future would have been secure, and Josephine's, too. And you already knew him, you were fond of him, and you had so much in common. We felt he was the perfect person for you, a far better choice for you than the penniless fifth son of a baron who would have hauled you off to the savage wilds of Africa."

For the first time since beginning this conversation, Kay felt her anger faltering. Whoever said there were two sides to every story had known what he was talking about. Her family story, she appreciated, had at least three. Perhaps more.

"What a shock it must have been," she murmured, "when my elopement became public knowledge and Giles threw me over."

"It was the most devastating blow of our lives," Magdelene said simply. "Your father was never the same man after that. He died heartsick, blaming himself, knowing you and Josephine would now be left with nothing."

Kay tried to shore her anger back up, but she couldn't do it. She wanted to hang on to resentment and blame, but what good would it do? Her duty remained the same, for Josephine's sake. Still, there was one thing she had to say, one thing she needed her mother to understand before this matter could be put behind them.

"I fully understand my responsibility, Mama, and I have no intention of shirking it. But I'm glad you mention Josephine, because in light of what you did, of how you and Papa deceived me,

I intend to be sure you have no chance at all to use Josephine in the same way. I intend to advise her to always post her letters herself, so that I may ensure she is never the subject of your machinations the way I was."

"Machinations?" Magdelene sat upright, looking affronted. "Haven't you heard a word I've said, Kay?"

"I heard every word, and I accept your explanations. I even forgive you for them. But I will not forget them."

"And will you tell Josephine about any of this?"

"No. And," she added as her parent sagged with relief, "we will not speak of it again. We will put it behind us. But I do that for Josephine's sake, Mama, not for yours. As for myself, I doubt I will ever be able to trust you again."

With that, she turned and walked out, and as she closed the door behind her, she tried not to care that her mother had just burst into tears.

Devlin stared down at the offer to purchase that his solicitors had forwarded to him from Lord Shrewsbury, but despite reading the typewritten lines for the third time, he could still not seem to comprehend their meaning. His mind, sadly, was not thinking of a house in Eaton Square, but of a suite on the other side of the Savoy Hotel, and a pair of sage-green eyes filled with pride and defensiveness and tinged with desperation.

A week had passed since the Mayfair soiree, and yet he could not stop thinking about that night, about the facts he and Kay had both uncovered regarding their elopement so long ago, about the perfidy of her parents, and the misunderstandings, chaos, and pain that had resulted.

He'd lost his heart to her the moment he'd taken her into his arms that night at Lady Rowland's ball, and her parents' disapproval of him had only fueled his determination to have her. He'd been young and randy and wild, but he had loved her, body and soul.

He stared down at the papers on his desk with unseeing eyes, remembering it all, from the night he'd first seen her at the ball to the secret assignations, the whispered conversations, and the hot, stolen kisses of those three months in London. He thought of their desperate, clandestine meetings where they'd plotted running away together. And that fateful night in Birmingham when she'd refused to go on with it. These memories swam through his mind with vivid clarity—the gardenia scent of her hair, the velvety softness of her lips, the blazing lust she could ignite just by flashing him a look with those strange, wonderful eyes. His frantic desperation to have her, the triumph when at last they were on their way to a life together. He thought of that night in Birmingham, of her in front of him nearly naked, and lust raging in him like a hurricane.

But he'd actually done the honorable thing. He'd kissed her within an inch of her life, and then he'd torn himself away and slept on the floor. It had been agony. It had also been the happiest night of his life.

And then, it had all gone wrong.

The duke's sisters had burst in, and like a bucket of cold water had been hurled over her, Kay had come to her senses. She'd looked at him, those eyes heartsick, and he knew deep down inside that he'd lost her.

He refused to admit that to himself at the time, of course. He'd gone to Wales, to Yorkshire, and then halfway around the world, and through it all—on the boat to Cape Town, during his trek from South Africa to Egypt—he'd propped up his hopes with each letter he'd written, determined to believe that somehow, some day, they'd be together. He'd consoled himself with memories of her for months on end, but looking back now, he recognized the strange unreality of it all, as if he'd been living in a dream. Her engagement to Giles had woken him up.

Then those memories of her had become not a solace to sustain him but a torment to torture him. His illusions irrevocably shattered, his love transmuting into resentment and hate, and then, slowly, all of it easing into some half-forgotten corner of his mind. He'd met Pam, and that had rather put the lid on things. At last, life had seemed worth living again, and he'd finally thought he was over the past, and that he could actually make a life with a woman who was not Kay.

He closed his eyes and tried to hang on to that—to the life he was building now, to the woman he would be marrying in a month, and to the future he would have with her, working to once again relegate Kay to that vague, hazy corner of his consciousness where she'd been before that fateful moment in the florist shop.

Pam, he reminded himself over and over, was his responsibility now. Kay was not. Kay had a fiancé of her own to take care of her, and though Rycroft might very well be a tyrant, marrying him was her decision and not his problem.

It was her decision, granted, but was it really a choice?

He muttered an oath and opened his eyes again. Yanking a pen out of its holder, he once again turned his attention to the document before him, forcing himself to read it all the way through.

His solicitors had assured him it was a fair offer, and he was inclined to agree. It would be an ideal investment property, likely to bring in a very high rent for many years to come, and though the asking price was steep, he could easily afford to pay it.

Not everyone, a little voice whispered to him, had that luxury.

Devlin sighed and leaned back in his chair, tapping the pen against the blotter on his writing desk, his mind drifting from his own comfortable financial situation to that of someone who had not been so fortunate.

It had never occurred to him that Kay could be in such dire straits. Thinking back fourteen years, he tried to remember if her father had ever shown any signs of financial impecunity, but it was hard to know. Peers tended to hide that sort of misfortune. Besides, his family and hers had not been well acquainted. The one time he'd visited Raleigh Grange in pursuit of Kay, he'd paid no notice to the conditions of the earl's estate. His thoughts had been on Kay, not her home.

He did know that the earl had seemed prosperous enough. He'd managed to somehow scrape together two thousand pounds to get rid of the man he'd deemed a fortune hunter. In hindsight, he could recall no signs that indicated the earl had been desperate for money. But then, he hadn't been looking for any.

If only he'd seen. Devlin tightened his grip on the pen in his hand. If only he'd known.

The moment those thoughts went through his mind, he almost wanted to laugh. Had he known her family was broke, would it have mattered? It probably would only have made his resolve to get her out of their clutches all the greater.

In the end, of course, none of it had mattered. Her determination to escape had faltered at the last minute, and he'd known she would never go to Africa.

If only he'd stayed.

Ah, but what then? The options for the fifth son of a peer who hated his guts were limited. God knows, he wasn't cut out for the clergy or the army, which meant he'd probably have become a barrister, or worked for a bank, or become some rich magnate's secretary, and he knew none of those occupations would have enabled Raleigh to give permission for Kay to marry him. And, to be brutally honest, Africa was where he'd wanted to be. It had been so easy to believe the earl, to take his money, and go where he wanted to go, confident he'd make his fortune and come back to Kay with something to offer her. He hadn't thought she would see his departure as an abandonment. How could he, given all the letters he'd written?

Looking back, the news of her engagement to Giles hadn't really been much of a surprise. A shock, yes, but once the shock and disbelief had worn off, he'd accepted her supposed betrayal as a fact without really questioning why she'd done it. And given that he'd never heard from her, it had seemed quite likely that she'd given him up willingly to marry someone else.

If only he'd refused to accept it. If only he'd come home, fought for her. If only he hadn't been so ready to believe the worst.

Devlin stirred impatiently. If only...if only...the most banal and futile phrase in the English language. He hadn't known her situation, he hadn't come home, and he hadn't fought for her. Instead, he'd allowed his anger and hurt to keep him away, and now she was forced to marry a man strictly for material considerations.

Anger flooded through him, anger on her behalf, anger at

Rycroft, at her father, and at society. Raleigh had controlled Kay's destiny from the moment of her birth. The malicious tongues of society had shredded her and smeared her good name for no reason other than for the entertainment of watching her downfall. And Rycroft knew, he must know, that he was in control of her. Rycroft was a ruthless bastard, but he was not stupid.

But though all that was true, none of it compared to the anger he felt at himself. It roiled within him, seething in his guts like molten lava.

Devlin's hand closed in a fist around his pen. He could have prevented this, but he hadn't. Bitter and broken and full of resentment, he'd done only the absolute minimum to salvage her reputation, deeming it her fiancé's office to save her, not his. And now, as she'd pointed out, there was nothing he could do to save her. She would marry Rycroft, and like her father before him, he would tell her what she could and could not do, who she could and could not associate with. He'd tell her what to feel and what to think, and she would be unable to do anything but comply.

Marrying for a dowry is a time-honored and perfectly acceptable tradition.

That, of course, was true. In their world, a dowry was always a consideration in marriage. It was how things were done. Had Kay's father offered him a marriage settlement, he'd have taken it without a thought, so he was hardly in a position to criticize the concept.

Her lack of choices, of alternatives, made him sick inside, and he knew that no matter what he'd known or hadn't known, what justifications he'd had for his thoughts and actions, he was to blame for what she was now forced to do. Because of him, her ability to move in society had been curtailed, her chances of finding someone else to marry, and the means to support her and her mother and sister had boiled down to only one choice.

All this time, he'd blamed her—for her lack of courage, her lack of faith, her weakness in turning to another man, but their conversation a week ago had forced him to put all that aside, to see past his bitterness over her actions and take a good, hard look at his own. Despite his shock and hurt, it had been far easier than it should have been for him to believe she'd thrown him over. He recognized now that his own youth had made it hard for him to have faith in anyone, even Kay, or that she could truly love him enough to stand by him. But those excuses didn't absolve him. The blame for this began and ended with him.

A sharp sound pulled him out of his reverie, and he looked down, staring in surprise at the pen in his hand, realizing he'd snapped the pearwood handle in half.

He tossed the broken pieces aside with an oath, plunked his elbows on the writing desk, and rested his head in his hands. Never in his life had he been filled with such profound remorse and regret, never had he felt as powerless and frustrated as he felt right now. But as hellish as these feelings were, he almost relished them. Because this hell was of his own making, and nothing less than he deserved.

10

The night of Josephine's ball, Kay's trust in her younger sister's taste proved amply rewarded, for the flowers and decorations were exquisite. And though Magdelene fretted that the vivid jade color of Jo's gown was "too forward" for a debutante, Kay's heart swelled with pride at how beautiful her sister looked tonight.

A week ago, Devlin had asked her if marrying a man she did not love was worth the sacrifice. As Kay looked around the crowded ballroom that boded so well for her sister to have a successful season, she almost wished Devlin were here so he could see for himself how obvious the answer was.

Jo, Kay thought, watching with delight as the Duke of Westbourne led the girl across the floor in the ball's opening dance, would never be a wallflower shredded by gossip columnists for her figure or her complexion. Jo would not suffer for the mistakes of her parents or elder sister. Jo would now be able to make a good marriage. And for all of that, she could thank Wilson. Delia, of course, had been a godsend, working all week to help bring Josephine out, and the duke's appearance here tonight would help as well, but if it weren't for Wilson, there would not have been a season for Jo, nor any dowry to ensure her future.

So, yes, it was all worth it, Kay thought fiercely. Jo was worth any sacrifice she had to make.

"Darling!"

Kay turned to find Delia coming toward her in a luscious concoction of tangerine silk, hands outstretched in greeting. "Fashionably late, I see," she teased, giving Delia a kiss on each cheek.

"Of course! You know I hate arriving anywhere on time."

"I thought Calderon might be rubbing off on you. You said he's a stickler for punctuality."

"So he is, but alas for him, that character trait of his is not one I'm inclined to adopt." She cast a glance over Kay's amethyst purple ball gown. "What a lovely dress you've got on. Speaking of dresses, Jo looks absolutely stunning."

"Just what I was thinking myself."

"The young men have certainly noticed," Delia added, nodding to the eager male faces watching the girl as she danced with the Duke of Westbourne.

"Some of the credit goes to you, Dee. And to the duke, of course," she added, nodding to the ballroom floor as the waltz ended and Westbourne escorted Jo back to Magdelene's side. "I am so thankful he was able to come down from Gloucestershire to attend the ball and lead her in the first dance. With the duchess expecting her baby in just a few weeks, I wasn't sure he'd be able to come."

"It's only for the night. He's going back tomorrow."

"Still, I do appreciate it so much."

"Don't give Max all the credit! Evie told him if he didn't come down and partner Jo for the first dance, she'd make him sleep in the dressing room for a year."

"A fate worse than death," Kay said, laughing.

"To a man in love, it is, darling!" Delia paused, rising on her toes to have a better look at the crowd. "And look at all the other fashionables who are here. It bodes well for your wedding. And I'm glad you didn't have to miss it."

"Miss it? Are you daft? I wouldn't miss Jo's debutante ball for anything in the world."

"You missed Simon's soiree a week ago."

Kay made a face. "Oh, that."

"I'm relieved to see you're feeling better now." Delia turned to look at her. "No fever, I take it? No chills?"

The twinkle in Delia's eye told Kay that her friend was not unaware of Magdelene's tendency to exaggerate. "Nothing like that. It was . . . just a headache."

"Was it?" Delia grinned, giving her a knowing look. "I thought you might have been attempting to avoid a certain person we both know."

"Oh, for heaven's sake," she grumbled, remembering Devlin's accusations. "Why would I care? I'm not a timid little rabbit, you know," she added with some heat, "bolting away at the sight of him."

"No need to be spiky! I was only teasing."

Deciding it was best to change the subject, she glanced again at her sister, who was now talking nineteen to the dozen with a slim blond girl of about the same age. "Jo seems to have found a friend in your future sister-in-law."

"Indeed. They took an immediate liking to each other when they met at the soiree last week, and Cassandra tells me they intend to brave the season together. They remind me of us."

"They do, rather," Kay agreed, smiling. "Without you, I'm not sure I could have endured my first season."

Delia's sideways glance was tinged with understanding. "I remember, darling."

"As for Jo and Cassandra, they've been joined at the hip all week, and I'm so glad. Jo hasn't had much opportunity to make friends since leaving school."

"No worries about that anymore, from what I can see. All our efforts on her behalf are paying off. I wish we could have roped in my cousin Idina to help more, but she's not doing the season, and even if she were, she has Rothmere's wishes to consider—"

"Say no more," Kay cut in, well aware that if anyone understood the need for a woman to placate the men in her life, it was she. "Idina has done what she can. It's not her fault her husband disapproves of me."

"We don't call him Percy Proper for nothing."

Kay laughed at the nickname Delia had bestowed on her cousin's husband years ago. "He is rather a snob, isn't he? But I'm so glad Idina is coming to my wedding anyway."

"Of course she's coming, and so are my other cousins, Nan, Audrey, and Pen. We're all coming to support you. Which reminds me...you're coming to my house party, I hope?"

"House party?" Kay echoed in surprise.

"Oh, that's right! I haven't had the chance to tell you. I'm having a house party to replace Max's usual Whitsuntide affair. You know he always does a big house party at Idyll Hour every Whitsun?"

Kay nodded. "It makes a nice respite from the frantic pace of the season, I've always thought."

"I'm glad you feel that way, because you're coming this year."

"But isn't it a family affair?"

"Mostly, but we always have a few of the county families and sometimes one or two close friends of the family, too."

"I'm flattered the duke puts me in that category, but I wouldn't have thought the duchess would want a big house party at this stage."

"She doesn't, believe me. That's why they aren't doing the house party this year. I am."

Kay felt compelled to point out the obvious. "But, Delia," she said, laughing, "you don't have a house."

Delia's dark blue eyes opened wide. "When have you ever known pesky little details like that to stop me?" she countered.

"Never," Kay admitted.

"Just so. I'm making the arrangements, but Simon will be officially hosting the party. It will be at Ivywild, his estate in Berkshire, which will be far easier to manage, since it's so close to London."

"He's willing to do that, even though he hasn't married into the family yet?"

"Willing? Are you joking? Simon jumped on the idea at once, saying it's a perfect way to entertain the investors as well, which means Wilson will be invited. Devlin will be there, too, of course," she added airily, "but that shouldn't matter to you, since you aren't some timid little rabbit who runs away."

Kay gave her friend a wry smile. "You really are a devil, Delia, when you want to be."

"Yes, so Simon tells me daily."

"And you don't care?"

Delia grinned. "Not a jot."

Kay felt a sudden, wistful pang. "I envy you," she murmured. "I care terribly what people think."

"It's different for me. I'm a rich widow. I have the luxury of not caring. But about the party, the date is set for the fifteenth. Audrey, Nan, and Pen will be there. Sadly, Idina can't come, for she's going to Scotland with Rothmere for a wedding. One of his cousins or something."

Kay made a rueful face. "Just as well, I suppose. I wouldn't want to make things awkward for the house party or cause any friction between Idina and Rothmere."

"Nonsense. I told Idina I was inviting you, and she wrote back heartily approving the idea. And," she added before Kay could recover from her surprise, "she's told her husband she wants to see more of you, and that he didn't have any say in the matter. He gave in with hardly a grumble. When a woman really puts her foot down, a man has to give in."

Kay thought of Wilson's hard face and was doubtful, but she didn't say so.

"So, you will come, won't you?"

"I'd like to," Kay replied. "I truly would. But..."

She paused, Devlin's words from the other night echoing through her mind.

So do you really want to spend the future repeating the past? Do you really want to live your life letting a second man dictate to you where you'll go and what you'll do?

Of course she didn't want that, but she also knew that things weren't as clear-cut as Devlin made them out to be. "But," she said at last, hedging, "I'm not sure I ought to attend. Between Jo's debut and the wedding plans, I'm just so busy right now."

It was true, and yet it also sounded terribly lame.

Do you really want to marry a man who will decide for you what friends you'll have and what parties you'll go to?

As Devlin's questions echoed through her mind, Kay's gaze slid to Josephine, who was now dancing with Lord Synby's handsome eldest son. "I really don't know how I'll get everything done before June as it is."

"I know it's only a few weeks before your wedding," Delia replied, "but surely you can spare one teensy little weekend away? I shall invite Josephine as well, of course, so do it for her, if not for yourself. She and Cassandra will have no end of fun, and Cassie can introduce her to some of the young people of the county. And don't worry about the wedding. I'll help you get everything arranged in time."

"It's not only that."

"Then what is it?"

Kay hesitated, knowing discretion was her wisest course, but the urge to confide in her friend was too great to resist. "I don't think," she said, the words like sawdust in her mouth, "Wilson would like it if I attended the party."

"Why ever not?" Delia laughed. "Surely, it's not because of Devlin Sharpe? What does he think, that Devlin is going to seduce you and take you off to Gretna Green in some bizarre attempt to repeat history? Heavens!" she added as Kay made a grimace. "That is what he thinks, isn't it? That's the real reason you didn't come to the soiree, isn't it? Because Wilson is jealous of Devlin?"

"I suppose he is, though it's ridiculous, really."

"Is it?" Delia smiled a little, her expression half wry, half amused. "You don't think it's reasonable for him to be jealous of a man nearly half his age and twice as good looking? A man," she added when Kay made an impatient sound, "with whom you have a romantic history?"

"Exactly," Kay agreed with an emphatic nod. "History is what it is, *history*, as in the past. Over and done with. Dead and gone. Buried," she added for good measure.

"All right, all right," Delia said, still smiling. "I appreciate your point. No need to keep hammering away at it. And since that's the case, are you really going to allow Wilson's unfounded jealousy to prevent you from coming to my party? Or is it that you don't want to come and can't bear to tell me so you're using Wilson as an excuse?"

"It's not that!" she cried. "As I already told you, I do want to come. But—" Kay broke off, swallowing hard. "Wilson is a complicated man."

"No man is complicated. And a little jealousy is good for them. The only way for a woman to deal with a man's jealousy," she went on as Kay opened her mouth to reply, "is to show him he has nothing to worry about. Which is impossible to do by the tactic of avoidance. Trust me on this. I've been married three times, darling, and I know what I'm talking about."

Kay had no doubt of that. But sadly, she did not have her friend's experience handling the vagaries of the sterner sex. "That's all very well, but I can't afford—that is, I don't want to antagonize him. It's not worth the risk," she added, reminding herself firmly of that fact as she spoke.

"Risk?" Delia's voice rose sharply on the word. "What risk?"

Kay decided she'd said more than enough. She'd already had one lecture on this subject from Devlin. She didn't need one from her friend. "I only meant I don't want a quarrel five weeks before my wedding."

Delia didn't seem satisfied, but thankfully, she didn't pursue the question. "I can ensure that your attendance at my party does not cause any friction between you and Wilson," she said instead, displaying all her usual blithe assurance.

"Even you can't move mountains, Dee."

"No? Well, the mountain in question is coming this way, so let's test your hypothesis, shall we? Mr. Rycroft!" she added, looking past Kay's shoulder and donning a wide smile. "How lovely to see you again so soon. And you've arrived at the perfect moment to settle a little dispute between Kay and myself."

"Oh?" Wilson paused beside Kay. "What dispute is that?"

"Simon, I understand, has invited you to his little house party two weeks hence? I have invited your wife-to-be, of course, but sadly, she is not sure she ought to come. She says," Delia added with a laugh, ignoring the nudge of Kay's slipper, "that she has far too much to do here before the wedding."

"So she does."

"Oh, but I've assured her that I'm happy to help with anything she needs before and after the house party, so she really has no excuse at all to refuse. And so many of our mutual acquaintances will be attending. My cousins, for instance. Not the duke himself, sadly, but three of his sisters will be there. They know Kay already, of course, though they haven't seen her for ages. All of them have said how much they look forward to seeing her again. If she's not there," Delia added with a sigh, "they'll be so disappointed. And so will I. You don't want us to be disappointed, do you?"

Kay choked at this blatantly manipulative tactic, but Delia went on serenely, "Rycroft, do, please, use your influence with Kay to make her change her mind. We simply must have her at the party. The duke's sisters are quite set on it."

"Hmm..." He paused, and though he might desire the goodwill of the duke's family, Kay could tell he was not pleased. She could only offer him a helpless shrug in reply.

"I'm not sure what I can do," he said after a moment. "If Kay feels that she's too busy, then—"

"As I said, I'm happy to help her," Delia assured. "She says she doesn't want to impose on me, but I've assured her that it's no imposition at all. Now that I've returned from Paris, I've plenty of free time, and I want to help, so please add your voice to mine and help me persuade her."

"Well, all right, then," he said with a heartiness that was unmistakably forced, the same heartiness, Kay appreciated now, that he'd displayed that night at Delia's opera supper, the heartiness of being pinned in a corner, and she could only cross her fingers it didn't backfire. "There's no more to say. Of course Kay will be happy to attend the house party."

At those words, a flicker of something crossed Delia's face, an emotion Kay couldn't quite identify. But it was gone in an instant, and Delia bestowed on Wilson the same melting smile that had enabled her to secure three husbands. "Thank you," she said reverently. "I won't forget this. And if there's anything I can ever do for you..."

Kay saw the look of understanding pass between them before Wilson gave them both a nod of farewell and moved on, making for the refreshment tables at the other end of the room.

"Well played, Delia," Kay murmured. "You realize you just

promised to help his daughter make her London come out in a few years?"

"Of course. The girl's not awful, I hope?"

"I've no idea. I haven't yet met her. But upon my engagement, she wrote me a very sweet letter welcoming me to the family. And if the miniature of her that Wilson keeps in his pocket is any indication, she's quite pretty, too."

"That helps. She'll have a generous dowry, I trust?"

Kay smiled. "Obscenely generous, I daresay. By the way, I noticed you didn't tell Wilson how the duke's brother-in-law disapproves of me and my notorious past."

"I didn't think it was necessary to go into trivial details about Percy Proper, especially since he and Idina won't be there. So, now that your fiancé has given his approval, are you going to accept my invitation? Or must I beat you about the head?"

"All right, all right," she capitulated, laughing. "After all that effort on your part, how could I refuse?"

"Absolutely right. Now that we've got that all settled, I'd best tell Simon to notify his housekeeper to prepare for three more guests. I'll leave it to you to give Josephine and Cassandra the good news."

Kay nodded. "I just hope," she added as her friend moved off, "that neither of us lives to regret this."

"I won't, darling," Delia promised over her shoulder. "And neither will you."

"Easy for you to say," Kay replied, crossing her fingers. "You're not the one with a jealous fiancé."

But her words were wasted. Delia, sadly, was already too far away to hear them.

Ivywild, Simon's country home in Berkshire, was a solid, rectangular structure of red brick and gray stone that, true to its name, was swathed in ivy. Set on a rise, the house overlooked gardens set amid wide expanses of lawn, beyond which beech woods, fields of newly planted wheat, and undulating hills of misty spring green stretched endlessly in all directions.

Devlin's room was a sizable one, with a comfortable bed and a bath just across the corridor. Despite the agreeable accommodations, however, he knew Kay was here, and that fact made him look forward to this house party with about as much enthusiasm as he afforded visits to the dentist.

Only through the first afternoon, and this party was already living up to his exceedingly low expectations. It hadn't escaped his notice that Rycroft had prevented Kay from eating a second scone with her tea, and afterward, when she'd said she was going for a walk, the American had insisted on accompanying her. Watching them, Devlin had wondered in exasperation if the man told Kay what time to go to bed and what time to get up and what dress to wear each day.

The idea that she was going to marry this man and that it was all his fault made Devlin want to pound his head into a wall. Three of the duke's sisters were also here, and their censorious looks in his direction didn't help his mood.

He could have made some excuse and stayed away, of course, but he feared that it would have made no difference. Over two weeks since he'd last seen Kay, and yet he'd been unable to stop thinking about her.

Despite his best efforts, his mind had insisted on returning repeatedly to their conversation the night of the Mayfair soiree, and every time he thought of it, frustration, anger, guilt, and powerlessness surged in him again.

But those emotions, he appreciated grimly, were the easy ones. There was a far deeper feeling, lurking down inside, one that was proving much harder to conquer than it should have been.

Desire.

It rumbled inside him every time he looked at her. It shamed him every time he looked at Pam. And it slayed him with self-loathing every time he looked in a mirror.

Still, there was nothing for it. He'd accepted Simon's invitation and that was that. He'd assumed, in light of what she'd told him the night of the soiree, that she wouldn't be here, but now it was too late to bow out. And after all his teasing about her being afraid to be in his company, avoiding hers would be a laughable display of hypocrisy.

He walked to the window of his room and looked out at the view, but when he saw the gardens below, he almost groaned. There, as if to torture him, was a boxwood maze.

His mind flashed back to another maze in another garden long ago, and he closed his eyes, working to shove memories away, striving to bring himself back into the present and a girl who was not Kay.

But when he opened his eyes, his efforts were for naught. Amid the guests taking advantage of the agreeably warm spring evening to stroll the labyrinthine paths of the maze was the woman who'd dominated his thoughts for the past fortnight.

A hat of pale straw shaded her face, but beneath it, tendrils of her bright hair curled at the side of her neck. Her figure, slim and lithe in a frock of apple green, evoked as much lust in him as the generous curves of her youth had done, and he began to fear that whether she was chubby or slim, seventeen or seventy-five, or anything in between, his desire would still be there, rumbling within him, ready to flare up at the slightest provocation.

After their first encounter in the flower shop, he'd thought things would get easier, but the opposite had proven to be the case. Seeing her, being near her was much harder than it had been seven weeks ago. Now, he could no longer prop himself up with anger and hurt pride. His resentment, his bitterness and rancor were gone, leaving only an awful aching vulnerability, the vulnerability of knowing that if he ever allowed himself to be that stupid, he could fall in love with her all over again.

She turned her head, lifting her face to say something to Rycroft, and when Devlin saw the wide smile that curved her mouth, a smile he'd seen many times in his youth, it hit him like a punch to the stomach.

He turned abruptly away. Pam, he reminded himself brutally, was waiting downstairs for him to take her for a stroll. They would not, he decided sourly, be exploring the boxwood maze.

Though Devlin had managed to avoid Kay after tea by escorting Pam and her mother through the rose gardens, ducking her that evening was more difficult. Calderon's drawing room was not a large one, and though Kay seemed as averse to his company as he was to hers, avoiding her altogether was simply not possible, especially since each of them had to pretend a casual amiability that neither of them actually felt.

He managed to keep up the pretense somehow—by sheer force of will, probably—through the aperitifs and small talk, but when dinner was served, he found himself in trouble. Though Lady Stratham had seen to it that they were not seated near each other, that fact, he soon discovered, was meaningless. Kay was seated a good ten feet away on the opposite side of the long dining table, but that only meant that every time he spoke with the person to his right—a social necessity at dinner—she was directly in his line of vision.

Beside him, Lady Marchmont rattled on about breeding terriers for ratting, and though he made a pretense of hanging on every word, he found his gaze wandering to the other side of the table again and again. Given how Kay looked tonight, he doubted even a saint could have resisted a peek or two.

Candlelight had always been Kay's element. Its soft, gleaming light lent an incandescent magic to the fiery riot of curls piled atop her head. Above the damnably low neckline of her soft pink gown, the candle glow gave her skin the translucent sheen of marble, and the pale brown sugar freckles scattered across her collarbone were plainly visible, just begging to be kissed. Every time he looked at her, the desire within him rumbled again, reminding him—as if he needed any reminding—that where Kay was concerned, he was weak as water.

He wished he could have diverted his attention with a glimpse or two of his fiancée, for Pam's stunning beauty might have been enough to haul him back to sanity and remind him of his priorities, but, sadly, she was at the very other end of the table on his side, and

Devlin could only see her if he leaned far forward. On the occasions when he did so, she was deep in conversation with Rycroft, who was seated beside her.

It was twelve courses of hell.

He got some relief when the ladies went through, leaving the men to their port, but it was a brief respite. When the men rejoined the ladies in the drawing room, Simon's sister suggested dancing and told the butler to bring the gramophone into the great hall. As the servants rolled back the carpets and someone put a waltz recording on the gramophone, any relief Devlin felt evaporated.

He turned to find Pam, but it was too late, for she was already dancing, locked in the embrace of a good-looking young man whose name Devlin could not remember, but who was clearly the best dancer in the room.

More couples filled empty space in the great hall, leaving only a handful of guests on the sidelines. Rycroft, for one, who was standing nearby, talking with Simon and several of the other hotel investors. A bit surprised by that, he glanced around the room, searching for Kay.

He found her, back against the wall on the other side of the room, rather reminiscent of the ball at Lady Rowland's so long ago. Before he knew it, his footsteps were taking him to her side of the great hall.

As he approached, he didn't know what to expect, but he supposed the alarm he saw in her face was not wholly unexpected.

"Please don't ask me to dance," she said at once, holding up one hand as if to ward him off.

He hastened to reassure her. "No fear."

"I'm not being a rabbit."

"I didn't say you were." He moved to stand beside her. "But that remark of mine at Lady Stratham's opera supper really got under your skin, didn't it? Sorry about that," he added when she made a brief nod of confirmation. "It was a boorish thing to say."

"Yes," she agreed, understandably in no frame of mind to let him off the hook. "It was."

"Again, I apologize." He turned, nodding to a man on the other side of the room. "I thought," he said, sliding her a sideways glance, "you'd be dancing with Rycroft."

Her profile remained impassive. "No," she said without looking at him. "Wilson doesn't really like to dance. He'll take a turn once in a while, but he really prefers to talk business." She lifted her glass of champagne, gesturing to the subject of their conversation. "As you see."

"Not very romantic of him."

For some reason, that made her laugh. "Says the man whose fiancée is dancing with someone else right now."

He laughed, too. "Fair point. Pam adores dancing, so she latched on to the best dancer in the room immediately, and I was happy to let her."

She tilted her head, studying him. "And you're not the least bit jealous?"

That, he almost blurted out, would imply passion. "Over a dance?" he said instead. "Hardly. I'm not that sort of man."

"Unlike Wilson."

"I didn't say that."

"But you were thinking it. The truth is," she added before he could admit or try to deny her accusation, "I don't much like dancing, either. So, you see?" She lifted her chin, and a hint of defiance shimmered in her eyes. "Wilson not dancing with me doesn't bother me in the least."

"You don't like to dance?" he said in surprise. "You seemed…" He paused, self-preservation warring with curiosity. "You seemed so keen on it whenever we danced."

"That was diff—" She broke off, but not before an odd sensation struck him—a feeling of triumph, and pleasure, and something else, something he couldn't quite define, something sweet and painful that he hadn't felt in about fourteen years.

"That was a long time ago," she said after a moment.

"Not so very long." He drew a deep breath. "I still vividly remember that night at Lady Rowland's ball."

"Devlin," she began, but he cut her off.

"I remember thinking how much I hate balls. And then," he added, clearly determined to be a glutton for punishment, "I saw you."

Her lips parted as if his words surprised her. He didn't know why they should, for with her, he always felt as transparent as glass. He stared at her mouth, and before he knew it, he was thinking of another ball from that London season.

It had been at the Marquess of Harrington's villa in Chiswick, he remembered, down by the river. He'd found her on the terrace, catching a bit of air, and when she'd turned, looking at him in the moonlight, he'd felt the earth shift beneath him. Without a word, without even a conscious thought, he'd taken her hand and led her down the terrace steps and into the garden. There, beside a fountain in the center of the boxwood maze, the gardenia scent of her hair filling his senses, he'd kissed her for the first time, and his fate had been sealed.

"Aw, hell," he muttered helplessly. "Kay."

She stiffened, pokering up at once. "You talk as if you don't like dancing," she said, a slight hint of desperation entering in her voice that told him she was feeling, at least a little, what he felt.

He forced himself to reply. "I don't, usually. It depends."

"On what?"

He stared at her lips, parted, full, and pale pink in the candle glow, and a slow burn began in his body. "On the partner."

"And Lady Pamela is not that partner?"

He lifted his gaze to hers. "No."

The moment the word was out of his mouth, he wanted to take it back, but it was too late for regrets on that score. "Pam and I are not madly in love, if that's what you're thinking. To quote you," he added, "I'm very fond of Pam, and she's very fond of me."

If he had hoped she'd display some hint of feeling—relief or pleasure or something like that—he was disappointed.

Her expression remained impassive. "I see."

"The truth is," he said slowly, thinking how to explain when he didn't quite understand it himself, "Pamela and I are both in this marriage for reasons that don't have anything to do with true love."

"What reasons?"

"Pam's mother is a lot like your parents. She doesn't approve of her daughter marrying me. Not because I can't support her, because I have plenty of money to support a wife nowadays."

"Why then?"

"Position. She feels that the fifth son of an inconsequential baron isn't much of a catch. Unlike you, however, Pam doesn't care two straws what her parents think. She wants to annoy her mother, so she adores the idea of marrying someone Lady Walston doesn't approve of. It adds tremendously to my appeal."

"And her father? Doesn't he have to agree, since she's not yet twenty-one?"

"That was an easy thing to manage. I told you, Walston's broke, and when I presented him with a very lucrative marriage settlement, he was happy to give both his permission and his blessing. So you see?" he added when she didn't reply. "Pam is not, by any stretch of the imagination, in love with me."

"And you?" She tilted her head, studying him with those strange, magical eyes. "If it's not love, what is your reason for marrying her?"

Just now, looking at Kay with memories of all their past kisses throbbing through every cell of his brain and his body, his reason seemed completely futile. "Escape."

Realizing he'd said too much, he turned to go, but her voice followed him as he walked away.

"But what are you escaping?"

He stopped. He tilted his head back, staring at the ceiling, not daring to look at her. If he made that mistake, if he turned and looked at her, he wouldn't be able to resist answering her question, and what good would that do?

He was marrying someone else, and so was she. Telling her the truth would be stupid and pointless, so instead, he resumed walking away, saying nothing, working to hang on to what little shreds of self-respect he had left.

11

Escape.

Kay didn't know what to make of Devlin's enigmatic comment, but for the rest of the evening, the word stayed with her, whispering in her ear as she mingled with the other guests, and echoing in her head late that night as she lay awake in bed, staring at the ceiling.

He was marrying Lady Pamela for escape. Escape from what?

She understood the desire for escape, of course. Hadn't she, honestly, agreed to elope all those years ago in order to do that very thing? To escape, to run away from home? Looking back with the benefit of hindsight, she was forced to admit that the prospect of getting away from her parents' stifling control had added to the allure of the whole thing. Africa had promised escape. Only in Birmingham had she stopped to consider the ramifications of what she was doing. She hadn't wanted to live in Africa, not really. She hadn't wanted to be thousands of miles from her home, and she certainly hadn't wanted to disgrace her family or disappoint them.

All that was true, and yet perhaps all that was just an attempt to rationalize the fact that her courage had failed her. Perhaps that was why Devlin teasing her about being a rabbit rankled so much. She'd thought of what elopement would mean—her reputation, her parents' disappointment, the gossip and the scandal, the cost to her sister—and her courage had failed her.

Well, if that was true, she thought crossly, she'd paid the price for losing her nerve. She'd paid in spades.

She'd thought, of course, that Devlin would stay, too. That he'd remain by her side, and they'd stand together against her father. The fact that he'd left without her had been a wound that had shaken her faith in him to the core, a wound that even her love had not been able to overcome, a wound that, even after all this time, still hurt.

She knew now that his reason for taking the money had been to build a future for them and that her parents had wrecked everything, but though she didn't blame Devlin anymore, the pain remained. A part of her still felt that he should have stayed. Together, they could have found another way.

In the distance, she heard the grandfather clock in the corridor chime three o'clock, and she groaned, grabbed her spare pillow, and rolled onto her side.

Hugging her pillow tight, she reminded herself that none of this mattered. In three weeks she was getting married to a man who she knew would never abandon her. She knew it because Wilson never relinquished anything that belonged to him.

That, Kay realized, biting her lip as she stared into the darkness beyond her bed, wasn't much comfort.

Do you really want to live your life letting a second man dictate to you where you'll go and what you'll do?

Devlin's question was a pointless one. But despite that fact, the question continued to echo through her brain like a relentless drumbeat, and it wasn't until dawn was breaking that Kay was able to silence it enough to fall asleep.

She woke about half past ten, unrefreshed and oddly restless. The day's program of croquet, badminton, and other lawn games, she discovered when she went downstairs for breakfast, had been canceled due to the misty rain falling outside. The men, who didn't seem to mind the dreary dampness, had gone fishing, much to Kay's relief. Having spent most of the night plagued by thoughts of Devlin and Wilson, she was quite glad to have a respite from both men.

Delia had planned an afternoon of charades and other parlor games for the ladies, but being cooped up in the house with her mother and Lady Pamela all day proved to be a trial to her nerves as well. Her troubled mood did not improve through dinner, for every time she looked down the table and met Devlin's thoughtful gaze or watched Lady Pamela listening rapturously to Wilson's explanations of Wall Street finance, she felt troubled and agonized and uncertain all over again.

Thankfully, no one seemed to notice her preoccupation. No one, of course, except Devlin, who brought her a glass of champagne after dinner and bestowed it on her, along with a penny and a bow.

She looked down at the gleaming disc of copper he'd just placed in her palm, and she laughed. "They're hardly worth it," she objected, looking up.

"No?" He tilted his head, his gaze roaming over her face. "I don't believe that for a second."

Her laughter faded away, her throat went dry, and she downed a swallow of champagne, working to don an indifferent air.

"Well, penny or not," she managed at last, "I'm not sharing my thoughts with you. But thank you for the champagne. That was kind."

He shrugged. "I was pouring some for myself and noticed you didn't have any, so I brought you some."

She held the penny out to him, but he shook his head. "Keep it. That way," he added as she moved to tuck the coin into the slit side pocket of her teal green evening gown, "I can call in the debt later."

For no reason she could identify, her fingers fumbled, and the penny slipped free. It dropped to the floor, bouncing off the carpet onto the hardwood floor and rolling away.

"Hmm," he said as they watched it disappear under a nearby cabinet, "it appears your thoughts are safe." He looked up, smiling a little. "Much to my regret."

She froze, her champagne glass halfway to her lips, as a sharp, sweet sensation suddenly pierced her chest, the same sharp, exquisite mix of delight and agony that she'd felt as a girl whenever he'd looked at her with those stunning turquoise eyes.

Feeling again like that shy, tongue-tied wallflower, she stared at him, the heat of a blush washing up into her face, her mind giving her the same frantic, desperate plea of long ago.

Don't just stand there gawping. Say something, you fool.

Fortunately, a voice intervened before she had to think of something.

"Devlin? Are you playing or not?"

Still looking at her, he didn't seem to hear, and in the silence that followed, Kay managed to find her voice. "I believe your fiancée is calling for you."

"Hmm?" He shook his head as if coming out of a daze. "I beg your pardon?"

She gave a nod across the room. "You're needed to make a fourth for bridge, it seems."

He turned to where Lady Pamela was seated at one of the card tables, along with Wilson and Delia.

"Of course. If you will forgive me?" He bowed again and moved away, but when Pamela put a proprietary hand on his arm and said something that made him laugh, Kay decided it was much too stuffy in the drawing room. She downed the rest of her champagne, set aside her glass, and went through the French doors to the terrace.

The damp spring air was intoxicatingly crisp and cool, a welcome relief to her flushed skin. It wasn't raining now and the moon was out, so Kay descended the terrace steps to the garden. She started along one of the flagstone paths, but her steps faltered almost immediately, more memories assaulting her at the sight of the boxwood maze.

Hastily, she changed direction and took a different course along a path flanked by lilac trees, breathing deeply of their heady fragrance, reminding herself that she wasn't a shy wallflower anymore. She wasn't, she told herself as she strode through paths of moonlit white roses, an innocent girl enthralled by a pair of turquoise eyes and the promise of escape.

By the time she had circled the entire rose garden and started back along the path of lilacs, she felt as if she'd regained her equilibrium. She was back in the present and ready to embrace the future—a future as a bride, a wife, and a mother. Her bout of cold feet, she concluded with relief, was over.

Fate, however, seemed inclined to test her on that point, for as she reached the terrace, she saw Wilson standing there, watching as she approached.

His back was to the lighted house, but the moonlight shining across his face showed that he was not in an agreeable mood, and Kay could only hope that his displeasure was not directed at her. She was in a better mood now than she'd been in all day, and she didn't want it ruined. The last thing she needed was another sleepless night.

"There you are," Wilson said as she started up the terrace steps. "I've been looking for you everywhere."

Of course you have, she thought as she ascended the terrace steps, suppressing a sigh. "I needed some air," she said.

"I daresay." He moved aside as she stepped onto the terrace. "Anyone would need air at this point. I knew it would happen," he added before she could ask what he meant by his previous remark. "I knew it was a mistake to let you come to this damned party."

Kay could have pointed out that he'd had the chance to prevent this circumstance, but she refrained. She also shoved down the hint of irritation that rose in her at how easily he assumed authority over her, reminding herself that she was not in a position to dispute it, as she herself had reminded Devlin not long ago.

"Well, it's done now," she said instead. "Nothing to be done now but get through it."

"Oh, I don't know about that," Wilson said grimly, staring out over the darkened garden beyond the terrace. "I'm thinking the best thing is to send you back to London on the morning train before that scoundrel has the chance to pull any more of his tricks."

As to the identity of the scoundrel in question, there could be no doubt, but though Wilson's description of Devlin was identical to what her own opinion had been just seven weeks ago, she just couldn't view him in that light anymore. It had been easy to blame him for everything before she'd heard his side of it. Now she knew it wasn't quite as clear-cut as she'd once believed, and he wasn't the blackguard she'd painted him to be.

She had no intention of telling Wilson any of that, however. "Tricks?" she repeated. "What tricks? I'm not sure what you mean."

Wilson gave an impatient snort. "Don't be obtuse, Kay," he said, turning toward her. "Last night, the minute my back was turned, he made a beeline for you. His own fiancée had to dance with someone else, poor girl."

"That's not quite how it was," she began, but Wilson cut off her attempt to set him straight.

"He's been doing this sort of thing all weekend. Staring at you through tea, and through dinner, drooling over you, pining away—"

"Pining?" she interrupted, and made a scoffing sound at such ludicrous accusations. It was obvious that Wilson's innate jealousy was making him imagine things. And yet, as absurd as it was, she nonetheless relished the idea a little. Truth be told, after the years she'd spent in Wales pining over Devlin, she rather liked the notion of the shoe being on the other foot, even if it was all a fantasy concocted in Wilson's imagination.

"You know he was, Kay. He keeps going out of his way to speak with you at every opportunity."

"Well, it is a house party, Wilson," she said. "You know how these things work. We are all expected to spend some amount of time speaking with the other guests. It would be rather a sad and dreary house party if we didn't speak to each other, don't you think?"

This very reasonable point was ignored.

"The minute we came through to the drawing room after dinner," Wilson went on, "there he was, by your side, being so solicitous and bringing you champagne. Who does he think he is, the damned butler?"

"Oh, for—" Kay stopped, biting back an impatient retort. "He was pouring champagne for himself and he noticed I didn't have any," she said in a more moderate tone. "He knows I'm fond of champagne, so he brought me some. That's all there was to it."

"He was panting over you like a dog, and with his own fiancée right there in the room, so don't make excuses for him, especially when your own conduct hasn't been much better."

All Kay's efforts to regain her equilibrium went to the wall. "My conduct?" she repeated. "My conduct?"

"Yes, Kay. Your conduct. Don't pretend you don't bear some responsibility. We agreed you would steer clear of him, and yet, every time I look up, there he is, popping up like a bad penny. And there you are, encouraging him."

"What?" she cried. The idea was so bizarre that she laughed, even as a cautionary voice inside her head warned her to guard her tongue. "That's absurd."

"Is it?" He glanced down over her. "That gown you're wearing is hardly meant to keep a man at bay."

She stared at him, her mother's words echoing through her head.

Wilson prefers the satin... he told me quite clearly that he wanted to be kept informed of all the wedding plans...

All the misgivings that had been keeping Kay awake at night came roaring back, along with Devlin's question.

Do you really want to live your life letting a second man dictate to you where you'll go and what you'll do?

She forced herself to say something. "This is merely the latest fashion. I'm not wearing it to entice Devlin Sharpe, believe me."

"No? All weekend, every time I look for you, I see you with him, your heads together, talking, laughing."

"Laughing?" She stared at him, beginning to think perhaps the man she was about to marry was a bit touched in the head. "What are you saying? That I'm not supposed to laugh, even when a man says something amusing?"

"You know what I mean, Kay. I expect my future bride to behave with some degree of decorum, and that means not flaunting your breasts and cozying up in a corner with the very man who ruined you, laughing at his jokes. What the hell were you thinking?"

"This is becoming ridiculous!" she cried, turning toward him, her own temper fraying at this unjustified and completely unreasonable attack. "Ever since we saw him at the opera supper, you've been hovering over me like a hen with one chick. You assume authority over my schedule, my friends, my amusements, and even how I dress. Even my wedding gown needed to be approved by you. Don't deny it," she added as he opened his mouth. "My mother already let it slip that she's keeping you informed of everything I decide. And, as if all that's not enough control for you, you're now dictating when I'm allowed to laugh?"

"Stop it, Kay. Now you're talking like a shrew."

"Am I?" she countered. "Perhaps that's because I don't appreciate being scolded and criticized and told what to do, as if I'm a child."

"Not a child," he corrected. "A future wife. And a husband, as you know, is fully entitled to order, and a wife is expected to obey. It's even in the wedding vows."

"But as you said, that's in the future. So I would appreciate it if you would refrain from behaving like a jealous, dictatorial husband until we're actually married."

In the light that spilled through the windows onto the terrace, she could see anger rising in his eyes, warning her that she was on very thin ice. When he spoke, his words confirmed the fact.

"Tread lightly, Kay," he said, his voice low and cold with anger, "or we may not marry at all. And then what will you do? How," he added as her insides twisted with sudden alarm, "will you pay your family's debts then?"

Placate him, she thought with a jolt of desperation. *Pour oil on the troubled waters. Apologize.*

She looked up, meeting his eyes, shoving down fear. "It's not your place to decide these things, Wilson," she said as if he hadn't spoken, her voice surprisingly calm given that her stomach was in knots.

"Not my place?" he echoed, his voice rising, warning Kay she was going too far, but she knew she could not stand down, or this would happen again. And again.

The more things change...

"It's not for you to choose my gowns, my schedule, or my friends," she said evenly. "I will decide these things for myself, and you will just have to trust me."

She turned to go, but suddenly, Wilson's hand snaked out, grabbing her by the wrist to stop her.

"Don't turn your back on me," he said, swinging her around,

tightening his grip when she tried to pull free. "Don't ever turn your back on me."

She was given no chance to reply.

"Let her go."

"You," Wilson muttered, keeping Kay's wrist locked in his grip. "I should have known you'd be sneaking about, looking to make trouble."

"I do adore trouble, I confess," Devlin answered, but though his voice was light and careless, Kay knew there was danger beneath it. "Let her go, or you'll have more of it than you can handle."

"Devlin," Kay began, striving to resolve the situation before it could get out of hand, but Wilson forestalled any attempt to make peace.

"This is none of your business, Sharpe," he said, looking past Kay's shoulder to give Devlin a hard stare that most men would have wilted under. "My fiancée and I were having a private conversation. Get out of here."

Devlin merely laughed. "No, I don't believe I will. I don't leave women to be manhandled by other men."

"I'm quite all right, Devlin," she said. "There's no need—"

"The one who needs to leave, Mr. Rycroft," Devlin cut her off mid-sentence, "is you. I suggest you let go of Kay and return to the party of your own accord. Otherwise, I shall have to make you do so."

"Threats of violence aren't surprising from a cad like you, I suppose."

"Not in the least," Devlin agreed. "I'm an absolute savage. Don't make me prove it."

Much to Kay's relief, Wilson's hands fell to his sides. "Come with me, Kay. We'll finish this conversation inside. In private."

He took a step toward the door, but when he noticed she was not following him, he stopped.

"Kay?" he said and held out his hand. "Come along."

She stared at his outstretched hand for a moment, then she looked up, met the cold anger in his eyes, and decided further argument tonight was something neither of them would want.

Slowly, she shook her head. "I think it's best if we resume our discussion on this topic another day, Wilson. We're both angry just now. It's only a few weeks until the wedding," she added, her voice as reasonable and conciliatory as she could make it, "and I should hate for either of us to say anything foolish in the heat of the moment, things that we might regret later. Best to give each other a bit of time to cool our tempers and regain our composure."

His jaw jutted forward, but to her relief, he didn't argue the matter. "Very well. But this is not over, Kay. We will discuss this again. Without an audience."

If his expression was anything to go by, that discussion would not be any more pleasant than this stupid argument had been, but she didn't say so. Instead, she nodded. "Of course."

Wilson bowed, and without another word, he turned on his heel and walked away.

"It seems my arrival was timely," Devlin murmured, watching the other man enter the house.

"I'm not so sure," she said, rubbing her sore wrist as she watched Wilson cross the terrace and reenter the house. "Your arrival has probably made everything worse. Wilson was right. I should never have come to this house party. What brought you out here anyway? I thought you were playing bridge."

"So I am. I'm dummy for this rubber, so I came out for some air. It's a good thing I did, too," he added, his gaze falling to her hands. "Are you all right?"

At once, Kay jerked her hands down. "Of course I'm all right," she said lightly. "Why wouldn't I be?"

He said nothing. He merely looked at her, something almost sad in his face, and Kay stiffened, looking away. She didn't need his pity. "Thank you for your concern," she said, working to keep her voice even, "but I'm perfectly all right."

The moment the words were out of her mouth, she almost grimaced. Of all the lies she'd been telling herself of late, that was probably the biggest one of all.

Devlin seemed to know it, too. His next words proved the fact. "Tell that one to the marines."

She gave up on pretense. With Devlin, it seemed to be useless. "I am a bit...muddled up, I confess." She made a rueful face. "For that, I blame you."

He smiled a little. "I'd say I'm sorry about that, but then I'd be the one lying."

"The truth is..." She paused and faced him. "Wilson has been showing this obsessive jealousy for weeks, and it's starting to set my teeth on edge. That's why, I suppose," she added, thinking it out as she spoke, "I didn't agree when he ordered me to stay away from you. I was angry."

"Kay, you aren't blaming yourself because he behaved like a lout, are you?"

"He didn't—" She broke off as Devlin raised an eyebrow, daring her to deny Wilson's conduct. "I'm not blaming myself. But it's undeniable that I could have avoided this argument with him tonight, and I didn't. In a strange way, I wanted it. I don't really know why. To test him, perhaps? To take a stand and see what he'd do in response? I don't know. But it was foolish."

"Perhaps it's much simpler than that. Perhaps you did it because you don't really want to marry him, and you're looking for a way out."

"We've already discussed this," she reminded, in no mood to rehash it again. "There is no way out."

To her relief, Devlin didn't try to debate the point.

"And anyway," she went on, "he's only being this way because of you." Even as she said it, she thought of Wilson following her across Yorkshire last autumn, and her words seemed more like wishful thinking than truth. Devlin's return may have made things worse, but there had been signs of Wilson's possessive, acquisitive nature from the very beginning. It might very well continue, even after their marriage was a fait accompli. Either way, however, it would serve no purpose to discuss any of it, especially with Devlin.

"It's true that jealousy can bring out the worst in a man," he said as she fell silent. "I know that well enough. But if I'm what brought this on, then why did he invest in the Mayfair? He knew—he must have known—I was an investor, too."

She decided not to get into the weeds by bringing up Wilson's desire for connections to the Duke of Westbourne and Lord Calderon. Instead, she shrugged. "It's clear he thinks it will be a lucrative investment, and things like that are important to Wilson. He never turns down a chance to make money. That's how he got so rich. And I don't think he thought you'd ever be directly involved. After all, you live in Africa."

"That's probably it. No doubt he'll be happy to see the back of me when I go, and with any luck, that'll be the end of it. I hope so, at any rate," he added, giving her a meaningful glance. "For your sake, Kay, I hope so."

At this confirmation of her own apprehensions, Kay shivered, misgivings dancing over her skin.

"But," he added when she didn't reply, "will it be the end of it?"

Slowly, gently, he picked up her hand, his thumb caressing her wrist through her glove in the very place Wilson had gripped her so tightly.

Kay shivered again, a feeling that had nothing at all to do with her fiancé or her fears of the future.

"If my departure isn't the end of it, Kay, what then?"

She stirred. "I should go."

At once, Devlin opened his hand.

Pull away, she ordered herself, staring at her wrist resting on his open palm. *Go inside*.

She didn't move.

"When I came out here," he murmured, "and I saw him grab you and refuse to let go, do you know what I thought?"

"No," she whispered, lifting her face, meeting his eyes in the moonlight. "What did you think?"

"I thought I'd have to break his arm to free you. I was almost looking forward to the prospect."

Warmth flooded through her, an odd feeling given the violence of his rhetoric. She parted her lips to reply, but no words came out. She didn't know what to say.

His lashes, long, opulent, and midnight black, lowered as he looked down, his gaze homing in on her lips.

Kay's heart slammed hard into her ribs, robbing her of breath, and she tensed. He seemed to feel it, for he stirred, letting her hand fall, then slowly, ever so slowly, he moved closer.

"I should go in," she said again, her voice strangled and desperate to her own ears.

"Yes," he agreed, but he didn't move.

Sadly, she couldn't seem to find the will to follow her own advice. "We should both go in," she said instead, a rather craven attempt to put all the responsibility on him, to get him to do what she could not find the strength to do herself. "We really should."

For some unfathomable reason, that made him laugh softly under his breath, his teeth dazzling white in the moonlight.

"Why are you laughing?"

"Hell, Kay," he said as he leaned closer to her, "when have you and I ever done what we should?"

"Never," she admitted with a sigh. "What did you—"

She broke off in the midst of her question, the same question that had been nagging at her for the past twenty-four hours. But though she was sure she was probably going to regret asking, she could not resist. "What did you mean the other night when you said you were marrying Lady Pamela for escape?" she whispered. "What are you escaping from?"

Still smiling a little, he put his hand on the side of her waist, then slowly, ever so slowly, giving her plenty of time to draw back, he slid his arm around her. "My fate."

She frowned, too aware of his touch to make sense of his reply. "What do you mean? What fate?"

"You, Kay," he muttered, his free hand sliding up her back to the nape of her neck, his thumb pressing beneath her chin to lift her face. "I mean you."

With that, he bent his head and kissed her.

The touch of his lips sent Kay hurtling backward in time and space, out of a garden folly in Berkshire to a ball in Chiswick, where Devlin had taken her hand, led her into a boxwood maze, and given her the first kiss of her life.

Devlin, she thought with a jolt of the same frantic yearning she'd felt for him in her youth. This was Devlin—his mouth, his embrace, his hard, strong body, blotting fourteen years of loneliness, shame, and disgrace from her mind as if they had never happened.

Suddenly, she was eighteen again, running out to meet him in the dark, with her heart beating like a mad thing, coming into his arms with exaltation and joy surging through her veins, returning his kiss willingly as burning, uncontrollable desire coursed through her body. In his arms, she wasn't a chubby, freckle-faced social failure or a ruined, dried-up spinster. She was beautiful, desirable, wanted.

It was glorious.

His mouth opened, urging hers to do the same, and when she parted her lips, the arm he had around her waist tightened, urging her even closer. Willingly, eagerly, she came, her hands slid up his chest and into his hair as she rose on her toes, pressing her body to his.

Against her mouth, he groaned, and she reveled in the sound, raking her fingers through the thick, unruly strands, tasting his kiss with all the abandon of the girl she'd been.

But then, his hips stirred against hers, and she felt the hardness of him. She jerked as if he burned, striving for sanity.

In less than a month, she was getting married, and not to the man holding her in his arms, but to a man whose one and only kiss had felt nothing like this, a man who did not evoke desire in her body and wreak havoc in her soul. A man who would never be able to break her heart.

She tore her mouth from his. "We can't do this, Devlin," she gasped. "It's madness."

"Absolute madness," he agreed, his arm tightening around her waist, his free hand caressing the nape of her neck. Suddenly, his fingers cupped the back of her head, and before she could reply, he recaptured her mouth, sending desire coursing throughout her body. She rose on her toes and wrapped her arms around his neck, relishing this kiss, glorying in it, and sanity floated away on the spring breeze like so much flotsam.

She'd forgotten, she realized as she raked her hands through his hair, what desire felt like. But Devlin was making her remember, in the taste of his mouth and the hard feel of his body pressed to hers.

How, she wondered wildly. How on earth could she ever have forgotten this?

"What is going on here?"

The sound of that demanding feminine voice was like a bucket of ice water being dumped on her head, shocking her out of her euphoric haze. Devlin must have felt the same, for he broke the kiss, lifted his head, and swore.

Kay opened her eyes and felt another jolt of shock at the sight of Devlin's grim countenance. He was looking past her at the doorway, and when she turned her head in that direction, she found herself staring into the beautiful, horrified face of Lady Pamela Stirling.

Making things worse, the girl was not alone. Wilson stood behind her, staring past her shoulder. As his eyes met Kay's, she saw his lips press together in a tight line and his expression turn cold, so cold that a shiver ran down Kay's back.

Oh, no, she thought, sick with dismay as she realized what they must have just witnessed. *Oh, no, no, no.*

Confirming that realization, Lady Pamela's face crumpled, she let out a sob, pressed her hand over her mouth, and turned away.

Wilson moved sideways to let her pass, then he looked at Kay, and with that look, she knew there would be no discussions, no reconciliations, and probably no wedding.

He said nothing, however. Instead, he turned without a word and followed the girl back into the house.

Kay stared at the empty doorway, watching the carefully constructed new life she'd tried to build crumbling into ruins all around her as the ramifications of tonight's events sank more deeply into her consciousness. Her sister's season and prospects—and possibly even her entire future—in jeopardy. Her mother living in poverty and debt. And herself, unmarried and childless, going through a lifetime of regret over the fact that for the second time in her life she'd allowed Devlin Sharpe to wreck her life.

She was an idiot. And he was a dog.

"Kay?"

At the sound of Devlin's voice, she turned toward him with a groan. "Why?" she cried in despair. She stepped back, tearing herself free, staring up at him through a blur of frustrated tears. "Why do you have to keep ruining my life? And why do I keep letting you?"

"Kay," he said again and took a step toward her, lifting his hands as if to touch her.

The move sent her momentary self-pity to the wall and galvanized her into furious action. "Don't," she ordered, flattening a palm against his chest to stop him. "Don't come any closer."

To her relief, he complied, coming to a halt, letting his hands fall to his side without a word.

"Stay away from me, Devlin," she ordered fiercely, even as her voice broke. "Just stay the hell away from me. Or I swear, I'll shoot you dead like the cur you are."

With that, she stepped around him and strode toward the door into the house without a backward glance.

12

Devlin watched Kay walk away, the hem of her teal green dress and the white petticoats beneath churning behind her with the force of her strides like turbulent ocean waves, her angry words still ringing in his ears.

She was right, of course. By any standards of gentlemanly conduct, he was a cur. He'd been flaying himself for days with what he'd done to wreck her life in the past, and yet, given the chance, he'd just done it again in the present.

In the space of about fifteen minutes, he'd ruined Kay's prospects, betrayed his own fiancée, and cuckolded another man, and he ought to feel guilty as hell about all that.

But, sadly, he didn't.

His father had always called him the devil's spawn, and perhaps he was, because his body was burning like hellfire, lust was raging through his veins, and despite how strongly he reminded himself of how abhorrent his conduct had been, he just couldn't work up the proper amount of regret over it.

That might be due in part to the fact that no hearts had been broken tonight. Love, as he well knew, had played no part in Kay's engagement to Rycroft nor his to Pam. And, thankfully, there had been no witnesses to carry the embarrassing news of what had happened tonight to the poisonous pens of London's gossipmongers.

None of that excused him, of course, and there would be repercussions for what he'd done, painful repercussions he would need to face and atone for to whatever extent was possible.

First, he needed to see Pam and apologize. Whether she'd accept it or not was open to question, for Pam had a considerable amount of pride, and he'd just shredded it to ribbons, so she might not see her way clear to forgiving him. She might very well end the engagement, but even if she didn't end it, he would have to do so.

A man was not supposed to break an engagement, but Devlin knew he could not marry Pam now. The illusions he'd held about how his life could be had been shattered tonight. There was no going back.

A few months ago, he'd felt sure he was ready to settle down, sure enough time had passed that he could finally build a future with someone who was not Kay.

But one taste of Kay's mouth had shown him just how thoroughly he'd been deceiving himself. Being free of her, he realized grimly, was a mirage. He could cross the world a dozen times, another fourteen years could pass, and yet he knew now that one thing would always remain the same. From the moment he'd seen Kay's silvery green eyes look at him across that ballroom floor so long ago, she'd captured his heart and sealed his fate. Kay was his destiny, and there was no escape from that.

His way forward now was crystal clear, but there was one gigantic problem.

He turned, staring through the French doors to the drawing

room, thinking again of Kay's anguished questions and angry departure, and he very much feared they did not have the same view about destiny.

Kay had no opportunity to speak to Wilson that evening. Not that she had any idea what she could have said to him given the shameless scene he'd just witnessed, a scene that had only confirmed that his jealousy had not been completely unreasonable. He deprived her, however, of the opportunity to say anything at all, for upon her return to the drawing room, she learned that he had retired for the night. Lady Pamela, too, had gone to bed, and after the mortifying events of the evening, who could blame her? Who could blame either of them?

Following their example, Kay also went to bed, but that did her little good. For the second night in a row, she found herself devastatingly wide awake, fuming, fretting, and staring at the ceiling, though for very different reasons.

Last night, she'd been plagued by doubts about her upcoming wedding, but if the look on Wilson's face tonight was anything to go by, there very well might not be a wedding, and with the acknowledgment of that possibility came not only the remorse of having subjected two innocent people to a humiliating spectacle, but also gut-wrenching fear, the same fear she'd experienced right after learning that Papa had left the family destitute.

If Wilson broke with her over this, she wouldn't blame him one bit, and if he did, she knew what would happen next. The bank that had been loaning her money based on her expectations would cut her off the moment her broken engagement became public knowledge, and they would demand repayment of what had already been borrowed. The Savoy would, understandably, kick them out of their rooms. They'd have to leave London, putting an end to Josephine's season before it had really begun.

Kay knew her own situation would be even more dismal. At best, another broken engagement would subject her to a fresh round of gossip and speculation. Worse, if Wilson or Lady Pamela chose to relay the events they had witnessed to anyone else, and the news spread, Kay would once again be deemed a strumpet. If that happened, Kay's past sins would come back to haunt her, and she doubted any amount of time and effort would rehabilitate her this time. She'd probably never mingle in society again. And that would put the lid on Josephine's marital hopes as well. Few men wanted a penniless girl and a disgraced sister-in-law. And even if such a paragon existed, how could Jo ever meet him? Without a season, carted across the country from hotel to hotel every few weeks, the prospects for the girl would be dim, especially if they were forced to go abroad.

And what about her mother? Some might say Magdelene didn't deserve any consideration after what she'd done to ruin Kay's chances years ago, but Kay, sadly, just couldn't work up the proper rage for such a view. She'd been driven to be desperate enough to marry a man for financial security, and despite Magdelene's deceit, Kay could not find it in herself to condemn her parent for having similar motives.

And Magdelene was no more capable of finding a way out of the mess now than she'd been a year ago, which put Kay right back in the same predicament she'd been in last summer: she had a mother and sister to provide for and very few options for how to do it.

Still, all was not lost, not yet anyway. First, she had to see Wilson, talk with him, try to explain what had happened.

But on the heels of that thought came the inevitable question, the one that made going to Wilson not only exceedingly difficult but probably futile as well. Yes, Devlin had behaved abominably. Yes, he had defied all rules of decorum and kissed her. But what had she done?

Had she wrenched free? Had she shouted for help? Had she even expressed the proper maidenly outrage and given him the resounding slap across the face he'd deserved?

No. Sadly, she'd done none of those things. She hadn't done a thing to ward off his advances, nor had she expressed a shred of outrage about them. She had, in point of fact, done the exact opposite. She'd kissed him back.

Suddenly, memories of that kiss overwhelmed her—the feel of his arms around her, of his hard, strong body pressed so intimately against hers, the taste of his mouth, the hunger of wanting him, and the heady delight of knowing he wanted her.

She'd forgotten, she realized. She'd forgotten all that. In the wake of his departure, in the certainty of his betrayal, she'd forgotten how his kiss had always made her feel. Her breath quickened, and she closed her eyes, her muscles tightening, her blood heating, her body aching with need she only vaguely understood. All of that had been pushed away, stored so deeply in her memory that she'd forgotten it was there at all. Until that kiss on the terrace had reawakened it.

Kay jerked her eyes open and rolled over with a groan, pressing her flushed face into the pillow and covering her head with the counterpane as she recalled in hot chagrin the entire humiliating episode. How she had slid her arms around his neck and returned his kiss with all the same heedless, willing passion she'd felt for him as a girl. How she'd raked her hands through his hair, glorying in the taste of his mouth and the feel of his hard body pressed against hers. Hell, she thought, grimacing as she touched her fingertips to her still-burning lips. Even now, she felt the imprint of his kiss like a searing brand.

No, she thought, anguished, there was no denying her own culpability. She'd returned Devlin's kiss with willing and wanton abandon, and she had relished every second of it.

Wilson, no doubt, had seen that for himself, so there was nothing to explain and no excuses to offer.

Still, despite that awful, nauseating fact, Kay knew one thing.

She flung back the counterpane, took a deep breath, and turned onto her back. She had to face her fiancé, apologize, and take her lumps. It might not work, he might not take her back, but she had to try.

After all, what other choice did she have?

For the second night in a row, Kay got almost no sleep, but upon rising the following morning, she at least felt better able to face Wilson than she had the night before. As she dressed, she went over all the things he might say and all the responses she might offer to any questions he might ask or demands he might make, but she invented no excuses, for there were none. She rehearsed no explanations, other than a sincere and heartfelt apology. What would happen after that, she could not begin to fathom.

But Kay had barely journeyed downstairs before Josephine waylaid her at the door to the breakfast room and put paid to any chance Kay had of offering Wilson an apology.

"Psst, Kay," Josephine hissed in a desperate whisper, causing Kay to stop by the door and glance around. "Over here."

Kay turned to find her sister skulking by a pair of enormous potted ferns, clearly waiting for her. When she stepped closer, Jo immediately did the same, grabbing her by the arm and hauling her without any explanations down a corridor, out a side door, and into the kitchen garden.

"What in heaven's name happened last night?" the girl demanded the moment the door had swung shut behind them.

Kay's stomach lurched at the question, but with an effort, she kept her expression neutral. "What do you mean?" she asked, absurdly proud of the nonchalant tone of her voice. "Has something happened?"

"Haven't you heard? Wilson's gone. Calderon's carriage took him to the train station first thing this morning."

So much for allowing her the chance to offer an apology, Kay thought ruefully.

"Cassandra told me," Jo went on when she didn't reply, "that Wilson told Simon a sudden, important business matter had come up, and he had to go back to London at once."

Kay sank down on the top of a low stone wall. "I see."

"There's more," Jo went on, moving to sit beside her. "One of the housemaids told Cassandra's maid that she saw Devlin Sharpe and Lady Pamela out in the garden earlier, and though the girl couldn't hear what was being said, she told Cassandra's maid that Lady Pamela was making an awful fuss—crying and carrying on and clearly very upset. And Sharpe wasn't even comforting her. He didn't embrace her or take her hand or anything. He just looked grim as death, the maid said."

"I'll bet he did," Kay murmured. "So he should."

"Why, what do you mean?" Jo asked. "So you *do* know what happened?"

"I only meant," Kay improvised quickly, "that if his fiancée was crying, of course he'd look grim. Any man would, I daresay."

Jo's face took on a hint of disappointment. "So you don't know anything about it? Could Pamela being upset have something to do with Wilson leaving, I wonder?"

"I don't see how," Kay said, wriggling as she spoke, her conscience smiting her, but thankfully, her sister didn't seem to notice. "I'm sure it's just a coincidence," she added firmly. "If Wilson got word of an important business matter and had to attend to it, then—"

"But that's just it," Josephine cut in. "Cassie and I don't see how that's even possible. The butler told her that no telegrams or letters had come for Wilson, and they're not on the telephone here, so how could any business matter have come up? What did his secretary do, sent him a note by carrier pigeon?"

Kay laughed at that, but it was a laugh tinged with a hint of both relief that facing Wilson had been postponed and dismay that perhaps the reason for his departure was that no apology would matter. She had no chance, however, to reply to her sister's question.

"So, you see?" Jo went on. "Something must have happened last night, or very early this morning. Cassie and I are wondering if Wilson and Sharpe had a set-to about you."

Kay made what she hoped was a convincing scoffing sound.

"Me? How ridiculous. You and Cassandra have clearly been reading too many romantic novels."

"Well, it would explain why Wilson left the party and why Pam is angry with Sharpe. But Calderon told Cassie he didn't know anything about any of it, and if you don't know anything, either, then I don't suppose we'll ever know the truth. Unless you were to ask Wilson about it..."

Jo paused, casting a prompting sideways glance at her, but Kay refused to take the bait.

"I wouldn't dream of doing any such thing," she said and rose to her feet. "Now, if you've finished regaling me with the latest gossip, I shall go in to breakfast."

"You are just no fun," Josephine accused with an exasperated sigh as Kay started back toward the house.

"You have no idea," Kay murmured under her breath, fearing that many things may have been spoiled last night. She could only cross her fingers and pray that her upcoming wedding wasn't about to be one of them.

If Kay had hoped to make her apologies to Wilson upon her return to town and perhaps effect a reconciliation, those hopes were dashed almost at once. Upon inquiring at the front desk of the Savoy, she was told that Mr. Rycroft and his secretary had departed from the hotel, leaving no forwarding address. Making matters worse, he had left her no note, leaving her decidedly in limbo less than a month before the wedding.

The only thing to do, she knew, was to carry on. The wedding invitations had already been sent out, and she couldn't write to all those people and tell them the wedding had been canceled, since she wouldn't know that until she and Wilson had settled things. So she visited Lucile for the final fitting of her dress, approved the flower arrangements she and the Savoy florist had discussed two months ago, confirmed the arrangements with St. Paul's for the ceremony, and discussed the wedding banquet menu with the Duke of Westbourne's London chef. But by the time a week had passed, any hope there might still be a wedding had faded away, for Wilson seemed to have vanished off the face of the earth.

To discover anything at all regarding his whereabouts, Kay was reduced to reading the gossip columns. But though Delilah Dawlish and various other so-called journalists reported that Lady Pamela Stirling and her parents had unexpectedly returned to their estates in Durham, while her fiancé remained in town, none of them conveyed even the tiniest hint about Wilson's whereabouts. It was a full ten days after the house party before Kay discovered what her fiancé had been up to.

"Oh, my God!"

Dumbfounded, she stared at the front page of *Talk of the Town*, and the ghastly headline spread across the top.

This can't be true, she thought, going numb with shock as she read the headline again. *This just can't be true.*

"What is it?" Josephine asked, looking up from her breakfast tray.

Kay didn't bother to reply. Instead, she shoved aside her chair and stood up. "Where's Foster? Is she in with Mama?"

"I don't think so, no," Jo replied as Kay turned away, stopping her in her tracks. "Before you got up, she said she was taking some letters down to post. She'll be back any minute, I imagine. Why?"

Kay handed her the newspaper, then turned away and started for her own room, adding over her shoulder, "You'll have to help me dress. Come on, there's no time to lose."

Without waiting for a reply, she crossed the sitting room and entered their bedroom, Josephine on her heels with the paper in her hands.

"This can't be right," Jo said, looking up as she came to a halt inside their room. "That woman's made a mistake, surely."

Kay was too preoccupied with yanking clothes out of her armoire to reply.

"I mean, she gets things wrong all the time," Jo went on, tossing the paper aside and coming to her side. "You know she does."

Kay had the sick feeling that wasn't going to be the case this time. This time, she feared Delilah Dawlish was very much on the spot. But she didn't express that pessimistic thought aloud. "Just help me dress," she implored, shoving a day dress of lilac-colored silk at her sister and shrugging out of her wrapper.

"Of course," Jo replied, undoing the buttons of the dress as she spoke. "But where are you going? It's terribly early still," she added, glancing at the clock on Kay's mantel. "Not even nine o'clock."

Kay was saved from having to reply by a loud wail that sounded like the mourning cry of a banshee.

The sisters looked at each other. "Mama," they said in unison.

"Delilah Dawlish isn't the only one who's gotten hold of this bit of news apparently," Kay muttered, pulling her nightgown over her head. Tossing it aside, she reached for a pair of lawn knickers and stepped into them. "It's clear the other papers have, too."

Magdelene let out another wail, impelling Jo to ask, "Should I go and comfort her?"

"No," Kay said and pulled a chemise over her head, thrusting her arms into the sleeves. "She doesn't need an audience," she went on, wrapping a corset around her ribs and doing up the hooks. "She's fully capable of having a fit of hysterics all by herself."

Kay was proven wrong about that less than a minute later. Jo had barely finished lacing her into her corset and started doing up the buttons of her dress when their mother came bursting into Kay's room.

"Have you seen the papers?" she demanded. "Have you seen them?"

"Yes, Mama. I have."

"Well?" her mother prompted when she said nothing more. "Did you know about this?"

"Of course I didn't. Jo," she added as her sister fastened the last button at the nape of her neck, "fetch my room key out of my handbag, in case I'm not back before the two of you go to luncheon with Delia."

"But where are you going?" Magdelene asked as Jo departed on this errand.

"Out. I don't know when I'll be back. Please give Delia my excuses."

"Our luncheon with her was to discuss your wedding and what preparations need to be made at Westbourne House." Magdelene began to cry. "What reason can we possibly give her for why you aren't there?"

"I doubt you'll have to invent a reason. Knowing Delia, she's probably already aware of what's happened."

Amazing, she thought as she pulled on her gloves, how calm she sounded when her life was falling apart all around her.

"What happens now?" Magdelene asked, her voice quavering. "They'll boot us out of our rooms, Kay, you know they will. And then where will we live? Oh, dear, oh, dear," she said, bursting into sobs again, "what will happen to me now?"

"Your flair for drama is only exceeded by your self-centeredness, Mama," Kay replied, as she buttoned her gloves.

"Don't get snippy with me, miss," her mother cried. "What would impel Wilson to do this? What did you do to him, Kay?" she added accusingly. "Did you quarrel with him? Nag him? Lose your temper? Oh, Kay, you did, didn't you? And less than a month before the wedding, too. How could you be so careless?"

Kay bit back the sharp retort that hovered on her lips and turned away to retrieve the newspaper from the bed where Jo had tossed it a few minutes earlier.

"I've warned you about your temper," Magdelene went on, following her as she went into the sitting room. "And how much men hate that. A lady never loses her temper."

"I didn't lose my temper. At least, not exactly."

"Well, you must have done something!" her mother wailed. "Otherwise this wouldn't have happened!"

She'd done something all right, she thought grimly. She'd allowed herself to be shamelessly ravished by a blue-eyed devil. Again.

The truth, however, was more than her mother could handle, and she was in no mood to invent lies. Instead, she crossed the sitting room to where Josephine was waiting by the door with her key.

"Thank you, darling," she said. Taking the key, she slipped it into her skirt pocket. "Look after Mama," she added as she opened the door. "Make sure she doesn't get carried away with her role of humiliated mother and hurl herself off the balcony. We are on the fourth floor, after all."

Her mother sniffed at that. "If I did such a thing, it would be no more than you deserve after this latest disgrace. And I don't understand where you could possibly be going."

Kay didn't reply because her mother was hysterical enough already. If she told Magdelene she was going to put her hot temper to good use by invading Devlin Sharpe's hotel room and throttling him within an inch of his life, Mama would probably drop dead of apoplexy on the spot.

Instead, Kay walked out without a word and shut the door behind her.

The knocking on his door woke him, but Devlin decided it was best to ignore it. For one thing, he knew he hadn't rung for room service. It couldn't be his valet, for he hadn't gotten around to hiring one. Nor could it be his now-former fiancée, who wouldn't dream of coming to a man's hotel room, and who wasn't speaking to him anyway.

Upon hearing his apologies for what she had witnessed, his request that they dissolve their engagement, and his heartfelt hope she would one day meet a far better man than he, Pam had burst into tears, unleashed on him a torrent of scathing criticism he completely deserved, tossed his engagement ring in his face, and stalked off, declaring over her shoulder as she departed the garden that he'd pay for this insult to her and her family.

No, he decided as the clock in his sitting room struck nine; it could not be Pam. In fact, the only person his befuddled brain could imagine being at his door this early in the day was Kay. Granted, Kay didn't shy at coming to his hotel room at inconvenient moments, but if her last words to him at the house party were any indication, she was not speaking to him, either.

Not that he'd made any attempt to test that theory. He knew Kay's temper, and he wasn't completely sure that she wouldn't make good on her threat to shoot him if he dared to even appear in her general vicinity. So he'd decided his best move for now was to keep his distance and give her time to cool her fire a bit before he made any attempt to talk with her.

Sadly, keeping his distance hadn't stopped him from thinking about her and the kiss they'd shared. For over a week now, the feel of her in his arms and the glorious taste of her mouth had tormented him, invading his mind, arousing his body, and dominating his dreams. Worse, it was such a sweet torment, he hadn't tried to stop it. Instead, he'd relished it, reliving that kiss in his imagination over and over again.

Nonetheless, after ten days of this self-torture, he'd decided some relief was required, and he'd spent most of last night sampling cocktails in the Savoy's American Bar. After too many Manhattans, martinis, and a few oh-so-aptly named stingers, he'd come back to his room and passed out cold, only to be awakened by this annoying knocking at his door. When the knock came again, he wondered vaguely if there might be a fire. Not that he much cared, for he already felt like death. A herd of elephants seemed to be pounding through his head, his mouth felt as if it were full of cotton wool, and he feared that if he tried to get out of bed, his skull would crack wide open. If he was going to die today, it was best to do it in bed, he decided, and promptly rolled over and drifted back to sleep.

Whoever was at his door, however, proved to have no mercy whatsoever, for the knocking became a constant, relentless drumbeat, and Devlin tossed aside the pillow with the foulest oath he knew. Moving with infinite care, he got out of bed.

He started to reach for his dressing robe, but then realized hazily that he was still dressed, more or less. His shoes and socks were missing, his white tie and collar button were undone, his jacket and pocket watch were on the floor, and his waistcoat buttons were unfastened, but other than that, he was still wearing his evening clothes from last night.

The knocking at his door had not paused. "I'm coming, I'm coming," he called as he raked his hair with his fingers into some sort of order and crossed the sitting room. "For God's sake," he added as he opened the door, "is the hotel on fire? Or—"

He stopped, staring in disbelief at the figure in the corridor.

"Kay?"

He thought he must be dreaming, but almost at once, he dismissed that possibility, since in all his dreams of Kay this week, she had never been wearing this many clothes. Besides, she looked angry enough to spit nails, and she never looked that way in his dreams.

Wondering if his vague half-formed idea of dying on his feet had been prophetic, he glanced down, but thankfully, she wasn't holding a pistol. The only thing in her hand was a rolled-up newspaper, and that wasn't going to do him any damage, even in his present, decidedly fragile condition. Bolstered a bit by his observations, he decided to meet her anger with as nonchalant an air as he could muster. His masculine pride demanded it.

"You again?" he said, managing to keep his voice light, though it took a great deal of effort. "We really have to stop meeting like this, Kay, or people will talk."

"Believe me, they already are." With that, she unrolled the newspaper in her hand with a flick of her wrist, slapped it against his chest, and as he took it, she let it go and pushed past him into the sitting room. "Only they aren't talking about us. Not yet, anyway."

"How refreshing," he said as he closed the door and turned to face her. "Not having our names spread across the scandal sheets is a nice change of pace, I must say."

"You won't think so when you've read the shocking news. Other side," she added as he frowned down uncomprehendingly at an article about the most fashionable hats for Ascot.

He turned the paper over, read the enormous headline at the top of the page, and grimaced.

TWO BIGGEST WEDDINGS OF THE SEASON CANCELED!

"Aw, hell, Kay," he said and looked up. "I know I'm to blame for all of this. Not that I'll be sorry, I confess, if you and Rycroft have called it off, because he wasn't right for you—"

He stopped as her eyes narrowed, and his hazy wits grasped for something better to say. "I know it's going to be embarrassing and difficult for you for a while, and I truly regret that part of it—"

"Embarrassing and difficult?" she cut in, staring at him as if she couldn't believe what she was hearing. "Is that how you'd describe this?"

He frowned in puzzlement, wondering if perhaps the aftereffects of last night's binge were preventing him from a proper understanding of the situation.

"Well, I'm not sure how else to describe it, Kay, to be honest," he said at last, trying to be as tactful as possible. "I don't find this news particularly shocking, at least not from my side of things. I knew Pam would be doing this."

That only seemed to deepen her bewilderment. "You knew?" she said, her voice rising a notch. "You knew and you didn't tell me?"

"Well, you really can't blame me for that, can you?" he asked, managing a weak smile. "You did threaten to shoot me the last time we spoke."

Kay folded her arms, showing she was not amused.

He coughed and tried again. "I haven't had the opportunity to discuss any of this with you as yet, but let me say that it's true that Pam and I have called things off. She was outraged by what she saw that night—"

"Understandably," Kay interrupted, her voice icy.

"Just so," he said hastily. "I spoke with her the morning after it happened, we talked things through, and in the end, by mutual consent, we decided to dissolve our engagement."

"Yes, but, Devlin—"

"Still," he went on, returning to the matter at hand, "I can't imagine how *Talk of the Town* got hold of the news that my wedding's been canceled. Pam would never have told them anything. She hates being the subject of gossip."

"Does she?" There was an odd inflection in Kay's voice that puzzled him. "Does she, indeed?"

"Yes. Granted, she was quite hurt and angry, but even out of spite, she'd never tell the gossip rags anything. And she certainly wouldn't tell a soul she and Rycroft caught us kissing, if that's worrying you. I doubt Rycroft would, either. Both of them are far too proud to ever let it be known that we found each of them less attractive than we found each other."

"Don't you dare speak for me and who I find attractive," she said hotly. "As for that kiss," she added, a wash of pink flooding her cheeks, "there was no 'us' involved. There was only you kissing me."

"Oh, really?" he countered at once. "I seem to remember you flinging your arms around my neck and kissing me back. Rather passionately, in fact."

"I didn't do any flinging," she muttered, tossing her head and confirming his memory hadn't played him false. "And anyway," she added before he could debate the issue further, "that's not the relevant point, for heaven's sake!"

"Then what is? I take it you didn't know your wedding was canceled until you read this drivel? Well," he went on when she shook her head, "it's a hard way to learn that he's breaking off the engagement, I grant you. You could sue him for breach of promise, I suppose, but I doubt you'd win, since—"

He broke off, but she finished his sentence for him. "Since he and Pam both saw you kissing my mouth off?"

"Something like that. Either way," he rushed on, "it's pretty obvious what happened. Rycroft heard about my quarrel with Pam the morning after, probably from one of the servants, and because he was angry with both of us, he decided to make trouble, so he told the papers both weddings were canceled, thereby spiting us both."

"Perhaps, but—"

"Don't try to defend him, Kay. He's a vengeful cove, and this rather proves it, don't you think?"

"Either way, it doesn't matter. Didn't you—"

"Is the fact that he didn't discuss things with you before going to the papers really all that shocking? I mean—"

"Devlin, for heaven's sake," she interrupted, "do stop rattling on about how the papers got hold of the story. That's not the shocking part, obviously."

"Then what is?"

"Didn't you read past the headline?" She stepped closer and tapped her finger forcefully against the words below the headline. "Pam and Wilson got married!"

"What?" He blinked, trying to comprehend this bit of news. "To each other?"

"Of course to each other!" she cried, lifting her hands in a gesture of complete exasperation. "Honestly, why are you so dense today?"

Admitting he'd gone on a bender over his lustful thoughts about her and was now suffering for it was not, he decided, a wise idea.

"They eloped to Gretna Green," Kay went on when he didn't reply.

He made a scoffing sound. "This whole thing's ridiculous. That Dawlish woman must have got it all wrong. They hardly even know each oth—"

He broke off, remembering the opera supper, and Pam hanging on Rycroft's every word about Wall Street. And at the soiree at the Mayfair, he recalled, they'd spent a great deal of time talking together. And the house party, with the two of them seated at the dining table side by side, their heads together.

He looked down, scanned the first couple paragraphs, and looked up again. "Maybe it is true, after all," he said and gave a low whistle. "I'll be damned."

"I have no doubt about the fate of your soul," Kay said. "But it's a relief to know we're no longer talking at cross-purposes."

"Well, well," he said, laughing a little as he glanced down at the paper again. "Rycroft and Pam? What's that line from Shakespeare? 'Of all mad matches, never was the like,' or something like that. Describes them pretty well, doesn't it?"

"Rather, but that's not the question."

"What is the question?"

"What are we going to do about it?"

"Do? I'm not sure there's anything we can do, Kay. It's not as if we can go chasing after them and stop them. The deed is done."

She waved a hand impatiently in the air. "I'm not talking about them. I'm talking about us. By the end of the week, everyone we know will be wondering what could have spurred this turn of events. They'll be nodding and ho-humming and saying inane things to each other—no smoke without fire, and how the fire had never quite gone out, and how Pam and Wilson must have seen it, too, and decided to start a little fire of their own, and rot like that."

He opened his mouth to reply that it wasn't inane rot if it was true, but when she spoke again, he decided it was best not to stress unpalatable facts.

"They'll say how they knew all along we really did elope and all our denials were lies."

"I daresay they will," he agreed mildly.

"I'll be a subject of ridicule. Or worse—pity. The papers will feed on it, don't think they won't. They'll rake up everything, including my broken engagement to Giles. Delilah Dawlish is probably already authoring the stories. I can just imagine them now. Poor, poor, Lady Kay, she'll write. Three engagements, but she just can't get to the altar. She truly is the bad luck bride, isn't she? Dear, dear, what does she do to drive all these men away?" She paused and took a deep breath as if bracing herself for the onslaught. "It will be humiliating."

"No doubt," he acknowledged, appreciating how hard it was going to be for her to go through all that, and reminding himself that it was all his fault. He had to make it right.

"You got me into this mess," she accused as if reading his mind. "Twice. Three times, really."

"So I did."

"Damn it, Devlin, don't just stand there agreeing with me! Come up with a plan. How are we to counteract all this? What do we tell the papers? Our friends? How shall we keep me from being a scandal all over again?"

Maybe it was the aftereffects of last night's alcoholic excess. Or maybe, even all these hours later, he was still slightly drunk. Either way, there was no denying the sudden exhilaration he felt. A bit like taking a leap into space. But it was the only thing to be done.

He took a deep breath and burned his boats. "The answer to all this is pretty obvious, isn't it? Pam and Rycroft have gone off together, have they? All right, then. Why don't we?"

He tossed aside the paper and reached for her hands. "Let's get married."

13

"Get married?" Kay stared at him, unable to believe what she was hearing. "You and me? Are you out of your mind?"

For some unfathomable reason, he laughed. "On the contrary, I don't think I've ever been saner."

Much to Kay's astonishment, he sank down on one knee. "Lady Kay Matheson, will you marry me?"

"No." She snatched her hands away. "For God's sake, Devlin, do get up. You're being ridiculous," she added when he shook his head and remained where he was.

"I'm not. I'm dead serious now, Kay. The two of us getting married makes perfect sense."

"As much sense as flying pigs or a flock of Amazonian parrots landing atop St. Paul's Cathedral," she muttered. "I was hoping—foolishly, perhaps—that you'd have something reasonable to suggest."

"Marrying me is perfectly reasonable."

"I've had enough of this nonsense. I'm leaving." She stepped around him and started toward the door, but he rose and followed her. When she tried to open the door he flattened one palm against it and pushed it shut again.

Heaving a sigh, she turned around, placed her back flush against the door, and lifted her chin, staring him down. "Detaining a woman against her will is truly beyond the pale. But from a scoundrel like you, it's not surprising, I suppose."

"Just hear me out, please. That's all I ask."

"Do I have a choice?"

He smiled, not the least bit apologetic. "Not really, no."

At the sight of that smile, her throat went dry and her stomach gave a nervous dip. It was the same dazzling smile he'd given her the first time he'd ever seen her at Lady Rowland's ball, the same smile that had captured her heart, had persuaded her into meeting him for secret assignations behind her parents' backs, had beguiled her into eloping with him to Gretna Green and running off with him to Africa, and at the sight of it now, Kay felt the exact same sensation she had felt then: a combination of overwhelming pleasure and stark terror.

How ghastly to think she was still susceptible to his charms. Hadn't she learned her lesson by now, in heaven's name?

She scowled. "Keeping me here by force, are you? And to think only a week or two ago you accused Wilson of being a bully. A case of the pot and the kettle if ever there was one."

Her point, of course, sailed right past him. "You came here asking for a solution," he said. "Well, I've offered you one. If we got married, that would resolve every problem you mentioned. For one thing, it would take the wind out of everyone's sails and leave them with nothing scandalous to talk about."

He was probably right about that, but she'd have died rather than admit it.

"In fact," he went on in the wake of her silence, "everyone will probably deem our marriage a fitting end to this business."

"Fitting?" she echoed, trying to sound as scornful as possible, but much to her chagrin, the word came out as an unimpressive squeak.

"Yes. Fitting. Our fiancés have betrayed us. What better solution, people will say, than for us to find consolation in each other?"

Kay pushed away any stupid girlish flutterings about his smile by taking a deep, steadying breath, reminding herself of all the ways he'd managed to make her life hell over the years. "Given that I'd be irrevocably tied to you for the rest of my life," she said, folding her arms, "I see no consolations here at all."

"Ah, but there are a few," he murmured, leaning closer, so close that his lips almost brushed hers. "If I kissed you, you'd remember some of them."

Kissing him had never failed to get her into trouble, and for him to use those kisses as leverage to bring her to heel now was damnable. "You are as conceited as you are crazy."

"Am I? Let's test that theory." His lips touched hers, and her heart gave a hard, panicked thump in her chest, but then he stopped and drew back a little. "Well? Is your memory stirring, or do you need more evidence?"

"My only memory is realizing how big a mistake I almost made fourteen years ago." Kay unfolded her arms and pushed his outward to free herself from his embrace. Much to her relief, his arms fell to his sides, and he took a step back. "I have no intention of making it again."

"Kay," he said, his voice gentle. "I know I am to blame for all of this, and I want to make it right."

"Why? To ease your conscience?" She sniffed, clearly unimpressed. "I didn't realize you had one."

"Well, I do. But what I really mean is that I want it for your sake. Is that so hard to believe?"

Inside, Kay began to shake, because suddenly, for reasons she did not understand, she wanted to believe him, which only proved that he could not only destroy her life, he could also destroy her sanity and make her as crazy as he was.

"You can't make it right, Devlin," she said. "Even if what you suggest solves everything—which I'm not conceding for a second, by the way—things will never be right. The damage is done."

"Damage? I saved you from making a disastrous marriage."

"And I'm supposed to be grateful for the favor?"

"No, of course not. I only meant that he wasn't right for you—"

"That wasn't your decision to make!"

For the first time, a shadow of what might have been guilt crossed his face. "It wasn't what I'd call a decision," he muttered. "At least, it wasn't a deliberate one. I just…lost my head."

"Well, your action makes it abundantly clear that you haven't grown up much in the last fourteen years. But I have, Devlin. I'm not a lovestruck girl anymore, I'm a mature woman. Even if marrying Wilson would have been a mistake—and I do not concede that for a moment—I have no intention of making an even worse one by going off half-cocked and marrying you. Especially not because of one passionate kiss."

For some unaccountable reason, that made him smile. "At least I've finally gotten you to admit that kiss on the terrace was passionate."

Unable to refute that contention, she tossed her head. "That's beside the point."

"Is it? Just think about this for a minute, Kay. People won't be able to accuse you of driving all your suitors away, will they? I'll wager the deed would scarcely be done before the scandal sheets would start gushing about our happy ending and how first love is the truest love."

She made a gagging sound, but all that accomplished was to make his smile widen into a grin, so she decided to be as brutally blunt as possible.

"Everything you say might be true. From the standpoint of sheer logic, it might make sense, and yet I remain unmoved. In fact, Devlin, after what you did, I wouldn't marry you if you were the last man on God's earth. Rather than reward your unspeakable conduct with my hand in marriage, I'd prefer to die an old maid, alone, in an attic garret in Bermondsey."

"Quite a poetic end, Kay, but completely unnecessary."

"But still my choice."

"You'd rather face gossip, embarrassment, and humiliation than accept my proposal?"

"Yes," she answered at once.

"You'd rather endure scandal and shame? Be stared at everywhere you go? Be whispered about and laughed at? You'd rather face poverty than marry me?"

Reminded of painful practicalities, she hesitated, but only for a second. "Yes."

"You'd rather watch your sister's chances diminish?"

Agonized by that prospect, she wavered, but then she reminded herself he was using Jo solely as a means of manipulation and control, and she wasn't about to let him do it. Wilson had tried that trick, too, and she was fed up with it. There had to be another way out of this mess, and since Devlin didn't have any solution to offer that she could possibly live with, she was going to find her own. Somehow.

She lifted her chin. "Yes," she said, absurdly proud of herself for the firmness of her reply. "Now, are you finished?"

"Yes, except—"

"Good," she cut him off and once again turned to go, but instead of stepping back and letting her leave, he remained where he was, his arms coming up on either side of her.

"Except," he resumed, his lips brushing her ear and making her shiver, "for one thing. Just what," he added as she pressed her forehead to the door with a muttered oath, "is your objection to my proposal?"

She whirled around, shaking her head, laughing a little in disbelief at that absurd question. "You really have to ask?"

"Yes, I do. You were ready to marry Rycroft to solve your financial problems, weren't you? So why not me? I'm reasonably well off nowadays—not as rich as Rycroft, granted, but I've got plenty of money to support you and any children we might have. I'll take care of your family, too. In addition to that, I'm also quite good company—"

"That's debatable."

"And," he went on, ignoring her skeptical rejoinder, "I'm not half bad to look at, even if I say it myself."

"You say it yourself because no one else will."

He grinned, the insult rolling off him like water off a duck's back. "Your sarcastic sense of humor is one of the things I've always liked best about you, Kay. So, please answer my question. I've made you an honorable proposal of marriage. No elopements, no concealments. And you're right to say we're not the young fools we once were. I'm not the boy with no prospects and you're not underage, in need of anyone's permission. There are no impediments to stop us this time."

"Except one. We hate each other!"

"I don't hate you, Kay. Oh, there was a time when I thought I did," he added as she raised a disbelieving eyebrow. "But I don't hate you. I never really did. And..." He paused, once again easing closer to her. "I don't think you hate me, either."

"You're right," she agreed, smiling sweetly. "'Hate' is not the right term. 'Revulsion' describes it so much better."

He laughed, a low, soft sound, and his turquoise gaze lowered, staring at her mouth. "If that's true," he murmured, "you have an interesting way of demonstrating it."

That mortifying reminder ought to have been like a splash of ice water. Sadly, it wasn't. Instead, her lips began to tingle, and tongues of heat curled in her belly.

Damn him.

"You should despise me, of course," he said. "And I've no doubt you want to do so. And maybe you really did once. But I don't think you do. Not anymore."

That, she feared, might be true. And that admission only made her more angry with him. "Your insufferable arrogance is truly a thing to behold."

"It's not arrogance. It's simply that that kiss makes a liar out of you. You lie to others, you even lie to yourself. But don't lie to me, because I know you couldn't have kissed me the way you did if you hated me."

At this moment, she might resent him like hell, she might want to slap his face or bash him with a newspaper, but he was right. No matter what he did, he'd always been able to find a way to penetrate her defenses. She'd built up layers of armor as a carrot-haired child, as a plump, freckled adolescent, and as a shy social failure, but one kiss from Devlin in a maze fourteen years ago had shattered all her protective layers. And now, in spite of everything, he might manage to do it again, leaving her vulnerable to yet another heartache.

But that could only happen if she allowed it. There could only be heartache if she let herself fall in love with him again. Far better, she decided, if she sent him back to Africa where he belonged.

"So, you want to do right by me now, do you? That's why you want to marry me?"

"Yes."

"Well, maybe it's silly of me, but I don't think guilt and remorse are a good basis for marriage."

"Right, because marrying for money is so much better?"

She gave him the most withering look she could muster. "If you're trying to persuade me, remarks like that won't help you. And unless you intend to tie me, gag me, and keep me a prisoner in here," she said, turning her back and reaching for the doorknob, "I'm leaving."

His hand closed over hers on the knob, his palm callused and warm. She jumped at the contact and yanked free, and she half expected him to refuse to let her go, but instead, he nudged her gently aside and opened the door, but if she thought his action meant he'd accepted her refusal of his marriage proposal, his next words disabused her of that notion.

"This isn't over, Kay," he told her as she stepped out into the corridor. "If I remember correctly, you said not long ago that you deserved a proper courtship from me? Fair enough. Courtship it is."

"What I want is for you to leave me alone and stop ruining my life. Go back to Africa."

He shook his head. "Not unless you marry me and come with me."

"Not a chance."

"I'll win you over," he called as she turned and walked away down the corridor.

"Ha!" she shot back over her shoulder without stopping. "That'll be the day."

"I am not giving up."

"Of course you're not," she muttered as she turned the corner and made for the electric lift. "Why should my luck change now?"

Devlin had meant what he'd told Kay about winning her over, but during the fortnight that followed her refusal of his proposal, he realized he had a long, hard road ahead. Winning a woman was not an easy thing to accomplish if the woman in question refused to even speak to you.

He tried to call on her, several times, but whenever he sent up his card with a footman, she refused to see him. He appeared at her door, unannounced, but she slammed it in his face. He tried letters. They went unanswered, even after he began paying a delivery boy to put them directly in her hand. He even tried a telegram. All to no avail.

When he read that she was attending a charity ball, he bought a voucher and attended it, too. But she refused to dance with him and didn't even bother to invent an excuse. She just turned him down flat and ordered him to leave her alone.

He knew he could not comply with that order. He would not.

She'd said marrying him would be a mistake, but he didn't see it that way at all. Marrying Kay felt absolutely right. He'd known that from the moment the proposal had come spilling out of his mouth. And his certainty didn't stem from any of the logical, practical reasons he'd given her. Nor did it stem from any sense of guilt or pangs of conscience. She was right that he'd taken her decision to marry Rycroft out of her hands, but he didn't regret it. Not a jot. He should, but he didn't. He just had to convince her not to regret it, either. A dim possibility at present, but as he'd told her, he was not giving up. Not by a long chalk.

That kiss had proved that despite all the years that had passed, despite all the resentments and misunderstandings and pain, the passion between them was still there, hotter than ever, though it was not quite the same sort of passion it had been then.

What he felt now, he realized, went far beyond the wild, crazy attraction he'd felt for her in his youth. This was, he realized, a deeper feeling. It was the passion of knowing without a doubt that Kay was his woman, but also of being willing to shoulder the responsibilities that came with that knowledge. Kay was wrong to say he'd never grown up, because he had. He knew now that to protect and cherish and provide for Kay was his destiny, and that meant far more than merely providing an income to support her. It meant standing by her side until he was laid in the ground. In other words, he was in love with her. In fact, he'd never stopped loving her, and all his efforts to deny that fact had been futile.

She didn't feel the same, but he could not let that deter him. This time, there would be no walking away. No believing the worst. No letting some man move in and take his place because he'd been foolish enough and naïve enough to leave her behind. Not this time.

Still, after a week of being cold-shouldered, Devlin knew more than determination and learning from past mistakes would be needed if he was going to win her over. The problem was that the scandalmongers were determined to shred her to ribbons in the meantime, and watching it happen was almost more than he could bear.

By the end of the first week, the news of Pam's elopement with Rycroft had given way to stories about Kay, and those stories were nearly identical to the dreck she had predicted they would print. They regaled the public with her supposed lack of attractions as a girl, a take that baffled and infuriated Devlin as much now as it had fourteen years ago. They dredged up the elopement, of course, and her broken engagement to Giles. Some made her an object of pity, while others deemed her nothing more than a desperate, grasping spinster.

By the end of the second week, the gossip columns were mocking her for being unable to keep any man long enough to walk down the aisle.

As bad as it was, none of it seemed to change Kay's mind about marrying him, however. And he didn't know whether to be frustrated by that or glad of it. He didn't want her to marry him merely to stop the merciless onslaught, but he did want it to stop, and he knew the only way to make it stop was to soften her stance, get past her pride, and persuade her to change her mind. But what could he do? Keep writing letters, sending flowers, and inserting himself in her path? Or was there something else he could do that he had not yet tried?

He knew from painful experience that pushing Kay too hard was a recipe for disaster. He'd done that fourteen years ago, and it had ultimately cost him the only woman he'd ever loved. Now, he was doing all the things suitors were supposed to do, and that wasn't working either.

What he needed, he realized, was a new plan of campaign, and allies to help him.

Allies. He considered the word. *Allies.*

Setting aside the latest edition of *Talk of the Town,* he finished his breakfast, got dressed, and headed for the Mayfair Hotel.

14

In any crisis of life, there were always one or two things to be thankful for.

Etiquette required that Kay return the wedding gifts that had come in and inform the invited guests that the wedding had been canceled, but she was not required to explain why. Not that an explanation was needed anyway, not with her name splashed across every paper in town.

Kay didn't read the articles. In a slew of fresh tears, her mother provided her with all the details every morning at breakfast, whether she wanted them or not. Josephine was a brick, of course, constantly asking how she could help, offering to keep her company, and inviting her along for any social occasion possible, insisting she was welcome. Kay, however, refused all these kind gestures, assuring Jo that she could be of the most help by carrying on with her season, especially since that meant Mama would have to chaperone her and wouldn't be glued to Kay's side, regaling her with recriminations and woeful prognostications of the dire future that awaited them. Jo, much to Kay's relief, appreciated her point and kept Mama occupied as much as possible.

In the fortnight following the infamous elopement, Kay also discovered and rediscovered who her true friends were, and predictably, they were not the paragons of society she'd been bowing and scraping to all these years.

Idina wrote, inviting her for a sketching holiday to Ireland, an offer she found both amusing and touching. She knew Idina had never had any talent for drawing, nor any interest in it, but she appreciated the kindness behind the offer and told Idina so. She wanted, however, to remain in town for Josephine's season, and declined the invitation. But she also expressed the hope that she and her old friend could see more of each other from now on, and to her happy surprise, Idina responded by inviting her and Jo to come for a visit after the start of the grouse, an invitation she happily accepted.

Some well-meaning and not so well-meaning acquaintances also came to call. Some were motivated by kindness, she knew, but others had more unsavory motives, and Kay soon wearied of all the sympathetic tut-tutting and thinly veiled curiosity about Wilson and Lady Pamela's shocking elopement, and despite all the years of effort she'd put in trying to win over these people, she soon began asking the Savoy footmen bringing up their calling cards to say she was not at home. In doing so, she discovered that turning them away was not particularly difficult. Climbing back up the ton's social ladder was probably a lost cause for her now. And, more important, she'd lost the impetus to try, for she found all this false sympathy irritating and the ghoulish curiosity distasteful.

There was, however, one person who called on Kay who knew instinctively what would do her the most good. One evening shortly after the news hit the papers, Delia arrived at her door with two bottles of the Mayfair's best claret, a box of French chocolates, and a tray of éclairs. She enveloped Kay in a heartfelt hug, asked in an offhand way if she wanted to talk about it, and upon receiving a resounding no, proceeded to open the wine and regale her with humorous tales of life as the general manager of a hotel. And though drinking that much claret and eating that much confectionery in one sitting caused Kay to wake the following morning with rather a headache, her friend's visit helped enormously to revive her spirits.

She did not speak with Devlin. Not that he didn't try. He called, he wrote, he approached her at a ball and asked her to dance. He even sent a telegram, of all things, but she steadfastly ignored these attempts to gain her attention.

She was still angry at him for the high-handed kiss that had thrown her life into this mess. But she also knew that by not shoving him away and slapping his face, she might have given him cause to believe he had a gentlemanly way to make up for his most ungentlemanly actions. And she wasn't about to let the scoundrel have such an easy way to ease his conscience.

After she pitched his ridiculous telegram in the trash, a week went by with no other word from him, and she hoped he'd given up. But two weeks to the day after she'd refused his proposal, the Savoy brought a delivery to her door, one that made Kay realize Devlin had not given up at all.

"Heavens, what's all this?" Magdelene cried, causing both Kay and Josephine to look up from their afternoon tea.

"Delivery, my lady," a male voice said from the corridor.

"What is it, Mama?" Kay asked. She leaned first one way, then the other, but from her seat at the table, there was no way to see past her mother into the corridor beyond.

"Something for Josephine, I think," Magdelene turned to her youngest daughter, her face lighting up with delight. "It seems you have acquired a most ardent admirer, my dear."

"Begging your pardon, my lady," the voice said from the corridor. "But these aren't for Lady Josephine. They are for Lady Kay."

"Me?" Kay rose from the table, and she could only stare in shock as her mother moved aside and a seemingly endless line of footmen entered the suite, each carrying an enormous vase of pure white flowers.

"Where should we put them, my lady?" the first footman asked, looking at Kay over the bouquet in his hand.

"Heavens, I don't know." Kay scanned the dozen bouquets lined up in front of her and made a helpless gesture. "Anywhere you can find room, I suppose."

"But who are they from?" Magdelene asked. She pulled the card from the midst of the bouquet closest to her, but Kay snatched it from her hand.

Ignoring her mother's protest, Kay walked to the card table by the door, retrieved a pound note from the drawer and handed it to the first footman. "I'm afraid I don't have enough change for each of you," she apologized. "You can split this out later, I hope?"

"Of course, my lady." He bowed and exited the suite, and the other eleven followed in his wake, each giving her a bow as they departed.

"Well, my stars," Magdelene breathed, closing the door behind them as Kay opened the card. "Who on earth would be sending Kay flowers?"

Kay did not respond to this rather unflattering inquiry. She was staring down at the card, and the sprawling handwriting she knew so well.

> *Your favorite flower. If you want to know how I know that, you'll have to stop ignoring me long enough to ask.*
>
> *—DS*

Blasted man, she thought, bemused and exasperated. Didn't he understand what the word "no" meant?

"But who are they from?" Josephine's voice interrupted. "Kay?" she prompted when her sister didn't answer. "Do tell us."

She might as well answer, since Mama would read the card the minute she was out of the room anyway. Taking a deep breath, she turned around. "They are from Devlin Sharpe."

"What?" Magdelene looked almost as delighted by that as she had by the prospect of Josephine having a suitor, making Kay more exasperated than before. "Devlin Sharpe is sending you flowers?"

"Not just any flowers," Josephine put in. "Gardenias, Kay."

"Yes," she agreed. "My favorite."

As she said the words, pleasure rose inside her, pleasure so keen it almost hurt. She lifted the card to her nose, breathing deeply of the scent she loved so well. Just how *had* he known? she wondered. She'd never told him—

"Gardenias are so terribly expensive, too," Magdelene said. "Especially at this time of year."

"He must still care about you, Kay," Jo said. "Why else would he send flowers?"

The pleasure inside Kay became sharper, keener, bringing fear as she realized her own vulnerability where he was concerned.

She jerked her hand down, shoving the card back into the slit of its wooden stake. "It's absurd!" she cried as she turned away from the flowers and returned to the table where tea had been laid. "Absurd to think a few flowers will change my mind!"

"Change your mind about what?" Jo asked.

She hesitated, but she knew she had to tell them what had happened. There was no way to keep Devlin's intentions a secret, not if he was so determined to pursue her in this ridiculous way. Taking a deep breath, she braced herself for the inevitable scene. "After Wilson and Pamela ran off together, Devlin proposed to me."

"What?" Magdelene cried in understandable astonishment, falling onto the settee almost as if it were a fainting couch. "Devlin Sharpe proposed? Honorable marriage?"

"No, Mama," Kay replied at once, rolling her eyes as she reached for a scone. "Illicit relations."

"Kay!" her mother admonished, sitting up. "Not in front of Josephine."

"I know what illicit relations are," Jo said impatiently. "What did you say?" she added, returning her attention to Kay. "It sounds as if you refused him?"

"Of course I did."

"Oh, Kay," Magdelene wailed, reminding Kay why she'd wanted to keep the whole silly business to herself. "But why?"

"Really, Mama! You needn't sound so stricken! Must I remind you that you can't stand him? You've been calling him That Horrible Man for donkey's years, and now you want me to marry him?"

Magdelene looked away. "Any port in a storm," she muttered.

"Oh, I see." Kay gave a humorless laugh. "Now that I've once again been jilted and I'm being ridiculed by the scandal sheets as a result, even Devlin would be acceptable? You are impossible, Mama!"

Magdelene looked at her, her mouth taking on a decidedly mulish curve. "I don't see why you say that, Kay."

"The man was engaged to someone else scarcely two weeks ago!"

"So were you. That was then, and this is now." Magdelene paused, fingering the edge of the newspaper beside her plate. "I heard he's become quite rich."

"Mother!"

"Don't look at me like that, Kay Victoria! I'm looking out for you."

"How unselfish of you."

Magdelene heard the acerbic note of her voice and bristled in response. "Well, someone has to think of the future," she cried. "After all," she added, rising to her feet as Kay groaned, "it's not as if there's anyone else for you waiting in the wings, is there? Not now that you've ruined things with Wilson and dashed all our hopes."

With a sob, she left the table and flounced off to her room.

"Well," Kay said, wincing as her mother slammed the bedroom door behind her, "at least he's not 'dear Wilson' anymore."

Josephine giggled, then sobered, looking suddenly thoughtful. "Kay?"

"Please don't tell me you think I should have accepted Devlin Sharpe's proposal," she said, holding up her hand, palm outward as if stopping traffic. "Mama's lectures are difficult enough. I couldn't bear one from you."

"I wasn't going to lecture you. And if you don't want to marry Sharpe, of course you shouldn't. Though it amazes me he'd dare to ask you, given your history and everything that's happened since."

"That man would dare anything," she said, and grimaced as she realized she almost admired him for that. "What did you want to say?" she asked hastily, happy to divert the conversation if possible.

"I haven't wanted to cause you any pain, so I haven't brought up the subject, but this whole thing is so strange. I can't believe Wilson cast you off, just like that." She paused and snapped her fingers. "And then Pam doing the same to Sharpe? And the two of them going off together? It doesn't make sense. Why would they do such a thing?"

With an effort, Kay kept her face expressionless. "I have no idea."

As the words came out of her mouth, Devlin's words rattled through her brain.

You lie to others, you even lie to yourself.

Just the memory of it made her wince, because it was true. She'd been lying to so many people for so long, it had almost become second nature to her. Pasting on smiles when she didn't feel happy, pretending to be fine with things she disliked, accepting things she didn't want in order to please others, all because she'd never felt as if she had a choice or because she wanted their approval or their love or to avoid the pain of being hurt. And in spite of all that mendacity, she'd lost everything anyway. More than once.

Perhaps, she thought, it was time to find a better way to be, one that enabled her to be true to herself. But what way was that? She wanted to be herself, but who was she? What did she want from life?

"You look terribly serious all of a sudden, Kay." Jo's voice broke in on her thoughts. "What are you thinking?"

She was saved from a reply by a knock on the door. "Heavens," she said and rose to her feet. "I wonder who that could be. I hope it isn't more flowers. Where would we put them?"

"It's probably a reporter," Jo said as Kay walked to the door. "I wouldn't put it past them to come up unannounced. They accosted me and Mama right outside Harrods yesterday, bold as brass. Thankfully, I was able to send them scurrying off before Mama could invent some dramatic tale for them."

"You're a darling," she replied with heartfelt gratitude as she opened the door.

A Savoy footman stood in the corridor with a card. "For you, Lady Kay," he said, presenting the card with a bow. "The gentleman wishes to know if he may come up?"

She hesitated, taking the card even though she didn't see the point, since it was sure to be Devlin, and she really didn't want to give him ideas. "Thank you," she said as she looked down. "And please tell him—"

She stopped, unable to quite believe the name printed on the calling card in her hand.

"Who is it?" Jo asked. "Sharpe, I suppose?"

"Actually, it isn't." Kay looked over her shoulder, shaking her head. "It's Wilson."

"What?" Josephine cried with lively scorn. "Send the blackguard off with a flea in his ear, that's what I say. He deserves that and so much more."

Kay, who knew there was plenty of blame to go around, did not bother to reply.

"Jilting you," Jo went on. "The cad. And for Pamela, who is one of the most useless ornamental nitwits in London!"

"Well, if that's true," Kay replied, smiling a little at her sister's choice of words, "then being chained to her for life is him getting what he deserves, don't you think?"

Josephine laughed. "Rather," she agreed, and nodded to the card. "What are you going to do?"

"I daresay you're right. I should refuse to see him. But I confess, I am curious why he's here. And," she added, considering, "it might be best to not end all this on an ugly note." Kay turned to the waiting footman. "Send him up."

When Wilson arrived, Kay was surprised to discover that her only thought at the sight of him was relief. No hurt pride, no guilt, and oddly enough, no regrets. Despite everything, as she looked into Wilson's ice-gray eyes, she knew one thing with absolute certainty, one thing that made regret impossible. She knew she had been saved from making an irrevocable mistake.

Not that she'd ever admit that to Devlin, of course. And if he—

"Thank you for seeing me."

Wilson's voice recalled her to the present moment. "Not at all," she answered and opened the door wide to let him enter.

He came in and took a quick glance around. "Did someone die?"

Kay gave him a rueful look, but she saw no need to tell him who'd sent all the flowers. It would only confirm his jealous suspicions and validate his decision to marry someone else.

"No," she said and waved a hand vaguely in the air. "It's just that it's the season. Jo's debut and . . . and everything."

It was a ridiculous explanation, of course, for no one sent a debutante twelve dozen flowers, but being an American, he might believe it.

Thankfully, he gave a nod, accepting her reply at face value. "Is your mother here?"

"She's resting in her room." Kay gestured to the tea things spread across the table. "Would you care for tea?"

"No." Even he must have sensed the abruptness of that reply. "No, thank you," he amended and nodded to her sister. "Miss Josephine."

Jo gave him a hostile answering stare and didn't reply, and he returned his attention to Kay. "I was hoping we could speak privately."

"I'm not leaving." Jo folded her arms, looking decidedly mulish, and Kay wanted to hug her. "At least," she amended with a glance at Kay, "not because you say so. I'll only go if Kay wants me to."

Kay smiled at that. "Why don't you go down to the restaurant and make us a dinner reservation for tonight? That will take about... fifteen minutes, I imagine."

Jo gave a nod of understanding, and with one last hostile glance at Wilson, she departed. As the door closed behind her, Kay moved to sit on one of the room's settees, gesturing for Wilson to take a seat opposite her.

"I understand congratulations are in order," she said.

"Hmm." He shifted his weight on the settee, looking, Kay was gratified to note, slightly ashamed of himself. "Yes, well, Pam and I rather hit it off at the house party. Perhaps that was because," he added dryly, "we sensed we had something in common."

What? she wanted to ask. A thirst for vengeance?

She bit the words back. "I suppose you did," she said instead. "And I hope the two of you will be very happy."

"Happier than you and I would have been, under the circumstances." His face hardened into merciless, unforgiving lines. "You must understand, I could never marry a woman who has demonstrated that she can't be faithful to me."

She grimaced, but though his assessment was brutal, it was also, sadly, fair. "I understand."

"As for being happy…" He paused and shrugged. "We'll be as happy as most married people, I expect. For one thing, Pam will be able to bail out that worthless spendthrift father of hers. What is it with you Brits, anyway? Spending yourselves into oblivion and refusing to work?"

"Gentlemen aren't supposed to work."

"How convenient for 'em."

"Convenient" wasn't quite how she'd have described it. She thought of Pam's father and her own, peers trapped in the morass of financial obligations associated with their rank and estates, obligations they'd never been allowed to prepare for and that their social position prevented them from doing much about. Desperation, she knew, had led to her parents' actions regarding her all those years ago. That, she appreciated, was why she'd been able to forgive. Desperation was something she understood quite well. She'd been desperate enough to marry a man whose need for absolute control would have given her a lifetime of misery, a man who, she realized now, would have been equally unhappy with her.

"Either way," Wilson went on when she didn't speak, "it'll be a good matchup, I think. She'll be able to rub her American husband in her mother's face every chance she gets, which is something I gather she's looking forward to tremendously. They don't get on."

Another thing, Kay thought with an inward sigh, she understood quite well. "Will you be living here permanently, then, instead of returning to New York?"

"Oh, no, we'll live in New York, of course. She wants a place here, too, which makes sense, since we'll come back for a bit when she brings Charlene out for your London season."

Kay nodded. "Of course. And in spite of her elopement, Lady Pamela's position in society is still far more established and secure than mine; she'll be able to do much more for Charlene than I would have been able to do. In fact, looking at it objectively, she's a far better match for you than I am."

"Yes. I'd—" He looked away. "I'd have preferred you," he muttered.

He looked at her again, and in his craggy, ruthless face, was a flash of something she'd never seen there before. She saw pain. And a hint of vulnerability.

"I loved you, you know," he said.

She blinked at this unexpected declaration, and she had no idea what to say in reply.

He smiled grimly, noting her reaction. "You seem surprised."

"So I am, rather," she murmured.

He gave a harsh laugh. "And here I thought my feelings were painfully obvious."

"It's been clear from the start you wanted me," she said. "But that you loved me?" She shook her head, still not quite able to believe it. "That never occurred to me, to be honest. You never declared it, and…" She hesitated, then added, "To me, your regard always seemed more like a need for possession than love."

He frowned, uncomprehending. "I don't see that there's much difference."

"No," she said gently. "I know you don't."

He stood up, not waiting for her to do so first. "I guess there's no more to say, then. I just didn't want us to part on angry terms."

A strange remark given his actions, but one that reflected a similar view to her own. She wondered, though, if his motive was not to make peace with her but was instead a belated attempt to salvage his connection to the Duke of Westbourne, for his daughter's sake.

She didn't express that rather cynical assumption aloud, however. Instead, she merely rose and walked him to the door. Opening it, she waited for him to walk through to the corridor. Then, when he turned, she held out her hand. "Good luck to you, Wilson."

He stared at her hand for a moment, then took it in his. Giving it a hard shake, he let it go. "And you, Kay," he said. "I hope you get what you want out of all this."

With that, he bowed and left her. "So do I, Wilson," she murmured under her breath as she watched him walk away down the corridor. "If only I knew what that was."

She closed the door and leaned back against it, her own words echoing to her in the sudden silence, bringing the obvious question.

Just what did she want?

She stared at the flowers all around her. What Mama wanted was obvious. Devlin offering her marriage was, from Magdelene's perspective, the perfect solution, but Kay no longer cared much what her mother wanted.

Josephine, of course, would reap the same benefits if Kay married Devlin that she would have if Kay had married Wilson. And yet even her beloved Jo wasn't enough to make Kay willing to make another attempt at marrying for security. She'd done it with Giles, she'd done it with Wilson, but she would not do it again. Fear and desperation had led her down that path, but though her situation was as dire as ever, she was suddenly no longer afraid. She didn't know what would happen, or how she would provide for her mother and sister, but whatever the future might be, she would meet it with whatever courage she could muster.

And now that the shock of her third broken engagement had worn off, she realized why she had turned Devlin down. It was time for her to stand on her own two feet, to find a way forward that didn't depend on a man or his money, that didn't require the goodwill of people who were not her friends. She didn't know what that way forward was, but allowing Devlin to swoop in and save her was not it.

All well and good, but what, she wondered, was that way forward?

As she asked herself that question, Wilson's contemptuous words rattled through her head.

What is it with you Brits?

Kay jerked, straightening away from the door as the answer came, an answer as obvious as the proverbial elephant in the drawing room.

She walked to her writing desk, shoved aside the latest pile of bills, and reached for pen and paper. She scribbled a note for her mother and Jo, then put on her hat, grabbed her cloak and her handbag, and went down to secure a cab. She needed to go to the West End.

The Mayfair Hotel, if Kay remembered rightly, had never been much of a hotel. Despite its prime location, nestled in the valuable wedge of real estate between Park Lane and Devonshire House, it had long been regarded as a second-rate hotel, only in demand during the London season, when any decent room in town was hard to come by. It had been, she remembered, a rather seedy-looking place, with sooty limestone walls and shutters in need of paint.

But now, looking at it as she stepped out of the hansom cab, Kay was impressed. As the manager, Delia had done some marvelous things to the place. The soot had been washed away, revealing the mellow, golden stone beneath, the shutters had been painted creamy white, and boxes of ivy and red geraniums adorned the windows.

A liveried doorman held the plate-glass door open for her, and Kay walked through it, crossing the inlaid floor of black-and-white marble to an oak desk with a wall of cubbyholes for letters behind it. A clerk looked up as she approached.

"May I help you?" he asked.

"I was hoping to call on Lady Stratham," Kay said. "Is she in, by chance?" she asked.

"I will find out. Who is calling, please?"

"Lady Kay Matheson." She handed over her card, and the clerk bustled away. Returning moments later, he beckoned her to follow him. "This way, my lady."

He led her down a well-lit, carpeted corridor to an office at the very end. It seemed to be an antechamber of sorts, where packing crates and filing cabinets lined the walls and the contents of some were scattered heedlessly across the floor. Picking her way carefully through the chaos, she followed the clerk to a closed door at the other end of the room. He opened the door, announced her name, and stood aside.

Delia looked up from her place behind a massive desk, its mahogany top barely visible beneath stacks of manila files and piles of correspondence. "Kay, darling!" she cried, beckoning her forward. "Come in, come in."

Kay accepted the invitation, stepping carefully around two more packing crates by the door, but she was only three feet into the room when she noticed a man rising from the chair opposite Delia's desk, and as he turned toward her, Kay froze in her tracks.

It was Devlin.

"You?" She sighed. "I knew I should have telephoned first."

"Lady Kay." He bowed, smiling a little. "I'm delighted to see you, too."

"Now, now, children," Delia chided. "Don't start squabbling, or you'll make me cross."

She once again waved Kay to come all the way in, but Kay hung back. "I don't want to interrupt," she said, her mind reaching for ways to make a graceful exit. "I'll do some shopping and come back later."

"No, no," Delia said, circumventing an easy escape. "We were just conducting some hotel business, and I think we're nearly finished. Aren't we, Devlin?"

"I believe so," he replied. "I'll be on my way, then, and you ladies can have your visit. Before I go, Delia," he added, "let me say how much I appreciate your help with this . . . project."

"I'll do what I can, of course," she replied, "but as I told you before, I'm not sure how much help I'll be. It will be up to you to make the most of any opportunities that may arise."

"I understand."

"I wish you the best of luck, Devlin. You'll need it."

"Of that, I have no doubt." He bowed to both of them, tipped his hat, and departed.

"Devlin?" Kay echoed, once she had determined he was safely gone. "Delia and Devlin? When did you and that man start using Christian names?" she asked, a bit nettled by this intimacy between her friend and the man who kept turning her life upside down.

Much to Kay's chagrin, Delia merely laughed. "We've been working together a great deal lately. Simon wants to expand the Mayfair Hotel conglomerate, and lots of work will be required in the weeks ahead. I'm in desperate need of help and advice, and Devlin has very kindly offered to extend his London visit and provide some of both."

Kay sniffed. "From what he said, I got the impression he was in need of your help, not the other way around."

"Well, this sort of thing works both ways in business." She gestured to the chair Devlin had vacated. "Do sit down and tell me what's brought you to my side of town. Did you come to have a look at the place?"

"I'd love a look around, of course, but I came for a different reason. One I hope you don't think is cheek. You see..." She paused and took a deep breath. "I'm rather at loose ends these days, as you know. And I've plenty of time on my hands. Josephine is fully immersed in the season, and my mother is driving me mad."

"I'm happy to get you out and about," Delia said at once. "The fuss about your broken engagement will die down soon enough, I daresay, and you'll be able to move in society again without enduring anyone's—"

"That's not it," she interrupted, cutting to the heart of her purpose, just in case Delia was about to make an offer to be her matchmaker and find her a wealthy man to marry her and solve all her problems. "I'm here because I want your advice. And perhaps your help."

"I'm happy to help you in any way I can, of course, but as for advice—" Delia broke off and laughed. "I've made a mess of my own life so often in the past, I'm not sure I'm qualified to give anyone advice."

"In this case you are. You see..." Kay paused and met her friend's gaze steadily, pride lifting her chin a little. "You already know my financial situation. And now that I'm no longer engaged to an American millionaire..."

"You can't borrow against your expectations," Delia finished when she paused again.

"Exactly. And we soon won't have anywhere to live. The Savoy has already asked me when we plan to vacate our rooms, and I'm sure a bill for what we already owe will be coming any day."

"If money's what you need, Kay, of course I'm happy to loan you—"

"No, please." She held up her hand to stop the offer. "That is so kind of you, and I adore you for it, but I didn't come to ask you for a loan. As I said, I'm here for advice. I'm wondering if you can tell me how I might embark on a career."

"A career?" Delia stared at her. "I do believe," she said after a long moment of silence, "that you're serious."

"I am. I must find a way to earn a living."

"You realize taking up a career will only give the papers more meat to feed on?"

Kay couldn't help a laugh. "What can they say about me that's worse than what they've already said?"

Delia acknowledged the truth of that with a grimace, and Kay went on, "I've decided I can't marry merely for material considerations. I've tried that twice, and I won't make the mistake of trying again, even if the opportunity arises, which is more unlikely than ever now. Taking up an occupation is the only thing I can do at this point. The thing is, I've never worked a job in my life. I need to find one, and I don't even know how to begin looking. Or what I might be qualified to do. I was hoping you could offer me some ideas, some guidance based on your vast experience—"

Delia's merry laughter cut her off mid-sentence, but if she thought her friend was laughing at her, she was soon proved mistaken.

"Darling Kay," Delia said with affection, "I can do far better than offer you guidance! I can offer you a job."

"You can?" Kay looked at her friend doubtfully. "I don't want it if you're just being kind. I genuinely want to be useful." She made a rueful face. "For once in my life."

"Kind?" Delia echoed and laughed again, as if heartily amused by the notion that she was some sort of Lady Bountiful. "Kindness has nothing to do with it. And if you don't believe me, just look around." She lifted her hands, gesturing to the folders and letters on her desk and the crates on the floor. "I am in desperate need of a secretary, as you can see."

Kay laughed a little, too, out of surprise more than anything. "I daresay you do," she acknowledged, "but I have to warn you, I don't know anything about being a secretary. I've never used a typewriting machine, or taken dictation—"

"Oh, don't worry about any of that. You can compose letters on my behalf as well as anyone, and you can handwrite them until you've mastered a typewriting machine. They have classes where you can learn typing and shorthand, so you can take a course in your spare time. And even if you don't take courses, you certainly won't be any worse than me, because I can't type, either. I'll pay you twenty pounds a month. And don't worry about where you'll live either. You can live here."

"Here?" Kay blinked. "You mean here at the Mayfair? Oh, but I can't afford that. And I can't take charity—"

"It's not charity. It's not," she insisted as Kay started to argue. "When I worked at the Savoy, they provided my rooms in the hotel as part of my compensation. When Ritz offered to take me to Paris, he offered the same. This sort of thing is done all the time. Not for maids or footmen or waiters, obviously. But for managerial staff, it's quite common."

"As your secretary, I would be part of the managerial staff?"

"Absolutely. Once you learn the ropes, you will have authority to make decisions on my behalf. In light of that, I am happy to provide a suite for you, your mother, and sister, but it'll have to be our least desirable one. It's on the top floor, so it'll be beastly hot in summer, and there's no view and no balcony. And the bathroom is down the corridor. But it's got two bedrooms and a sitting room, and it's yours if you want it."

"Oh, Delia," she breathed, laughing, her relief so great, she felt dizzy. "Are you sure? Shouldn't you ask Simon first?"

"Ask Simon?" Delia echoed in lively surprise. "Heavens, no. I'm the general manager, so Simon has given me authority to make all hiring decisions here, and I want to hire you. But," she added as Kay opened her mouth to accept, "there is one more thing that needs to be addressed."

Kay felt a hint of alarm at her friend's suddenly serious expression. "What's that?"

"Devlin is a member of the board. Wilson's not; he's only a minor shareholder and has very little say in things, so you don't have to worry about him. Devlin, however, is another matter. He is vice president of the company."

Kay tried to imagine Devlin objecting to Delia hiring her, but though she had once thought him vengeful enough for something like that, in light of everything she knew now, Kay could not even begin to imagine it. Far more likely he'd spend the next month or two proposing marriage every fifteen minutes.

"My concern," Delia went on, "stems from the fact that there are several projects Simon wants Devlin and me to handle for the company before Devlin returns to Africa, but I just can't find the time. As my secretary, you'll have to work with him on those projects in my stead. Will you be able to do that?"

She didn't have much of a choice. "Of course."

"I only ask," Delia added, "because you and Devlin haven't been rubbing along very well since his return."

Kay's mind flashed back to that extraordinary kiss on the terrace at Ivywild, where they'd rubbed along a bit too well, but with an effort, she kept her face expressionless. "That will not be a problem," she said firmly.

"Are you sure? Think about it. You might be seen together, and that will be cause for curiosity and gossip."

"We'll be careful."

"Also, you two will have to find a way to get along and work together. And if he gives you an order, you'll have to follow it. No crying to me."

Kay drew herself up. "I would never do such a thing."

Delia clapped her hands together, obviously delighted. "Then you'll take the job? Please say yes. Otherwise I will have to stop procrastinating and begin the tedious task of finding someone else."

Kay didn't hesitate. "I'll take it."

"Excellent." Delia turned in her chair, bent down, and began rooting around beneath her desk. After a moment, she straightened again, a massive stack of folders in her arms. She plunked them down on top of the others cluttering her desk with a thud. "When can you start?"

15

Devlin's meeting with Delia had gone well, better than he'd thought it would. He had chosen to take her almost fully into his confidence, explaining that in light of Wilson and Pamela's unexpected elopement, he had proposed to Kay. He did not reveal what had precipitated Pam's elopement, but he took full responsibility for the fact that during the past fourteen years, none of the things that had hurt Kay would ever have happened if not for him. He wanted, he explained, to right the wrong done to her.

He also confessed that despite his efforts to get on with his own life, his love for Kay had never truly been extinguished, and though Kay had refused his proposal, he was not taking that answer as final. He needed to win her over, he explained, and for that, he admitted freely, he needed help, especially since she wasn't even speaking to him at the moment. All he wanted was a chance to court her properly, but how, he'd asked, could he even begin, if she refused to speak to him?

Delia had listened, and at the end of his little speech, she had agreed to do what she could to help broker a truce. But Kay had arrived before they could get down to specifics, and he'd been forced to make his exit, leaving him rather in limbo, until a few days later when a note from her arrived in the morning post.

Remember what I said the other day about opportunities? I may have one for you. Come to my office this afternoon at three o'clock. After that, it's up to you.

—Delia

PS—given your quest, you may want to consider moving to this side of town. It'll be easier.

"How intriguing," he murmured. He couldn't imagine what Delia had in mind, or how moving to the other side of London would help him, but he'd happily do whatever was necessary. Promptly at three o'clock, he was walking through the doors of the Mayfair Hotel.

When he arrived at Delia's office, he stopped in surprise at the sight of a woman in the antechamber. She was putting file folders in a cabinet, and her back was to him, but there was no mistaking the rich, bright color of her hair. "Kay?"

She turned, and to his complete amazement, she actually laughed. "You look as if you've been struck by a lorry."

"That's rather how I feel," he confessed. "What are you doing here?"

She nodded to the stack of manila folders in the crook of her arm. "Delia has hired me to be her secretary."

"Secretary?" As he said the word, Devlin began to get a vague inkling of what Delia had in mind. "Well, you certainly look the part," he added, glancing down over Kay's plain white blouse, necktie, and blue serge skirt. "But I didn't realize you knew anything about secretarial work."

Her freckled nose wrinkled up ruefully. "I don't, but I've signed on for a course in typing and shorthand so I can learn. In the meantime, it's trial and error, I'm afraid. You don't object, I hope?"

"Object?" he echoed in surprise. "Not at all. Why would I?"

"Well..." She paused and bit her lip. "I did refuse your proposal."

"And you feared I'd be spiteful?" He shook his head, remembering the first time she'd come to confront him in his rooms at the Savoy and her assumption that he'd started the rumors about their elopement for revenge, and he grimaced. "You really do tend to think the worst of me, don't you?"

"No, no, it isn't that. I realize," she added as he raised a skeptical eyebrow, "that I have tended to believe the worst about you in the past, but now—" She broke off, lifting her free hand to tug self-consciously at a loose tendril of hair at her neck. "Now, I don't know quite what to think, Devlin, honestly. Every time I think I have you pegged, you do something wholly unexpected, and it forces me to think again."

He grinned, his hopes rising a bit. "That's part of my charm."

She didn't smile back. "To answer your question," she said earnestly, "I thought you might object to me working here because of the project Delia wants us to collaborate on."

At that surprising bit of news, Devlin's theory of just what opportunities Delia had been referring to seemed confirmed, and his hopes shot up another notch, but with an effort, he kept his face impassive. "Will we be collaborating on a project?" he asked.

"Well, yes. Didn't Delia tell you anything?"

"Very little," he replied truthfully. "But," he added, feeling his way carefully, "I assume it's why she's asked me to come. So that she could give me the details."

"That was her intention, but when she set the appointment with you, she forgot she already had one for the same time. Merrick's Employment Agency."

"Employment agency, eh? Is your position here only temporary, then?"

"No, no, it's permanent. But the hotel is still short-staffed, and she's gone to interview more applicants. But as to what she wants you to do, Lord Calderon has asked her to take something on, and she doesn't have time, so she'd like you to handle it for her. To that end, she's asked me to assist you."

Delia, Devlin appreciated, was a very clever woman. "I see."

"That's why I was worried you might object. I feared you might find working with me a bit... awkward. Under the... ahem... circumstances. You see," she rushed on, looking decidedly nervous, "I need this job."

"Kay," he said gently, "you don't need to explain. I understand, and I don't feel the least bit awkward about working with you. And even if I did, that would be my lookout, not yours. I've no intention of queering your pitch, I promise."

She visibly relaxed, underscoring just how precarious her financial situation was. "Well, that's good."

"I confess, you've made me quite curious. Just what is this project we're taking on?"

"I can give you all the details," she said. "Just let me finish putting these files away."

He glanced around as she resumed her task, noting that the

packing crates were gone and the room was much tidier than it had been on his previous visit. "You seem to have put a great many things away already," he commented.

"You have no idea. The past few days, I've felt as if I'm Hercules cleaning out the Augean stables. But I'm ever so grateful for the job. Especially since the Mayfair is providing a suite for me, my mother, and sister as part of my compensation. We couldn't have afforded to stay on at the Savoy."

So that was why Delia had suggested he move to the West End. More opportunities to see Kay and make his case. His hopes rose another notch, but he didn't show it. "I see."

"She said it's often done."

He wouldn't have said often, and practically never for a secretary, but he wasn't about to point that out. "Oh, yes, quite often." He paused, then added diffidently, "In fact, I'll be moving into the Mayfair as well. I'm bringing my things over in the morning."

He was watching her as he spoke, and though her back was to him and he couldn't see her face, he did notice that she froze for just a second before dropping another file into the drawer.

"After all," he went on, "the only reason I was at the Savoy to begin with was that Pam was there. Now she's gone, so it makes much more sense for me to stay here. So, I suppose it's my turn to ask the question you asked me. You don't object? If you do, then of course—"

"Not at all," she cut in, shoving a file into place without turning around, the brisk, perfunctory tone of her voice telling him nothing. "As you say, it makes more sense for you to stay here. Why pay for your accommodations if you don't have to?"

"It's not the expense," he rushed to reply, lest she think him cheeseparing. "It's just that London traffic is beastly, and if I'm to help Delia, I'd prefer to be on the spot rather than all the way across town."

"I understand, believe me. I've only been working here three days, but I've already come to appreciate how convenient it is to live where you work."

Kay dropped the last file into the cabinet and shut the drawer, then moved behind the oak desk beside Delia's door. She sat down, and when she gestured for him to take the chair opposite her across the desk, he couldn't resist teasing her a bit.

"This is certainly a day of surprises," he murmured, accepting the offered chair. "I never thought you'd even speak to me again, much less invite me to sit down, given the ruthless way you've treated me these past two weeks."

"Ruthless?" She made a scoffing sound. "Oh, please."

"Last time I saw you, you heartlessly refused to dance with me. The time before that, you slammed a door in my face. And then, when you didn't send my flowers back straightaway, I was sure you intended to deprive them of water and let them wither to a depressing condition before returning them."

She did smile at that, just a little. "I considered it, I admit. Not the withering part," she added at once. "But I knew I ought to send them back. In light of the fact that I had refused you, returning them would have been the correct thing to do."

He couldn't resist pointing out the obvious. "And yet, you didn't."

"No. I—" She broke off and looked away. "It...it seemed a shame. I mean, you'd already spent the money, and it's not as if the Savoy would take them back."

"All very sensible reasons to keep them," he said gravely.

She gave a sudden laugh. "You should have seen them. They filled up the entire suite. When Wilson saw them, he asked if someone had died."

Devlin frowned at that. "Rycroft saw them?"

She nodded, her smile widening, as if she sensed his displeasure and was savoring it, the little devil. "He called on me," she said, "when he and Lady Pamela came back from Scotland, or wherever they'd spent their honeymoon after eloping. The footmen had just delivered the flowers a few minutes before."

"What the hell did he come for?" Devlin demanded, his ire rising. "To gloat and rub your face in it?"

"No, I don't think so." She paused, propping her elbow on her desk and resting her cheek in her hand. "Funnily enough," she said thoughtfully, "I think he wanted to make peace."

"Him?" Devlin made a sound of derision between his teeth. "I doubt it."

"Well, his desire to make peace probably has something to do with my long-standing friendship with the Duke of Westbourne's sisters. It's a valuable connection, and I imagine he'd like to salvage it."

"That sounds more like him."

"Either way, I don't care."

"You don't?"

"No. You see…" She straightened and looked up, meeting his gaze. "The truth is, I'd already been getting cold feet. He was becoming irrationally possessive, and it was really beginning to get on my nerves. It was a good thing he came to see me, because that's when I realized that marrying him would have been a horrible mistake."

"Oh, really?" Devlin's mood brightened at once.

She frowned at him. "Stop smiling like the Cheshire cat," she ordered sternly. "Just because I realized Wilson wasn't right, that doesn't make what you did any less wrong."

He wiped the smile off his face at once. "Of course not," he said, doing his best to look appropriately chastened.

"Anyway, I wished them both happiness." She paused, tilting her head. "Do you think they will be? Happy, I mean?"

He considered. "It's hard to say. If you want my opinion, I think it's a case of the unstoppable force meeting the immovable object."

"You may be right. But," she added and flashed him an unexpected grin, "which is which?"

He gave a shout of laughter. "Good question."

She laughed, too, and as he watched her wide, radiant smile light up her whole face, he felt his throat go dry. "Well, look at that smile," he murmured. "Now, that's a bit of all right."

Her smile faded, but she didn't look away. "Still," she said, "twelve dozen gardenias? A bit excessive, Devlin, don't you think?"

"That depends."

"On what?"

He let his gaze fall to her mouth. "On what one hopes to achieve."

He thought he heard her catch her breath, and he thought she was going to ask him how he'd known gardenias were her favorite, but she didn't.

For that impudence, he decided a little revenge was in order. Slowly, he reached out, tucking a loose tendril of her hair behind her ear. He let his hand linger, relishing the blush in her cheek and the velvety softness of her skin against his fingertips, then he drew his hand away, leaning back in his chair.

"So," he said, somehow managing to sound coolly businesslike, "what is this project?"

"Project?" She shook her head and gave a little cough. "Oh, yes, the project."

He thought her voice sounded a little bit breathless, indicating that she wasn't as immune to his touch as she'd probably like to be, and he had to work hard to keep a smile from his face. She reached for a file on her desk, opened it, and extracted a sheet of paper.

"This," she said, holding the sheet out to him across the desk, "is a list of London hotels that are currently for sale or that might be in financial trouble. Delia would like you to investigate them," she went on as he took the sheet from her fingers, "and put together a report for Lord Calderon and the Duke of Westbourne as to which ones you think the Mayfair Hotel Company may want to purchase. I am to give you any assistance you might require."

He looked up, and this time, he couldn't help teasing her. "Any assistance I require?" he murmured, earning himself a frown in return.

"Within reason," she clarified. "And that most certainly does not include reading your letters or dancing with you or accepting marriage proposals from you."

"Spoilsport," he murmured, gratified when she laughed.

He glanced over the list of a dozen names. "I can tell you already that the Algonquin is not a likely possibility," he said. "It's owned by Lloyd Pierce, and he's an obstinate chap. The hotel has been in his family for generations, and even if it's bleeding money, I doubt he'll ever sell. His creditors will have to drag him out of there by his heels."

Kay reached for a sheet of paper and a pencil. "Shall I cross that hotel off the list?" she asked, scribbling notes. "Or do you want to approach Mr. Pierce anyway?"

"It's worth a try, I suppose. Find out if he'll see me and if so, make an appointment."

He looked down again at the list of names, pretending vast interest in it as he considered what his best move should be.

He knew he could not push Kay too hard or too fast. He'd done both fourteen years ago, and it had been the biggest mistake of his life. This time, he decided, slow and steady was his best bet.

"I see that nine of the other hotels on this list are represented by house agents," he said, after a moment. "Contact them and secure orders to view." He leaned forward, putting the list back in front of her on the desk. "We'll tour each property and assess their potential."

"We?" she echoed. "You want me to come with you?"

"Of course. I'll need you to take notes. So bring a clipboard. And a measuring tape."

She nodded. "Anything else?"

Best not to push his luck, he decided, and stood up. "I don't believe so. Let me know when you've got those orders to view."

With that, he departed, but before he'd even reached the lobby, he was grinning like a schoolboy.

"Thank you, Delia," he murmured with heartfelt appreciation as he crossed to the front desk to reserve himself a room. She'd given him this chance, and now it was up to him to make the most of it.

16

She could still feel the warmth of his fingers against her cheek, and her insides still felt as if she'd swallowed a jar of butterflies.

So long, she thought, since she'd felt this way. So, so long. She'd forgotten what romance felt like. She gave a dreamy sigh and lifted her hand again to touch her face, then realized what she was doing. With a groan, she folded her arms and buried her hot face in the crook of her elbow. She didn't want to feel this way. Not again. It was too hard. Too painful. And too risky, she added, lifting her head to look at the open doorway to her office.

What if anyone had walked in and had seen him touch her like that? Word of it would spread through the hotel, and would probably get back to Delilah Dawlish or some other reporter. More gossip was the last thing her family needed. And she certainly couldn't afford to be distracted.

With that reminder, she worked to put any idiotic notions of romance out of her mind and tried to forget how Devlin's touch had made her feel. She'd already turned him down, for heaven's sake. And besides, she had a job now, a job she badly needed, and letting herself be distracted by thoughts of him and what had once been between them was not going to help her keep it.

She concentrated instead on the task he'd given her, and by the next afternoon, she had obtained orders to view for the first four hotels on their list, and sent him a note to that effect, inquiring if the following day would be a convenient time for them to begin touring those properties. His reply was affirmative, and by the time he arrived at her office at ten o'clock the following morning, Kay had picked up the hotel keys and was ready. She had also put her priorities firmly back in order, for she did not want to be as much a sensation to the scandal rags in the future as she'd been in the past.

Devlin's first words to her, however, demonstrated that she didn't have to be caught doing anything untoward to be the subject of gossip, and also proved Delia had been right to caution her that even working with Devlin would be cause for curiosity.

"Best if we go out the back way," he advised as she put on her hat. "When I came down a few minutes ago, I happened to look out the front windows as I crossed the lobby, and I saw Delilah Dawlish skulking on the opposite side of the street."

Kay gave a groan of exasperation. "Oh, that woman! She is the absolute end!"

"She is tiresome," he agreed as they left the office, walked out the back door of the hotel and into the alley behind it.

"'Tiresome' is a kind way of putting it. She's tried to catch me out several times since Pam and Wilson eloped, hurling questions in my face. 'How do you feel, Lady Kay, about being jilted again? What's it like to be such a bad-luck bride?' Rubbish like that. She's done it to my mother and sister, too, and several of our friends."

"Yes, she's done it to me as well. I have perfected the art of the reply: 'I have nothing to say.'"

"Me, too. But my mother, sadly, always has something to say. And it only gives that odious woman more meat to feed on."

"I know this isn't much comfort, but it will all die down again eventually."

"In all honesty, I've stopped caring what the scandal sheets say about me," she assured him. "I just don't want it to hurt Josephine. This is her first season."

"Is it hurting her?"

"It doesn't seem to be, not yet. I mean, I'm rather a laughingstock at present, but she's found a group of friends, including Lord Calderon's sister, and there are several young men hanging about her as well, so I think she'll do well enough, in spite of my troubles. Of course, it helps that she's beautiful."

"Is she?" He stopped just before they reached the sidewalk, compelling her to stop as well, and when she looked at him, he was smiling a little. "I hadn't noticed."

Kay's heart twisted in her chest, a pang of pleasure so sweet it was almost like pain, and it was so much like how she'd felt in those heady days so long ago, that she couldn't seem to breathe. *Say something,* she thought desperately, but when she opened her mouth, no words came out.

He didn't seem to notice she'd gone stupidly mute. Instead, he turned away as if to resume walking, but when she took a step forward, he stopped her, stretching out his arm to block her path.

She inhaled sharply, the feel of his forearm against her tummy doing strange things to her insides as he leaned forward and peeked out of the alley.

"I think the coast is clear," he said looking up and down the street. "I don't see Dawlish anywhere. Or anyone else that looks like a reporter."

"Well, that's a relief," she managed as his arm fell away.

"Where shall we go first?" he asked as they emerged from the alleyway.

She pulled the list out of her pocket. "I thought the Grenville first, since it is the closest."

He gestured with a flourish. "Lead on."

The Grenville Hotel was only a short walk along, a tidy little hotel in a quiet little side street, with whitewashed steps and a brightly polished brass plate proclaiming its name.

"It looks quite nice," Kay commented, opening her handbag to rummage for the key. "Shall we go in?"

But instead of answering in the affirmative, Devlin was already shaking his head. He pulled the list from her hand, read the particulars the house agent had given her, and shook his head. "Not worth the bother," he said and handed the sheet back to her.

"It seems a nice little hotel," Kay remarked, looking it over. "Why are you against it?"

"It's very close to the Mayfair. We don't want them competing with each other."

"But why did you agree to see it, then?"

"Well, if it turned out to be a bargain, it might be worth buying anyway. But given the small number of rooms and the very high asking price, it's not a bargain. Where to now?"

She looked at her list and pointed in the direction of the Marble Arch. "The Marchmont Hotel. It's in Marylebone, just above

Cavendish Square. So we'll need a cab. A closed carriage is best, I think?"

He agreed. "Walking is one thing. After all, we might happen to be going in the same direction, but a carriage is different. The last thing we need is for someone we know to see us and report to the Dawlish woman that we were gallivanting around London together, unchaperoned."

Fortunately, they were near Park Lane, where cabs were thick on the ground. He went off to fetch a growler, and twenty minutes later, they were standing in the courtyard of the Marchmont Hotel, an ancient five-story structure of crumbling red brick with uneven flagstones and weeds popping up between them. It didn't look particularly enticing to Kay's eyes, but as they paused on the sidewalk to study it, Devlin said, "This has possibilities."

"It does?" She nudged a piece of broken flagstone with her shoe, dislodging it. "I have my doubts."

He turned, making a sweeping gesture to their surroundings. "This is one of the most prosperous parts of London. Rich, professional men—bankers, industrialists, and the like—live and work around here."

"Agreed. And?"

"It's a good location for a quality hotel, but this building is for sale at quite a reasonable price."

"That could mean it has bad drains and smells," she pointed out.

"True. Best go in and have a look."

She shoved the particulars sheet into her handbag and handed him the key. They crossed the courtyard, past an eroding stone fountain, and he unlocked the main entrance door.

They passed into an enormous lobby with a well-worn terrazzo stone floor, columns of dark purple mahogany, and a domed ceiling of leaded glass. Thankfully, it did not have the sulfurous odor that spoke of bad drains, but most of the ceiling's glass panes were broken, and rain had got in, damaging the mahogany and staining the floor with the sooty London air.

"See?" he said. "I told you it had potential. The architectural lines are stunning."

Kay eyed the broken ceiling. "I see what you mean, but won't the dome cost the earth to repair?"

"That's something we shall have to find out. I think it is worth an engineer's report, provided the rooms are all right. Let's have a look around."

For the next two hours, she followed him through the offices, kitchens, and rooms of the hotel. Clipboard in hand, she scribbled notes, taking down every comment he made about the place, from its non-functioning lift to its surprisingly decent bathrooms, to its recently installed electricity. By the time they left the building, she had five pages of notes.

"How do you know so much?" she asked him as their cab took them toward St. James and the Woodville Hotel for their third viewing of the day. "About hotels, I mean."

"Trial and error. I own three hotels of my own, and I have interests in several others."

"In Africa?"

"Mostly, but also in Constantinople, Athens, and Cyprus."

"Goodness," she said. "You proved my father utterly wrong about your prospects, didn't you?"

"A fact which has given me a great deal of satisfaction over the years, I confess, though without the loan he gave me, none of it would have been possible. Sadly, my own father is still not the least bit impressed by my success."

"Sod him," she said, earning herself a shout of laughter from him. "Who cares what he thinks?"

"Quite right," he said as their cab slowed to a halt and the window in the roof slid open.

"Duke Street, guv'nor," the driver told them through the opening. "Sixpence for the fare."

"Here's your tanner," Devlin told him. "And a joey for a tip."

A gnarled hand reached through and took the coins. "Much obliged, guv'nor."

The hand disappeared, and a moment later, Devlin was helping Kay alight from the vehicle.

"It's right here," she told him, gesturing to the modest building of white stone and black wrought iron nearby as the cab rolled away. She pulled out the key, but when she started up the front steps, he didn't, and she turned in surprise. "Aren't you coming?"

"I just thought of something I have to do." He gave a nod to the front door of the building. "You go in. I'll catch up with you in a quarter of an hour."

"I'll come with you, if you like?"

"No need. Go in and start looking around. I'll be interested to hear your opinions when I get back."

"But I don't know anything about hotels," she protested as he started walking away down Piccadilly. "I've only been working for the Mayfair for a week."

"You know more about hotels than you think." He paused and looked at her over his shoulder. "You've been assessing them with me for over three hours. And besides," he added before she could point out that three hours was hardly an adequate education on the subject, "you've stayed in dozens of 'em. You told me so."

With that, he turned and resumed walking down Piccadilly the way they'd come.

Kay watched him for a moment, baffled. He really was the most unaccountable man. Where was he going? And why was he leaving her to assess this place on her own?

Still, perhaps he had a point. If she considered this place from a customer's point of view, what would she think?

Intrigued by the challenge, she turned her attention to the building in front of her.

The Woodville wasn't much to look at. A modest three-story building of white painted brick and wrought-iron railings. But it was at least clean and tidy. She went inside, trying to follow Devlin's advice in forming her opinions, assessing it with the business considerations he had mentioned during their time at the Marchmont and with her own experience of having lived most of the past year as a hotel guest.

The lobby, she decided, was quite nice, if somewhat old-fashioned, with its walnut pillars and malachite floors. The kitchens and laundry, she noted, had no hot water taps, only cold, which meant a boiler would have to be purchased and more plumbing added—a major expense. Worse, however, was yet to come.

When she reached the first floor, she tried to look beyond the worn and faded carpets and the stained cabbage rose wallpaper, for those could be replaced, but as she began to explore the rooms, she was reasonably sure Devlin would advise against purchasing this building.

For one thing, the rooms seemed awfully tiny. There was no furniture to provide a sense of scale, however, and unwilling to trust her eyes, she pulled out the tape measure Devlin had asked her to bring.

"Eight feet by nine feet?" she muttered. "That's not nearly enough room." Put a bed, armoire and dressing table in here, she thought, looking around, and there'd be no room to move. There were storage lockers for customers' luggage downstairs by the laundry, but even so—

"Kay?"

At the sound of Devlin's voice floating up the stairs, she snapped the tape measure, causing it to roll up inside its casing, and shoved it in her handbag, then she stepped out into the corridor.

"I'm up here," she called down the stairs. "On the first floor."

"Well, come down. I've had an idea."

"I'll be right there." She retrieved her clipboard and jotted down the measurements she'd just taken, then shoved her pencil behind her ear and went down to the ground floor, where she found Devlin standing by the front desk, an enormous picnic basket at his feet, the basket's origins stamped in big black letters on its side.

"Fortnum & Mason?" she cried in delighted surprise.

"I thought we could do with some lunch."

"Rather. I'm famished."

"Where shall we dine?" He glanced around the dim and dusty foyer. "Doesn't seem to be anywhere suitable in here."

"Perhaps the kitchens?" she suggested. "I saw a deal table in there and a few chairs. Not much else, though."

"That'll do." He bent and picked up the basket. "Lead me to it."

She complied, taking him across the foyer and down the long, dark corridor to the kitchens. "Here we are," she said, gesturing to the battered table and a trio of rickety-looking ladderback chairs. "It's not much, but from what I've seen so far, this is the only furniture in the entire place."

"That doesn't surprise me. If they went bankrupt, all the furnishings would have been sold." He set the basket on the table, reached inside, and pulled out a napkin, laying it across the wooden seat of one of the chairs. "Your seat, my lady."

"Playing waiter, are you?" she asked as she sat down and began pulling off her gloves.

"Well, someone has to play that role, and it can't be you. You outrank me."

She laughed at that as he unfolded a second napkin with a professional flick of his wrist and spread it across the table.

"Now," he said, rummaging in the basket, "let's see what we have in here."

He pulled out plates, a knife, a chunk of ham, a pot of mustard, a wedge of bright orange Gloucester cheese, and a baguette of bread. A bottle of claret followed, along with two glasses and a corkscrew. "Unwrap the ham, will you?" he asked and began to open the wine.

"I thought you were the waiter," she teased, reaching for the ham. "Isn't this your job?"

"Well, when you've hired only one waiter, you have to help him out."

"Fair enough." Taking up a knife, she cut the twine netting and unfolded the cheesecloth wrapping, then began slicing it while he poured the wine.

"A shame we don't have candles," she murmured. "It's quite dim in here. There's gas jets," she added, nodding to a point high up on the wall behind him, "but no electricity."

"That's not uncommon in a hotel kitchen."

"It isn't? Well," she added when he nodded, "there's no electricity in the rooms, either. To add it would be costly, I imagine?"

"Through the entire hotel? Very. Do you think it's important?"

"Don't you?"

"Forget what I think." He paused, pushing a glass of claret toward her and reaching for the wedge of cheese. "I'm asking what you think," he reminded as he began paring cheese.

"Oh." Startled, Kay set down her knife and sat back with a slice of ham and cheese, laughing a little, feeling suddenly self-conscious. "It's so seldom a woman is asked what she thinks, unless it's about clothes or something equally trivial. We're never consulted about anything important."

She paused, nibbling on ham and cheese as she considered. "I think," she said after a moment, "there's probably two kinds of customers. The ones who care about tradition and keeping with what's familiar and the ones who prefer the latest modern comforts. So putting in electricity rather depends on which sort of customer you wish to cater to, doesn't it?"

"Quite right." He took a slice of cheese and his wineglass and leaned back against the wall behind him. "You must be the modern sort. After all, you are a woman with a career. That's very modern."

"I've had this career for a week," she reminded. "I'm not sure it counts. But I do prefer electricity, I confess. Mama hates it. When we first came to the Savoy, she fretted about all the vapors in the air. Jo and I both tried to explain that electricity isn't like gas, and there are no vapors, but we don't think she quite believed us. Either way,

I think electricity is the way of the future, and that putting it in would probably be worth the cost. Unless, of course, there's heaps of other work to do to the place."

He nodded. "Are there any water closets?"

"I saw only one on the first floor, but I don't know how many others there might be. There's no boiler, so no hot water. And the rooms are very small. Still, the location is first rate. It is St. James, after all. So, even if you had to gut the building or demolish it altogether, it might be worth it, depending on the—what?" she broke off as he began to laugh.

"And you said you don't know anything?" he chided. "If we do this much longer, you'll be more knowledgeable about the hotel trade than I am."

"With three hotels to your credit, I doubt it. How did you do it? What got you started? And even with the money from my father, how did you ever afford it?"

"Oh, well, that last question's easy. After I landed in Cape Town, I spent the first year just exploring, trying to determine where I wanted to settle and what I might want to do. I had my education as a mining engineer, so I thought at first I'd get myself hired on with some British mining firm, but somehow, I just didn't fancy it. So I wandered through South Africa for a bit, looking for the right opportunity. I toured some of the mines at Kimberly, and De Beer offered me a job, but I didn't want to be a cog in their wheel. I did safari work in East Africa for a while, then I wandered through Rhodesia. It was there that I stumbled onto a gold mine. And I mean that literally. I'd like to brag that it was my extensive education in mining that led me to it, but no. It was just instinct. When I saw the terrain, I just had a feeling there was something there."

She eyed him dubiously. "A feeling?"

"Yes," he said firmly. "A feeling of knowing, of…destiny. It's hard to describe, but it's just a certainty that something important is happening, and I'd best pay attention." He paused, tearing a hunk of bread off the loaf between them and smearing it with butter. "I've had it a few times in my life."

Suddenly, his hands stilled, and he looked up, meeting her eyes across the table. "I had it the first time I ever saw you."

"Me?" Kay stared in astonishment. "You did?"

"I did. I looked across that ballroom, and saw your face, and I had that feeling."

"My face?" Kay shook her head, bemused. "My round, freckled face? The one Delilah Dawlish deemed round as a ginger biscuit and equally unremarkable?"

"I love ginger biscuits, I'll have you know, so forget what the Dawlish woman said. Besides, I am a far better judge of feminine beauty than she will ever be. Have you ever looked at the woman? Face like a rocking horse."

Kay laughed at that. It wasn't true, of course, not really, but she enjoyed hearing it just the same.

"Anyway," he said, setting aside the butter knife and piling ham and cheese onto his bread, "it's not fashionable standards of beauty that make a woman attractive. It's about what a man feels when he looks at her."

He paused, his eyes meeting hers across the table, and something in their turquoise depths made her catch her breath. "I looked at you, and I knew somehow that knowing you was going to hurt like fun." He smiled a little. "And I was right. It hurt like hell in the end, but the fun was worth every bit of the pain."

Kay stared at him, too astonished to think of a thing to say.

"Anyway," he went on, resuming his previous light, teasing tone, "what did you think when you saw me?"

Recovering, she picked up a piece of bread and butter. She couldn't tell him how she'd felt—how her knees had gone weak, and her wits had vanished. She couldn't tell him of the panic she had felt as he'd crossed that ballroom, or how the moment he'd taken her in his arms, she'd fallen in love with him. She could only tell him one part of the truth. "I'm not sure I thought anything," she said.

"Ouch."

"No, no," she said, laughing a little. "I didn't mean it like that. I mean that I was too stunned to do much thinking, especially when you walked over to me." She wriggled on her seat, not quite sure how to put it. "You see, men as good-looking as you—"

"Wait," he ordered, cutting her off. "You think I'm good-looking? I seem to recall you saying something completely different the day I proposed to you."

Caught out, she tossed her head. "I only said that because I was still angry with you about that kiss," she muttered. "I didn't really *mean* it. Besides," she added as he began to smile, "you are good-looking and you know it and you don't need me to validate that opinion."

"No, no, I really think I do," he said, setting aside his half-eaten sandwich and leaning forward to prop an elbow on the table and rest his chin in his hand. "Tell me more."

She tried to give him a quelling look, but it hardly had the desired effect because she couldn't quite hide her smile. "My point is that men who look like you don't usually ask girls like me to dance. I was too shocked to do much thinking."

He frowned. "If you say one more word to disparage yourself, I will dump my wine over your head," he told her. "I hate it when you do that."

She smiled, remembering. "You always did hate that. Still, there's no denying my looks aren't what anyone would deem swoon-worthy, and I wasn't by any stretch of the imagination a social success. But let's stop arguing about my looks. I want to hear the rest. You had this feeling about that land . . . so, did you buy it?"

"I ordered a surveyor's report, and what I saw was favorable, so I put together an investment group, and we bought it. I used the money from your father and my savings from my safari work to buy my shares. I also roped in Simon as one of the investors. He was in the army and was stationed there at the time, and we'd become friends. We both invested every cent we had, and it paid off. We hit an enormous vein, and within four years, all six of us had made a bloody fortune."

He paused to take another bite of his sandwich, then went on, "But then the mine petered out, and we closed it down. Simon had gotten out of the army by then, and he decided to go back to England, and I went back to being a wanderer. Back up through East Africa, and then I caught a boat out of Mombasa, sailed the Red Sea through the Suez Canal, and ended up in Egypt. The first time I took a trip up the Nile, I fell in love with it. The sky seems endless and the sunsets are like nothing you've ever seen. They take your breath away. And to be sailing along, and all of a sudden, you come across enormous pyramids thousands of years old, just sitting there along the bank. In Egypt, you trip over history with every step. It's amazing."

"It must be," she murmured. "I've never been any further away than the Isle of Wight." She felt a wistful little pang as she spoke, and she half expected him to remind her that she could have seen it—could still see it—if she'd accepted either of his proposals.

But he didn't remind her of that, and she didn't know whether to be relieved or disappointed when he merely said, "Well, travel is much harder for a woman to do on her own than it is for a man."

He ate the last bite of his sandwich, brushed crumbs from his fingers, sat back with his wine, and went on, "Anyway, coming into Cairo, I saw this tract of land right on the river, very close to the British Consulate, and I had that feeling again, so I bought it. And that's where I built my first hotel."

"Why a hotel, particularly?"

"Simon had told me a great deal about the hotel trade—he'd been raised in it, you see—and something about it appealed to me. And Britain was in charge of Egypt by then, so Cairo was packed with British tourists who were having a devil of a time finding proper accommodations. The British, you see, want to see the world, but they also want the world to be British."

Kay laughed at how true that was. "What you mean is that we Brits want to see the pyramids in the morning, then have our tea and eat scones with jam in the afternoon, while we gaze out over the Nile and talk about merry old England?"

"Exactly so," he said, laughing with her. "I was sure a hotel that catered to wealthy British tourists was bound to make money. I also loved Cairo. It's one of the most exciting, vibrant cities you can imagine. So I built my hotel, and once the hotel was profitable, I built another, and then another. I also built myself a house right beside my first hotel in Cairo. Very modern," he added. "Electricity, bathrooms, hot and cold laid on, all that."

"Did you..." She hesitated, lowering her gaze to the table, tracing little circles with her finger, then she took a breath and looked at him again. "You never thought of coming home?"

He held her gaze steadily across the table. "No, Kay. Not after Giles. I felt as if we'd rather crossed the Rubicon there."

She nodded, seeing in his eyes the same pain that still lingered inside herself. "You mean you felt I had forsaken you."

"Yes. From what you told me, you felt the same."

"Yes."

They both fell silent, the past suddenly between them again like a wide, unbridgeable divide. She wasn't an infatuated girl, and he wasn't a wild, adventurous youth, and they weren't caught up in the frantic, reckless throes of first love. That was all over, they were completely different people now, with completely disparate lives, and one could never go back.

Abruptly, he pushed back his chair and stood up. "It's getting late. We should get on, if we're going to tour this place before it gets dark."

She nodded. "Of course."

They gathered up the remaining food, put it in the basket, and left the kitchen. They left the picnic basket by the lobby door, and for the remainder of the afternoon, their conversation was strictly professional. But as she jotted down notes and took measurements and discussed the potential of the property they were viewing, the past still rattled around in her head, and she wondered suddenly what her life would have been like if she hadn't been sensible. If she hadn't cared what her parents and friends thought. If she'd listened to her heart instead of her head.

Would their wild, passionate infatuation have grown into a mature love that would last? Or would they have fallen into the typical stale, loveless marriages so many other people had, realizing they had nothing to say to each other and nothing in common?

She'd never know now. And to be honest, she wasn't sure she wanted to know. Because regrets were a waste of time.

17

The day after their tour of the hotels, Devlin made sure to stay away from the Mayfair as much as possible, for he knew that the game of romance required both pushing forward and strategic retreat. But the next day, when he received another note from her, inquiring if the day following he was free to view more properties, he was glad to answer in the affirmative.

Though his goal was courtship with a view to matrimony, he knew he could not endure the excruciatingly sedate wooing that involved long strolls side by side under the watchful eyes of chaperones, dancing only once at each ball, and having afternoon tea with her mother, and he very much doubted such efforts would bring Kay any closer to changing her mind.

Touring the hotels gave him opportunities to be alone with her, as Delia had shrewdly surmised, but he suspected that even that wouldn't be enough. She hadn't quite forgiven him for that kiss at the house party, but he sensed that if he could only kiss her again, hold her in his arms, awaken her passion, he might get somewhere. If she didn't haul off and slap him, of course. And a few kisses might eventually persuade her to agree to marry him. It was a risky strategy, though, for he didn't want to compromise her, not again, and he would have to tread carefully.

With that in mind, he appeared at her office at the appointed time. Kay, however, didn't seem to notice his arrival, for she was standing behind her desk, staring at a slip of pale pink paper in her hand, a wide smile on her face.

He tapped his knuckles on the doorjamb, giving a cough, and she looked up.

"Good morning," he said and nodded to the paper in her hand as he came in. "You look as if you backed a longshot and won the Derby."

She laughed. "No, no, nothing like that. But look."

She held out the paper with a triumphant flourish as he halted in front of her desk. "I just got *paid*."

She said the word almost reverently. He leaned closer, studying the bank draft a bit dubiously, not sure a mere five pounds was worth such veneration. "Well, yes," he murmured. "That's rather the hope when one obtains employment. That one will be paid."

"I've never been paid wages before. I mean, I get a dress allowance from Giles, of course, but that's different." She looked down at the check and laughed again. "I worked for this. I earned it."

She sounded almost...awed. She lifted her head again, her smile so happy, it made him smile, too. "Why, Kay, you seem almost giddy."

"So I am! You're laughing at me," she accused, still smiling.

"I'm not," he denied. "Well," he amended at once, "maybe a little."

"Oh, I'm sure five pounds a week is a tiny fraction of what you earn in a year, but..." She paused, waving the check in the air. "It's so gratifying to feel one is *useful*."

That took him back, rather. "You don't feel as if you are useful?"

"Most women don't," she countered, making a face. "We pay calls and do the season and go to house parties. We buy clothes and write letters, we garden, we embroider cushions, and raise funds for charity... but it's all for the sole purpose of killing time. Until we're married, we have no place, no real purpose but to be decorative."

"That's rather true for gentlemen, too," he pointed out. "We obtain educations that prepare us for no trade, occupation, or profession. We live off our quarterly allowance—well, not me, since my father disowned me ages ago and I kicked against the pricks and trained as a mining engineer, much to my family's embarrassment, but what you describe is true for most gentlemen we know."

"I suppose it is." She waved the check in the air. "This is so much more gratifying."

"Yes," he agreed, smiling at her, savoring the joy he saw in her face. "But I'd happily pay you a hundred pounds every day if I could see you smile at me like that."

Abruptly, he looked away, suddenly, oddly embarrassed. "We had best be going. I've hired a carriage for the entire day. I thought it better than trying to find cabs. If you're ready?"

"I am." She put the bank draft in the top drawer of her desk, then retrieved her handbag from beneath her desk, then she rose, hooked her handbag over her arm, and started for the door.

"Did you see Delilah Dawlish lingering out there anywhere, waiting to pounce?" she asked over her shoulder as he followed her.

"I didn't. Perhaps she's moved on. Perhaps someone else's scandal has pushed us off the front page of her wretched paper."

Kay brightened. "I know I shouldn't find that to be a happy prospect..." She paused, making a face. "But, sadly, I do."

"Well, I ordered the driver to pull into the alley, just to be on the safe side."

Kay took her straw boater hat down from its peg on the coat tree and pulled her hatpin from the crown. "That was wise of you," she said as she put on her hat and secured it in place.

They left the hotel, and Kay ordered the driver to take them to Red Lion Square.

"Holborn, eh?" Devlin said, assisting her into the carriage as the driver climbed up onto the box.

She nodded. "We have four hotels to see today. Holborn, Bloomsbury, Soho, and ending in Marylebone."

Their tour took them most of the day to complete, but Devlin found little opportunity for anything more than conversation. The first two hotels they visited were still in operation, with dozens of people milling about. They had lunch in a crowded Bloomsbury tea shop, and the third hotel, in a very poor section of Soho, had boarded up windows, broken shingles, and peeling paint. It wasn't, they decided, even worth a look.

But in Marylebone, the Portland Hotel gave him cause for hope. It was empty, for one thing, and as they began to explore the rooms on the first floor, Devlin saw a heaven-sent opportunity for a little romance.

"One thing's certain," he said, nodding to the walls of the suite's sitting room. "The wallpaper will have to be replaced."

"I'm afraid so," she agreed, running a hand over the peeling paper. "There's no saving it."

"It's a shame, though." He moved to stand behind her, stretching out his arm above her shoulder. "Gardenias," he said, tracing the petals of one of the flowers. "Your favorite."

"Yes," she agreed with aggravating indifference.

"Go on," he coaxed when she fell silent. "Ask me how I know that."

"No." Her voice was firm. "I'm not asking."

He flattened his palm against the wall, his chest brushing her shoulder. "Don't you want to know?"

"Of course."

"Then why aren't you asking me?"

Her face was in profile, but he didn't miss the faint smile that curved her mouth. "Because you so badly want me to."

"You devil," he murmured. He leaned even closer, playing with fire. "C'mon, ask me."

She made a choked sound—a stifled laugh—then pressed her lips together, shaking her head. "I won't."

"C'mon," he murmured in her ear. "If you don't…"

Beneath the brim of her hat, her eyebrow lifted in a delicate arch, daring him. "If I don't?" she asked.

"If you don't, I might have to send you pineapple lilies next time."

"Pineapple lilies?" She turned her head, and he pulled back a fraction. "What are those?"

"They grow in South Africa. They're quite pretty, but they smell like a dead body."

"Lovely."

"I'll send a footman with them while you're out. That way, the room will be divinely wretched by the time you return." He gave her a look of apology. "I advise you not to test me on this."

"Oh, very well, since you are determined to use blackmail…" She paused and turned toward him. "How did you know gardenias are my favorite? I don't remember ever telling you that."

He smiled back at her. "You didn't."

"Then how did you know?"

"I made a calculated guess." He paused, leaning closer, inhaling deeply, relishing the arousal that began rising inside him even as he reminded himself to keep his head. "Your hair always smells like gardenias. Scented soap, I imagine?"

She tossed her head and looked away, making a scoffing sound that wouldn't have deceived a child. "That seems like pretty slim evidence to me."

"On the contrary. No woman would ever wear a scent she didn't love."

She sniffed as if unimpressed. "I daresay you know a great deal about what women love."

He grinned at that. He couldn't help it; she sounded so prim. "I know enough," he said. "But I also overheard you in the flower shop at the Savoy, saying you wanted a gardenia for your hat. And..."

He paused again, his grin fading as his arousal rose higher.

"And," he resumed, bracing himself for the torture he knew was to come, "the first time I ever saw you, you had a gardenia in your hair. Right here," he added softly, lifting his hand to her temple. Her hair felt like silk, and without thinking, he leaned forward as if to kiss her, but he jerked back in time, letting his hand fall and reminding himself sternly not to ruin the moment by rushing things.

She was staring at him as if in disbelief. "You remember the flower in my hair? After all this time? Most men, I daresay, wouldn't even know what flower it was, much less remember it fourteen years later."

He lowered his gaze to her full pink lips, then lifted it again to look into her eyes. "I remember everything, Kay."

Her tongue flicked over those lips, calling to the desire inside him. "You do?"

"I do," he said, and took a deep breath, summoning all his control, "I remember that night in Chiswick in the maze, when I kissed you for the very first time. The moon was nearly full, and I remember it made your eyes look like silver. I remember the scent of your hair and the feel of your body in my arms."

He watched the color wash up her neck and into her face, telling him his words were having an effect, and when her lips parted, he decided to push his luck a little further. "I remember all the times we snuck out of some ball or party, how we talked and laughed." He lifted his hand again, cupping her cheek, caressing the plump curve of her lower lip with his thumb. "All the times we kissed."

She was as pink as a peony now, and he pushed on.

"I remember Birmingham," he said, his voice unsteady to his own ears, "and that inn where we stayed. I remember watching you take down your hair and how it looked like liquid copper in the firelight. I remember your silhouette behind that screen as you changed into a nightgown—the fullness of your breasts, the curve of your waist, the flare of your hips—and I remember that it took every shred of willpower I possessed not to fling the damn screen aside, haul you into my arms, and make love to you right then and there. I remember heartily cursing myself for doing the noble thing and sleeping on the floor because we weren't married yet, and I remember the torture of lying there in the dark with you so close by and me with raw, unrequited lust coursing through every cell of my body. Hell," he added with a hoarse laugh, "it's hard not to remember all that, since it's precisely what I'm feeling right now."

Her breath was coming faster now, quick little puffs against his thumb, and though he knew making love to her with words was a tactic that seemed to be working, he also knew that he was at the brink.

He wrenched his hand away, and when he took a step away from her, it felt as if he were ripping himself in two.

"It's getting late," he said. "We should go back."

"Yes," she agreed in a whisper. "But then..." She paused and looked at him, and something in her eyes made him fear that all his efforts to be noble were about to be absolutely shredded. "When have we ever done what we should?"

He didn't know quite who moved first, but suddenly, the clipboard between them was clattering to the floor along with her handbag, and she was in his arms. As his hands pressed into her back to pull her even closer, she rose on her toes, and then, to his stunned surprise, she wrapped her arms around his neck and kissed him.

At the touch of her mouth, all his resolutions about courtship seemed absurd. His arm wrapped tightly around her waist, and his other hand cupped her cheek.

Her skin was soft and warm, her lips were like velvet, but it wasn't enough. He slid his hand to the nape of her neck and opened his mouth against hers to deepen the kiss. When her lips parted in surrender, the soft moan she made into his mouth sent his desire rising even higher.

Kay, he thought in joyous agony. *Kay.*

His tongue entered her mouth, and he tasted deeply of her as he slid his free hand up her ribs to brush the side of her breast. He lingered there, but the hard whalebone rigidity of her corset stood in the way of any possible explorations there, and he moved his hand down again, over her waist to her hip.

The scent of gardenias filled his head, desire was coursing through his body like a flood, and his heart was thudding so hard, he thought it would come right out of his chest.

He dipped at the knees, pressing his hips to hers, and the pleasure was so sharp, so exquisite, he tore his lips from hers with a groan. Fighting to stay on his feet, he rocked against her, relishing the low moan she made in response.

He pulled back again, but only to grasp her skirts, pulling them upward to get his hand beneath.

She made a faint sound that might have been a protest, and he froze, waiting in an agony of tension, but when she said nothing and didn't push him away, he moved again, gliding his hand slowly up her thigh as he tilted his head, to press kisses along her jaw to her ear. Then, slowly, giving her plenty of time to object if she chose, he eased his hand between her thighs.

She gave a shuddering gasp, and he kissed her, capturing the sound in his mouth as he slid his fingers inside the slit of her drawers.

All those years ago, they'd never gone this far, and as he touched the soft, slick wetness of her, the pleasure was so great, he almost sank to his knees.

He caressed the crease of her sex, and he relished the low, soft sounds she made in response. As her breathing quickened to desperate pants and her hips worked frantically against his hand, he knew she was nearing climax, and once again, he used words to arouse her further.

"You're close," he murmured, delicately caressing her clitoris with his thumb. "So close, my love. Let it happen. Come for me. Come."

And then she did, giving a sharp, keening cry that was like the sweetest music he'd ever heard. Again and again, her muscles clenched hard around his hand as he continued to caress her, wringing the last few spasms of pleasure from her. Then she collapsed, panting, her knees buckling beneath her. He caught her, pulling his hand from beneath her skirts and wrapping both arms around her waist, holding her tight against him.

He was painfully aware of his own throbbing need, but this wasn't the way to sate it. Not like this. Not in an empty hotel, against a wall. The way was courtship and romance, culminating in a big wedding for everyone in society to see. That was what she wanted, and he intended to give it to her.

Hat askew, loosened tendrils of red-gold hair falling around her face, she looked deliciously rumpled. She stared up at him with those strange, magical eyes of hers, reminding him of that first night when he'd asked her to dance. As if... as if he was her hero. And he almost wanted to laugh, because right now, with lust coursing through every cell of his body, he felt anything but heroic.

"Why did you stop?" she panted.

"Because we can't." He pressed a quick kiss to her mouth and stepped back, forcing himself to let her go. "Not now. Not like this."

He turned abruptly away. "I'll wait for you in the carriage," he said. And then, as he had done so many times when they were young, he turned away from her with his body on fire.

"But for God's sake, Kay," he said over his shoulder as he walked away, "give me a minute or two before you come down. Or I really don't know what might happen."

He started down the stairs, and he didn't look back. Because he knew that if he turned, if he looked at her again, with her rumpled skirts and wide eyes and just-kissed lips, the honorable courtship he'd embarked upon a few weeks ago would be nothing more than a bad joke.

He crossed the empty lobby and walked out the front door, into the warm afternoon sun. Leaning his back against the brick wall beside the door, he closed his eyes, breathing deeply of the sultry summer air, working to contain his lust, just as he had when he was a lad of twenty.

No wonder he'd wanted to elope all those years ago. Courtship, he thought caustically, was a hellish business.

18

Kay closed her eyes as Devlin's footsteps faded away, her head in a whirl, her body still pulsing with all the strange, glorious sensations he had evoked with his touch. She wasn't completely naïve about these things, but she hadn't known—hadn't ever dreamed—it could feel like this. In all the frantic kisses of their youth, never once had they gone this far.

She opened her eyes, and as she stared at the wall opposite, she knew that for the rest of her life, she would remember that peeling, stained, absolutely beautiful gardenia wallpaper.

Down below, she heard a door open and close, reminding her that they had to go back, back to reality where she had to be proper and decorous and careful. How tiresome.

Kay straightened away from the wall, tidied her skirt and hat, and retrieved her clipboard and handbag from the floor, but even as she did these things, she still felt as if she were in a dream.

As the carriage took them back to the West End, neither of them spoke. Kay was still too overwhelmed by what had happened between them, and she felt a bit shy in consequence. In addition,

Devlin stared out the carriage window for most of the journey, causing her shyness to give way to uncertainty.

There were things she badly wanted to ask him, but his demeanor didn't invite questions, and it wasn't until the carriage was nearly at the hotel that she found her nerve.

"Devlin? Are you all right?"

He still didn't look at her, but to her surprise, he gave a chuckle. "No," he said. "For that, I fear a dunk in a very cold bath will be required."

Given the fiery episode of half an hour before, she had at least some idea of what he meant. "Oh," she murmured, her face heating.

"What about you?" he asked.

"Me? I feel..." She paused and sighed. "I feel wonderful, actually."

"I'm glad."

Encouraged, she took a deep breath. "Why... why did you stop?"

He turned toward her, but he didn't quite look at her. Instead, he bent his head, staring at his hat in his lap. "You deserve a proper courtship," he said simply. "And that means our first time ought to be after we're married. Not against a wall in an abandoned hotel." Suddenly, he smiled a little. "Besides, I didn't want all the other times I actually did the honorable thing and stopped in time to have been wasted sacrifices."

That made her laugh.

The carriage turned into the alley, and he lifted his head, looking at her at last, a direct, steady gaze that brought her amusement to an abrupt end and made her catch her breath. "I love you, you know."

The carriage stopped, and the driver hopped down from the box and opened the door before she could reply. They exited the vehicle, Kay's mind still reeling.

He loved her still? After all this time? After everything that had happened? She stared at him, stunned, and she had no idea what to reply.

The accepted mode, of course, was to say she loved him, too, but was it love?

Thankfully, he didn't seem to expect an answer, for he was already walking to the hotel's back door.

She stared after him, unable to define what she felt right now. Glorious, alive, happy, still reeling from the incredible sensations he'd evoked in her, sensations she'd never even dreamed existed. Was that love, or was it infatuation and the euphoria of sated desire? Or worse, was it really just a desperate, grasping effort to recapture what they'd had and lost so long ago? She didn't want to declare love unless she was sure, and she wasn't sure.

She knew she was painfully vulnerable where he was concerned, that he could still make her head swim and take her breath away, and make her mad as a hornet. Was that love?

He paused by the door, opened it, and turned. "Are you coming?"

Dismayed that she was standing there like a lovestruck adolescent, she moved to follow, passing through the door he held open for her, trying to pretend a nonchalance completely at odds with her topsy-turvy emotions.

Still, despite her inability to define how she felt about Devlin, she knew she didn't want this wonderful day to end, not quite yet. When they paused by her office door, she seized on an excuse and gestured to the corridor behind him. "I thought I'd fetch my letters," she said. "The afternoon post is here by now, I expect." She paused, took a breath, and added, "Walk with me?"

His smile was her reward, and the sight of it tilted her heart sideways. "What an excellent idea."

They traversed the corridor side by side. Neither of them spoke, but it was, somehow, a companionable silence.

At the front desk, they each found a handful of letters awaiting them. Devlin, however, also had a cable.

"Came just ten minutes ago, Mr. Sharpe," the clerk told him, holding out the folded slip of paper.

The moment Devlin opened it, Kay knew from his grim expression that something was terribly wrong.

"Not bad news, I hope?" she murmured, her joy in the day faltering.

He looked up, meeting her gaze, and her stomach clenched with dread. The news, whatever it was, was very bad indeed.

"There's been a fire," he said tersely, and looked down at the slip of paper in his hand. "My hotel in Cairo."

"Oh, dear God. How awful." Kay covered her mouth, dismayed and heartsick. "Have they put it out? Was anyone killed?"

"I don't know if there's any dead. But the fire doesn't seem contained, since my secretary says other buildings are in danger as well. He advises me to return immediately."

"Oh, Devlin, I'm so sorry."

He didn't reply. "The Calais-Méditerranée is probably the fastest way," he murmured as if thinking out loud. "Six days...maybe eight."

He looked at her again. "I've got to go to Cook's at once and see what can be arranged. And I have to see Simon, let him know what's happened."

"Of course. You'll let me know, once you…" She paused, her voice wobbling as it finally penetrated her shocked senses that he was leaving, and her heart sank.

He seemed to sense it. "I'm sorry."

Kay took a breath, reminding herself that this was not the time for him to be thinking about her feelings. He didn't need that burden after this devastating news. "There's nothing to be sorry about, Devlin. You'll…" She paused and swallowed hard. "You'll let me know once you know your travel plans?"

"Of course. It will probably take a couple of hours. I'll call on you the minute I return."

"I'll wait in my rooms," she began, then remembered. "Blast it, I can't. I won't be here. I've got the Farthingtons' dinner party tonight, and I promised Jo I'd be there. She's sweet on Lord Farthington's son, I think, and she wants me to meet him. It would be a good match for her. She'll be terribly disappointed if I miss it, but—"

"Don't miss it. We can talk tomorrow morning. The Calais-Méditerranée express doesn't even leave from Dover until the afternoon, so we have plenty of time to…" He stopped and took a deep breath. "To say goodbye."

Don't make it harder for him than it needs to be, she told herself firmly. *He doesn't need that now.*

"Come to my office first thing," she said. "I'm always at my desk by nine. Now, go," she urged when he hesitated. "You won't be able to arrange anything standing here."

He nodded and turned away, and as she watched him go, she felt a strange, unmistakable foreboding about his departure for Cairo.

What if he doesn't come back?

At once, she tried to shove the question aside, but no matter how she tried, she couldn't, because she knew, better than anyone, that nothing in life was sure. She also knew, as she watched him walk away, that she loved him, too. And now, just as she was figuring that out, he was leaving, walking out of her life again before she even had the chance to tell him how she felt, and there wasn't a damn thing she could do about it.

Or was there?

Kay considered the question as she watched him exit the front doors of the hotel and vanish. She'd decided to take charge of her own life, hadn't she? She'd resolved to start going after what she really wanted, hadn't she? Well, perhaps it was time to put those fine resolutions to the test. Her mind made up, Kay turned and marched toward the lift.

Devlin returned to the Mayfair at midnight. He'd spent most of his evening sending cables to Cairo and waiting for replies, but it wasn't until an hour ago that he had gotten any definitive news from his secretary.

> *Fire out but hotel and dock total loss. No one dead. Some boats may be salvageable. Insurance company notified. Need you here posthaste.*
>
> *—Morse*

Devlin set the cables on his dressing table, staring at the top one, both relieved and worried. Mercifully, no one had been killed, because in June, the hotel was nearly empty. In January, it would have been different. Every room would have been occupied, and the death toll could have been catastrophic.

The investors would be worried, nervous. He knew he had to get home as quickly as possible and take charge. Morse was a good man, but a secretary couldn't pacify a group of skittish businessmen. He'd have to assess the damage, meet the insurance agent, make a plan of how to rebuild…

Naked, he fell into bed, his body tired, his mind still reeling. Cook's had made his travel arrangements by the quickest route possible. He'd be home in a week.

But what about Kay?

He rolled onto his back, staring at the ceiling. He hated to leave her now, just when he felt as if their future together had a chance. She hadn't said she loved him, and that hurt, he had to admit. He'd wondered in that moment if she'd ever fall back in love with him the way he had with her. But he had shut that pessimistic fear down at once, refusing to indulge it, reminding himself that all he could do was hope that, given time and a patient, gradual courtship, she'd come to feel as he did. But now, there was no time.

He gave a groan and rolled onto his stomach, burying his face in his folded arms. Was Fate ever going to give them a chance? he wondered in despair.

The soft tap on the sitting room door lifted his head. *Kay,* he thought, and though he knew it was more likely to be additional news from Cairo, his heart gave a leap of joy and he was out of bed like a shot.

He'd only taken three steps, however, before he remembered he didn't have any clothes on. Cursing, he stepped back, and grabbed a dressing robe, sliding into it and tying the sash as he crossed to the sitting room door and opened it.

His first guess had been right, for it was indeed Kay who was standing in the corridor, her glorious hair loose around her shoulders, a lamp in her hand. She was also, he noted, looking down, wearing nothing but a nightgown and robe.

He didn't know if he was ecstatic or dismayed, but he did know one thing.

"God, woman," he muttered, hauling her inside before some other hotel guest decided to use the corridor bathroom in the middle of the night, came out of their room, and saw her hovering at his door in a state of undress. "This is becoming quite a habit with you," he added as he shut the door behind her. "What are you doing here at this hour?"

She set the lamp on the table beside the door. "Is there any news?"

He stared, nonplussed. "You came to my room at this hour to ask me that?"

"Yes." She paused, touching her tongue to her lips as if they were dry, making his desire for her, the desire he'd been desperately banking all day, flicker to dangerous life. "Among other things."

He met her eyes, resolving he would not look at her luscious mouth again, or anything below it either. "The fire's out," he said, keeping his gaze firmly locked with hers. "No one died."

"That's good. When... when do you go?"

"I'm not leaving until noon tomorrow, so we'll have plenty of time to see each other in the morning and say goodbye. Now," he added, taking her by the elbow and reaching for the doorknob, "if that's all..."

She put her hands behind her, covering the doorknob before he could get to it. "It's not all."

He sighed, his arms dropping to his sides. "Of course it's not," he muttered.

"I'm really here because you're leaving, and we don't know when you'll be back—"

"But I will be back, Kay. I promise you. Just don't go getting engaged to someone else in the meantime, if you please."

She laughed, but it was a decidedly nervous laugh. And so it should be, he thought sardonically, since they were both standing here in his hotel room at midnight. Nearly naked.

And with that reminder, Devlin felt his desire flare into hot, blazing lust, and he knew he had to get her out of here, now.

"Kay, for God's sake, if you don't leave this instant, I swear I'll come undone."

"You will?" Her smile widened. "I think I'd like to see that."

"No," he denied, growing downright desperate. "No, you wouldn't."

"But I would," she whispered, letting go of the doorknob and stepping forward to close the distance between them. "That's why I came. I decided that before you go, we needed to finish what we started."

Trying to steady himself, he took a deep breath, but he inhaled the luscious gardenia scent of her hair, and his fortitude slipped a notch. "Kay, we can't. I told you, this is a proper courtship."

"We've never been proper before," she reminded him, lifting her hands to finger the edges of his robe, putting all his honorable efforts in serious jeopardy.

"Well, no," he was forced to agree, "but—"

She stepped closer and wrapped her arms around his neck, cutting off whatever he'd been about to say. "Why start now?"

He wrenched free, grabbed her wrists, and pulled them down, deciding it was time to be ruthlessly blunt. "Damn it, Kay. If you stay I'll take your virtue. Do you know what that means?"

She actually seemed nettled by the question. "Of course I do. I'm not a child. I'm thirty-two, for heaven's sake."

"Then you know if I give you what you're so sweetly asking for, the result could be that you're with child. And I'll be on the other side of the world, with no idea when I'll be back."

"Yes, well..." She paused and gave a little cough. "I...ahem...I thought of that."

He couldn't believe what he was hearing. "You did?"

She nodded. Pulling free of his hold, she reached into the pocket of her robe and pulled out a long, flat envelope of red velvet. "That's why I brought this. It prevents pregnancy, I understand?"

"My God," he muttered, rubbing his hands over his face, praying for fortitude, fearing such a thing was quite impossible at this point. "My holy God."

"It's called a French—"

"I know what it is." He grabbed the envelope and the condom he knew was tucked inside out of her hand. "Where in blazes did you get this?"

"I saw an advertisement for it once in one of Mama's ladies' magazines. A shop in Soho has them. So, after we parted this afternoon, I went there and bought one."

"How could you have done? Only men and married ladies can buy these."

"Yes, so the advertisement said. So I took Mama's wedding ring out of her jewelry box and put it on my finger. And I took off my gloves while I was there. That way," she added as he gave a groan, "they'd believe me when I assured them I was married."

Devlin's control was slipping further into oblivion with every word she spoke, but he had to try, one last time, to dissuade her. "Kay," he began.

"I love you, too, by the way," she said, cutting the grass from beneath his feet in an instant.

"You do?"

She bit her lip, nodding as she looked up at him.

"Well, you might have said so this afternoon, Kay," he replied, feeling quite nettled all of a sudden. "I said it first, and you didn't say it back, leaving me in an agony of suspense, wondering if you were ever going to fall in love with me again."

"I didn't want to say it unless I was sure, and when you said it, I wasn't. But as I watched you walk out of the hotel, headed for Cook's, I thought of how it would be, me here and you thousands of miles away for weeks or months or maybe even years, and how much that was going to hurt. And I knew I was in love with you. Fourteen years ago, we had the chance for a night like this, Devlin, and we let it pass by. Are you really going to make us wait any longer for a second one?"

Like a dam breaking, all his resolve crumbled to bits, and he caught her in his arms, pulling her hard against him. "Hell, no," he muttered. "I never make the same mistake twice."

With that, he bent his head and kissed her.

19

Desire was clawing at him already, but he kept the kiss soft and tender as he slid an arm around her waist and pulled her close. He lifted his other hand to stroke her hair.

It felt like liquid silk, and he lingered a moment, toying with it, twisting strands around his fingers, then, wrapping tresses around his fist, he tilted her head back and deepened the kiss.

Her mouth opened at once in surrender, and as he tasted deeply of her, his heart began to pound hard in his chest. But even this luscious kiss wasn't enough. He wanted more.

He broke the kiss, pulling back enough to slide his hands between them to untie the sash of her robe. When he pulled the edges of the garment apart, his knuckles brushed her breasts, and just that was enough to send sharp shards of sensation through his body and threaten to break the precarious hold he had on his control.

But he knew he could not let that happen. It had taken them fourteen years to get to this moment, and he wasn't about to ruin it by rushing things. He had to slow down, so he reluctantly slid his hands away and took a step back, letting her go and earning a cry of dismay from her.

"You're not stopping?"

Her anxious voice was loud enough that he cupped her face and pressed his thumb to her lips.

"Believe me, Kay," he said, his voice unsteady to his own ears, "I couldn't stop now if my life depended on it. But we've got to keep our voices down. We're in a hotel, remember? There's probably guests on both sides of us."

She nodded, but when she lifted her hands as if to remove his robe as he had done hers, he grasped her wrists to stop her. "I want this to be right for you, and while I realize that you are no longer a girl of just eighteen, but a very sophisticated woman of thirty-two, I also know that when it comes to lovemaking, I know a bit more than you."

"Oh, really?" she whispered, frowning a little. "And just how did you acquire this knowledge, hmm?"

"I knew about this before we ever even met," he assured her, wisely steering clear of the fact that he hadn't exactly been celibate for the past fourteen years. "Because of that, it's important that you let me lead."

"A bit like dancing, then."

"Very much like dancing."

"Oh, very well," she said meekly, but when she flashed him a wicked smile, he feared remaining in charge of this from start to finish was going to prove a Herculean task, and her next words confirmed the fact. "But if you dance too slowly, Devlin, I'm taking over."

Despite her threat, he let her go and drew back, then raked a hand through his hair and took a moment for a long, deep breath. Having already spent most of the day in a very acute state of unsated sexual arousal, he willed himself to keep his own desires securely in check and concentrate on hers.

"All right, then," he said at last and reached up to push her hair back from her shoulders, a move that showed the outline of her hardened nipples beneath the thin fabric of her nightgown, requiring him to take another slow, deep breath, then he lifted his hands and cupped her breasts through the fabric.

There was no corset to get in the way, and he gave a groan of appreciation as he felt her breasts in his hands. She might be slimmer now than she'd been as a girl, but her breasts were lush and full, and he relished the fact as he toyed with them for a bit, embracing their shape and brushing his thumbs over her nipples. Unable to resist, he bent his head, and through the thin muslin of her gown, he took one of her nipples into his mouth.

She gave a sharp gasp, and her knees buckled. Instantly, he wrapped his arm around her waist, but he did not stop. Holding her upright, he suckled her, relishing the quickening of her breathing and the way she shivered in his hold.

After a few moments, he pulled back, but only because he wanted more. "I want to see you," he said, grasping folds of her nightgown in his fists. "Lift your arms."

She complied, raising her arms to the ceiling, and he pulled the gown upward and over her head, baring her body completely.

Her skin was flushed a delicate shade of pink, making the freckles scattered across her face, shoulders, and bosom look more like brown sugar than ever. Her breasts were every bit as perfect as his explorations had told him they would be. Her nipples were turgid, showing her arousal, and he once again took her in his arms and bent his head, pressing kisses to her hot cheeks and her chin, then lower, along her neck and across her clavicle, then lower still to those exquisite breasts, but to his surprise, she stopped him.

"Wait," she gasped. Pulling free of his hold, she reached for the sash of his dressing gown. "My turn to look."

He groaned and grasped her hands. "I'm leading this dance," he said sternly.

"But I want to see you," she whispered. "Fair's fair."

He hesitated, for he was fully aroused, and he had no idea what she'd make of that, but she had as much right to see his body as he had to see hers. "Well, when you put it like that," he muttered and let her go.

She untied the sash and pushed the dressing gown from his shoulders, but as it fell to the floor behind him, she didn't look where he thought she would. Instead, her gaze paused at his bare chest. She touched him, and he inhaled sharply, tilting back his head and bearing it as she slid her hands across his shoulders, over his nipples and down to his abdomen, where she stopped.

"Oh!" she said, her startled exclamation telling him she'd seen him in all his flagrant glory. "That's not what I..." She lifted her head, frowning a little. "You don't look anything like the statues in the British Museum."

He gave a shout of laughter. "What were you expecting?" he teased, tilting his head to look into her face. "A fig leaf?"

She made a face, pressing her hand to his shoulder and giving him a playful shove for his impudence. "No, of course not. But..." She paused and looked down, and her cheeks turned absolutely scarlet. "Goodness."

She reached out as if to touch him, but that would be a bridge too far. He was in a precarious enough state as it was. "Oh, no," he groaned, pushing her hand away. "We're not to that point in this dance just yet."

She started to protest, but he bent down, sliding one arm behind her back and hooking the other beneath her knees, then he lifted her into his arms and silenced her laughing squeal with a long, deep kiss as he carried her into his bedroom.

He laid her on the bed, but he didn't join her. Instead, he stood beside the bed, letting his gaze roam over her, from her coppery hair spread across the sheets to her adorable face to her perfect breasts to the deep curve of her waist, to the generous curves of her hips. His gaze caught there, on the red-gold triangle between her thighs. He grasped her hips in his hands, turning her body and easing his own between her legs as he sank to his knees.

He put his hands on her thighs, pulling her legs wider apart, then he bent his head.

Guessing his intent, she stiffened, giving a startled gasp, and her thighs clenched, her knees pressing against his shoulders.

He lifted his head, waiting until she did the same. "Kay," he said softly, his fingers touching her most intimate place as their eyes met. "I want to kiss you here. Let me do this. Trust me."

Her eyes were wide as saucers, but she nodded, relaxing a fraction, and he slowly bent his head to press his lips to her fiery curls.

She gave a long, soft wail at the contact, and he reveled in the sound, smiling as her head fell back against the mattress. Still watching her, he ran his tongue over the crease of her sex to her clitoris, and this time, she gave a startled cry. Instantly, she stifled it with her hand, and he smiled, knowing the tension of having to be quiet would only arouse her further.

Closing his eyes, he allowed his other senses to take over. She smelled like flowers, and she tasted like heaven, and as he caressed her again and again with his tongue, he relished her stifled sounds of pleasure and the thrust of her hips against his mouth.

"Devlin," she whispered. "Oh, oh."

She was so close. He continued this carnal kiss, stroking her relentlessly, until, with a final sob of pleasure, she came.

He continued to kiss and caress her and nuzzle her, wringing more orgasms from her, then finally, with one last kiss, he stood up.

Kay lifted her head to look at him. She wanted to say something, but the feelings within her were so overwhelming, she couldn't find words.

He lifted her legs and turned her body, stretching her out on the bed. Then he left her, going into the sitting room, and when he returned, the French letter was in his hand. As he moved to the other side of the bed, she dared a peek at him, and though the lamplight that spilled through the door from the sitting room was faint, it was enough to confirm that his manhood was still jutting out proudly in front of him, and she realized with sudden insight just what that French letter was supposed to do.

He paused by the side of the bed, pulled the sheath of vulcanized rubber from its velvet envelope, and unfolded it. Tossing the envelope aside, he slid the sheath along the length of his shaft, and she felt a sudden, strange pang of fear.

He looked up, making her realize she had made a shocked sound, and instantly, he was on the bed beside her, kissing her.

"I love you," he said against her mouth, then he pulled back to look into her face. "Do you love me?"

Without hesitation, she nodded. She didn't quite know how all this was going to work, but her love for him was absolutely certain. "Yes," she said, reaching up to touch his face. "I love you."

He bent his head as if to kiss her again, then paused. "Just to clarify things, you are going to marry me, aren't you?"

Talk of honorable marriage seemed strange when they were both naked and aroused and about to do something that was strictly forbidden outside marriage. "What a question to ask at such a moment," she murmured with a chuckle.

"I mean it, Kay." His voice was strained, his face suddenly hard. "Without marriage in the offing, I'm not taking your virtue. Yes or no?"

"Yes," she said happily and kissed him. "Yes, yes. I'll marry you as soon as you come back."

"Thank God," he muttered. "I thought I was going to have to toss you out and take another cold bath."

He moved then, easing his body on top of hers, and she gladly opened her arms, but then, he stopped again, resting his weight on his arm, suspended above her as his hand maneuvered the hard, sheathed part of his body between her thighs.

"One thing you need to know." His voice sounded hoarse, his breathing labored, and he paused, his face grim, as if he was striving for control. Sweat glistened on his chest, on his forehead, and his breathing was quick and harsh. "I've got to warn you about this. You've never been with a man before, so it's probably going to hurt."

That news was a bit alarming, but then he rocked his hips against hers, and as the hard part of him rubbed the place he had kissed so wickedly a short time ago, she forgot to be afraid. With a moan, she closed her eyes, savoring the sweet, aching delight of it.

"God, Kay," he groaned. His free hand slid between them, his fingers touching her, opening her. Then he lowered his body onto hers, sliding his hand out from between them as his hard shaft pressed against her, and then, with a hard thrust, fully into her.

She gasped, the sharp, stinging pain snapping her eyes open. "Devlin?"

He kissed her. "It'll be all right," he said. "I love you."

With that reassurance, he slid his arms beneath her, buried his face against the side of her neck, and flexed his hips, a move that thrust him more deeply into her.

Thankfully, the pain had already begun to subside, and she wriggled her hips, trying to accustom herself to the strange fullness of him inside of her.

The move seemed to ignite something inside him, for he quickened the pace, each thrust stronger and deeper than the one before. His eyes were closed, his lips parted, and it was almost as if he'd forgotten about her, but he was stroking her hair and saying her name, and she realized it wasn't that at all. He was caught up in the pleasure of this joining.

With that thought, she relaxed beneath him, and with his next thrust, she pushed up to meet him. Then she did it again, and again, urging him to a faster pace, and faster still, as an aching, hungry need rose within her, the need for more of those amazing, explosive sensations that he had evoked with his touch and his mouth.

Suddenly, it happened. She reached the peak, waves of that sweet, earth-shattering pleasure rippling through her.

"I love you," she whispered against his ear, her legs tight around him, her body clenching around his shaft as the pleasure kept coming. "Oh, Devlin, I love you so."

With those words, shudders suddenly rocked his body and he cried out, a smothered cry against her neck. He thrust against her several more times, and then collapsed, his breathing hard and labored against the side of her throat.

She raked her fingers through his hair and stroked the hard, strong muscles of his back and shoulders. When he kissed her hair and murmured her name, happiness rose within her like a fierce, surging tide.

She was so glad she had come tonight. Because she'd spent so long—too long—being afraid. Afraid of doing the wrong thing, of earning disapproval, of making mistakes, of what people would say. It had gotten her nothing but worry, aggravation, and pain.

Now, the only thing she cared about was him and their love, and she knew that no matter how long they were separated, she would have the beauty of this moment and her newfound courage to sustain her.

20

Devlin woke to the scent of gardenias, and that told him that what he'd experienced wasn't a dream. Kay had come to his room in the night, shredded all his honorable intentions of proper courtship, and mercilessly seduced him. What a woman.

Eyes closed, he smiled, imagining how she'd looked with her copper hair spread across the pillows, her adorable, freckled face flushed with arousal. Making love to Kay had been the most beautiful, extraordinary experience of his life.

Still smiling, still half asleep, he rolled over, hoping perhaps they could enjoy each other a little longer before she had to sneak back into her room, but when he opened his eyes, he knew it wasn't to be. Morning light was streaming in between a gap in the curtains, and the place beside him was empty. The scent of her still lingered on the bed linens, but she was gone.

He groaned and grabbed her pillow, holding it tight as sudden desolation swamped him. This, he knew, was how it would be for some time to come. Waking to nothing but memories of her until he could return. He thought of those early days in Africa, and he didn't know if he could endure all that again.

Wretchedly cruel of fate to do this now, just when everything seemed to be coming right for them. But he had to go. He had a duty to his investors and to the people who worked for him and depended on him for their livelihood. And she had to stay.

Unless...

Devlin flung aside the pillow and got out of bed. There just might be a way for history to repeat itself, but with a much better ending.

Kay stared listlessly at the letter she was trying to write. Somehow, telling Baroness Voytevsky that they would be happy to reserve her a suite, but that, alas, they would be unable to accommodate her seven Pekingese dogs just wasn't holding her attention.

She turned her head, glancing at the clock on her credenza. Nearly ten o'clock already? How could time pass so slowly and yet so quickly at the same time?

Devlin would surely be here any minute to say goodbye, and dread at the prospect was like a stone in the pit of her stomach.

He'll come back, she thought, plunking her elbows on her desk and burying her face in her hands, willing it to be true. *He will come back.*

A sound lifted her head, and when she saw Devlin in the doorway, the dread inside her intensified, twisting in her guts. It was time.

She took a deep breath and stood up. "Good morning."

He took off his hat and bowed. "Sorry I'm late. I know we agreed on nine o'clock, but..." He paused, a faint smile curving his mouth as he came in and shut the door behind him. "Some ripping redheaded siren invaded my rooms last night and seduced me, sapping all my energy."

She almost smiled back. "You were sleeping like the dead when I left. I'd have stayed, but..."

Now it was her turn to pause, her throat closing up, for she couldn't tell him that as he'd slept, she had lain beside him as long as she could bear it before tearing herself away. She couldn't tell him that had she stayed a moment longer than that, she'd have woken him and begged him to stay.

"I understand," he said. "Hotel staff are always up before dawn. Wouldn't do for anyone to see you."

She seized on that with relief. "Exactly. Yes, quite so."

There was a sudden, awkward silence.

She forced herself to break it. "Are you packed?"

"Yes. The bellboys are loading my trunks into a cab as we speak."

Already? A sob rose in her throat, and she choked it back. "And when is your train?"

"The train for Dover leaves Victoria Station at one o'clock. Then across to Calais, and the train to Nice."

That was hours away, but she understood. What was the point of long, drawn-out, agonizing goodbyes?

"The Calais-Méditerranée, I assume?" When he nodded, she went on, "You'll take a boat from there to Cairo?"

He nodded. "Steamship. It's the fastest way."

"Of course."

There was another silence, then suddenly, he moved, crossing her office and coming around to her side of the desk. "Come with me."

"What?" She stared, stunned, thrilled, overjoyed. And then she remembered why that was impossible. "I can't, Devlin," she whispered, wretched once again.

"Yes, you can." Tossing aside his hat, he hauled her into his arms. "It's simple. You pack your bags and put them in the cab with mine, and we're off. There is a Cook's office at Victoria Station," he added when she didn't reply. "We buy your tickets, and there we are, on our way to Egypt together. We can be married when we get to Cairo."

"Elope, you mean."

"Yes."

She was tempted, oh, so tempted. But it was impossible. "Devlin," she began.

He stopped her, cupping her face and pressing his thumb to her lips. "I know it's a scandal, but does that matter now?"

"I'm afraid," she said softly against his thumb, "that it does matter."

He slid his hand to the back of her neck, his thumb caressing her cheek. "But why? What can the scandal sheets say about us that they haven't already said?"

"It's not that."

"Is it the opinion of the ton that's got you worried? Sod them. Our friends will stand by us."

"I know. It's not that, either."

He frowned, still clearly baffled, his hand sliding away. "Then what is it?"

"I don't care anymore what drivel the scandal sheets print about me, or what the ton thinks of me. But, Devlin, my darling, it isn't about me at all, or you, or us. It's about Josephine."

He blinked. "What does your sister have to do with it? Are you afraid she won't have a dowry? Of course I'll provide her with—"

He broke off as she shook her head. "It's not that, either," she said. "I know you will give her a dowry, of course you will. And even if you couldn't, it wouldn't matter. I've come to realize that marrying a man you love is far more important than marrying the one your family wants, or the one who can best provide for you. I'd marry you if you didn't have a bean. But I can't elope with you."

"Because that will hurt her chances."

"Yes. If she were married already and had a strong social position, I wouldn't hesitate. But that's not the case. She's barely halfway through her first season. More important, she hasn't been presented at court. And if we elope, she won't ever be. That alone could wreck her chances of making a good marriage. I couldn't bear it if that happened just because I couldn't wait a few months or even a few years to secure my own happiness. I ruined things for her once before she was even out of pinafores, Devlin, and it took me years to atone for that and return our family to a halfway decent social position. I can't ruin things for her again. I won't."

He didn't reply, but his face was grim, and she tried to smile. "At least we don't have to worry about a baby," she said. "I made sure of that."

"And I let you." He lowered his head with a sigh, rubbing four fingers over his forehead. "A decision on my part that in hindsight seems extraordinarily stupid."

She didn't reply. She waited, and at last, he looked up.

"So," he said, squaring his shoulders, "it's no, then, is it?"

"I'm afraid it is. It must be. I can't cause Josephine the same pain and humiliation I suffered. I just can't do that to her. Do you understand?"

He didn't reply, but the pain in his face tore at her, ripping her heart out.

"Oh, Devlin," she cried, suddenly fearing the worst. "Please tell me you understand!"

"Of course I understand." His arms came up, wrapping around her as she sagged with relief. "I hate it, Kay," he muttered, his lips brushing her hair. "I do. I won't lie. I hate it, and I resent like hell the stupid rules and tight-laced morality that governs all our lives, but I also know the pain you've suffered and how much you love your sister and how you want to spare her that same pain. And as frustrating as it is and how hellish it's going to make our lives for the next few months, it only makes me love you more."

A sob came from her, a sob of wrenching pain and overwhelming love, and also a tiny little speck of disappointment that he hadn't rejected her reasons, hauled her over his shoulder, and carried her out here by force, taking the decision out of her hands.

He heard it, that sob, and his arms tightened, holding her so strongly, it took her breath away. "I'll be back," he promised fiercely.

"Of course you will," she mumbled against his lapel.

She must not have sounded convincing, for he grabbed her arms and pushed her back to look into her face. "Listen to me," he ordered, giving her a little shake. "I'll get things straightened out as quickly as I can, but it won't happen overnight. It'll take a few months, maybe a year, before I can come back to England."

"I know." She took his face in her hands and looked into his beautiful eyes, putting the best face on things, for his sake. "At least no one's going to suppress our letters this time. And even if they do, I won't lose faith in you or in us."

"Neither will I."

"And I won't be holed away in Wales, thank heaven, with only my mother and little sister for company. I have my work here at the Mayfair, and that will give me something useful to do while you're away."

"When I come back, we'll get married, and it will be the biggest, grandest wedding the ton's ever seen."

"Damned right it will."

He smiled a little. "Just don't go getting engaged to anyone else while I'm gone, all right?"

Laughter bubbled up inside her, ending in a sob. She choked it back. "I won't, I promise."

The clock on her credenza chimed the half hour, and she couldn't bear it another moment. "You'd better go," she said, her voice suddenly, surprisingly resolute.

He pulled her close, bent his head and kissed her, hard. Then, he let her go, picked up his hat, and turned abruptly away, walking toward the door. He opened it and started to walk out, but then he paused again to look at her one last time. He didn't speak. He just stared at her for what seemed an eternity, then he said, "I will come back to you, Kay. However long it takes."

"I know."

He didn't reply. Instead, he stepped backward into the corridor. And then he was gone, vanishing from her life once again.

Kay stood there long after his departure, staring at the empty doorway, his last words echoing through her mind like a dismal dirge.

However long it takes.

She feared it was going to take a long, long time.

Suddenly, desolation swamped her, and all her courage vanished into the wind. She sank into her chair, folded her arms on her desk, and buried her face in the crook of her elbow. She would have burst into tears, if a beloved voice calling her name hadn't stopped her.

"Kay?"

Josephine's voice came floating to her along the corridor, and she sat up, grabbed her pen, and assumed the pose of the efficient secretary as her sister came into her office.

"Where have you been?" Josephine demanded.

She paused in her nonsensical scribbling and tried to look surprised. "Here, of course. Where else would I be?"

Josephine waved a hand impatiently and crossed to her desk. "I mean last night," she clarified, pulling up a chair and sitting down across from Kay. "I woke up in the middle of the night and you weren't in your bed."

Kay felt a jolt of alarm. "You didn't tell Mama, did you?"

"Tattle to Mama?" Jo gave her a censorious look. "What do you think?"

Reassured, she tried to smile. "Thanks, Jo. You're a brick."

"But where were you?"

Kay opened her mouth to invent a lie—she couldn't sleep, she'd gone for a walk, gone to the bathroom, she'd been sleepwalking, anything—but memories of where she'd actually been swamped her, and she couldn't utter the words of a fabricated excuse. The pain she'd been holding back ever since leaving Devlin at dawn could suddenly no longer be contained, and a sob erupted from her before she could stop it. "Oh, Josephine!"

"Oh, my God!" Jo jumped out of the chair and came around her desk. Bending down, she wrapped Kay in a fierce hug. "What is it? What's wrong?"

"Nothing," she choked, shaking her head, trying to regain her control.

"Stuff!" Jo cried. "Tell that to the marines!" She straightened, hauling Kay to her feet, shaking her fiercely. "What is wrong? Tell me, this instant, and don't lie. Not to me."

Echoes of Devlin.

"He's leaving," she blurted out before she could stop herself.

"Who's leaving?"

"Devlin. His hotel caught on fire and he has to go back to Egypt. Now. Today. He's already gone."

"And that's what's got you crying like your heart's going to break? Sharpe?"

Kay stared into her sister's face, noting the girl's understandably confounded expression. Biting her lip, she nodded.

"But...but..." Jo paused, studying her. "You're still in love with him."

It wasn't a question, but she nodded, answering it just the same.

"And you're sure of that? In spite of everything?"

She nodded again. "And he still loves me," she said, though she didn't know why, for there was no point in telling Jo all this. But somehow, she couldn't stop herself. "He asked me to go with him. He wanted us to elope. Again."

"Heavens!" Josephine paused, digesting this bit of news, then to Kay's complete astonishment, she said, "Well, then, what in blazes are you doing here? Why didn't you go?"

Kay stared back at her. "You know why. It's your season. You have to be presented. If I elope—"

"Don't you dare!" Josephine scowled. "Don't you dare turn down his marriage proposal because of me!"

"Goodness," cried another feminine voice from the doorway before Kay could reply. "I could hear your voices from halfway down the corridor. What's the fuss about?"

Josephine turned as Delia came in, answering her question before Kay could regain her composure enough to do so. "Sharpe has to go back to Egypt. His hotel caught on fire."

Delia nodded. "Yes, I know. I was with Simon when Devlin gave him the news. Terrible. But at least no one was killed." She waited, giving Kay an inquiring look, but again, it was Josephine who replied.

"He asked Kay to marry him. To elope and run away with him to Egypt, but she was a complete noodle and said no! Because of me, she says. I ask you, Dee, what can one do with such an impossible sister!"

"I had to say no," Kay cried. "Otherwise your season would be ruined. You haven't been presented yet, and you wouldn't be if I eloped. The scandal would ruin your chances."

"Hang my chances," Jo said fiercely. "This was *your* chance. Your second chance to be with the man you love. How could you let it pass by?"

"He'll be back," Kay said. "By spring, he'll be back. Maybe summer. And we'll get married then."

"Will you?" Jo gave an inelegant snort. "Given your history, I very much doubt it!"

Kay took a deep breath, calm settling over her, replacing her momentary hysterics. "We will get married when he comes back," she said again. "And your reputation remains intact. And mine, too," she added as Jo opened her mouth to fire off a reply. "Devlin and I will wait."

"Wait?" Jo echoed. "Good heavens, haven't you two waited long enough?"

Kay turned, appealing to Delia for support. "You agree with me, of course."

"No," Delia said to her complete astonishment. "I don't agree with you at all. Or you," she added, turning to Josephine. "Neither of you can be trusted to have a bit of sense on this topic, it's obvious."

Kay was too dumbfounded to reply, and Josephine seemed to feel the same, for they both stared at her, speechless.

Delia made a sound of impatience and crossed the room, halting before Kay's desk. "Your problem is easily solved, because I—" She paused, pressing a hand to her bosom and giving an exaggerated bow, "am here to be your problem-solver, my darling friend."

Kay shook her head, her wits too scrambled to even try to figure out what Delia was talking about.

"Of course Josephine's reputation needs to be protected," Delia went on. "And," she continued, overriding the girl's protest, "she absolutely needs to be presented, especially given your rather checkered past. And it's true that you eloping for the second time would ruin that prospect and probably also ruin her chances of a good marriage."

"Thank you!" Kay said. "That's what I'm saying."

"But," Delia went on as if she hadn't spoken, "that's where I come in. Kay, you do not have to elope. I've been married three times, and I'm about to get married again, so trust me when I say I know all the ways, respectable and not so respectable, that a girl can tie the knot."

"But—"

"Listen, will you? As I said, you don't have to elope. I'm a countess, darling. I will take over for your mother and present Josephine at court. Especially fitting, since I'm the one who submitted her application in the first place. I will see that she is properly presented, and I will chaperone her for the rest of the season. Meanwhile, you, Kay, darling, will pack your bags and your mother's, too, and the pair of you will go off with Devlin to Egypt."

"But when can they get married?" Jo asked before Kay could speak.

"A British woman who is over the age of consent can get married to a British man anywhere under British control. You just have to establish residence and read the banns. I happen to know this because I ran off to Italy with my soon-to-be second husband and we got married in Gibraltar." She turned to Kay. "Egypt is currently a British protectorate. You can be married from there. And with your mother along, it's all perfectly acceptable. Your mother sails home in time to join Josephine and me at all the autumn house parties and you and Devlin live happily ever after."

Kay caught her breath, hope and joy rising within her. "Oh, Delia, you'll do that for us? Really?"

"Of course I will, you goose. What are friends for?"

"But what about Mama?" Jo put in. "She'll miss seeing me presented. Will she agree to go?"

"To see your sister finally be respectably married, of course she'll go," Delia replied. "And if she doesn't, well, I'll chaperone Kay and your mother can stay here."

"But what about your own wedding?" Kay cried.

"Simon can come, too, and we'll all get married in Egypt. Now, go."

Kay laughed and started for the door, but she'd barely taken a step before she stopped. "Money," she said. "Heavens, what do I do for money?"

"I'll loan you the money," Delia said. "Now do stop throwing obstacles in the path of my brilliant idea, because we don't have much time and you still have to pack. Knowing how your mother dithers, that will take forever. Devlin's already gone, of course. I saw his cab leaving twenty minutes ago, but you can take your own cab and follow him to Victoria. And you can get your tickets at Cook's there. I'll see the hotel cashier and cash a bank draft for you while you pack. You can purchase your traveler's checks at Cook's when they issue your tickets. Now, go. What are you waiting for?"

Kay needed no more urging. "Delia," she said, circling around her desk and racing for the door, "you are the best friend in the world. Jo, get me a cab."

Not waiting for a reply, she ran for the lift. It seemed to take forever, but it was probably only a few minutes before she reached the top floor and raced for her suite.

"Mama?" she cried as she came in. "Mama, where are you?"

"In bed, Kay. Having breakfast. Where else would I be at this hour?"

She ran for the bedroom and paused in the doorway. "Well, get up, Mama, right now. And Foster?" she added to her mother's maid. "Fetch our trunks and suitcases and start packing. Summer clothes, the lightest ones. I want Mama packed and ready to leave in fifteen minutes."

"But where are we going?" Magdelene cried. "We can't go anywhere just now—"

"Egypt, Mama," she said and laughed. "We're going to Egypt."

21

Devlin paused in the main hall of Victoria Station and pulled out his pocket watch. An hour and a half before his train departed, and only seven minutes since the last time he'd checked the time. He'd come far too early, he supposed, but then, he hadn't been able to bear the idea of hanging about the Mayfair any longer. Once Kay had refused to come with him, there was no reason to stay. Long, drawn-out farewells at that point would only have made things harder on both of them.

Even so, at this moment he'd give his right arm to see her one more time before he left. Just once more. There was time, he supposed, to dash back to the Mayfair—

Muttering an oath, he put his pocket watch away and resumed walking, taking his fourth turn around the main hall. He couldn't go back to the hotel now, he knew, or he'd never leave again. And it wasn't as if he and Kay would be parted forever. Six months. Maybe a year.

Even a day seemed too long.

Kay, he thought, anguished. *I have to go, but how can I, when I promised you I'd stay?*

He stopped and turned, leaning his back against a wall, closing his eyes, imagining her as he'd seen her last, but the sadness in her face was too much to take, and he opened his eyes again, straightened away from the wall, and kept walking.

He went round the main hall yet again, this time pausing at WH Smith and Son. There, he bought three novels, half a dozen newspapers, and a copy of the *Strand Magazine*. He'd need them all, he feared, if he was to get through this journey without going out of his mind.

He checked his watch again. Still an hour and a quarter to go.

Again he put his watch away and resumed walking, but he didn't take a fifth turn around the main hall. Instead, he made for the Chatham terminus, where the trains departed for Dover. His luggage was there already, having been taken by a porter upon his arrival to be safeguarded until his train pulled in and it could be loaded.

A train must have just arrived, for everyone seemed to be coming in the opposite direction from his destination, making him feel a bit like a salmon swimming upstream. But he reached his platform eventually, and he found a seat on one of the long, backless benches. Resigning himself to the wait, he set the books and newspapers beside him and opened the *Strand Magazine*.

"Mr. Sharpe?"

He looked up to find his porter standing nearby, and he rose to his feet, tucking his newspaper under one arm. "Your train won't be in for about an hour, so I've stored your luggage. When the train comes, you can board when you like, and the conductor will punch your ticket. You don't need to find me."

"And my luggage?"

"I'll load it when the time comes, never fear. And it'll go straight through to Calais. There, of course, you'll need a porter to transfer your trunks to the Calais-Méditerranée."

He nodded and reached into his pocket for a shilling to tip the fellow, since he wouldn't be seeing him again. "Thank you," he said, holding out the coin.

"Thank you, sir." He took the tip and held out a small pink ticket. "And here's your claim check. You'll need it for the porter to transfer the luggage. Even the Archbishop of Canterbury," he added with a laugh as Devlin took the claim check, "couldn't get his luggage without that!"

Devlin froze, staring down at the slip of pink paper in his hand. *The Archbishop of Canterbury?* he thought. *Of course.*

The porter was already walking away as Devlin looked up. "Porter?" he called, but the man didn't hear, and Devlin started after him, breaking into a run.

"Oh, dear, oh, dear," Magdelene clucked, looking over the trunks and suitcases as the bellmen carried them past where she stood and loaded them onto the boot of the cab that was waiting to take Kay and her mother to Victoria Station. "I do hope we haven't forgotten anything."

"If we have, I'm sure we can purchase it along the way," Kay told her. "Do stop fussing, Mama."

"Going somewhere, Lady Kay?"

She turned to find that loathsome woman, Delilah Dawlish,

standing nearby, a notebook in one hand and a pencil in the other, and she suddenly appreciated that Devlin was right. Mrs. Dawlish really did look a bit like a rocking horse.

Giving an irritated sigh, she turned away, facing Delia and Josephine. "I'll cable you when we've arrived," she told her friend. "Take care of my girl."

"Of course I will," Delia replied. "So don't worry. And I shall hire a photographer to take pictures of her in her court gown so you'll know how gorgeous she looked when she was presented."

Kay nodded. "Thank you, Dee. You think of everything," she said, and turned to her sister, opening her arms.

Jo's beautiful face suddenly broke up, and she hurled herself at Kay. "I'm going to miss you so much!" she cried.

"Stuff," Kay said, her voice stern to hide the fact that she was starting to cry, too. "You'll be far too busy flirting with all your suitors for that. Listen to me," she added, interrupting her sister's indignant denial and pushing her back a bit so she could look into her face. "You are to do whatever Lady Stratham tells you to do, you understand?"

Jo nodded. "Of course I will."

"And don't cry," she added with a sniff, cupping her sister's chin and trying to smile. "I'll write you every week," she promised. "And I'll come for a visit next summer. Everything in Egypt should be settled by then."

"Is that where you're going, Lady Kay?" Mrs. Dawlish asked, sidling closer. "Egypt? But what about your job?" she added when Kay didn't reply. "Aren't you working as Lady Stratham's secretary now? And working with Mr. Sharpe, too, I hear. How does it feel to be working with the man who ruined you all those years ago?"

That was too much. Kay turned. "The only person who's ever tried to ruin me is you," she shot back. "And," she added with a scowl, taking a threatening step toward the other woman, "if you don't stop pestering me, I'll slap your face right here in front of everyone, something I daresay half the ton has wanted to do at some point in your odious career."

"Hear, hear," Delia said, coming up beside her. "Please leave, Mrs. Dawlish, before I have you removed from the premises."

The woman retreated, but only as far as the sidewalk, where she continued to watch avidly as Magdelene said goodbye to her younger daughter and moved to step into the cab.

The driver held out his hand to assist her as Kay gave Josephine one last hug. She turned to follow her mother just as a hansom pulled into the courtyard, and Kay froze, paralyzed, hardly able to believe her eyes.

"Devlin?" she cried.

He didn't wait for the driver, but flung back the hansom doors and exited the vehicle before the man had even climbed down from the box. He started toward her, and she met him halfway. Heedless of Delilah Dawlish and all the other people milling about, she flung herself into his arms with enough force to send his hat flying off his head.

"Kay, my darling!" He wrapped his arms around her, kissing her everywhere he could—her cheek, her nose, her forehead, her mouth—making her laugh with joy. Until she remembered.

"But what are you doing here?" she cried, pulling back, staring at him, joy giving way to chagrin. "You left for Victoria Station over two hours ago!"

"I'm not going."

"What?"

"I promised you I'd never leave you again, remember? How can I go without you?"

"But the hotel. The fire. You have to go."

He shook his head. "It can wait. Listen," he added as she started to protest. "I can go to the Faculty Office in the morning and apply for a special license. It'll take about a week. We'll get married at the Registry Office and take the next train we can get. I'll be delayed, but we'll be respectably married, and we won't have to be apart."

She laughed. It was so wonderful, so absurd, and so typical of their tumultuous fourteen-year, on-again-off-again romance, she couldn't help it.

"What?" he said, laughing with her, clearly baffled. "Why are you laughing?"

"Because you nearly missed me. I was leaving."

"Leaving?" He looked past her to the waiting growler and her mother watching them through the window. "Leaving for where?"

"Egypt."

He swerved his head to look at her again. "What?"

She nodded, still laughing. "You don't have to get a special license, and you don't have to delay your trip. Delia's going to present Josephine at court and chaperone her while Mama and I come with you to Cairo. And we'll get married there. All very proper and aboveboard."

He let go of her, raking his hand through his hair, looking utterly confounded. "And to think we almost missed each other," he muttered.

"But we didn't. That's destiny, don't you think?"

"Absolutely." He lifted his hand to cup her face. "I love you," he said. "I love you more than my life."

"And I love you," she said.

"A good thing indeed, since we're getting married." He moved to take her in his arms again, but she pulled back, turning toward the woman staring at them from the nearby sidewalk.

"Did you hear that, Mrs. Dawlish?" she said. "Devlin Sharpe and I are getting married. We're going to Egypt and getting married there, with my mother along to chaperone us. So put that in your gossipmongering pipe and smoke it!"

She turned back to Devlin and wrapped her arms around his neck. "We're not being nearly scandalous enough for her, I fear. Getting respectably married is so terribly mundane. Should we give her one last scandal to write about before we go?"

He grinned, his arms coming up to wrap around her. "Like what?"

"Kiss me, you wretched man."

He lifted one eyebrow dubiously. "Here?"

"Right here. Or do I have to shamelessly fling myself at you and kiss you first?"

Fortunately, he didn't let it come to that. Bending his head, he captured her mouth in a long, hot, totally satisfying kiss that had her mother squawking like a bilious pigeon and caused everyone else watching them to burst into a round of applause.

Except Mrs. Dawlish, of course, who, when Kay and Devlin drew apart, was still scribbling in her awful little black notebook.

"Heavens," Kay said, trying to catch her breath as she looked again at the only man she had ever loved. "You always could kiss me senseless."

"I wanted to give you a kiss they'll talk about for years."

"I hope you succeeded, my darling." She tightened her arms around his neck, giving him a wicked grin. "I certainly hope so."

About the Author

New York Times bestselling author Laura Lee Guhrke spent seven years in advertising, had a successful catering business, and managed a construction company before she decided writing novels was more fun. The author of thirty historical romances and a two-time winner of the Romance Writers of America RITA® Award, Laura lives in the U.S. Northwest with her husband and two diva cats. Laura loves hearing from readers, and you can contact her at:

LauraLeeGuhrke.com
Facebook/LauraLeeGuhrkeAuthor
Instagram @Laura_Lee_Guhrke
X @LauraLeeGuhrke